Digital Circumstances

ISBN-978-1-291-93901-9

Brian Stewart worked in education, and was a maths teacher for more years than he can count. He now focuses on his writing, and lives in the Scottish Highlands with his wife. He has two grown-up children who live elsewhere in Scotland.

Follow him on Twitter @BRMStewart, visit www.brmstewart.co.uk, or email brianrmstewart@gmail.com.

The cover design is by Malcolm McGonigle, from images on morguefile.

To my wife Sally
for making it all possible.

The beginning of the end, and the beginning

Chapter 1

Now - Kirkwall

The hotel room itself is silent, save for a slight creaking of the old wardrobe, but I can hear the wind howling outside and the rain smashing against the window panes as I look out. It's not long after noon, and only early September, but out there it's very dark. I can see part of the outer harbour, with two ferries pulling restlessly at their ropes against the northerly gale. Somewhere further on are the small north isles, and beyond that Shetland and the Arctic, which doesn't feel so very far away. I've moved my chair so that I can sit with my feet on the old cast-iron radiator, and the room thermostat says it's twenty degrees in here, but I feel cold.

The window flexes against the wind.

It's been a journey and a half to get here. BA Glasgow to Faro, EasyJet from Faro back to Glasgow, EasyJet again from Glasgow to Malaga, car hire to Gibraltar and then back to Malaga, train to Alicante, Ryanair to Edinburgh, train to Inverness, Flybe to Kirkwall, taxi to the hotel. Ideally, I would have done each leg with a different fake passport, using different credit cards, covering my tracks. But I'm just an ordinary guy: one passport, two credit cards, a debit card – all in my own name. I'm not quite sure who wants to find me the most, but if they have the resources and the contacts, they surely will.

Assets? I've got fifty pounds and five hundred Euros in my wallet, and about two million pounds split over three bank accounts in Gibraltar, and half a million Euros in a Spanish bank account (though that could suddenly be worth fuck all any day now with the way the economy is going). I can access almost all of my money online, but one of the Gibraltar banks would need me there in person – that was the arrangement. I've got other investments in a string of companies, and a scattering of ISAs which I've lost track of, but they're probably all out of reach now.

Possessions? I've got a suitcase – weighing just less than 15kg of course – and enough technology to see me through: a MacBook, an iPhone, and an iPod.

All of that is enough for a forty-two-year old single man to be going on with, except for that particular word 'single'. I have no lover – not any more. No friends, no security. I can't even contact anyone I know – updating my Facebook status is probably out of the question.

I smile at that thought: Martin McGregor is hiding in Orkney. Sad face.

The hard rain turns to hail, and I can see my reflection in my hotel room window. My unshaven face looks tired and gaunt, a product of irregular hours and irregular eating. I need to relax, to sleep, but part of me expects a knock at the door to pour scorn on my attempts to run and hide.

Just a year ago, I thought I had it all. But it all went wrong.

Chapter 2

Alvor, a year before

Where did it all go wrong?

Well, it really went wrong way back when Charlie Talbot appeared at my school and I ended up at his party, met his dad Ken, and… But it really *really* went wrong that day on the Algarve, in the middle of my holiday with Helen, when Charlene appeared.

*

I find the Atlantic surf pounding onto an Algarve beach, when it's big but still safe to swim in, absolutely exhilarating – once you've had the sharp intake of breath when a wave first hits your groin, and then not minded how stupid you look as you've tried to dive through a wave only to find yourself beached as the wave recedes.

The difficulty of getting into the ocean is only matched by the difficulty of getting back out again. I thought I'd judged it perfectly, as I planted my feet down and began wading confidently ashore, but then the next wave smashed my in the back, knocked me over, and dragged me back out of my depth. I rose to the surface coughing and surprised, found I could stand up, started wading ashore again, and then the next wave caught me. By the time I stumbled up the beach, my swim-shorts were sagging round my knees, filled with rough sand. Helen was laughing so much that her iPhone was shaking as she jabbed at the screen.

I staggered across the hot beach to our sunbeds and the shade of the pointed, wicker umbrella. 'Oh, come on!' I said.

'There's a couple of likes in already,' she giggled, and leaned up on one elbow so I could kiss her mouth as I reached for my towel and my sunglasses.

I knew that was probably an exaggeration – Portugal didn't seem to have good Wi-Fi, certainly not on the beach – but I laughed anyway. Helen lay back, plugging in her ear buds and pulling her NYPD baseball cap over her forehead. I looked at her as I towelled myself, admiring her figure, her short black hair, the intelligent dark brown eyes hidden behind big sunglasses, the full lips. I smiled with a satisfaction bordering on smugness. OK, there had been tough times, tough decisions in my life – some of which I wasn't proud of – but I felt in a good place now.

I looked around. Many of the beaches on the Algarve are tiny coves, hard to get to – and I love them – but the one at Alvor runs for over a mile, formed by the river estuary turning sideways just before it gets to the ocean. We were on the last, most westerly rectangular group of loungers and umbrellas, close to where the courtesy bus from the hotel dropped us. The beach further on was deserted. In the other direction lay the travesty of high-rises that had been built during the seventies tourist boom, and then the beach ran into the sandstone cliffs. Just beyond them was the larger town of Portimao.

I scanned it all, still grinning. All I had to do was finish my plan to get out of various... *entanglements* I had. Then I could have and enjoy it all.

I was about to lie down beside Helen when I caught sight of a couple walking along by the water's edge. This was early October; the beach was by no means empty, but now that the weekend was over there weren't that many people around. As I looked at this couple I realised they were looking at me.

They were an odd couple. She was small and blonde, wearing only the tiny lower part of a bikini. He was much taller, heavily built, with coarse features. He wore swim-shorts and carried a manbag. As I watched, they turned away from the shore and started walked straight towards me, no expression on their faces.

I was aware of Helen sitting up, pulling an ear bud out and pausing her iPod. 'You'll certainly know her the next time,' she commented. I gave a small murmur that I hoped was non-committal. 'The word you're looking for is 'pert',' she added.

'They seem to be coming this way.'

'Do you know them?'

'Don't recognise them at all.'

As they came nearer, Helen reached for her T-shirt to cover herself and swung her legs off the lounger, her bare feet on the sand. I gave my hair a last rub with the towel and dropped it onto my lounger. The couple got closer and closer, still looking straight at me. I looked straight back.

They were now directly in front of us. He stood with his feet planted firmly in the sand, looking at me: he had a square face, with a prominent forehead – straight black hair combed forward over it – and a single, long eyebrow, and thick lips. His body looked strong, but not particularly athletic. His chest, legs and arms were thick with dark hair. She was just perfectly formed, like some film director had asked the CGI people 'make me a cute little blonde with a perfect body and a pretty face'. Her face was expressionless, flat. She stood with one knee bent, shoulders back, almost daring me not to admire her. She looked like she was in her early twenties, he was maybe around thirty. I saw wedding rings, the gold chain round his neck, the barbed wire tattoo round his upper arm. She had a small dolphin on her shoulder. There were perfect little pearl earrings in her perfect little ears, red nail varnish on her fingers and toes.

'Hello again, Martin,' the man said, in a very rough Glasgow accent.

I sensed Helen looking at me. I frowned, and reached to shake hands – his grip was dry, firm, but I sensed reserves of pressure. 'Hi – er..?'

'We met at Colin Strachan's a couple of years ago, remember?'

My smile froze. What the fuck… 'Colin Strachan's. Sorry, I can't remember your name.'

'Jimmy Anderson. I'm a friend of Ken Talbot.'

Oh shit, I thought. The relaxed, safe holiday mood slipped off me. What did this guy want?

'Not surprised you don't remember,' Anderson said. 'You were pretty well gone that evening. It was quite a party.'

I might very well have been pretty well gone 'that evening', but it wasn't at Colin Strachan's party. I hadn't spoken to Colin since he'd left the company four years ago, and I'd never had any need or desire to. I'd definitely never met this guy before;

he was mentioning Colin and Ken Talbot in order to get my attention, and probably frighten me a little. It had worked.

‘This is my partner Helen,’ I said.

They shook hands, and then Helen and I both looked at the cute blonde, who didn’t react.

‘This is my wife Charlene.’

She didn’t offer her hand, but kept giving us the blank look, so we just nodded at her and said hi.

‘We’re going for lunch,’ Anderson said. ‘Why don’t you join us?’ And he began to walk towards the wooden walkway that led up the beach, Charlene by his side.

Helen pulled my arm. ‘Stop leching, Martin. And can you tell me just what the fuck is going on?’

I started gathering our stuff together, and she helped, face in a frown. ‘Don’t worry,’ I said. ‘Might as well have lunch now anyway.’ But I knew I looked worried, and that wouldn’t be reassuring for her.

We paused to wash the sand off our feet at the taps by the walkway and put on our sandals, then went up past the café bar where we usually had lunch and a drink – the waiter gave us a wave as we went by, though he was clearly focused on Charlene. As we left the beach, Anderson passed her a T-shirt and she shrugged it on.

We made our way over the rough track flanked by scrub, past the sports ground and the fishing businesses, to the promenade. On our left the water was filled with small boats, and then we reached the first of the line of café bars.

Anderson sat at a table by the wall, his back to the shoreline, and Charlene sat beside him, shaded by the standard conical wicker umbrella. Helen and I sat opposite, the metal legs of the chairs scraping on the concrete.

The waiter materialised, white shirt and black trousers, a round tray under his arm, nodding to me and Helen like he maybe recognised us but giving a cautious look to our companions.

'Bom die,' I said.

'Good afternoon,' the waiter replied. 'What can I get for you?' He gave the tabletop an unnecessary wipe, and repositioned the ashtray.

We ordered drinks – beers for me and Anderson, a large glass of red wine for Helen. Anderson ordered Charlene a sparkling water without asking her. Three of us made small talk about the fabulous weather and how lovely the town was, and where we'd visited. Charlene sat half-turned towards Anderson, looking behind him to a narrow pontoon at the end of which was the large Portuguese-style wooden boat that took tourists on trips. I wondered what Anderson wanted from me.

We ordered food – Helen and I shared a cataplana, with more beer and water and a bottle of wine, Anderson had a burger and chips, and he ordered Charlene a salad, which she picked at disinterestedly. She still hadn't said a word, and it wasn't clear whether she was following the small talk. I began to think she didn't speak English.

After a bizarre but not unpleasant hour – Helen was now pleasantly lunchtime-sloshed, and looking almost relaxed – Anderson stood up. 'Can we go for a wee walk, Martin? I'd like a chat in private.'

He stood up and started walking away, in the direction of the town. I shrugged at Helen's wide-eyed look, her hands indicating Charlene with a glare that said 'what the fuck am I supposed to do on my own with her?' and followed him.

We walked slowly through the heat along the promenade, past the stalls noisily advertising boat trips, and the strange totem-pole, and then turned up along one of the narrow roads that ran through the old town, lined with traditional Portuguese restaurants and the odd Italian, an English-themed pub; down a side road was an Indian restaurant. I followed him patiently.

At the end of the restaurants, beyond the small shops, almost at the end of the old town, he turned off into an even narrower residential street and stopped beside the empty skeleton of a small building where a major renovation had been started and then abandoned in the recession. The street was deserted, shutters closed against the heat and dust of the early afternoon.

As I realised we were completely out of sight here, and how quiet it was, Anderson turned and reached to hold my arm while his other hand went into his pocket. And pulled out a smartphone, which he unlocked and dialled one-handed. When he heard someone answer, he passed the phone to me.

'Hello?' I said, hearing how thin and nervous my voice was.

'Hi, Martin. How's it going?' The voice was the low Glasgow growl of a million cigarettes and a lifetime of hard living.

'I'm fine, Sandy. Enjoying the sunshine.'

'Good, good.' A dry cough, and the sound of a cigarette being lit and sucked on, my earpiece crackling as he exhaled. 'I won't spoil it. The people at your end have a job for you – won't take long, won't cause you any hassle. Just do what they want, and that'll be just fine.'

I frowned at that. 'What sort of job?'

'Nothing too difficult, I expect. Just do what they ask – that'll keep you and us all square, and us and them all square too.'

I looked at Anderson, and he looked back at me with his dull eyes, still gripping my arm. 'Who are these people, Sandy?'

'Just people, Martin – people with things to get done. Don't worry about them, don't ask any daft questions. Just do the wee job for them.'

'And afterwards?'

His voice seemed surprised. 'Afterwards? Nothing. You just get back to your wee holiday with the lovely Helen, and then get on home to Glasgow.'

'Nothing else?'

He gave a wheezy laugh. 'Just do this wee job, Martin. For the business.'

And he hung up. I gave the phone back to Anderson and he put it away, but continued to grip my arm, looking hard at me, and I took a deep breath and let it out slowly.

His voice was precise: 'In Portimao, there is a road that runs along the beach, towards the marina, called Avenue Tomas Cabreira. On that road, about a mile from the marina, is a pub called the Kingfisher. Do you know it?'

'No,' I said.

'You'll find it no bother. Be there at one in the afternoon tomorrow. Someone will come in and tell you what to do. OK?'

I took another deep breath. ‘Yes, fine.’

He let go of my arm, and we walked back down to the marina, past the couples and the families in the café bars and restaurants. As we neared our table, his voice was a whisper: ‘One pm, Kingfisher Bar, Avenue Tomas Cabreira. Just you yourself.’ There was no threat in his voice, no ‘or else’.

I nodded to show I’d heard, and tried to think of the story I could tell Helen to excuse myself the next day, knowing she was going to be really pissed off by this.

As we approached the table, Charlene stood up and started to walk away, back in the direction of the beach. Anderson grabbed his manbag, fished out a few Euro notes which he dropped on the table, and followed her.

I sat down and drank the rest of my beer. Helen was staring at me, her mouth wide. Then she laughed. ‘What the fuck was all that about, Martin? Do you know she didn’t say a bloody word to me? Just sipped at her fizzy water, and gazed around. What did he want?’

I was trying to think what the hell to say to her, and decided on something that had elements of the truth in it. ‘He works for some clients of B&D. They’ve got a problem and they want me to help out – I’m the only one who can. They obviously found out I was here, so…’

‘Couldn’t he just have emailed you?’

‘It’s all a bit sensitive.’

’Oh.’ She took a gulp of her wine and filled it to the brim with the last of the bottle, pushing it to the middle of the table. ‘So what is it you’re doing?’

'I told you, it's sensitive.' I tried a grin, but she just frowned back, and I took a big drink from the glass.

We finished the wine as we watched the comings and goings of the local boats and the tourist trips in the marina, paid for lunch with Anderson's money and some of our own, and then made our way back up through the old town and into the newer part where our hotel was. We showered to get rid of the salt and the dust, and then made love. I dozed off for a time, and awoke to find Helen stroking me, a smile on her face. 'Did that wee blonde turn you on, then?'

'Not as much as you do.' But it was undeniable: there was something in Charlene that was very attractive - compelling.

We made love again, and then Helen gave a contented, sleepy sigh. 'Love you, darling,' she murmured, and slipped into sleep, a little smile on her face.

I lay for a couple of minutes almost dozing, and then got up, showered again, put on shorts and a polo shirt, and went out to our balcony with a bottle of water.

I sat and looked out over the hotel gardens, the big pool, then the town, the ocean hidden by the high rises near the beach. I sipped at my water.

My mood of optimism from earlier had wilted as I realised that there was a crack in my plan, a crack in my life – a fault line that ran all the way back to that day in Glasgow, the party twenty-five years ago, when everything had changed.

I needed to get clear, get away. Do this 'wee job' and get out. It felt more urgent somehow.

*

I found the street easily enough, but was past the pub before seeing the sign: I don't drive much abroad, so I really have to concentrate. I managed to find somewhere to turn, and then drove past the pub again and squeezed into a line of cars at the side of the road.

It was another fantastic day, temperature in the high twenties, a clear blue sky. Helen was back at the hotel pool, sulking, having refused to go down to the beach on her own. She'd quizzed me again about what I was doing and why she couldn't come, and was either seriously pissed off at me or was pretending to be seriously pissed off. It didn't matter either way, I reflected, as I headed under the sign at the entrance to the pub, deciding to sit out of the sun. The place was smaller inside than it looked, with small round metal-legged tables and wooden chairs. I took off my baseball cap and sunglasses, and sat down near the door. The aircon was turned up high, and I almost shivered in my shorts and T-shirt.

'Bom die,' I said to the waitress.

'Good afternoon,' she replied. 'What can I get you?'

'Just a coffee – Americano. Please. No milk.'

The place was almost empty. There were four old men who looked like locals huddled over small glasses of beer at the bar, and a family of tourists at a table - a couple and their two young children, poring over maps, drinking cokes, chatting about their day.

My coffee came. 'Obrigado.' 'You're welcome.'

One o'clock came… and went.

At one thirty I ordered another coffee, with a corresponding trip to the toilet. The family left amidst excited chatter, and were replaced by two young clean-cut couples in shorts and T-shirts, sunglasses tucked in their hair, studying maps, drinking beers, speculating about their day in loud middle-class voices. I began to think that no one was coming for me.

And suddenly there was a figure sitting beside me, calling for a beer from the waitress and placing a wide, battered straw hat on the table. He reached to shake my hand. 'Mr McGregor?' He sounded local.

I nodded. He was shorter than me, with longish thick black hair shot with grey, and dark leathered skin that had spent its life in bright sunshine. He wore jeans cut off at the knee, a loose, dark polo shirt, and old sandals. His dark arms showed muscle and sinews like steel wire as he lifted his beer glass, and conversed with the waitress. She laughed, and reached to rest her hand on his arm as she turned away.

He drank quickly. 'Please, we have to hurry.' He dropped some coins on the table, and I left a five Euro note.

A moment later we were back out in the full blaze of the day. I followed him into an old, battered, open-top short wheelbase Land Rover; he crunched the gears as he pulled into traffic to a blast of car horns, picking up speed. Without slowing down or seeming to look around, we cut left past modern apartment blocks, right at the roundabout – oblivious to the other traffic – and along a wide avenue with olive trees scattered on either side, the estuary and the ocean away to our left. We raced down the avenue, swung round another roundabout, and then were bouncing across rough ground to skid to a halt at the end of a line of parked cars in front of the marina. He let the engine stall, and climbed out.

I followed, putting my baseball cap back on, and grateful to get away from the stench of diesel.

'Come.'

He climbed over the short wall that bordered the marina, and walked, almost stooped, along the path by its side, with me just behind him.

The marina was huge, split by a complex of apartments. There were boats of all sizes, from small cabin cruisers to enormous, fully-crewed vessels. I couldn't begin to guess at the amount of money I was looking at.

He unlocked a gate to a pontoon; we stepped onto it, and walked out for about fifty yards to a relatively small fishing boat, painted bright blue. It had a small wheelhouse, a narrow metal drum winch at the front for fishing nets, and it looked incongruous amongst all this display of money. He leapt down with practised ease onto the afterdeck, went straight for the wheelhouse, and fired up the inboard engine, letting it idle. Once again I felt the smell of diesel as I cautiously stepped aboard, amongst the lobster pots and buckets half full of water.

He turned to me, looking back along the pontoon. 'Please, sit down.' He reached into a locker and pulled out two bottles of Cristal beer, knocking the caps off on the edge of a wooden locker, and handed one to me. He stood beside me, the engine running, drinking from the bottle and looking along the pontoon. 'Ah, this weather,' he said. 'Is like July, not October.'

'Good for tourists,' I said, sitting, feeling the condensation on the beer bottle. He bobbed his head ambivalently. Then he gave a wave to someone, and I turned my head to look, hearing him go to the bow.

A short, slim woman was walking towards us, along the pontoon, carrying a rucksack. She had on a baseball cap and big sunglasses, a T-shirt, and jeans cut off as high as they anatomically could be. I half-recognised the confident – arrogant – walk, but it was a minute or two before I identified her as Charlene from the day before. I watched her approach, and the man untied the rope at the front of the boat then went back into the shade of the wheelhouse, looking over his shoulder at her.

She pulled the aft mooring rope from its bollard, and stepped past me onto the deck, letting her rucksack down gently and tidying the mooring rope into a neat coil beside it. She sat on the bench opposite me as the engine was revved and we pulled away from the pontoon. She didn't look at me, but I found myself examining her perfect profile: every time I turned away, my eyes were drawn back to her. She bent to pull a bottle of water from her rucksack, the neck of her T-shirt falling open. I sipped at my beer. I assumed her husband Jimmy would meet us at the other end of the trip.

We steered into the main exit channel, past the end of the harbour wall, and round into the ocean, but almost doubling back immediately, heading diagonally across the estuary. There was more of a swell here, the breeze cooler, refreshing.

On the west bank was an ancient wooden tall-ship flying the Portuguese flag, and further on was another marina. Further on still was the road bridge, and beyond that the arcs of the railway bridge, and then the bridge carrying the motorway, chaotic storks' nests on top of its towers. I'd first come here, on the way up to Silves, with the woman I'd loved – and still did, if I was honest – and then again with the woman I thought I had loved. I had been looking forward to sharing the experience with Helen, and wasn't enjoying the feeling that it was being hijacked for some other purpose.

We headed towards the east bank, to a tight collection of villas with their white walls and red tiled roofs. There was a sandy bay, and another inlet busy with small boats. We rounded a breakwater, and made for a modern concrete pier. As we neared it, Charlene stood up and stumbled, almost falling onto me. I held her arms to help her get her balance, feeling her smooth skin, sensing her body, looking into her eyes. She smiled and sat down again. It was the first display of any emotion I'd seen on her face, but I couldn't understand what she'd been trying to do.

We glided to a perfect turn and stopped by a flight of concrete steps. Charlene tossed the rope up onto the wall, swung her legs onto the steps, and raced up them to tie us up. The skipper threw up the forward mooring rope, and she tied us off with that too. I looked around, not sure what to do. The skipper helped himself to another beer; as he opened it, he gestured me away, up to Charlene. She stood on the sea wall, arms akimbo, and watched while I tentatively climbed from the boat onto the steps –the first few covered with seaweed – and up to her.

She shouldered her rucksack, and headed off into the network of narrow streets and modern villas, me following. After a couple of dead-ends and circuits, after which I'd completely lost my bearings, we stopped at one particular villa. It wasn't one of the largest ones. It looked to be very new, with closed freshly-painted blue shutters, a couple of satellite dishes on the roof pointing to slightly different parts of the sky, containers of shrubs arranged on the gravel front garden.

Charlene was at the door, trying to turn a key in the deadlock. It seemed to take some effort, but then it was open and I followed her in, taking off my sunglasses and tucking them in the neck of my shirt – gradually my eyes got used to the darkness of the interior, where the only light was sunshine leaking round the edges of shutters. We were in the main part of the open-plan house. There was a leather sofa, a large TV set with a Sky box and another satellite decoder underneath, a glass table. The place felt empty, as if only occasionally used. Charlene looked around, and then she took the rucksack off her shoulder and moved towards what looked like a small cubbyhole.

The cubbyhole was actually a tiny study. There was a closed laptop and docking station, with a 27” screen on the desk, piles of papers beside it. Shelves were covered with books, all in English, roughly half-in-half thrillers and books on travel. Charlene switched the laptop on, and the monitor, and we watched as we were asked for a password.

Here we go, I thought. She expects me to somehow guess the password, or bypass it, the way they do in the movies or on TV. I wondered how I might break it to her that this just didn’t happen. At the same time I felt relief: the trip was pointless, the ‘wee job’ couldn’t be done. I could get back to my holiday.

Charlene pulled her iPhone out of a pocket in her shorts – god knows how there was room for it there – and her thumbs moved rapidly across the screen. She bent over the computer keyboard and typed in characters. The screen opened up to the standard Windows desktop screen, showing two columns of icons. I watched, mildly impressed. But the sense of relief had evaporated: this was deeper than I had thought, and I was going to have to do the wee job after all.

She stood back and turned to me. ‘We need you to do two things.’ I was taken aback by her voice: it was soft, polite

English with something either Welsh or Northumberland in there – not what I expected, but I couldn't have said what I did expect; I'd begun to believe she didn't speak English at all. Her face was still expressionless. 'We want you install a keylogger, and we want you to find some files.'

'I don't…'

She bent from the waist, the T-shirt falling open again, and reached into the rucksack, standing up with a USB stick in her hand. 'There's one on here.'

OK, but she could have done that herself, I was sure. 'What sort of files?' She was clearly not a computer illiterate, so why did she need me?

'He does financial transactions, and hides them. That's why you're here. You know where to look and what to look for. You're familiar with the kind of thing he's doing – moving money around, laundering it.' She checked her phone. 'You have two hours.' And she stepped away from the computer chair.

I sat down – no choice. I swallowed, and then the old work instinct just kicked in, because I had to do what she asked, and it wasn't outwith my field of expertise. 'I'll do the keylogger last – no point logging my own keystrokes. Let me know when I have fifteen minutes left.'

As I started to work, she placed a bottle of cold water on the desk beside me.

I started by looking at all the documents on the hard drive, and how they were organised, and what he stored in the cloud. It took a long time of searching – I could hear an imaginary clock ticking beside me, but I stayed with a systematic search, resisting the urge to panic and just search frenetically and fruitlessly, all too aware how working at a computer can just suck all of time away. I kept looking, leaving windows open and parked so that I knew where I'd been and could work up and down the trees of folders. The owner of the machine had actually structured his files fairly logically, and that helped me: it helped me find the anomalies, because he wouldn't have put folders accidentally in the wrong place – he'd have done it deliberately. I found a spreadsheet which unlocked with the same password that the computer used, and opened to reveal a list of other passwords; I scanned them and continued working.

'One hour,' Charlene said at one point. Her voice was calm. She was sitting on the big leather couch, fingers tapping and stroking the screen of her phone.

I finally found something promising – a folder buried several deep within 'family photos' but not containing photos. There were four documents, and three spreadsheets. They all needed a password, but they were in the password file, clearly identified.

'Think this is it,' I said. It hadn't been that difficult after all.

I opened the files and had a cursory look: names, addresses, dates, lists of people and money, bank account numbers and sort codes. Charlene came over and stood by me, leaning to look at the screen. I could smell the light scent of her perfume, feel her left breast pressing against my shoulder.

'That's it,' she said. 'Store them on the USB stick. I've got another if you need it. Forty minutes,' she added.

I copied the files across, spending the time continuing my search of the hard drive and the synchronised cloud folders, watching the painfully slow copying process. Then a last look for any other files that might be important, and finally it was done.

'OK,' I said, 'ready for the keylogger. What have you got on here?' I opened the folder on the USB stick and looked at the two files with the meaningless names.

'One is a packet analyser, the other is a form grabber,' she said.

I nodded. Between the two, they would pick up Internet transactions, catching passwords before they were encrypted and sent over the internet, and sending them on to an FTP server or an email address. I installed them, telling the anti-virus program and the firewall that this was all perfectly safe. Whatever it was that the owner of this computer did, Charlene would be able to monitor it and then do it herself on another computer.

I finished everything, ejected the USB stick, and stood back to let Charlene shut down the machine and finish off. Silently, she put the empty water bottles in the rucksack, and wiped the keyboard clean of our fingerprints, along with the surface of the desk and the door-handles – and we went out to the sunshine, putting on our sunglasses but still screwing our eyes up against the light.

We went back to the harbour through deserted streets – siesta time – and I awkwardly went down the steps and into the boat, Charlene waited till the skipper started the engine then cast us off, threw the rope down, and nimbly climbed down and aboard. The skipper opened three beers and the throttle, and Charlene and I settled on the bench in the stern while he steered us back across the estuary. I drank the beer slowly, trying to stay calm but realising my heart was beating fast. What now? She'd cleaned our fingerprints away, but there would be traces that we'd used the computer: the files would show when they'd last been accessed, if anyone cared to look – unlikely maybe, because the owner would assume that password-protection kept him secure. I wondered how Charlene had got her hands on the password.

We reached the marina, and slowly made our way back to our berth. Charlene leapt out, tied us off, then shouldered the rucksack and started walking away quickly along the pontoon. I looked at the skipper questioningly, and he shrugged. 'I drive you back.'

We stepped off the boat and followed Charlene along the pontoon. By the time we got out of the marina and up to the rough ground where he'd parked the Land Rover, there was no sign of her. The skipper drove me back to the Kingfisher, with rattling engine, diesel fumes and no regard for any other traffic – occasionally he blasted his horn as some tourist dithered in his path, and he lifted his hands in despair: 'Rental!' he hissed.

I found my car, gave the skipper a wave as he let out the clutch and did a U-turn in the road in front of other cars, and I drove back to the hotel and went up to our empty room. From the balcony I could see Helen by the pool, so I changed into swim-shorts and went down to join her, ordering two large rum and cokes on my way through the bar to the outside decking, indicating to the waiter where I'd be.

She was lying back wearing only a bikini bottom, sunglasses, and her baseball cap. I crouched beside her and tugged one white bud from her ear as I leaned over to kiss her lips and then her left nipple.

'Are you going to tell me what the fuck that was all about?' she asked, not looking at me. I knew now that she was seriously pissed off with me – this was not pretence. I also remembered that she'd said, early in our relationship: 'Never lie to me, Martin. I won't stand for that.'

Well, a large part of my life had always been a lie, but it was coming to a head, even without the appearance of Charlene. 'Honestly, darling, it was just a wee computer job some old friends wanted me to do. Forgive me?'

The waiter arrived with our drinks, and she sat up and moved her legs aside so I could sit by her on the lounger. 'We'll see. We'll drink these and then you can be very nice to me.' There was no warmth in her voice.

'Oh yes, I promise.'

*

Three evenings later, when we had been in town for dinner and were wandering back to the hotel, we stopped at the last café on the very edge of the old town, as we usually did, for what Scottish pals would call a 'ditcher'. The place was by the main road, and had no view, but the drink was very cheap, and locals drank there. We sat inside, because the evening was dark and cool, a sign that the summer really was about end, that the last hot week had been an anomaly.

As we sipped our rum and cokes, I looked up at the TV news channel, and felt a shock as I saw the house I had been in with Charlene: I recognised the double satellite dishes. There were police cars and an ambulance, and a picture of a man: in his fifties, in a suit, balding and chubby-faced, a moustache. I watched, horrified, as the captions came up, my mind decoding them: assassinado, comerciante, milionário, crime organizado – with a question mark.

Through my haze of good food and lots of alcohol, I tried to work out if that afternoon could have had anything to do with this, and thought that it was too much of a coincidence if it hadn't. My mind raced through possibilities, but a cold certainty descended on me: this man's colleagues, or clients, had discovered their data had been compromised, and that he had become a liability, and they had killed him.

I knew this because of my previous experiences with gangsters. It's how they work. The crack in my life had opened up, the fault line that led all the way back to an August Saturday in Glasgow, a lifetime ago.

Chapter 3

Glasgow – twenty five years before

The phrase 'the day when everything changed' is much over-used these days, but for me, and for Davey Collins, there really was such a day – a mild, unusually dry August day in Glasgow.

It began with breakfast at around eleven o'clock. I'd had a shower, and found my grey trousers and the short-sleeved white shirt with my name-tag, unwashed from the Saturday before but useable. With a heavy heart I went downstairs to face mum's on-going anger.

She was frosty-faced as she paused from doing the washing-up to watch me get a bowl of cereal. The letter from the exam board that listed my failures, one line at a time, still lay accusingly by the kitchen sink. We'd been through the recriminations several times a day since Tuesday, as she realised that all the times I'd said I was doing homework with Davey up in my room, or over at his house a couple of streets away, we were really just reading computer magazines or coaxing second-hand machines back into life, writing programs to make them do tricks, playing games on them. I'd weathered the storm, miserable because I knew she was right. She'd only once said how disappointed my dad would have been, had he lived to see this day, and that hurt deeply. She never mentioned my brilliant little brother Peter, who had died of a brain tumour aged nine, but we both knew she was thinking it. 'You're clever, Martin – why are you throwing it all away?' And every time after the outburst, she'd leave the room in tears.

Now we'd moved into a new phase. The recriminations had stopped, though a cold glance from her was enough to remind me of everything she'd said. Now she was beginning to get angry – angry that I didn't give her anything towards the rent, or do any cooking or cleaning, angry that she was carrying the weight of running the little council house on her own shoulders. She was looking older and more tired day by day before my eyes. But it was too soon for me to try to make amends; I needed to ride out this angry phase. Somehow, I would make it up to her, I promised myself that. Inside, I knew it was all true what she'd said, though she hadn't said it as succinctly as I now thought it: my life was fucked.

I finished my cereal, and she grabbed the bowl, not letting me wash up myself.

'Are you off out tonight?' she asked, her back to me.

'Ah – yeah, probably. I'll go round to Davey's, maybe goin' out later. I'll be home for tea after work first, but.'

'Good of you.'

I stood for a moment, doing nothing, listening to her silent anger and feeling the well of my own disappointment at myself. Then I just grabbed my old anorak and went out to walk down to the bus stop on Drumchapel Road, past the kids playing football in the street, the old cars – one of which hadn't moved in weeks – the scabby front lawns, rotting fences and a dead spacehopper, groups of men of all ages standing around, nothing to do. I said hi to them on the way past, seeing my future life in their empty eyes – 'Hey, Martin, want to get us one of them fancy fuckin' stereos frae Dixons?' 'Aye, sure.' It wasn't a bad area – I never found it threatening – but every day there seemed to be more people just hanging around, more empty cider bottles in gardens, more hypodermic needles and broken glass by the primary school.

Once on the bus, I relaxed a bit. She'd get over it. I'd try to get more hours at Dixons, or at another shop. I agreed with her: I couldn't go on like this, but I didn't know what other options I had. I looked out at the streets of the council estates, and then the nice private bungalows with men out tending their gardens or washing their cars. On Maryhill Road I saw a young couple walking with arms round each other down the busy street, laughing and stopping to kiss and hug: she was a young blonde girl, he was tall and good-looking, well-groomed. They had it all, I had nothing. My life was completely shit. But I had no one to blame, not really.

Davey Collins and I had been well known at school as being very clever but total under-achievers; we'd have been called ultra-geeks if that expression had been used then. We hung around together all the time, so that we were regularly accused of being poofs, which was unfair – we hadn't had sex of any kind, with anybody. We spent our time with comics, electronics, science fiction, and cult TV shows and films that nobody else liked, and cassette recordings of unknown bands, taken off the radio because we couldn't afford to buy records. We didn't listen to the news: when the bright kids at school raged about 'that bitch' Thatcher being re-elected and the continuing destruction of the working classes that was leading to the social problems in council estates like ours, we shrugged and went back to analysing listings of computer programs.

We read about computers avidly, and Davey managed to get his hands on a BBC Micro and a Commodore 64 that people were practically giving away because they were old and broken; he had fixed them. I was more interested in programming, and would spend hours typing in programs for magazines, and writing my own. Our guide and mentor was Mr Jackson, a crap maths teacher who had started teaching computing instead, which he was also crap at; but he let us hang around his room and gave us free reign, never seriously asking where we should be instead of with him ('Study period, Mr Jackson.'). He let us learn, and seemed to enjoy learning along with us while hating and despising the other kids. In school we had an Apple II, a couple of BBC Micros, and a class set of Sinclair Spectrums, half of which didn't work at any one given time. We were aware that the world was moving over to faceless, beige IBM clones; they didn't interest us, but we read everything, absorbing it all.

By fifth year we were pretty much spending our whole time in the computing department, and other teachers had stopped marking us absent because they assumed we'd left school. We learned a huge amount about computers and software. We'd got good passes in our exams at the end of fourth year, and managed to persuade ourselves that our natural ability would see us through our Highers. That letter, by the kitchen sink, was the cruel evidence that we had been wrong. It seemed obvious after the event that not attending classes meant that you didn't learn anything about those subjects, and wouldn't pass the exam. We didn't even pass the computing exam, because I skipped half the syllabus there – all the hardware stuff – and Davey skimped on the software side; both narrow fails, but fails nonetheless.

We'd gone into school the day after the results came out because my mum and Davey's dad said we had to, and we suffered the derision and the 'I told you so' routine and the sarcasm, and vowed we'd never go back. I continued with the Saturday job in Dixons, gained because I was vaguely presentable and could talk to people. But Davey was unemployable: his long hair was always greasy, he had very bad acne, and he couldn't hold eye contact with anyone for more than a moment.

That Saturday afternoon, Charlie Talbot swaggered into Dixons to look around the stereos and the big TVs. He was my age, but centuries cooler, more confident; high cheekbones and long, fine, blond hair, always with girls hanging round him as he had a cigarette outside the school at breaks, the staff never challenging him - almost as if they were half-afraid of him. The story was that he'd been expelled from two schools, including a private one. Nobody knew what his dad did for a living, nor whether he had a mother.

Somehow, he seemed to quite like me, but I treated him with extreme caution. Soon after he'd arrived at our school, a couple of the local neds had grabbed him at home time and roughed him up gently. I'd hung back with Davey – neither of us inclined to interfere, partly because it didn't look like a serious roughing up, mostly because we were scared – but went up to him afterwards to check if he was OK. They'd said they wanted some money tomorrow off him, or they'd duff him up more, he told us.

The next day after school, I'd been surprised to see Charlie head out of the school gates with his normal confident swagger, and cross the road towards the neds, who nodded and smiled, perhaps expecting a handover of some cash and a regular income. Davey and I watched, mystified. But two men emerged from a car parked close by – small, wiry, badly dressed men, who grabbed the kids and punched them to the ground. Charlie got to the spot and started kicking the bodies squealing there, only stopping when the two men suggested he lay off. One of them bent and said some words, grabbing a fistful of hair until he seemed satisfied with the response he got.

Charlie recognised me in Dixons of course. 'Hey, man – how you doing?'

We made small talk, discussed a couple of stereos, and then, as he was about to leave, he said: 'Hey – want to come to the party tonight?'

I shrugged. 'Yeah.'

'Great.' He turned to go.

'Where is it?'

'My place.'

'Oh, yeah. Right. Where's that?'

He looked puzzled. 'You never been there?' I shook my head, and he gave me the address – in Bearsden, only a couple of miles and a golf course from where I lived, but socially light years away. 'Bring that weird pal of yours – should be a laugh.'

An hour after he'd left, Andrew Russell came in, and looked slightly bemused to see me. 'You working here, Martin?' He was smaller than me, slightly chubby, with glasses and massive tightly-curled long hair.

He realised his question had been pretty stupid when I pointed to my name badge. He ummed and erred and then asked: 'How did the exams go?'

‘Crap,’ I said. ‘Failed them all. How about you?’

He shuffled his feet awkwardly. ‘Five As.’

‘Well done. Sixth year and then off to Uni?’

He nodded, his limp hair bobbing. ‘Maths and stats. Glasgow.’

‘Well done,’ I said again, and watched the life I could maybe have had walk out onto Sauchiehall Street, feet dragging.

*

That evening Davey and I eked out a couple of cans of lager at his house while trading across the galaxy in Elite on the BBC Micro and a tiny colour TV Davey had rescued from the roadside beside a bin and fixed. Then his dad got home, so we ducked out from his baleful stare and went to the local pub. They never IDed anyone because they needed all the customers they could get: there was little profit in unemployed men who front-loaded with home-brew or supermarket cider or fortified wine and then nursed a pint and a packet of ten fags for the whole evening, making conversation out of a day spent doing nothing.

Davey and I talked about the very hard time we were getting over the exam results and the lack of prospects, but mainly we spoke of computer games which we’d never be able to buy, but which I had become good at pirating if I could get a copy. The idea of hiking across to Bearsden had been discussed and dismissed, but after a second pint we both tacitly agreed that we didn’t want to go home and couldn’t afford to drink here any more, so we went. To Charlie Talbot’s party in Bearsden, to change our lives.

The house was in a quiet, narrow cul de sac near the golf course. It didn’t look overwhelmingly posh from the outside, apart from the black Mercedes-Benz in the drive. Charlie answered the door and greeted us enthusiastically, pulling us into the darkness and the noise of the thudding synthetic synthesiser beat, and the sweaty heave of bodies. 'Fuckin' brilliant night, man,' he shouted at us. 'Where have you been?'

We stood in the hallway and tried to take in our surroundings: wooden floors, a glimpse into a front room containing leather chairs and wooden furniture and a huge TV, while elsewhere came the very loud hammering beat of some disco rubbish.

He dragged us through to the kitchen, which looked like it came out of Tomorrow's World with silver and metal surfaces and machines, and he thrust a can of Tennent's lager into each of our grateful hands. We prised them open and drank. He seemed not to have noticed that we hadn't brought a carry-out ourselves, but we could now pretend we'd just set it down amongst all the other drink. We didn't feel too out of place at first, until we took a good look around and noticed what people were wearing.

Charlie himself was dressed up like he was auditioning for a stint as a camp Pharaoh – he did the silly desert shuffling walk, and I looked blankly at him. Davey and I were dressed in jeans and T-shirts, as ever. As I slugged the lager, I looked around at the other bodies in the huge kitchen – and through the sun lounge to the patio outside – and realised everyone was dressed up in various stupid ways: a couple of guys in sharp suits with girls in short black dresses and 40's make-up, somebody carrying a sledgehammer (which, luckily, seemed to be fake), somebody with an outrageous mane of blonde hair. Davey and I looked at each other, realising that everyone else was in on something. We were out of place after all, and there was that moment where we thought we ought to just finish the can and bail out, back to our own world, which was normal and understandable. It was the sensible, right thing to do.

'Another can?'

Fuck it, we'd give it a go, till the drink ran out. What else were we going to do? 'Just going to the bog first – where is it?' I put my freshly opened can down.

Charlie led me out of the kitchen and shoved me through a heavy wooden door into the most exotic toilet I'd ever seen in my life. Tiles and towels, and little bowls of soaps and other stuff. There was a shower and a huge antique loo that I felt I might just fall into.

Afterwards, I went back through to the kitchen. There were loads of couples and small groups, chatting and shouting and screaming with laughter, but no sign of Charlie or Davey. There was a girl standing by the spot where I'd set down my can, on the sort of island unit where the cooker was. I hesitated and then said hi to her and indicated that she was blocking the way to my beer. She looked up at me and blinked, and then seemed to come to her senses and gave a wide smile, showing even, perfect white teeth: 'Sorry!' She turned and handed me my can. 'I'm Fiona.' The smile stirred something inside me.

I gulped. 'Martin.' Her smile widened. She continued to look at my face.

In those days, girls at my school didn't really do computers, so I was seldom in their company. I was 17, and not only a virgin but with simply no experience whatsoever of interacting with girls socially or in any other way. I appreciated pretty girls, and had sexual desires, but had never sought out any kind of relationship that might have led somewhere. And girls didn't exactly seek me out either. I was shabby and untidy and poor. I was the opposite of Charlie. I was away at the end of a spectrum of desirability as far as girls were concerned. I had nothing to offer them. I would never be that guy on Maryhill Road with the gorgeous blonde on his arm.

So, I had never experienced someone like Fiona looking at me. I didn't know what she was thinking, didn't know what she wanted. I hadn't a clue what to do.

She was quite small, and very dark – short dark hair and dark, loose clothes, with loads of mascara, her skin tanned. She looked quite attractive – so why was she looking at me? – and her accent was fairly cultured, not like mine. She was holding a glass of red wine like she was accustomed to doing such a thing.

'Who are you dressed as?' she asked me.

'I'm dressed as Martin.' She laughed, and I had a strange feeling inside. 'How about you?' Gosh, I was having a conversation with a girl!

'I've come dressed as Fiona.'

We nodded, and then we both laughed, genuinely and loudly, together. It was an exhilarating moment.

'So what do you do, Martin?'

Ah, here we go. I took a long drink from my can, and she drank from her glass of red wine. I made a decision just to talk to her, openly and honestly, no bullshit. 'I've just left school, nothing planned. Hoping to do something with computers, but I'm not sure how to get into it. I'm really good with computers.' More lager. Oh god, this sounded dull even to me. 'We kind of pissed around at school – apart from the computer stuff, which I mentioned – so I haven't passed any exams, so Uni is a bit out of the question.' She nodded sympathetically. All of that came out in a bit of a rush, but I could now pose the next question: 'How about you?'

She took a long time to think about that. I gave a frown of concentration and folded my arms. 'I've just finished first year at art college.'

Ah, so she was at least a year older than me, and cleverer, as well as being classier. And attractive. The tiny spark that had ignited – the idea that we might somehow hit it off – died.

'Don't think I've passed, so not sure what I'll do after the summer.'

I nodded wisely. 'What options do you have?'

'Probably just go round Europe. My dad lives in Italy, so I might just make my way out there. Play the sympathy card, maybe get some cash off him.'

God, she was seriously out of my league; they could make a movie of her life, already. 'Your parents divorced?' I guessed. She nodded. 'My dad's dead,' I heard myself say.

'Oh dear.' Genuine concern passed across her face. 'What happened?'

'Cancer – a few years ago. He smoked like a chimney, so...' I realised I hadn't thought properly about him for some time, not even when mum had used him as a weapon in the failed-exam arguments. Suddenly, unexpectedly, I could feel myself welling up, and I couldn't speak.

'Hey.' She took a step towards me, and put her arms round me and her head on my shoulder.

This was a new experience for me, and I didn't know what to do. Unfortunately, my penis knew exactly how to react to the close proximity of an attractive young woman, and I had to ease her away from me. I guessed from her lack of outrage that she was probably well-used to getting that reaction from boys who held her tight.

I finished my can. 'I could do with another beer. Want a drink?' I looked round.

'I'll get you one,' she said.

I watched her ease through the crowds to the fridge. She disappeared from view, and my heart sank a little. Then she reappeared holding a can and a half-empty bottle of red wine, and her smile was the most wonderful thing I'd ever seen. She came back over, and stood very close to me. This was already the best evening I'd had in my life. I desperately tried to think of interesting things to say. Did she like computer games maybe?

'So,' she said, 'we're just two souls who don't know where we're going.' We started on our drinks. She really was standing very close to me, and looking at my face. I was conscious of my old clothes, that I was a bit sweaty.

'That's a poetic way of saying it, but it serves me right for pissing about.'

The music had been loud, but suddenly it got even louder. I couldn't hear myself think, and I grimaced as Fiona said something. 'What?'

She smiled again and shook her head. Then she said something which I didn't hear, and reached for my hand and gently led me.

She took me upstairs and found a small spare bedroom, led me in, and firmly closed the door behind us. We sat in the gloom, on the bed, close together, drinking. The music thudded away elsewhere in the house.

We talked about my dad, and those horrible months as he died – four years ago. I had never, ever talked to anyone about that before, especially not to Davey, my only real friend. I hadn't realised the effect it had had on me, and on mum. She had become different after that – distant, lonely, unhappy. She hadn't got on to me about school, hadn't seem interested, until the blow-up when my spectacular failure came to light, probably partly blaming herself. I suppose my getting into computers had been a kind of withdrawal from the real world.

We talked about my clever wee brother Peter who had died a couple of years before dad, and who had become some kind of unspoken saint, a ghost in the house, a benchmark for all of my failures.

We talked about Fiona's mum and dad. Her dad – he was Italian – and had simply walked out on Fiona and her younger sister two years ago, leaving her mum pretty financially screwed, except that he'd left her the house. Fiona had felt betrayed, still did: she had loved her dad, and couldn't understand how he could have left them.

We held each other tight, and then she put her face close to mine and I kissed her, the red wine from her mixing with the lager on my breath. At first I copied what I'd seen in films and on TV: I based my technique on the many scenes where Captain Kirk sweeps the beautiful alien off her feet. But after a few minutes it just became natural.

We kissed and kissed. And we put our drinks down and our hands started moving, and I just gasped with the thrill and the pleasure of it all – that was what those things felt like! God, this was one for the autobiography.

And as I started fumbling with her clothes to get to the feel of her skin, amazed that she was letting me do this, she smiled and pulled back. 'I'll do it.' She took off her jumper and her bra, and then stood up to undress completely. I watched in disbelief till she was naked. A naked girl, in front of me, in real life. I tried to memorise everything.

She smiled. 'This is a bit one-sided, Martin.' She slipped past me and under the covers.

I took my clothes off – it had never been so difficult. I thought she would laugh at the sight of my pale scrawny body, but she didn't.

In bed, we held each other and kissed, and my hands were everywhere, gathering impressions. And then she parted her legs and I lay between them and prodded like the amateur I was.

'You're trembling,' she said. 'Calm down. You're so lovely, so gentle.'

I clumsily manoeuvred and panted. A few seconds later I groaned. 'Oh, god.'

'It's alright – don't worry.' She held me tight, and kissed me, and – miraculously – I was ready again.

'Don't mind my asking,' she said as we fumbled, 'but is this your first time?

'Ah, yes,' I mumbled into her hair. 'Sorry.'

'Don't worry.' She gave a sexy chuckle, and reached down between us and her soft fingers guided me in.

I was awash with excitement, wonder, delight, fear. 'How about you?' I asked. 'Are you a – er – '

'No.' Her voice sounded sad.

What followed was absolute magic, and the time just flowed as we held each other, stroking and kissing. At the end, she was writhing under me, and cried out as she squeezed me tight, and we lay back, sweating and panting. I can still recall that first feeling of satisfying a lover, the best feeling in the world.

'Well done, Martin,' she gasped. 'You're a natural.' I lay on my back, cradling her in my arms, holding her tight. I didn't want this to end, ever. Stop the world, let me stay here.

Rather late, I thought of a question: 'Are you on the pill?'

She gave that sexy chuckle again. 'Actually I forgot for a few days, but took a double lot this morning. I should be OK. Don't worry.'

Rather late, I thought of another question, but decided not to ask. AIDS had been a problem in San Francisco and was spreading rapidly through Britain, but I was pretty sure it wouldn't have reached Bearsden yet.

I suppose I must have dozed off. When I awoke, Fiona was dressed. 'I'm going to get a drink,' she said. 'Back soon.' She picked up her glass and my empty beer can and opened the door, checked outside, and then closed it softly behind her.

I lay grinning like an idiot, arms behind my head, and tried to fix every moment in my mind. God, I felt so good. I was a man. I'd had sex. A woman had wanted me – and she was lovely! Which meant I must be quite attractive too! Brilliant!

Desperate for the toilet suddenly, I got up and dressed. I found a loo, just two doors down. When I came out, there was no sign of Fiona, so I decided to head downstairs to find her.

On the landing was a door which was ajar. I looked in automatically as I passed it. There was a desk with an anglepoise light, and what looked like an Amstrad PC on a computer desk. There was a man sitting on an office chair, and as I looked at him he started a string of swearwords. I stopped outside the door. He turned and stared at me, still obviously angry.

'Can I help you?' His voice was a low growl. He had short grey hair, receding at the front, and a tough, angular face. His eyes were clear, cold blue. His long neck was a network of sinews and veins. He wore a shirt and jeans.

'Sorry – I'm Martin, one of Charlie's pals from school. At the party.'

'Oh, right.' He turned back to the VDU.

'Are you having problems?'

He didn't look round. 'Fuck off, son.'

'OK.'

But before I had gone two steps his growl came again. 'Do you know anything about these fuckers?'

I stepped back to the doorway. 'Yeah, quite a bit actually.'

'This fucking machine is driving me mental.' He dropped his hands from the keyboard to his sides, and sat back.

I took that as an invitation, so I stepped into the room and looked at the screen. He had a blank spreadsheet open. He was holding a 5½" floppy disk in his hand and looked like he had tried to shove it into the 3" disk drive on the Amstrad.

I glanced round the room – obviously a study – and saw the BBC Micro with its monitor and twin 5½" disk drives (and the 6502 co-processor unattached beside it) on another desk. I also saw the bookshelves and the steel filing cabinet with the security lock over the drawers, but it was the BBC Micro that told me what I needed to know: a previous flirtation with computing that had been abandoned until someone had talked him into trying again in the new world of the IBM clone.

'That won't fit,' I said.

He took a deep breath and was about to say something sarcastic that began with F.

'And even it did, you wouldn't be able to read the data off it.'

He exhaled slowly. 'OK,' he said.

'Were you using ViewSheet on the BBC?'

He raised his eyebrows and turned to me, realising that I really did know what I was talking about. 'You a fuckin' psychic?'

'And you're using Supercalc on the Amstrad?'

'Yes.' The word tailed into a hiss.

I nodded. Cheekily, I just looked at the VDU, and said nothing more. He had a blank spreadsheet on the screen.

'So, what can I do?' He got up and leaned past me to close the door. Then he retrieved a chunky, crystal glass full of whisky from beside the computer, and took a good drink of it.

I thought for a minute. Between us, Davey and I would be able to sort this out, and it would only take us an hour or so. Should I offer? Should I mention a charge? Should I suggest it was really hard and would take us a day or two?

'Me and my pal could sort this out for you. We might need to get a lead, but apart from that it won't be a problem. It should only take a couple of hours.'

I could sense he was thinking whether to offer money. 'That would be... good,' he said. 'I'll pay for the lead of course.'

'Great.' Davey probably already had a suitable lead, but we'd charge anyway.

'And if it works I'll pay you for your time. Can you get here this afternoon – ' he had glanced at his huge gold wristwatch – 'at around three?'

I nodded. 'Sure.'

I headed downstairs to find Davey and tell him what we were doing the next day and to find where Fiona had got to. The party seemed to be quietening down.

I found Davey, slumped on a settee with a can of lager dribbling down his chest. I managed to wake him up. I tried to explain what was going on before he lost consciousness, but he didn't understand. 'Look, I'll come round for you at one o'clock tomorrow,' I shouted at him. That seemed to register. 'Make sure you're in. We have a wee job to do. I'll explain then.'

He nodded again and his head lolled back. Obviously I had to get him home. But first I had a good look round the party: no sign of Fiona. I collared Charlie. 'Have you seen Fiona?' 'Who?' 'Wee, dark hair, dressed normally – no outfit.' He seemed to think, then shook his head. 'No idea, mate.'

I spent ages looking around, checking the bathrooms, the other rooms, and back up to the wee bedroom where we'd had sex – if I ever became famous, would they put a wee blue plaque on the door? – but she wasn't there. I didn't even know her second name. I asked a few people – Abba, and the guy with the sledgehammer – but nobody knew her.

But I still had my warm, happy feeling as I staggered home with Davey through the empty suburbs. OK, she was gone, but others would surely follow. I grinned. What a night.

The day when everything changed. Suddenly I didn't care about the exam results. I was a man. I'd had sex. I could do anything.

*

'My name's Ken, by the way. Ken Talbot.' He was wearing a suit and tie today. Standing up, he wasn't as tall as me, but had a presence about him. He was always looking, his narrow eyes focused, always thinking.

We'd got back to Charlie's dad's house on time on the day after the party, as promised, despite Davey's killer hangover. I was still high from my first sexual experience – and I really wanted to see Fiona again – and probably still drunk. I couldn't keep the smile from my face, and Davey was starting to get pissed off.

Davey was the hardware man, and I was doing the software. I hadn't used an Amstrad before, but I'd read all about them and the CP/M operating system, and I knew what to do: it was an ability I had - still do. Davey attached the serial lead, and got the computers talking to each other, and then he slumped in the corner, eyes half-shut, but ready in case I needed help or advice.

In under two hours, even with hiccups over dropped connections, we had all of Talbot's spreadsheets across from the BBC discs to the Amstrad, and I did a bit of tweaking. Talbot sat down and checked that they opened properly, that his data was intact. I was looking over his shoulder, but he turned and suggested that 'you two kids' go downstairs till he called us. I nodded. I had seen a list of names and addresses – people and businesses - with amounts of money and dates beside each, going on for row after row.

Davey and I went downstairs. Charlie was in the kitchen, drinking tea and looking immaculate. The kitchen, and the whole house, seemed to have been restored to normality – no sign of so much as a beer bottle cap or a crisp or a ring-pull tab on the kitchen floor. I looked around at the cupboards and the appliances, and thought of my mum's ancient gas cooker, our tiny fridge.

'Fuckin' brilliant party, eh?'

I agreed, and Davey nodded, not trusting himself to speak – he looked like he was trying not to be sick. His long black hair was spectacularly greasy today, hanging over his pale acned face.

I tried again to find out about Fiona. 'There was a girl – Fiona,' I said. Charlie frowned and shook his head. 'Wee, dark-haired. Wasn't in any kind of outfit, just a dark jumper, dark trousers. Been to art college. Ring a bell?'

Charlie shook his head. 'Sorry, mate. What's her second name? Where does she live?'

I shrugged, suddenly hopeless. I didn't even know which art college she might have been to. Shit. Oh yes: 'She's probably got a kind of Italian-sounding second name.'

Charlie shook his head again. 'Want me to ask around?' Then his face lit up: 'Did you shag her, yah dancer!'

I nodded, trying not to look smug.

'So, no more a virgin nerd, eh? Never mind, Davey, your time will come.'

There was a shout from above, and we went upstairs again to his dad's study. Talbot pointed to the screen with its lists of names, and started asking us questions: could he put it in order of amounts of money? Could he flag up rows with amounts over, say, a grand; could he copy certain columns or rows onto another sheet so that certain people could only see certain information? I answered all his questions, explaining about hiding rows (he understood that), and conditional formatting (he looked blank). Finally he nodded, eyebrows raised, and stood up. 'Come on down and get a cup of tea and we'll have a wee chat.'

We sat in the kitchen again, but he told Charlie to leave us alone, which he did, saying he was heading into town. Talbot made us cups of tea.

'Right, boys,' Talbot said, 'what do I owe you?'

Davey told him what the lead cost – 'might as well keep it here in case there's other stuff you want to copy over' – and then I said: 'and there's our time of course.'

'Of course.' He was still standing with his wallet in his hand. 'What do I owe you for 'your time'?'

'Eh… a tenner? Each?' I suggested.

He laughed, and handed it over. 'A tenner each.' He put his wallet away, and stood up. 'OK, boys, I need to chase you – I have things to see, people to do.' He laughed again.

'If you need any more help, just give us a shout,' I offered. 'You want my phone number?'

'If I need you, I'll find you. Don't you worry.' His voice was cold now.

Outside, I laughed aloud. I had had sex, and I had a tenner in my pocket. And part of me realised I had a skill that could maybe earn me more tenners, but I wasn't sure how. Meanwhile, this money was going straight to mum – that might keep her sweet, show I was going to pay my way.

Life was suddenly good. Promising, in a vague sort of way.

Chapter 4

Last autumn – Portugal and Glasgow

For the rest of our holiday after the murder in Portimao, I was on tenterhooks.

'Ever since that Neanderthal guy and little-miss-perfect-blonde appeared, you've been on edge. What's going on?' Helen would say, regularly. She knew something was preoccupying me; that wouldn't of itself have bothered her too much, but the obvious fact that I was keeping a secret from her did. It struck at the heart of our relationship.

'I'd like to explore Portimao, and we need to do that boat trip up-river to Silves that we planned. And we've hardly used the hire car: let's explore along to Sagres, or into the mountains.'

I agreed of course, though I sensed that it was not going to be comfortable for me.

We drove to the same rough car park by the marina, but to a different area. The boat was big, with the whole of the flat roof covered with solar panels. The two hosts greeted us with smiles and chat, and we joined the other eight passengers. They were three British couples and two single Dutch women, all in their sixties or seventies.

Our two hosts – one young guy, barely twenty, and an older man around my age – gave a continuous flow of banter and jokes, which kept everyone amused; but my smiles were rather fixed, and my laughter the quietest of us all.

I re-lived my journey from that day – no sign of the fishing boat in that big, crowded marina – as we crawled past the bunkering station, then round the harbour wall, towards the estuary. As we turned to head upstream, I could clearly see the houses on the other side, a couple of police cars parked, a couple of GNR police wandering around, keeping an eye on things – but otherwise the area was deserted.

A thought came into my head and I looked around the harbour area for CCTV cameras, but there was nothing I could see. I remembered that Charlene had wiped the house clean of our fingerprints – but what price getting trace DNA from my sweaty fingers on the computer keyboard?

But even if – somehow – the police tied me to the house, surely there was no way they could implicate me for the murder. Maybe the murder had nothing to do with our visit at all.

I settled back in the boat as we cruised underneath the motorway bridge, with its storks' nests. Helen looked at me, and I gave her a wide smile, and held her tight. It would be OK, I told myself.

We had a lovely trip up to Silves, and then a couple of hours to browse round the steep streets of the city, and up to the castle. On the way back, we were plied with beer and wine, and fed a chicken salad. The crew got funnier and more outrageous, and I relaxed.

Helen and I only had a few days of our holiday left. We drove out to Sagres, from where, apparently, Columbus had set sail westwards. We drove up into the mountains, and ate chicken piri-piri while gazing down at what seemed like the full stretch of the Algarve. We had another day on the beach, making love in the afternoon and again after a last meal in what we chose as our most favourite, most expensive restaurant.

And then we flew back to a cold, wet Glasgow, and back to our flat in the West End and work.

I tried to find out what I could about the murder in Portimao on the first evening back, but no British people were involved so there was nothing in our papers. I found stuff online, including descriptions of the victim, and talk of money laundering and connections to organised crime. When I read that, I stopped looking.

*

On the Monday after we got back, Helen was up early and into her study in our flat, on her laptop and blackberry, clearing emails, chasing up people, resuming discussions on deals that were under way. Several of the conversations were with my ex-wife Elizabeth: they both worked in publishing, trying to make sense of – and money at – the new digital world: helping promising writers publish on e-readers, picking up authors who had already self-published on e-readers and had established a track record, developing magazines and books for tablets. She seemed glad to be getting back to work, and I hoped she'd just forget about some of the events in Alvor.

After breakfast I took a taxi through the rain and the cold down to St Vincent Street and my office – 'B&D Software Solutions' – near the highest point of that road, looking east to the city centre, west to the motorway and on along Argyle Street to where it all began. The buildings here were two hundred years old, home to lawyers and accountants, small creative companies. And us.

Inside our offices on the second floor, we had established a quiet, calm atmosphere: modern and stark, with comfortable chairs, a coffee machine, and a very pretty secretary to welcome prospective and returning business customers. Three offices led off the main reception area, and there were a couple of small meeting rooms, and a larger conference room with projection facilities.

Claire looked up as I came in. 'Hi, Martin. Good holiday?' Her smile was wide, her long red hair curling past her shoulders in slow, thick waves, intelligent green eyes shining.

'Great, thanks.' I tried to sound enthusiastic. I made myself a coffee – Claire shook her head – and sat across the desk from her. 'Fabulous weather, and a great chill-out.'

'So what did you get up to?'

'Well, mainly sea, sun and sex,' I grinned and she laughed.

We chatted a bit about some of the things Helen and I had done – no, Claire had never been there: her skin couldn't handle strong sunshine – and where we'd gone.

'Is Sandy in?' I asked eventually.

Claire shook her head. He went away for a few days – due back tomorrow.' She was on the computer, checking his calendar. 'He was in Portugal too.'

'Was he?'

''Carry over'… or something like that.'

'Carvoiero?'

'Yes, that's it. Anywhere near you?'

'Not far,' I murmured. Not far at all, I reflected: just a few miles on the other side of Portimao. So, what had that thing in Portugal been about really?

'Anyone else coming in today?'

'Yes.' She peered at her screen. 'Graham has a pitch at two, a law firm. In the conference room. It's booked till six, and then he's planning to wine and dine them. He'd like you to join him, to help field any questions – he's sent a meeting request.'

'OK,' I stood up and fixed myself another coffee. 'To work.'

I went past the other two offices to mine. One door had a dark, gluey rectangle where the nameplate had been hurriedly prised off, when Colin Strachan had left suddenly, four years ago. Sandy Lomond used this office when he was around. The second office was Graham Turner, with the label 'Head of software sales'. My office had my name on it, and the title 'Head of software development'.

Inside, I closed the door and sat in my big leather chair, switched on the two computers – the iMac with its 27" screen, and the PC I'd inherited from Colin – and looked at the photograph of Helen on my desk. I reached to touch it. I'll get out and make this all OK, I said; I promise.

I sipped my coffee, and my mind went in two directions: one was trying to motivate myself to work, the other was still on my plan to get out of all of this. It was urgent now, after the Portugal business. I thought about Colin Strachan, and how he'd got away – Sandy hadn't even been angry, and I wasn't aware that he'd ever tried to find Colin. Maybe I should try to contact him; he'd left me a mobile number, but I'd never called, and maybe he'd changed it after all this time. I could even go to see him, wherever in the world he was.

Most urgently though, I needed to talk to Andrew Russell again – my old schoolmate and nowadays my personal financial adviser. I nodded to my reflection in the computer screen. Portugal had scared me.

I picked up the phone and speed-dialled. As I waited to speak to Andrew, I watched the emails and appointment requests pour in.

'Hey, Martin – how's it going?'

I could hear background chatter. 'Hi, Andrew.'

'Good holiday?'

'Yes – fabulous weather, good chill out.'

'Sea sun and sex?' he said.

'That's pretty much it. Listen. Can we meet up this week some time?'

'Sure.' A keyboard clacked. 'Solid this week, mate. How about…'

'How about after hours?' I interrupted.

'Sure.' More clacking. 'Tomorrow at six thirty? Blackfriars?'

'Perfect.'

'To do with…?'

'Same as before,' I said. 'But I'd like to step up the pace.'

Andrew sucked in his breath. 'Double-dip recession, Martin – maybe a triple. Not a good time to get out. And you risk attracting attention.'

‘I’ll need to take that chance,’ I said. ‘I need to get a move on with this, Andrew.’

‘OK. See you tomorrow, Martin.’

I put the phone down, and settled to work.

It took most of the morning to catch up with what had been going on. We had four people along Argyle Street in what had been our original premises, ‘Bytes and Digits’, back in the day. The two Franks were primarily hardware people, and Ian and Craig did most of the software, leasing out work to an agency in India as necessary. We had a string of clients across Scotland, from fairly large businesses down to shops and one-man operations, and a bunch of loyal hobbyists. We installed hardware and software for them, and kept it all up-to-date and safe. Well, safe from other people.

I checked that all of that side was working properly, that Ian and Craig were sorting out any problems – they kept me informed of anything major – and that our client database was up-to-date; I left it open on screen, showing the table of IP addresses and admin passwords and sorted by the date I had last changed those passwords. Most days I did some research into the latest developments in online security, reading press releases and following the forums. I would also usually phone around a few clients, checking that they were happy, maybe suggesting some hardware upgrade or replacement that might be useful for them, organising it if they said yes. It all kept our customer base loyal and grateful.

But today I had other things to catch up on.

I booted the PC into our bespoke version of Linux and logged on with my password. I stayed with the command line here: no windows environment or visual cues, just my memory. I typed 'strangle10', and that program started up, giving no clues that anything was happening at all until it put up two numbers, a nine-digit and a six-digit. On my phone, I sent a text to a contact called Straiton containing those numbers. This person would access the identified bank account, and transfer whatever money was there to other accounts, including mine. Hopefully there were enough steps in that process to obscure any direct connections between B&D – specifically me – and the people out there.

Now I typed woz84. Again there was just a long pause while the program went out to somewhere on the Internet and came back with a list of six numbers: IP addresses this time. I angled the monitor and went over to our customer database on the Mac. The IP addresses corresponded to six of our clients. I worked my way down the admin passwords that hadn't been changed in the last month – most of each password stayed the same, but I changed digits in there using the date of change as a key; except for the clients that Woz84 had given me: these stayed the same, because the people out there were getting on-going returns from those clients.

And finally I typed Gregory on the PC, and got a ten-digit number back from somebody somewhere, and a question-mark prompt. The number was divisible by nine, which meant that all was OK, the whole system was safe. I made up a ten-digit number that was also divisible by nine and typed it in, then pressed return. After a minute or so I got the command-line prompt back.

All that remained to do now was to check for updates for the operating system. I did that, and agreed to download and install them from the repository.

While it got on with that, I went to get another coffee, had a brief chat to Claire, and came back to stand and stare out of the window.

Out there was a person, or maybe a whole organisation, called Gregorius. We basically sold him access to our customers' computers, and from there they could step across to all of their clients' computers. We had also left gaps in the security of the software systems we had installed, so that Gregorius could install its own software without any alarms being raised – or, if a problem arose, the customer would phone us and I would go round and 'sort it'. The software could be anything: I didn't know and I didn't want to know. But it would be the kind of form-catcher and keylogger I'd installed in Portugal, which our anti-virus installation would say was perfectly fine. Gregorius could harvest details of bank accounts, email addresses, passwords; they could go on to steal money, carry out identity theft, or set up a computer as part of a botnet which might be used at any time for anything from sending out mass spam emails to bringing down computer systems belonging to commercial organisations or even governments.

None of this was of my doing. Colin Strachan had set it up, but I'd been left running it all when he'd vanished that day. And I just had to keep doing it, until I in turn managed somehow to get away from here. Sandy knew about it of course, and Ken Talbot probably did too. I wondered whether either of our programmers had any suspicions, or had done any investigating.

I finished my coffee and turned back to the PC: all done. I shut it down with a sigh.

Helen phoned. 'Hiya, darling – how's it going?'

'Busy busy,' I said. I pulled the iMac out of its sleep. 'We have clients coming in this afternoon – if that goes well, we'll have survived the recession for another day. How are you?'

'In the middle of lunch with Elizabeth. It's looking good. The whole Scandinavian crime thing is still going strong – our problem is getting good translators.'

'Good stuff.' No mention of Portugal – maybe it had all blown over.

'Anyway, are we free for dinner tonight?'

'Yes,' I said, and then wished I'd checked on the reason for the question.

'Curry with Jim and Catherine – they were on the Algarve in the summer, loads to talk about.'

Yes, I thought: Catherine was a literary agent, so she and Helen would have loads to talk about. I'd met Catherine but not Jim, though I knew he was a schoolteacher: I had never forgotten the reaction I'd got when my mum had tried to get me back into school to try again with my exams, never forgiven. But I was down on Brownie points: 'Sounds great! Where and when?'

'Oran Mor at seven, Balbir's at eight. OK with you?'

'I'll be tight getting back to the flat – might just go straight to the pub.'

'No problem. See you then. Love you.'

'Love you, darling.'

*

The sales pitch that afternoon seemed straightforward. Graham was the sort of guy who oozed massive confidence that hid little actual knowledge – I supplied that, stepping in to answer or head-off questions, explain the jargon that Graham spouted effortlessly but had only a limited understanding of. I watched his easy style, jacket off, sleeves rolled up, no tie, short hair spiked with gel, the young handsome face, the smile – the less he understood a question, the wider the smile became. He got us clients like this because people saw him as one of them, and hence trustworthy.

Well, maybe it wasn't so straightforward this time. One of the clients – she introduced herself as Rebecca, was dressed sharply in a dark suit with heavy-framed glasses, and never smiled – asked a lot of good questions about security: she knew her stuff. I could see her colleagues were slightly embarrassed in the way she pressed Graham, and that they were largely baffled, as was he.

Graham explained about our own anti-virus software.

'Why wouldn't we use a commercial product?'

'Ours is better?'

'In what way?'

'It just is.'

'How can it be better that something like Kaspersky, which has an international database, sharing knowledge of viruses, and can be customised too.'

Graham's smile split his face, and I leaned forward. 'Our anti-virus has access to other international databases, and we share our knowledge.' This was true: the last thing we wanted was some other bastard stealing money before we could steal it. 'And our product – free, as part of the package – is based on other similar products, actually Trend. But ours understands the environment you are working in, and will not pester you with false positives: it lets us know here if there is a problem, and we can patch it, as part of our on-going commitment to keep your system secure and your business safe and operational. So you have the advantage of a tailored product, with all the features of a normal off-the-shelf one.'

Graham was still grinning like an idiot, but I could see Rebecca wasn't convinced; none of her colleagues was about to argue with her knowledge – she was the key person in the room, and Graham hadn't spotted that, because she wasn't pretty: he had been talking mainly to the men.

I made the judgement call. 'But we are more than happy to install the anti-virus software of your choice on the system, and help you customise and manage it, including updates. It'll be more work for us, but we're happy to do it.' It would be more work for Ian and Craig: I wasn't going to be touching this one. We'd do a straight install.

Rebecca nodded, and she smiled for the first time: 'That would be good. Sorry about the interruption – carry on, Graham.'

'No problem,' Graham said. 'We want our customers to be happy – we rely on you feeling safe and secure. We want to protect your data like it was our own.'

He had ordered wine and canapés for after the business part of the meeting, along with lager and orange juice. Rebecca steamed through a large glass of red and seemed relaxed as Claire topped her up. As far as the male clients were concerned, having Claire around was the clincher: their eyes lit up as she smiled and leaned forward unnecessarily to fill their glasses. They admired her long legs, and didn't notice her engagement ring.

Just after six, I made my excuses. Graham walked with me to the main door of the office. 'Thanks, Martin.'

'She knows a lot about Internet security,' I said, indicating Rebecca. I found myself thinking about the lost opportunities here: lawyers could have interesting contacts and clients. Then I shook my head: Jesus, I was thinking like a criminal. 'Have you seen Sandy recently?'

'He's in the Algarve, apparently. Some business thing came up that he had to go and deal with. I think it's all done now, so he's just having a break.'

I nodded. 'Do you know a friend of Sandy's – short blonde girl, young, very pretty.'

Graham shook his head. 'I'm sure I'd have noticed.'

I sighed. 'You certainly would have.'

*

On the way back to Byres Road in the taxi, I realised I was a bit drunk. With the swaying of the taxi, and then the cold fresh air as I got out, I suddenly felt very drunk indeed: Claire had kept topping up the large wine glasses, and I hadn't managed to grab any lunch.

I stumbled up the steps of the converted church into the wooden, beery busy-ness, and the first thing I made out was Helen's frown. Jim and Catherine were already there: him tall and white-haired, a smiling affable look on his face, Catherine just as tall, stick-thin with bobbed brown hair with patches of red.

I greeted them at the table: Jim insisted on getting the round in – I thought a beer would be a good idea – while I sat down heavily.

'Busy day?' Catherine asked.

'Clients,' I said. 'We had to get them drunk to clinch the sale.'

'And you were on orange juice?' Helen suggested.

I caught her look: the serious pissed-off look from Portugal was back, I wasn't forgiven, and turning up drunk wasn't helping. What had happened? We'd never been like this before.

Red wine makes me thirsty, so I drank the pint of the pub's own lager very fast, and felt myself inevitably get even drunker.

There was inconsequential chat about the Algarve – 'Lucky with the weather', 'Lovely breeze in the evening', 'The people are so nice', 'recession's hitting them hard' – and then it was time to wander down a dark damp Byres Road to the Indian restaurant at its far end, past the record shop, coffee bars, the tube station, obscure posh grocers – many that were clients of ours. The road was filled with people, middle-class like us, but also students and homeless people: all of Glasgow on the one street.

We made it to the restaurant, were seated at a table in a busy corner, and ordered beers – Kingfisher. I stared at the name on the beer glass, and Helen frowned again, obviously thinking I was going mad. We spoke more of the Algarve – 'Gorgeous little beaches', wonderful food', 'Did you explore much – oh, Sagres, how wonderful' – and I gratefully pounced on the popadoms, and then my pakora starter.

I began to sober up a bit with the main course – my usual chicken tikka chilli garlic with a couple of chapattis and a spoonful of someone's rice, and another Kingfisher. Catherine and Helen got into discussion on books. I had heard most of it before: self-publishing on Amazon's Kindle store at low prices, or for free, in the hope of gaining recognition and maybe actual money further down the line; the 'game-changing' tablet market; the threats and the hopes.

Jim was a depute head-teacher in a secondary school on the south-side. We talked of the impending winter, hoping it wouldn't be as bad as the years before, and then inevitably he spoke of education cuts, having to use out-dated technology, the struggle to do more with less. I tried to point out that this is what everyone was doing during the recession – Catherine and Helen came in on my side on that one – and got nowhere, so we backed off before that became a serious point of dispute.

And he asked about me.

'I work in computers,' I told him, knowing that I was about to tell him how well off I was, and how easy my life was, and that wouldn't go down well with a teacher working in a tough Glasgow secondary school. But he would never know what lay behind all of that, and how I'd got to where I was, and how it was all in danger, and maybe my life was in danger too… All of it slipped through my mind in a moment. 'I'm a partner in a company here in Glasgow – B&D, on St Vincent Street, and we have another place on Argyle Street, in Finnieston.'

He gave me that affable smile over the rim of his beer glass. 'So you're surviving the recession.'

'It's tough,' I lied. 'But we have a good track record with clients – that's how we get new business, really. And our margins are tight.' Well, our official margins were tight, and often non-existent.

'How did you get started?'

'We started up a business way back in the late eighties, just after I left school – no qualifications, just me and my best pal Davey.'

I caught my breath, like I always did when thinking of Davey or mentioning his name. 'That was the Argyle Street shop. We fixed computers, helped folk out installing software, helping them use what they had. We expanded, started building and selling IBM PC clones, software installation and – most importantly – support and after-sales. And then in the nineties we got into the Internet quite quickly. Then Internet commerce, and Internet security. Setting up websites for people like travel agents and shops. Made a lot of money from doing that. And we floated some of our own ideas – lots of stuff that was complete bollocks, never earned anything, but people thought it was and bought it off us.'

'The dot com bubble.'

'That was us.' I laughed. 'We had one website where restaurants could advertise their specials for the evening – '5 o'clock specials', I think we called it.'

'Imaginative.'

'Customers could then rate the specials, and choose where to go based on that rating, and then give feedback on the restaurants. We got a huge amount of investment, ran it very successfully for two months, and then sold it on. Just before people realised what complete shite it was as an idea and the share price collapsed. We did that a couple of times.'

Jim sipped at his Kingfisher, pausing in the middle of his chicken tava. 'Any ethical issues there, Martin?'

Oh, fuck off, I thought. Fuck right off. I nearly said that aloud. 'It's the business world, Jim, not the public sector. Yes I got out before a collapse, but I didn't lie about the business' prospects. I thought up the idea, genuinely thought it was a good one, even though it looks like crap now – I didn't set it up as a con. If I'd stayed with it and gone down the pan and was living off Helen's money, would that be ethically sound?' I didn't mention the other side of the business, of course – that really was a pretty clear-cut 'ethical issue'. 'In my world, for all those years, every day could bring disaster. I could have lost everything at any point.' My voice was cold and angry, and Helen was watching me. And that statement wasn't fatuous: I felt I really was standing on the edge now, about to lose everything – about to lose Helen.

Jim pursed his lips: 'Another pint?'

I was really pissed off with him. Granted, I wouldn't have his job if you'd paid me twice the money I earned, but that wasn't the point. He was safe, my life was on a knife edge: apparently I worked with people who knew people who would kill people.

We talked about other things: sport, films, theatre, music. It was a long evening, and I was glad when it was over.

Helen was happy, laughing as we walked arm in arm all the way back up Byres Road after saying cheerio to Jim and Catherine, who had grabbed a taxi outside the restaurant.

Back in our lounge in the flat, she put the iPod in its dock, a playlist of her favourite songs. We sat listening to Beth Nielsen Chapman, sipping rum and cokes, me on the couch, she on the floor, against my leg, pretending we were having that ditcher in Alvor.

'What a great night,' she said. 'What a lovely couple. How did you and Jim get on?'

'OK. We had a bit of private sector versus public sector argument at one point, and I think we rather pissed each other off.'

'Oh dear. I did overhear some of it.'

I shrugged and yawned. 'He's no idea what it's like, what I've had to do over the years…' I stopped, and took another drink.

Her head tilted back: she had been stroking my calf with her fingernails, but now she stopped. 'Are you referring to last week and your mystery trip?'

I shook my head. 'No, no, not that – that was just a wee job, for a friend of a client, not an issue. No, I think I'm just getting a bit jaded – everything's plateaued…' I didn't quite sound convincing even to myself. 'Maybe I should move to something else…'

I had intended that to reassure her that – even if there had been something dodgy to worry about with the Portimao job, which there wasn't – things were going to be different, and good. But I sensed I had worried her more.

'Why won't you tell me what that was about?'

'I did tell you: it was just a wee computer job.'

'And nothing to do with that guy getting shot.'

'Of course not.'

'And you didn't have a quick fling with that gorgeous little blonde.'

I bent to kiss her. 'Chance would be a fine thing.'

She frowned and ducked aside from the kiss. 'I'm off to bed – busy day tomorrow.' Her tone seemed cool. 'Don't be too late,' was her parting remark. She left her drink on the coffee table, unfinished.

I sat alone, listening to the songs and the sweet voices. Oh god, I thought, my life was slipping through my fingers like sand. How can I get out of all of this?

Chapter 5

Glasgow – twenty five years before

In the two weeks after the party, and that experience with Fiona, my initial optimism was draining away. In fact, I felt worse than I had before. I had been shown a glimpse of another life, a life of money and sex and good living – I could be that guy with the gorgeous blonde on my arm – and was now being reminded that it wasn't for me after all.

Mum had been pleasantly surprised by my gift of the tenner. She was less impressed on the following Friday when I asked to borrow it back. She'd insisted we go back down to the school, together, to try to get me back in to repeat my Highers. I knew what would happen, and it did. The assistant head gave me the same sarcasm as before: pointless if I came back, attitude was wrong, wasting my potential, blah blah blah. Where I had ridden out the storm last time, I now saw mum becoming upset, and I got angry and shouted at him – I think I told him to stick his fucking school up his fucking arse, to which he spread his hands as if my outburst vindicated his opinion of me.

What I was keener on was finding a job fixing computers and helping people who had problems with their software, or just couldn't work out what to do with what they'd bought. Davey and I roamed the west end and beyond, finding wee computer shops that had sprung up offering the services we wanted to offer, asking for a job. On Argyle Street, around Finnieston, there were several of these shops, mostly staffed by Indian or Pakistani guys. We chatted to them, got on with them, but their businesses were tight: they had no need for extra staff, no room to expand. These were all one- or two-man operations. They were apologetic, but firm: no deal.

My mum seemed to appreciate that I was making an effort to find something, but we both silently agreed it was hopeless. As I stared out of my bedroom window at the greyness around me, visualising myself joining the men on the corner with their fags and cider to do nothing and talk about nothing, I was nearly in tears. Mum would do OK without me: she had her job as a secretary at the health centre, and I knew that there was money from dad in the bank.

Early one afternoon I was woken by a persistent ringing at the doorbell. I took a peek out of my bedroom curtain, and saw a big man in a suit at the front door. There was a black Mercedes-Benz at the kerb, and the groups of men from the estate were being drawn in by its gravitational attraction. I chapped on the window and the man looked up and saw me; I indicated I was coming down. I threw on yesterday's clothes and staggered downstairs.

The big man had wandered back towards the car, and was talking to a couple of local guys. I recognised them but didn't know their names: they were small, skinny, dirty – aged forty but looking sixty. He was saying something to them, and they were nodding, holding their hands up in supplication, then backing away from the car. The big man turned to me, smiling as he lit a cigarette.

He looked about thirty or so: his hair was reddish and receding, cut to a stubble. He was clean-shaven. He was taller than me, and bigger – partly fat, but mostly muscle; he stood with his feet slightly apart, balanced, braced.

'Martin McGregor?' The voice was deep, the Glasgow accent heavy.

I nodded.

'I'm Sandy Lomond. I work for Ken Talbot. He'd like to see you.'

I nodded again.

'Now,' he added. 'If that's convenient.'

'Oh – right. Can you give me five minutes – I need to go for a... I mean, I need to have a quick wash.'

'No problem, Martin.'

Ten minutes later I was pulling the door shut behind me. Sandy stood smoking by the car, looking round, his face impassive. When I appeared, he threw his cigarette away and got in and started the engine. I climbed in the front, marvelling at the leather seats, the dials. Mum didn't drive, so we'd sold dad's wee Fiesta after he died, after it had lain unused for a year. This car was much bigger, silent and comfortable.

We picked up Davey from his place – same estate, identical house – and the two of us were driven, baffled and overawed, back to that big house in Bearsden, where Sandy reversed into the driveway and we all climbed out into the damp afternoon. Sandy opened the front door, and took us upstairs to the study we'd been in before. The memories of the party came back, and the anguish of not getting enough detail on Fiona to be able to track her down; I looked up to the bedroom where we'd been.

'Hello boys.'

We nodded. 'Hi, Mr Talbot,' I said. Davey was looking at the Amstrad, head bowed.

Ken Talbot stood in the middle of the study, wearing smart casual trousers and a diamond-pattern sweater over a blue polo shirt. He patted the monitor of the Amstrad. 'This fuckin' heap of shite isn't working. It was slow as fuck, kept asking me to insert this fuckin' disc and insert that fuckin' disc, and now it's fuckin' broken. The shop that sold it to me won't come and fix it, and I sure as fuck am not taking it to them. I'd like you two boys to have a go. If you need to get any bits or bobs for it, or anything else, Sandy here will drive you, and he'll pay for it. Clear so far?'

I looked to Davey – this was probably mainly a hardware problem – and he bobbed his head. 'Yes, fine,' I clarified for Talbot. 'We'll have a go.'

'Good. I'm off to play golf – Sandy will come back here after dropping me off. It would be really good – *really* good – if this was working by the time I got back.'

'We'll sort out what we can. Have you got the disks that came with the machine?'

He waved his hand to a box high on a shelf of the bookcase. 'Do you need anything before Sandy takes me to golf?'

Davey cleared his throat. 'Just a couple of screwdrivers – flat-head, cross-head – and an adjustable spanner,' he said, to the carpet.

'And a cup of tea.'

We got all of that, and then Sandy vanished with Talbot and we took a deep breath and got to work. Apart from using the toilet a couple of doors down, we didn't go anywhere else in the house; we didn't dare.

The machine wasn't starting up at all. We delved into it – the guts of the machine were all inside the monitor case, which made it all tricky. We found a couple of leads which had come away, and re-attached them, thinking we'd done the job. Now the machine started up, but the disk drives didn't do anything. Back into the monitor, and a decision that the disk drives were faulty. I knew that this model had a single-sided and a double-sided drive, which were stacked sideways to the right of the monitor screen, and wondered how easy it would be to get replacements.

Sandy returned at some point during all of that, and sat impassively on an armchair in a corner of the room, reading the Glasgow Herald and looking across every now and again.

'We think we need to replace the floppy disk drives,' Davey said loudly to Sandy, but looking at me.

Clearly having no idea what we were talking about, Sandy drove us to a computer shop on Argyle Street – one of the places we'd tried to get work. The Pakistani guy there sold us a box of floppy disks, which Sandy paid for, but didn't have a spare 3" drive. We had a little small talk, but he seemed nervous of Sandy. 'You guys found some work?' 'Yes, thanks.' 'Good – really sorry I couldn't use you here.' 'I understand.'

At another shop we bought two new 3" floppy drives that would fit the Amstrad, but were only single-sided – I didn't think that would matter. Again Sandy paid, and again we got the same apologetic story that they couldn't take on me and Davey, but were pleased we'd found work.

Back at the house, we replaced the disk drives, and everything worked. Then we copied all the system disks and the data disks as backup, explained to Sandy how valuable this process was, and then wrote out instructions of how and when to do subsequent backups, and how to label and store the disks. 'Keep them in the filing cabinet,' I suggested, indicated the big, grey locked monster in the corner.

When Talbot got back after golf – it seemed he had won – we showed him a working system, and his joy was unbounded. He took us down to the kitchen and gave us a beer each, unsteadily pouring a large whisky for himself into a giant crystal glass.

'What do I owe you, boys?' He fished his wallet out of his back pocket.

I did the maths. A tenner last time, but this had taken longer, and we were invaluable to him – this was important work we had done for him. Surely we could ask for more. But how much…

'You decide,' I suddenly heard myself saying. 'You know how much your machine and your data mean to you, what would happen if you lost it. So you decide what our work was worth.' I could feel Davey staring at me – he wanted that tenner.

'OK.'

And he put his wallet away in his back pocket. I groaned inside, imagining what Davey was going to say when we got out.

Talbot took a sip of his whisky, and seemed to be thinking. Davey and I drank our beer. Shit, shit, shit.

‘What did you boys say you were up to? Left school?’

We nodded.

‘University? College?’

We shook our heads. ‘Didn’t pass the exams.’

‘So you’re good with computers but fuck all else.’

‘That’s about it,’ I said. I tried to force a smile, but it didn’t work.

He paused, and sipped the whisky again. ‘Tell you what I’ll do, boys.’

We were listening, but couldn’t imagine what he was about to say.

‘I’d like to talk about a business proposition with you, but I need to sort out a few things first. You boys can fix computers, that’s for sure. Any experience of selling?’

We shook our heads. ‘We’ve tried to get jobs in computer shops, but they’re all very small – no room for extra staff. And the big shops wouldn’t touch us without formal qualifications.’

Talbot looked like he hadn’t heard, was still thinking his own thoughts. ‘We’ll pick you up Friday, 1pm.’

Davey looked at me, and I asked the question: ‘Where are we going?’

‘Not sure yet. I have to work out some details.’ He looked at his big wristwatch. ‘Right. Sandy will take you home now.’

I stood up, and coughed. ‘Eh – about the payment for today’s work, Mr Talbot - ’

He smiled. 'Look on it as an investment, my boy. And a lesson.' He clapped me on the shoulder, a little too hard.

*

Talbot took us to an empty shop in Argyle Street around Finnieston, down from two computer repair shops where we'd tried to get work in the previous weeks and where we'd bought the stuff the other day. We were not far from the really rich parts of the west end, but this was a thriving area in its own right: small shops of all kinds, restaurants, and some interesting pubs, all of it changing as the shipyards were swept away.

The shop had been a Pakistani grocer's, and was set up that way, smelling of spices and dust. It consisted of a large rectangular floor space, with a tiny toilet, washroom and a storage room at the back. Davey and I stood in the middle of the floor and looked at each other, then at Talbot.

'Listen carefully, boys – here's the deal,' Talbot said in his low growl. 'I'll get this set up as a computer shop, and you boys will repair computers for anyone who comes in that door, just like you did for me. We'll give you a float to buy stock – whatever sort of shite a computer shop sells – and all the tools and bits you'll need.'

Davey was grinning widely, head up, looking around.

I was excited, but the practicalities shouted in my mind. 'Just a few things,' I said.

'Yes, Martin.'

I tried to prioritise my questions. 'How do we get it set up? We don't know anything about how to do that.'

'Come in first thing Monday morning. A guy named Ian Mackenzie will be here. Tell him exactly what you need, how you want the place to look, how you want it set up, and he'll get it ready – you have a think before then. His bills will come to me. Tell him you want to be open next Saturday and I'll break his fuckin' arm if you're not.'

OK, I thought. I looked round, and from a blankness in my head I suddenly could see what such a shop needed to look like – similar to the others we'd seen, but better. I looked at Davey, who had drifted towards the back room, away from where customers would be, and I could see that he had visualised his workshop.

'Will we sell computers too?'

'Maybe. If you make enough money to get stock.'

'So how much do we charge?'

'Up to you.'

'How much will you take?'

Davey looked at me sharply, but Talbot just smiled. 'Nothing at all, till Christmas. If it's still a going concern at Christmas, we'll talk about contracts and all that fuckin' nonsense. But not before. Till then, you just take the money you get. If anyone pays cash, you can keep it – but spend it wisely, and you'll need to renew your stock. If it's a credit card, or you give a receipt, then it needs to go through the till.'

There was silence for a minute, and I thought it all through. What else… what else… 'How about doing all that stuff - sending out invoices and things, and collecting money, and taking orders, handling enquiries?'

Talbot nodded. ‘We’ll get a wee lassie for you. She’ll be here Saturday morning when you open. I’ll pay her. We’ll make sure she knows how to cash up and use the night safe at the bank.’

Davey and I looked at each other. We were grinning, and then his face dropped.

‘Just one problem,’ he mumbled to Talbot. ‘There’s two computer shops up the road – one is where we got your stuff yesterday. We’ll be competing with them.’

‘So – you’ll just have to fuckin’ compete, OK?’

I thought of the Pakistani guys that ran that shop, young and keen, as were the Indian guys in the other shop. But maybe we knew more than them. Maybe we were better – bugger it, we’d have to be. We were intelligent, and we were young and keen too – we could take them.

There was a blur in my peripheral vision, and I ducked and reached, and caught the bunch of keys that Talbot had tossed to me, just before they hit my face.

‘Don’t forget to lock up, boys. There’s an alarm, so you’d better read the instructions.’ And he turned on his heel and was gone, Sandy smiled at us as he handed me his business card – ‘Just call me if there are any hassles; Mr Talbot doesn’t like to be troubled by detail’ – and turned and pulled the door shut behind them.

‘Jesus,’ I said. Then I laughed. ‘God, is this too good to be true or what?’

Yes, it was too good to be true, but we had nothing to lose and everything to gain. For a couple of nerds with no other job prospects, there was no decision to be made. We were naïve enough to ignore the weight of responsibility that had just been placed on our shoulders, and young enough to think 'Fuck, let's go for it'. Earning money for doing the stuff we did all day for nothing. Brilliant!

'OK,' I said. 'Let's think out the layout – till and counter there, by the door, where it was in the original shop – obvious place – but everything else gets ripped out. How about we leave it all open, so folk can see us working on the computers, know we're not ripping them off…'

We talked for an hour and worked out how it should look. Then we spent an hour getting our heads round the burglar alarm and how to set a new code we could both remember – half the instructions had worn away with time.

Finally, we were outside with the door locked and the alarm not going off. 'Fancy a pint?'

There was a pub called Krajewski's diagonally across the road, on a corner, and we went over and in. We liked it immediately: wooden floors, traditional layout, booths with big tables and pews. They had a good selection of beers, and looked like they sold food too. And they didn't ask us for ID, even though we were under-age and looked it. We paid the tall, thin waitress with the tufts of red hair and the nose piercings, and sat at the bar and toasted ourselves. 'Here's to a couple of lucky bastards,' we said.

'We'll need a name,' Davey suddenly said.

'And a phone line – two phone lines, one for the shop and one for a modem.'

'We'll sort that out on Monday.' We clinked glasses. 'Here's to the future,' we said.

We were back on track, looking good.

*

Ken Talbot and Sandy Lomond walked across the street and round the corner to where their car was parked.

‘You think this will work, boss?’

Talbot shrugged. ‘Don’t care. They know their stuff and I think they’ll work hard. We’ll keep them afloat till Christmas, and then see how we’re fixed. Meanwhile we can leave cash in their accounts for stock, move it in and out. We need a lassie who’s obedient but not too bright.’

Sandy opened the car door. ‘Plenty of them in Glasgow,’ he murmured.

Chapter 6

New York – early last winter

Mark Grosvenor had taken the packed A train from his home in Brooklyn, got off at Fulton Street and walked up through the extremely cold but dry day along the narrow Nassau Street into the wider, tree-lined streets of the financial district, towards Federal Plaza. He was huddled inside his black greatcoat, a woollen cap on his mass of white hair, gloved hands holding his briefcase, breath steaming through the bushy white beard. He knew the exercise was good for him, but it exacerbated the arthritis in his hip and made him walk with a limp – many people assumed he had been shot in the line of duty, and sometimes he didn't clarify for them that the real reason was so mundane.

In truth, he was glad he'd got the phone call the day before and had the chance to get away from home for a spell of work. His thirty-two year old son, along with wife and child, had moved back home after he lost his job. After years of getting accustomed to a calm, peaceful environment, Grosvenor and his wife found themselves again at the centre of constant activity, noise, and untidiness that seemed impossible to control.

Grosvenor made his way up to the 23rd floor, and along to the small, windowless conference room. Kurt Jackson was already there, with another younger man, both of them dressed in dark suits. Grosvenor shuffled off his coat, stuffing his cap and gloves into the pocket, and sat down at the long table, while Jackson got him a coffee from the jug.

'Hi, Mark. Cold out there, eh? Oh, by the way, this is Maxwell Stuart.'

Grosvenor cradled the coffee cup and stretched his legs under the table. 'Hi Maxwell.'

The young man bobbed his head. 'Morning, sir.' He was thin and pale, with hair that was short, black and gelled; he sipped from a bottle of water as he played with the trackpad on the laptop in front of him, keeping it from going to sleep. His voice was soft and Southern, a contrast to Grosvenor's deep New York growl.

Jackson sat down at the top of the table, sipping his own coffee, running a hand through his limp, thinning grey hair. 'Thanks for coming in, Mark. Steve Roberts, one of our IT guys, had first shot at some intelligence that came in and reckoned there was something in there, so he passed it up the line. I've read his report and I'm satisfied that the intelligence indicates that there is a real cyber threat to the US. It therefore falls under the remit of the FBI. The two of you will form a Cyber Action Team to investigate the implications of this intelligence, reporting to me.'

Grosvenor nodded at the standard formalities, and shifted his chair to look at the screen on the wall.

'That said, I think we'll get to it. Max, in your own time.' Jackson sat back, looking at the screen.

Grosvenor saw the young man wince slightly at the short form of his name.

'OK,' Stuart began, hunching over the laptop, stroking the trackpad. He coughed and his voice grew firmer. 'This is where we start.'

On the screen came the picture of a man's face; he was aged around forty five, with well-tanned skin, balding dark hair, a big moustache, a bullet-hole in his temple.

'This man is Aleixo Ramires. He was shot to death – a single gunshot – in a villa he owns in a town called Portimao on the Portuguese Algarve, on October 4th this year. Local police carried out the investigation, but found no clues at the scene. No fingerprints, no DNA.'

'A hit,' Jackson clarified, and Grosvenor nodded: 'You don't say.'

'Ramires was a self-employed accountant. Portuguese police are positive that, amongst his clients, were several criminal gangs, some organised, some disorganised. They were sure he was involved in money-laundering, and probably helping himself to more than his 'fair' share, as these people often do.'

Stuart's presentation zoomed out, rotated, and zoomed back in, to a map of the Iberian Peninsula, with Portimao and Lisbon marked. 'This is a map of Portugal and Spain,' he said.

Grosvenor got up stiffly to get himself a top-up of coffee from the jug. 'I know where Portugal is, Max.' He sat down again, scratching his beard.

'Ramires has his main home in Lisbon. Local gossip was that he'd been involved with escort girls since his wife left him two years ago; some of them are also run by organised crime gangs.'

Jackson sensed Grosvenor's growing impatience. 'So we have clear and obvious links to major crime – pretty definite.'

Grosvenor nodded and gave a small grunt.

'OK.' Stuart stroked his laptop, and the presentation whirled to a picture of a high-end laptop. 'The Portuguese police agency concerned – GNR – retrieved this laptop from the house in Portimao, presumably belonging to Ramires. They've spent a month or so trying to get stuff off it.'

Grosvenor frowned. 'So this was nothing to do with retrieving or stealing information: it was a revenge hit.'

Jackson nodded. 'Looks that way.'

'Anyway – ' another whirl and a page of numbers filled the screen. 'The disc was password-protected but not encrypted. Key files on it were also password protected. We've no idea at present if there was a backup to the cloud or a network drive somewhere. Portuguese IT forensics have spent the months trying to get names and addresses off it, with minor successes – they confirmed links with major criminals, but also found a few names on our most wanted list – including Alexandr Bobnev.'

Grosvenor sat back and gave an appreciative low whistle. 'So this guy wasn't just laundering money for local gangs: if he was connected to Bobnev, then he's been involved in international money laundering. And carders?'

Jackson repeated: 'Looks that way. Much bigger than they thought. Carry on, Max.'

'At this point GNR contacted our Computer Analysis and Response Team – this was three weeks ago. They sent over a mirror of the hard drive from the laptop, and Steve Roberts and other guys got to work on it. CART didn't find any more names, but they did trace credit card numbers from the hard drive, and a couple came back to US citizens – couple of guys in New York: they're clean, innocent – numbers were probably harvested from Internet sales, and then Internet bots got back to their computers and started gathering email addresses and other stuff. The usual kind of thing. These guys were pretty shook up when we told them.'

'So,' Jackson said, getting himself more coffee while Stuart sipped at his water. 'We have opened a case-file on this.' He sat down and leaned forward on the desk, Grosvenor copying him. 'Two lines of attack. Max here is working on more analysis of the hard drive. We have purchased the infected computers from their owners, and Max will see whether he can follow the trail back to the source – matching code fragments, checking email metadata from Prism, that sort of thing.'

Grosvenor nodded. 'You want me to start investigating the hit.'

'Yes. It may be that the hit was purely local gang-related, and you'll just help the GNR tidy up a case that's growing cold. But it may be that it was something to with Ramires' cybercrime connections, and the link to Bobnev, in which case you might be able to uncover something significant.'

Both men sat back in their chairs, and Grosvenor looked at the screen which again showed the map of Portugal. 'They'll give me access to anything I want?'

'Yes. I've given GNR your name. I've emailed you their contact details.'

There was a few minutes silence, while Stuart kept stroking his laptop, Jackson looked at Grosvenor, and Grosvenor looked at the map of Portugal, sipping his coffee.

‘Hotels there keep records of guests, don’t they?’

‘Yes.’

‘I’ll start there – pull in the names of guests in hotels around that time, in the immediate area at first. Run them past known sightings and contacts and the usual suspects. If that doesn’t give anything, I’ll also want flight lists of people coming into Portugal at the time, from anywhere.’ He sighed. ‘It’s gonna be a heap of names. Even with the computers crunching it all, it’ll take time.’ He frowned, thinking. ‘No CCTV near the crime scene, I suppose.’

‘No.’

Grosvenor finished his coffee. ‘OK, then, it’s just going to be a lot of work. I’d better get to it.’ He stood up.

Chapter 7

Glasgow – twenty five years before, almost Christmas

Ken Talbot's accountant was a wee guy with cropped hair and glasses, wearing a suit. He introduced himself as Tom, shook hands with us all, then sat himself at a desk in the corner of the workshop.

'Sam will give you anything you need,' I said. He nodded.

He sat there all morning, refusing cups of tea, or coffee from the takeaway place up the road, systematically going through the folders of receipts and takings Sam had kept, asking about a couple that had slipped through our net – customers who had paid cash, which we'd pocketed, but forgot to tear up the evidence.

Sam was our receptionist, a small thin teenager who wore black jeans and a baggy black top, chains draped around her waist, wild thick black hair which covered most of her pale face. Some days I thought she was attractive, and she would remind me a bit of the Fiona I had never found again, but those evenings when she came to the pub with us, she sat silently, responding to questions with nods or single words. She served customers well, and directed enquiries efficiently, but at quiet times she would just stand staring out of the window at the passers-by.

Davey and I had our usual busy Monday – customers would do silly things with computers over the weekend, like installing demos from games on magazine cover disks that didn't work on their system and they couldn't get rid of properly. We shook our heads at their stupidity and ignorance, but couldn't deny it was making us a nice living.

In fact we were making a very nice living indeed. An early boost had come when the computer shop a few doors up from us had closed down, just a couple of weeks after we opened. They'd been robbed on a Saturday afternoon – which was odd, because I felt there were better places to rob nearby – and then the two young Pakistani guys who worked there were mugged one evening after they left the shop. Next thing, they'd sold up and, in beautiful symmetry, it had been reincarnated as a Pakistani grocer's shop. When confused customers arrived, they looked around, clutching their computers, and saw our shop – they were so grateful it was almost pathetic. We'd branched out into selling software too, and printers, and were wondering whether to now start *selling* computers. The market was strange: the variety that we'd grown up with – Atari, Commodore, Acorn, Dragon, it was endless – was disappearing, and people were now fixating on IBM PC clones, largely Amstrad PCs and word-processors. Somebody brought in an Apple Macintosh one day, and we loved it; others had copied the WIMP idea, as indeed Apple had originally, but Apple did it best, we felt.

We were selling modems too. People were using email, and could get information from Prestel.

Home life had eased in one respect: I was giving mum rent money, and our relationship had been improving as a result – she saw me working long hours, earning money, dodging the life of standing on street corners that had seemed to be my destiny. Then Alan had appeared in her life. He was a primary school teacher, physically small, who took off his glasses and shut his eyes when he spoke to me. The little council house was crowded on the weekends and nights he stayed over. Worse, he quizzed me about the business, and about Sandy Lomond and Ken Talbot – he told me to be careful of them, like he knew anything about them, or the computer business.

Davey and I spoke about getting a flat together, near the shop. We could walk to the shop instead of getting the bus, walk to the pub, dead easy to get into town, walkable to the new Scottish Exhibition Centre – the 'big red shed' – which had been built on the now-disused Queen's Dock and was emerging as a major concert venue. The whole area around us was being re-developed, and it felt like a better place to be rather than Drumchapel. It was an attractive dream, but we couldn't yet commit to it.

Finally, around midday, Tom closed the last folder and gave it back to Sam. He made a short phone call, and then asked us for a coffee – Davey went for it.

As he came back through the door, three men followed him in. One was Sandy, one was Ken Talbot. The other was Charlie, almost unrecognisable in a suit and a camel coat. He gave us a wide smile. 'Hi, guys.' He locked the door behind him, and turned over the sign to show we were closed.

We stood awkwardly around: Tom the accountant sat at his wee desk, Sam leaned over the counter, chin resting on her hand.

Sandy had shaken our hands. He looked happy. 'OK, Tom. Your show first.' Ken Talbot stood back, his face impassive.

Tom took off his glasses and looked at his notes. 'The official turnover is very healthy indeed, and if we factored in the black cash income I'm sure we'd double that. Out of that comes what have been so far hidden payments: rent, heating, business rates, staff salaries, national insurance and various injections of cash for additional stock, but you're still doing better that most small businesses at this point in time.'

Sandy nodded, turning to Talbot to check he didn't disagree. Charlie had gone over to stand beside Sam. As Tom spoke, Charlie leaned over to whisper something in her ear: I saw her blush – I'd never seen so much colour in her face – and then nod as he kept on speaking; I saw him lightly rest his hand low down on her back.

'OK, Tom – listen up, Charlie – what's the prognosis?'

Charlie straightened after a conspiratorial nod to Sam. She gazed at him, her face like a hypnotised chicken.

'Huge scope for growth. The purchase of hardware and software should be expanded and re-focused on small business users rather than hobbyists. This requires capitalisation. I think you could do with another engineer working here. Regular accounting checks, of course – it needs to be more rigorous, but still with scope for 'exceptional' cash flow in and out when appropriate. Your wee Goth lassie has done very well, but she needs a bit more training – I recommend a college course; you'd need a temp, some overlap first.'

'Cut to the chase, Tom.'

'Set it up on a proper footing, given all the checks and controls of course. It's a runner.'

He finished his coffee and stood up. He handed over two sheets of paper to Sandy. 'I've drafted a contract and proposal. You can fill in the names and details and either change it and get me to check it, or just fire ahead. I'll leave you to it.' He nodded to me and Davey on the way past, and let himself out into the street. Sandy snibbed the door behind him, and he and Talbot started looking at the contracts.

After a few minutes they put the papers on the table, looked at each other, and Talbot nodded. Sandy smiled at me and Davey.

'Here's the deal,' he said.

And there followed a blizzard of technical business talk in the original Klingon that just baffled me. The only things I really caught were: Davey and I were partners in the business, and between us we had forty-nine per cent of the shares; we had a salary of seven grand a year – a fortune that made me dizzy with the thought – and a pro rata share of the profits, dividends and bonuses; we would have day-to-day operational control over buying stock, and pricing; we could hire people to help, and determine their salary.

'So,' I said, shell-shocked as Davey looked at me with an amazed face, 'we don't have to pay out anything?'

Sandy gave his smile. 'Technically at this time you are in debt for your shares and for the stock and the premises – ' he pointed to a tiny line on the bottom of one of the sheets of paper – 'but in actuality Mr Talbot will pay that all up front and you don't have anything to worry about. Just sit back and enjoy the ride.'

‘How about the other fifty one per cent?’ I asked. ‘I assume Mr Talbot controls that?’ I found it odd talking about him in the third person when he was standing a few feet away.

Sandy smiled again. ‘No. Mr Talbot has a number of business interests, so he is putting Charlie in charge of the company.’ He turned to Talbot, who was still just gazing impassively at me.

At this point Charlie stepped forward from Sam’s side, beaming, sweeping his long blonde hair back from his forehead.

Davey looked aghast and turned to me. ‘But Charlie knows fuck all about computers.’ I blurted out, voicing his thought.

‘True,’ Charlie said, not in the least offended. ‘And I know fuck all about running any kind of business, but this is my chance to learn.’ And he came over and put his arms round each of us. ‘We’ll do fine, boys. I’ll let you get on with things and make us all a lot of money. I won’t interfere, I promise. Now.’ He let us go. ‘Sandy will take the two of you to you to lunch to talk through some other details of this venture. I’m going to take Sam here off somewhere to further her education.’

As he spoke, Sandy and Talbot slipped out of the door: I could see them, standing talking on the pavement.

Charlie laughed at his own suggestive remark, Sam blushed but smiled, and I frowned. Charlie saw me and gave me a playful punch on the shoulder. ‘You’re not making any moves, Martin, so don’t concern yourself. Still pining over wee Fiona Andretti?’

The implication of what he said hit me straight away, and he wasn’t far behind; his right eye flickered.

‘You said you’d tell me when you found out anything about her. You said you didn’t know her name.’

'Sorry, mate. Yeah – found out just the other week when talking to a pal. Knew I'd get a chance to tell you soon enough.'

'So, do you know where she lives?'

'No.' He saw the expression in my eyes and added: 'But she's working in the Kelvingrove Museum.'

I had the urge to emulate The Graduate, and rush off to gather her in my arms, but it had been a few months now, and at that age a few months is a long time. So I drew breath – no rush: I'd think it through. After all, she hadn't tried to track *me* down, so maybe she wasn't that impressed. Maybe she'd found someone else. A memory of that night came back, and – after the self-satisfied glow passed – I thought with horror that maybe she was pregnant with my child. Christ. I wanted to see her, of course I did, but I was suddenly scared.

I needed to think it through. But I'd definitely go down there. Soon.

Sandy came back through the door on his own, and brandished a gold pen: 'We need a couple of signatures, boys. And a name – for the company. Any thoughts?'

Had to be something very computery – my first idea was absurd: Bytes and Digits – but Charlie leapt on it. 'Brilliant. Write that down, Sandy.'

And that was it. We were doomed to have students wandering in after a lunchtime beer asking if we did finger-food, each one believing he was the first to think of the joke.

*

The week after we signed the contract, we were in a place of our own: a tenement flat just up the road from the shop, owned by

Ken Talbot but he allowed us to stay there rent-free. We scavenged some crappy furniture, and a two-bar electric fire that ended up costing us a fortune to heat the place that winter. And we now had to learn to cook and keep a place clean.

But it was ours. Mum was sad; her boyfriend Alan couldn't conceal his delight – though he still had a cautionary word for me: 'Sure you know what you're doing, Martin? Careful with that guy Talbot, and his kid.' I told him I could take care of myself, and he gave a grim smile.

And one morning I summoned up my courage and left the shop, heading along a frosty Argyle Street to the Victorian sandstone splendour of Kelvingrove Museum, and up the broad steps and into the main entrance that faced the park, and then the huge main hall, looking at every member of staff. Mid-week, this place was the haunt of pensioners and bleary-eyed students. There was a primary-school class too, a young teacher babbling away at them, excited, while they gazed, open-mouthed, at the huge space around them.

I made my way upstairs to halls where there were art exhibitions, and the huge Dali painting – Christ of St John on the Cross – but I tore myself away from it. My heart was thumping and I was nervous as hell. I looked at everyone. There were loads of staff, but I couldn't see Fiona – maybe she'd changed her appearance; could I remember what she looked like? It had been so dark at the party, and in the bedroom, and she'd been dark, wearing dark clothes; even her skin, when she was naked, had been dark.

I wondered what to do if she was there – what to do if she wasn't there, half phrases in my mind. 'Long time no see.'

'Fancy bumping into you here.' 'How are you doing – gosh, great to see you!' 'That was a great shag, by the way.' Oh God.

I went round the whole floor twice, then upstairs, then down to the basements. Loads of dinosaurs but no trace of Fiona. I went back to the art exhibition floor and stood looking down into the main hall, looking hard. Time was getting on – I had to get back to the shop soon.

'Martin?'

I turned, and stepped back.

Of course I remembered her: her dark hair was now even shorter, but I did remember her face – her lips smiling, her brown eyes glinting, looking at me. She was wearing dark blue trousers and the uniform jacket, with her name on a badge.

I wanted to… all the emotions went through me, and I didn't know what to do, what to say. My voice squeaked and I coughed: 'Hi, Fiona. It's so good to see you again.'

Her smile widened and she stepped forward, her hand reaching to hold my arm. 'Are you here to see the exhibition? It's very good – well, some of it.'

I took a deep breath, and then my words came out in a rush: 'I came to see you. I only just found out you worked here. I only just found out your second name.'

She frowned at that. 'I saw Charlie the week after the party, asked if he could get in touch with you, tell you where I lived – I gave him my mum's phone number.'

We took that in, and both simultaneously said: 'What a *bastard.*' And we laughed, and then I reached and held her tight. She felt so good, warm and soft.

'You left the party – I looked for you.'

She pulled her head back, a serious look on her face that even I, with such very limited experience of dealing with girls, knew wasn't entirely serious. 'I came back with a beer for you, saw you in with Charlie's dad, playing with his computer. I said hi, but you didn't hear me – you were so interested in your bloody computer. Charlie's dad saw me, waved me away, shut the door on me.'

Oh shit. I hadn't noticed that at all.

'I waited downstairs for a bit, then my pal Julie was getting a taxi home because she was so drunk, and I just went with her. I was a bit annoyed with you. But I saw Charlie a few days later and told him to give you my contact details. When you didn't get in touch – well. You can guess what I thought.'

I pulled her to me. 'So sorry,' I said. She liked me, she really liked me. It wasn't a one-off that night. I was – maybe – about to have a relationship with somebody. Bloody hell. 'I saw Charlie the day after the party, asked him to look out for you – I didn't even know your surname, couldn't look you up.'

'You guessed it was Italian,' she grinned.

'Yeah, like looking for an Italian name in Glasgow would cut things down a bit.'

And we held each other again, letting all of that just go, and getting ourselves emotionally and logically to what was really the day after we'd had sex. What now?

'What are you doing these days?'

'Davey and I set up this computer business – fixing them, installing software, sorting software problems, and we're now expanding into selling hardware. Charlie's dad financed it, and Charlie is nominally the boss – he's such a tosser: all he's bothered about is shagging our receptionist. So he doesn't get in our way.'

There was a slight frown on her face. 'Is it all above board? I don't like Charlie, and I'm not sure about his dad.'

'It's fine,' I said. 'The business is really taking off. Even if it all went pear-shaped with Charlie and his dad, Davey and I know enough now to be able to set up on our own. Anyway, how about you?'

An older woman, in the museum staff uniform, was closing in on us: 'Fiona!' Her voice was a hiss.

Fiona and I broke off our clinch, and she turned to the woman: 'Sorry – this is an old friend I haven't seen for ages. Can you give me a couple of minutes?'

The woman frowned and moved on, but glared back at us, twice.

I smiled and Fiona suppressed a laugh. 'I'd better get back to work.'

'When do you finish?'

'Five o'clock. How about you?'

'Could be any time. Fancy a drink tonight?'

'I could come along to your shop after work – where is it?' She was holding me tight again.

I knew I'd have to work late. 'How about something to eat – maybe around seven?'

She smiled and nodded. 'Fine. That'll give me time to go home and change. Sure you can afford it?'

I grinned. 'Yeah, I can afford it. Where do you fancy?'

'There's a wee Italian just around the corner of Argyle Street, not far from here. Do you fancy a wee Italian?'

My grin widened, and I pulled her very tight to me and kissed her mouth. 'Oh yes, I fancy a wee Italian.'

And it was like we'd never had that hiatus. I could even forgive Charlie for being such a bastard – he was a nasty piece of work: I would never fully trust him.

Fiona and I slept together that night, and it was as good as the first time. And then again the night after, and over the following few weeks she moved more and more of her clothes over to our place, and mysterious toiletries and other things appeared in the bathroom. Davey didn't seem to mind – the two of us still went for a pint after work on a Friday and Saturday, and he would come with us to the pictures with me and Fiona. He drew the line at art exhibitions or the theatre.

As winter gave way to spring, I felt really good, happy. Just keep it like this, I thought: I've no other ambitions, this will do me just fine. Don't change anything, not ever.

Chapter 8

Last winter - Glasgow

Helen was away in London at a publishers' conference, staying overnight. My ex-wife Elizabeth was going too, and I thought back to that Internet conference in London where I'd met her, and ended up in a doomed marriage.

Something was going wrong with Helen and me: I couldn't say what exactly, but where there had been harmony and trust between us, there was now a crack. We didn't understand each other's moods well any more, often disagreeing on whether to go out or stay in. We were suddenly, after Portugal, not entirely happy together. We made love less often, and it felt... less satisfactory somehow, like it was simply a need we had, nothing more.

I went into the office in St Vincent Street every day, and worked on the code and watched the numbers, and checked all was OK. I marvelled at the way people would open up spammed links on their Facebook page and type in their login details, letting us into their personal information and that of their friends, allowing for wider phishing. I researched Internet fraud, keeping up to date with threats so that our clients could sleep soundly, unaware that their main protector was their worst enemy.

I only briefly saw Sandy: he brushed off any conversation about the events in Portimao – 'Just a wee job for a client of a friend, Martin. Nothing to worry about. That murder was absolutely nothing to do with what you did: trust me' – and didn't seem keen to swap holiday stories.

I met Andrew Russell a few times after work, usually in Blackfriars in the Merchant City. It was a traditional pub, always busy and noisy, always with good guest ales on tap, though Andrew drank gin and tonic. It had become a tradition for us to meet there, away from the west end.

'So, how is it going?' I asked him, after we'd caught up with the day-to-day chat about the weather and the economy and the government.

'It's difficult,' he said. 'I'm making some progress. Slowly.' He sipped at his gin and I swallowed some beer. Andrew had short hair these days, and dressed like he was back in the Thatcher era: clean-shaven, red braces, a Porsche Boxster S. He was an independent financial adviser. We'd never been close at school, but there seemed to be some kind of trust between us because we'd survived our beginnings in Drumchapel and become, on many measures, successful. We both had two marriages behind us, and he had told me he now thought he was gay.

'I'd like to move things on a bit faster,' I said.

He frowned. 'It's bloody difficult, Martin. Talbot's business concerns range far and wide: names change, ownership changes, and change again. You're a director in some businesses, a shareholder in others – but sometimes there are gaps in the chain, and some companies just don't physically exist. I'm finding it hard to map the whole network. I'm making some progress, and I'm managing to transfer your shares to your new dummy companies and bank accounts. But it's bloody slow and difficult.'

This had been our plan: we'd created new companies with different names – companies that existed but did nothing, though Andrew had some kind of back story – and my money was buying shares in them, capitalising them. From those companies in turn, Andrew would sell the shares to another of my companies, and move the money into various online bank accounts that I had, here and abroad, also in various names. At times it looked like a perpetual motion machine as the money went round and round. I wasn't bothered about making a profit on the shares in Talbot's companies, because I'd never actually bought them in the first place; I just needed capital, so I could get away from my entanglement with Talbot. Behind me would be left the debts and liabilities, but they would be isolated: it would be very, very hard for anyone to link the money that I would have squirreled away with the debts that existed. And while the money didn't really belong to me, the debts didn't either. It was a web that had been spun around me by Sandy Lomond and Ken Talbot.

At least, that was the plan. There was no way of knowing whether it would really work, no way to test it. One day I'd cash in and run – then I'd find out.

Andrew finished his drink and stood up: 'Let's have another. This is a three-gin problem, as Sherlock never said.'

It was fully five minutes later before he spoke again. 'I wonder if we could find out more about Talbot's companies.'

I started on my fresh pint. 'Who would have that information?'

'I'm guessing the police would.'

I frowned. ‘You think they’re on his case?’

‘I’m positive. There have been big moves against Glasgow organised crime recently – Operation Lockdown – and seizing assets is a priority, so they’ve got to find the assets first. They build up the picture, make the case, and then round up the bad guys.’

What he said sounded reasonable, but I couldn’t see how it helped, and said so. At the back of my mind I realised I was one of the ‘bad guys’. Were they planning to come after me? I shifted in my seat, suddenly feeling insecure; I looked round, and tensed as the pub door opened.

He nodded. ‘It could be very dangerous to start talking to any policeman involved in investigating organised crime in Glasgow.’ He sipped at his gin. ‘But it would be good to know what they knew. It would help.’ He left another pause, and another sip of gin. ‘There might be a way I could get some information.’

‘How?’

‘Private detectives usually have links with the police, and some have links that border on the illegal. I’m not accusing anyone of being a criminal here, but sometimes information is traded for favours. Or cash. I know a few. Want me to try?’

I nodded. ‘Yes, fine. Try anything you can to get the information.’

He gave a small cough. ‘I’ll get a contact for you, but then *you* do the talking, Martin. I need to keep at arm’s length.’

‘OK.’ I appreciated immediately what he meant: he was dabbling close to someone – me – who might be considered to be a criminal. He wanted to help me, but he had to protect himself. But I was feeling a chill wind, like people were creeping up on me, that time was running out.

'What do I do with the cash, Andrew? Ultimately. The papers are full of scare stories.'

He agreed. 'The big multi-national banks are safe now – no one can afford to let them go down the toilet – but foreign-based ones, especially in the Euro-zone, may take a hit at any time over the next few years. If you want your *money* safe, then keep it in concealed accounts in this country – spread it out; the money laundering regs are tight, so always be able to account for cash and transactions, and don't ship it back and forward. If *you* want to be safe then put your money in concealed accounts in offshore banks – Gibraltar would be a good option: it's technically British, but their financial institutions work differently. There are also some foreign online banks which are specialising in money laundering.'

'Could I lose it all?'

'Certainly – even if the police or HMRC don't get interested in you and track down your assets and seize them, the Euro could devalue more, or it might break up. In Spain, the property companies have taken the bullet. In Greece, nobody's taking the bullet, so the whole place is in meltdown, and they may drag the Euro down with them. If that happens, then nobody is going to predict anything. All you can do is spread your risks and cover your tracks, but the police have *very* good forensic accountants.'

We finished our drinks, and shook hands as he left. I stayed for another beer and something to eat. I looked out at the rain and the bodies huddling forward against the wind. I was committed now, that's all there was to it.

Chapter 9

Into the nineties - Glasgow

Davey and I got back to the flat late that Friday, after a couple of beers in the pub with our new co-worker Frank.

We'd expanded, and I'd discovered the joys of being an employer – hiring and firing people. We had needed a new engineer, and advertised in the trade papers, and also in the university union. We devised a simple test: hand somebody a broken computer and get them to diagnose the problem and either fix it, if it was simple, or describe what they would do: easy test first, harder one later.

Some of our applicants were rubbish: one guy just suggested reinstalling windows 3.1, when the fault was a broken monitor. Another didn't notice the monitor wasn't plugged in, and started hitting it.

We hired a guy who lasted three weeks. When a young customer came back saying that his new graphics card wasn't any faster than his old one and could I take a look, I found that it hadn't been replaced at all, and there was no paperwork – our guy had done nothing but pocketed the money from this trusting soul. I sacked him and fitted a new card for free.

But Frank was all right. He had trouble making eye contact, and didn't do much small talk, but he was OK. Davey at least looked at *your* shoes when he spoke to you.

All around us, Glasgow was changing. The shipyards had long been swept away now, and the riverfront continued to develop as a middle-class paradise with flats overlooking the river, all catalysed by the Garden Festival a few years back. Our area was now home to more little cafes and restaurants. Further over, Byres Road was moving further up-market.

The only problem we had was with Charlie.

Sam was now at college two days a week, so we had a temp, Stevie – also a girl. She was about Sam's age, but more personable – bright and chatty. She dressed smartly too, with leggings and tight tops. If Fiona hadn't been there, I would definitely have taken a fancy to Stevie, with her long strawberry blonde hair. Davey took a shine to her, but hadn't yet had the courage to ask her out.

'She must have a boyfriend,' he said. 'Look at her. She's gorgeous.'

'Give it a go,' I said. 'What have you got to lose?'

But he didn't.

One afternoon I'd been out to get some parts from another shop, stuff we needed urgently. Davey was home in bed with a hacking cough and a temperature. I got back to the shop and found the door was locked and the venetian blinds turned. I thought it was odd, but just used my key and went in.

Stevie was in the corner, arms across her chest, tears streaming down her face, which was half-turned away. 'Don't,' she was pleading. 'Please don't.' Her blouse was loose, half-unfastened.

Charlie was in the middle of the shop, swaying. He was wearing his suit, and I could smell the alcohol in the air.

'Charlie!'

He turned, almost falling over. 'Hey, Martin, wee man. Pal.'

His trouser zip was undone, and a tumescent penis waved at me. 'Just getting to know wee Stevie here. Fuckin' lovely, isn't she.' His words slurred into each other. He turned back to face her, and again she hid her face from him, crouching.

'Aw come on, hen. Just a wee suck o' ma cock. Come on. You be nice to me and I'll be nice to you. Come on.'

She almost screamed: 'No. Get away from me.'

'Charlie!'

He turned back to me, frowning.

OK, options, I thought. I could beat him senseless with the chair that was near me, and no doubt he would return the favour when he recovered, and might just kill me. Or I could kill him first – no, maybe not.

Option 3: 'Charlie! She's Davey's girlfriend. You have to leave her alone.' In the background I could see Stevie take that in – maybe she thought this was a worse option. Charlie slowly absorbed the information. 'If you hurt her, he won't be happy, Charlie. He would leave. We couldn't replace Davey. The company would be ruined. Your dad wouldn't be happy.'

I had to go through that several more times, till finally he didn't turn away from me. He zipped up his fly, tucked his shirt into his trousers. ''S OK wee man. 'S OK.'

He stumbled towards me and shook my hand warmly. ''S OK.'

And I helped him out of the door. I could have phoned a taxi, phoned Sandy to come and get him, or… but I shut the door behind him once I'd made sure he was still staggering away from the shop. I went over to Stevie. 'You OK?'

She was still crouched down, still sobbing, not looking up. I sat on the chair, wondering what to do.

Charlie reappeared two days later like nothing had happened. He didn't refer to that afternoon, and didn't comment on our new temp – a fifty-five year old spinster, who was personable enough and efficient, but who was never going to arouse Charlie's libido, or anyone else's, for that matter. I never saw Stevie again: we sent her a month's wages in lieu. I didn't tell Davey what had happened, in case he took it upon himself to avenge her honour.

*

One Friday evening when we got back to the flat very late, Fiona said she wanted to discuss something with me. Davey obligingly went off to his room: he had a Sega Megadrive and a wee TV in there, which kept him amused.

I sat by her in the lounge, and yawned. 'God, I'm knackered.'

She nodded sympathetically. 'I'm pregnant.'

I couldn't think of a reply. I looked at her to sense her mood – was she happy, devastated?

'How?' She frowned at me, a sardonic smile. 'I thought you were on the pill.'

'I was always a wee bit careless with taking them - sorry. And you're a very prolific lover.' She smiled broadly, reaching to stroke my hair.

‘So how…?’

‘Three months. What do we do?’

OK, options, I thought.

Her eyes seemed to know what one of the options was, so she chose to clarify one thing: ‘Remember I’m an Italian Catholic. I’m lapsed, but not that much.’

I nodded again, and she waited. Options. I saw my life with her, and the kids – because there would be more – a bigger flat. Me in the business, her at the museum, maybe finishing her art diploma. She was gorgeous, we got on so well – what more could I hope for?

But we were both just into our twenties – did we really want to nail down our lives in this way?

I looked at her, and she looked back at me as she stroked my hair, and I saw her smile start to dim and the panic rise in her brown eyes as they scanned my face – and I reached for her and held her tight, and she started to cry.

‘I’m so sorry, Martin. I know this isn’t what you wanted. We’re too young.’ I could feel her tears on my neck. I held her tighter.

‘I love you, Fiona,’ I said. ‘I want to be with you forever, and I promise you I will be.’

*

A month later, Fiona and I had a quiet Catholic wedding, if there is such a thing. Her family made up most of the crowd – aunties and uncles and cousins, and her younger sister Janine, who was just sixteen but had an astonishing Italian dark beauty and sultry sexuality about her. At one point Fiona nudged me: ‘Keep your mouth closed, Martin.’ She smiled, and then, seriously: 'She's big-headed enough. I don't want her thinking that my husband fancies her as well.'

Fiona's dad turned up. He was greeted politely enough, but embraces were tentative and the atmosphere cool around him. I talked to him, and found him good company – he was a businessman, and ran a couple of restaurants in Sorrento. I told him I'd never been there. 'You must come and visit. You can sip wine on the terrace of my restaurant and look across the bay to Mount Vesuvius. Stay in my apartment.'

He was a wee guy, immaculately dressed in what looked to me like an expensive suit; he was tanned, dark hair peppered with grey – I could see Fiona's and Janine's beauty in his good looks. Not that Fiona's mum wasn't lovely, but she was paler Glasgow stock.

My mum and Alan were there, and my Uncle Bert, who worked as a janitor in a primary school, and Auntie Chrissie. Davey was there too, with a girl, Jane. She worked in the pub we always went to: she was a wee round redhead, like a shorter version of Stevie whom Davey had fancied but never tracked down again. And Frank, who had somehow remembered to put on a jacket and tie.

At the reception we had lots of drink and food, and then a dance with a Scottish band and everyone we knew invited. Late in the evening, Fiona and I got a taxi to the Holiday Inn at Glasgow Airport. In bed we talked about the rest of our lives: the baby, my business, finding a child-minder in a couple of years so she could finish her art degree. Davey had already found another place – bought by Ken Talbot through the company, but in effect it was Davey's. Fiona and I would need a bigger flat when the baby was older, and we wanted to move up Byres Road: I reckoned I could afford a mortgage, get out from Talbot's patronage.

We were so young and as successful as someone our age could hope to be, though god knew I was working hard.

The next day we flew to Faro, took the coach transfer to Alvor and a hotel on a hill overlooking the town, the beach just out of sight. It was expensive, but we agreed it was going to be our last holiday on our own for a while. Fiona had been to Italy a lot, of course, but after her father had left her mother, they hadn't been particularly well-off. The gorgeous, enigmatic Janine had apparently been the favourite child, and her private education at an all-girls' school in Glasgow was being paid for by him. (Fiona had implied that this was an attempt to stop her getting shagged by all and sundry, thus distracting her from her studies.)

We had a fantastic week living the good life in Alvor, and I vowed to return whenever I could. It was my first taste of expensive meals and good wine – and all that when I was so young. I thought with some smugness about my school pals who had gone to university and who would not be able to afford a life like this.

Life was so good, I could taste it. The future was fantastic, there was nothing we couldn't achieve. All this from a guy who'd failed all his Highers – I lay on the beach and remembered report card comments from my teachers about how I needed to apply myself more (true) and how I would never, ever amount to anything (up yours!).

Towards the end of the week, Fiona was a bit sick from the heat and the baby. So were glad to get back to Glasgow.

I went back to work, and Fiona took to her bed to get over whatever it was. She was hardly eating.

Then I got a phone call from her to say she had stomach cramps: something was wrong with the baby. I called a taxi, and rushed her down to the Western. They took her into maternity. I waited and waited, and then someone came to take me to a little room: she'd lost the baby.

She was inconsolable, and immediately offered me a divorce. I laughed that away, and said we'd try again, and wouldn't that be fun.

And we did try again. After two further miscarriages in less than two years, we decided to stop trying for a bit. It had left her looking very thin, and she seemed almost permanently tired. But we still enjoyed a good life. I was confident she'd recover. I wasn't that bothered about having kids anyway.

Getting in, and getting out

Chapter 10

Kirkwall

It's been a week and a half since my arrival and there has been no knock at my door, no one looking for me. The weather has improved and I've hired a car – cash, but on my own driving licence of course – and been exploring. I've immersed myself in the history of the place, from the ancient history of Skara Brae – which puts my short little life into perspective – to the wars, Scapa Flow, and the drive along the Churchill barriers.

I'm beginning to feel safe, but I know that's an illusion. Maybe I am, but maybe time is running out as someone tracks me down, and I should prepare to move on, perhaps further to the north isles. Every day, as the Flybe flights come over, I wonder whether someone I really don't want to see is about to come for me.

I get to know a few regulars in the pub, and a few people who appear in the hotel for a few nights – though they leave, and my heart sinks because I can't. It's good to talk to people, but I have to be careful about what I say. I gradually evolve a cover story that isn't so far from the truth: I'm retired – yes, very young, thank you! – after working in computers for years, my own company, sold out – you wouldn't have heard of us. I alternate my story: sometimes my company was based in Glasgow, sometimes in Edinburgh, sometimes vaguely ‘online’.

There’s a woman that catches my eye, partly because she’s on her own: she’s about my age, and what I notice most about her is her mass of rich brown hair which reaches to her shoulders and falls over her face as she eats her dinner and reads her Kindle. She wears a severe dark suit in the mornings at breakfast – she’s usually leaving as I come down – but jeans and a mannish shirt in the evenings. She doesn’t drink alcohol: she eats her meals, gives a wide smile to the waitress, and vanishes back to her room. She wears a wedding ring.

On the Thursday evening I find I’m sitting in the hotel lounge bar at a table near her, and can make eye contact – which we do, and she smiles: she’s recognised me, but her Kindle is more interesting than me. I look at her face: no make-up in the evenings, bright eyes that quickly take in the room when someone comes in and then return to her reading, occasionally giving me a half-smile on the way past.

The hotel is quiet this week. I’m the only fugitive, from what I can see. There are a few people in suits, like my lady, and a few others who wear overalls. Some local families come in for dinner too – one evening there is a table of twelve for a birthday party, a grandfather and his extended family.

She finishes her meal – the haddock and chips – and looks like she’s going to finish her chapter, and then her coke, and then go back to her room as always.

‘Food’s good here,’ I venture.

She looks up, and gives me a wide smile. ‘Yes.’ Then back to her book.

'The hotel's pretty good.'

Head up, smile, 'Yes,' head back.

'You here with work?'

Head up, smile, 'Yes,' head back. And then a moment later she closes the cover of the Kindle, and finishes her coke. She stands up, and gives me another wide smile: 'Enjoy the rest of your evening.'

I get back to my lasagne.

The next morning – Friday – she's at reception, with her suitcase and a laptop bag and an enormous handbag, checking out.

'Safe journey,' I offer.

She gives me another of her big smiles. 'Good to be getting home,' she says. And then a fractional pause. 'But back next week.'

'I'll still be here,' I say, and our eyes hold contact for a little longer than necessary, before I turn away and wander down to the lounge bar where breakfast is served. This place maybe isn't so bad.

*

I've come to an agreement with the hotel: I'll stay for a week at a time, pay my bills, and re-negotiate an extension; if there is a danger of them becoming full, they'll let me know and I will decide whether to stay on and let them know immediately.

I've change my Euros into pounds, and checked that I can still access my current account through the ATMs in town, and my other accounts through the Internet. All seems to be fine, but I still have that creeping paranoia that someone is out there, monitoring every ATM and web transaction, looking for me; I'm on the hotel's open Wi-Fi, so anyone could be listening.

On Monday evening I am a bit disappointed to see that the woman from the week before isn't there. There is no reason for a flight delay, and no reason not to check in here. More suits in the lounge, eating in singles and threes, a group of five workmen in overalls, an elderly couple out for dinner, eating silently.

She isn't there at breakfast the next day either, and I am letting that little fantasy – the thought that I could have a proper friend here - slip away as I head out for a stroll round the town in the early evening, and a pint in the pub down the road. I am walking away from the back of the hotel, where the car park is, when I hear a taxi pull up. I turn my head and see her emerging from the taxi – she doesn't see me. My heart lifts a little; someone to talk to.

I walk around, have my pint, and then go back to my room to leave my coat, and, a spring in my step, wander down to the lounge, picking up a copy of the local paper. I see her out of the corner of my eye at the table for two in the corner, wearing the same style of clothes as last week, and notice that she looks up. I catch her eye and we exchange a smile, but I continue to the bar to order a beer.

I take a few sips and then walk slowly, looking at the headlines in my folded paper, holding my beer, towards her. I look up, she sees me, we smile – 'Hello again', 'Hi' – and I sit with an empty table between us, studiously reading my paper.

As she finishes her dinner and walks past me, I look up again: 'Good flight?'

‘Yes,’ she says.

‘Work to do?’

‘Yes. I need to crack on - homework. You?’

‘On holiday.’

She laughs, a throaty chuckle that is music to my ears. ‘Lucky man.’

We say goodnight.

The next evening I time it to perfection and I arrive in the lounge just after her. I get my pint from the bar, and sit at the table beside hers. We exchange pleasantries, and she reads her Kindle while she eats, and I read mine – we acknowledge that too, with gestures and smiles.

At the end of the meals, she declines the waitress’ offer of anything else, but she lingers over the last of her coke. She yawns and stretches. I ask for another pint, and close my Kindle.

‘It must be hard, working away from home,’ I say.

She nods. ‘It can be.’

‘What do you do?’

‘I work with Investors in People.’

I nod – I know of them, but we, of course, never used them.

‘I’m up here for a couple of weeks, helping small businesses.’

‘Husband at home with the kids?’ That doesn’t get the warm reaction I was expecting. ‘I’m sorry – I just assumed…’

She shakes her head. ‘It’s OK. Just one of those things.’

‘Listen, do you want another drink?’

She looks at her watch and I can almost see her thoughts, her dilemma. 'OK then. I'll have a glass of white wine – anything but Chardonnay.'

I ask the waitress when she comes with my pint, and tell her to put it on my room. After a few minutes we clink glasses, turn our chairs to almost face each other, sit with arms and legs mirroring each other. 'My name's Martin, by the way.' 'Nicola.' We shake hands and give a mock bow to each other.

'So how long are you here for?' she asks.

'I don't know. I'll play it by ear.'

'Where's home?'

'Glasgow. I have a place in the West End, just off the top of Byres Road.'

'You married?' Her eyes look hard at me over the top of her glass, probably used to getting a lie in answer to this question.

'No, not any more. Used to be.'

'Relationship?'

And that memory hurts. 'I'm afraid I sort of blew that. I'm on my own.' It's the first time I've said that out loud: I'm on my own.

She seems to relax a bit.

'So,' I say. 'What about you?'

She takes a drink of her wine, and raises her eyebrows as if surprised that it's palatable. 'Complicated,' she says. 'The wedding ring is to just to hide behind – if anyone tries to chat me up I just point to it. It's actually my mother's – she's divorced, I rescued it from a drawer.

So, I think: she didn't point to the ring when I appeared, she stayed for another drink, she asked me about my status straight up.

She is looking at me with bright eyes, and a smile playing on those lips. As she lifts her glass again, she brushes her hair back from her face, and I feel a great thrill run through me. 'So what do you do, Martin?'

Ah, what a question. I want to be honest, but I can't be. I wing it: some truths about the computer business and all the legal things I did, and a story about selling it all off and looking for something else to do after an extended holiday.

The time flashes past. She doesn't want another wine – 'Work to do' – and we say goodnight.

*

I have a restless evening in my room: I can't settle to anything on TV, or on the Internet. Finally I head back down to the bar with my Kindle. There are a few people in, but most of the action seems to be through in the public bar. I get myself a pint and sit at a table for two. I sip and read, sip and read.

I'm lost in concentration when I feel the presence beside me and hear her voice: 'Another pint?'

I look up, snapping out of my book. 'I'll get it.' I half rise to my feet.

'No, it's my turn. What kind is it?'

'Scapa Special.'

She's back a few minutes later with the beer and a large white wine, and I drain my first pint and put my Kindle down. We chink glasses. 'Cheers.'

'What are you reading?'

I sip the fresh pint. 'It's a history – about Scapa Flow. I've been getting kind of immersed in the whole war thing.'

'I've never really got into that. I visited St Magnus Cathedral, saw the memorial to the Royal Oak. Must have been horrific. Those poor men.'

'Yes.' HMS Royal Oak had been anchored in Scapa Flow in 1939 when U-47 had made the impossible journey round sunken blockships into the Flow, a great feat of seamanship. It had found Royal Oak and fired a torpedo, then dived and turned tail. When it heard no explosion, the captain stopped and cautiously checked the periscope: the torpedo had missed, but no alarm had been raised. So they went back and fired another, and this time it hit. 'Over a thousand men on that ship,' I said. 'Over eight hundred died. The ship's still down there.'

'Along with the German fleet that was scuttled at the end of the first war.'

'I was reading about that: most of them were re-floated and salvaged, amazingly enough.'

She smiles and raises her wine glass to her lips. 'So, you're broadening your mind on your holiday.'

I grimace. 'It's actually not too much of a holiday,' I find myself saying.

'Oh?'

'More of an escape.'

There's a pause, and then: 'From your relationship?'

I give a sigh. 'Some business partners. There were some things going on with the company.' I can't say any more. I look at her as I lift my pint, but luckily she's not recoiling in horror from me: she's looking concerned. 'Nothing too bad,' I say. 'It was a sort of computer fraud type thing.'

'So you're the one with all the Nigerian clients who want to leave me their money in their will?'

I smile. 'You got me.' Then I decide to clarify: 'It was them doing it all – nothing to do with me.'

There is a pause, but nothing tense or strained. 'You said you were married twice.'

'You said you're in a complicated relationship.'

She laughs the kind of laugh that isn't forced but decays into sadness. 'I love him,' she says. 'I really do. He's clever and kind and witty and knowledgeable and sociable.'

'What does he do?'

'He's a newspaper reporter in Edinburgh. Was working for the Scotsman, but he's freelance now.'

I nod: that sounds like quite a person. No doubt tall and good looking, and not on the run from gangsters and police in three countries. 'But?' I suggest.

'He drinks too much. I mean, way too much. It's a hazard of the profession, of course, but he's taken in to a whole new level. It's affecting his health, it cost him his job, and I don't think I can live with it any more. I've given him an ultimatum.'

I can't really think of anything to say, so I drink my beer.

'Sorry,' she says. 'I don't know why I'm laying this all out on you. You've got enough problems.' We laugh.

'It's always good to talk to someone who isn't involved. I'm guessing you feel this is all partly your fault.'

'You sound like an expert.'

So I tell her about Fiona and Elizabeth, and then Helen. She listens, and refuses another glass of wine; I really want another beer, but don't want to look like the kind of drunk she's trying to walk away from.

'So what went wrong with Helen?' she asks.

I can't begin to tell her all of that, but I have to tell her something. 'Cracks appeared in our relationship,' I say, which is true. 'And I suppose I didn't do enough to keep us together. I don't think she realised how much I cared about us.' My voice catches.

She picks up her room key. 'I really need to go and finish off my work. It's been lovely talking to you, Martin. I hope it all works out for you.'

'And for you.'

She stands up, and I watch her walk out, then get myself that pint of Scapa.

*

I get down to breakfast, slightly late, and catch her on her way out of the hotel, dressed for business. 'See you at dinner?' I suggest. She nods: 'Need to see how the day goes.'

I drive around for the day, and fill up with outrageously priced diesel. I buy a simple pay-as-go mobile, because I've decided I might just need to keep in touch with someone, and I daren't switch on my old one. I enjoyed talking with Nicola last night, and I'm looking forward to seeing her again this evening. I wonder about her appearance in the bar: had she sought me out, guessing I'd be there? I smile as I stand on the edge of Scapa Flow, staring out over the graves of thousands of men.

When I get down to dinner, I discover she's almost finished hers. I ask if I can join her, but she says she's just about to go up to her room to work, so I sit at the table next to hers. I can see she's distracted, sitting fiddling with her mobile, constantly checking it.

'Anything wrong?' I ask.

She shakes her head, and checks the phone again. 'It's him,' she says, in a voice I can barely hear.

And before I can phrase my next question, she gets up and slips away with only a vague: 'I'm sorry,' hanging in the air behind her.

I eat my meal, more alone than ever. Should I try to call her room? No, definitely not.

Later on, I come back down to the bar and nurse a pint of Scapa Special till it becomes obvious that she won't be down tonight. I hate sitting there alone, with that looming feeling that I might never see her again. She might be back here for work, of course, but perhaps in a different hotel. We might miss each other.

I go to reception, borrow a piece of notepaper and a pen, and write down the number of the new mobile I'd bought that day. I ask the man to give Nicola – 'the woman: tall, brown hair; works for investors in people' 'Oh aye, I know the one you mean.' - the piece of paper.

I lie awake till the early hours, wondering at my stupid gesture. When I groggily stumble down to breakfast, the man at reception calls to me: ‘She’s checked out for the early plane, but I gave her your message.’

‘Thank you.’ The day in front of me feels like a yawning empty void, and all the empty days after that are queuing up to infinity.

Chapter 11

Spain – Spring, this year

I flew into Malaga with EasyJet, emerging into the air-conditioned terminal building. The serious girl on passport control looked at my passport, swiped it, and then seemed to read something on the screen for a few moments; finally she pressed a couple of keys on the computer, and handed me back my passport with a tight smile, her eyes still scanning me.

I just had hand luggage with me, so I got down to the concrete bunker of the car-hire hall quickly. I walked up and down twice before fully registering that the company I'd booked with wasn't there. Finally I saw their booth out in the actual underground car park, and cautiously went through the doors: the warning signs said that return was impossible.

I did the paperwork – negotiating the advanced car-hire maths problems of extra insurance, whether to return it with a full tank – and then found the little black Seat. I rigged up my satnav, and headed out into the blazing daylight. It wasn't difficult getting out of the city, though I always have initial horrors at roundabouts when driving on the right – it feels so wrong, but the satnav helped. As I got onto the A-7 then the E-15, heading south, and the sun that we hadn't seen in Glasgow all winter shone down on me, I felt better. Helen hadn't been happy at being left behind, and wasn't convinced by my excuses: she thought this was another job for lumpen man and cute blonde, and I wondered if she really did think I was having a fling. And I wondered if I cared; I was starting to get pissed off with her coolness, and the new lack of symbiosis between us.

It took about and hour and a half to get to the town where Colin Strachan lived – on the coast, south of Marbella, near Manilva. It took a further hour to find the way in to the development where he stayed, find a parking space, and then negotiate the maze of alleyways to find his stairwell. It was a relatively modern development, but almost had that feel of an old Moorish village. There were a few obvious tourists around, and some grey retirees, but mainly the residents seemed to be young Spanish couples and families. It was quiet.

I remembered the day we'd discovered that Colin had vanished from Glasgow. I'd arrived to find Claire standing baffled, looking into his office, tidied and cleared, the filing cabinet empty, an envelope with Sandy's name on it on the desk. I got her to call Sandy, who appeared an hour later. He strode in, frowning, and lit a cigarette before opening the envelope and unfolding the two sheets of A4. As he read, I watched his eyes narrow, his teeth clench, and then he just gave a smile and folded the top sheet of paper and put it in his inside jacket pocket. He kept hold of the other, shaking his head as he read through it, then passed it to me. He shook something out of the envelope – a USB stick – and handed it to me as well.

So he'd got away, I thought; the bastard had got clean away, and Sandy wasn't storming out to find him and rip out his throat – in fact he looked relaxed as he shooed Claire out of the office and closed the door. 'Looks like you're taking over Colin's work,' he said. 'Does that make sense to you?'

I read the paper, and nodded. There were instructions on how to use what was on the USB stick – a version of Linux, and a few programs – and details of emergency procedures if things went wrong.

'I don't want to do this,' I said.

Sandy sucked on his cigarette. 'You've no choice, Martin. Remember our discussion? Remember Davey?' His voice was quiet.

And I closed my eyes and nodded.

Colin had got in touch with me soon afterwards by good old-fashioned letter, to my home. The address said 'In the sun', followed by a line that said: 'Burn after reading - seriously.' The postmark was London. It was a short letter, an apology for dragging me into the cybercrime. There was a statement that he would try to give me any help he could in the future, but that the scope for this was probably limited. There was a mobile phone number, starting 34, and a remark that he really hoped we'd meet again one day, under happier circumstances. I'd stored the number on my own mobile with the name Fred Bloggs, and shredded the letter. At that time I had no intention of ever contacting him, not ever.

But a week ago I'd called the number and found myself, to my slight surprise, speaking to him. I said I'd like to visit, alone. He didn't sound fazed to hear from me, but he was cautious. He'd told me where he lived, and said he looked forward to seeing me again.

Now I went through the open iron gate guarding the stairwell, up to the top floor, and knocked on the heavy wooden door, its own protective iron gate hooked open. The door opened, and Colin grinned hugely at me – with a glance over my shoulder first, as if checking I was alone – and we shook hands with genuine warmth. He pulled me inside.

'It's good to see an old familiar face, Martin. How are you? Coffee? Drink? I'm so glad you got in touch.'

'I'll have a beer, thanks.' This was a man I had hated a few years before, and who had probably wrecked my life, but I would set that aside, for the moment at least: he seemed really pleased to see me – and I needed information and his help.

We were in the small lounge-kitchen area, and I noticed a large bedroom and a small box-room with a desk and a MacBook. The furniture was a couple of old sofas, and a table, small units for storage, cupboards on the wall round the sink, and a huge fridge-freezer. There was a large TV with a Sky box underneath it on a stand. It was small, cosy. And hot.

Colin opened the beers and we chinked glass and drank.

'Come out onto the balcony.'

There were two plastic chairs at a small table, a padded sofa and a couple of comfy reclining chairs; we sat on those, with our backs to the red-tiled roof with its pottery chimneys. We were looking over a golf course built onto the side of a hill, with villas and chalets at the top. Away to the left was the coast, and to the right was the skeleton of an apartment block, unfinished and abandoned.

The first beer vanished in no time at all in a blizzard of small talk about the flight and what Glasgow was like these days, and we had another.

Colin was looking good. He was over fifty now, and his hair had gone very white, balding on the crown. His face was tanned, of course, and relaxed with crinkly smile lines everywhere; he'd grown a neatly trimmed white beard. He was smaller than me too, and looked incredibly fit. 'In the sea every day, Martin. Golf three times a week – ' he indicated the course – 'and walks round the town. We usually have dinner out down at the marina – we'll take you to our favourite tonight. Life is brilliant here. Good broadband – ' he caught my look and held up a hand: 'All completely innocent these days. No…' His voice tailed off, and then he shrugged. 'Just the sheer enjoyment of life.'

We heard the front door and a greeting shouted, returned by us. Bags were put down heavily, accompanied by sighs of relief, and then the curtains across the open patio doors parted. We stood up. 'This is Elaine,' Colin said. She smiled at me and we embraced, with two air kisses.

'I'm going to get a beer, darling. You guys want anything else?' She was English, slightly Yorkshire.

We nodded.

'I'll prepare some bread and cheese for lunch, bring it out. Need to go to the loo. Back in ten minutes.' And she vanished into the darkness of the flat.

Colin smiled at me, and I raised my eyebrows appreciatively. His smile turned into a cat-with-cream grin. 'That's Elaine.'

She had a lovely, happy face, with messy highlighted brown hair and bright eyes. She was tall – taller than Colin – and wore a patterned dress that was loose and long, but didn't hide a full, curvy figure and nice legs. She was at least fifteen years younger than Colin.

Colin and I chatted about the company and the old days, the people we'd worked with – things we'd probably never done at the time – and Elaine brought us more beers. He was cautious at first when she was with us, as if worried that I would say anything out of turn. She brought out a tray with crusty fresh bread, oatcakes, cheese, pickle, tomato and salad. And more beers. I was slightly pissed already, and relaxed as a result.

Colin and Elaine spoke about how busy the town was, and whom she'd met in the supermarket and at the grocer's, and what a nice day it was. 'It's lovely this time of year, Martin,' she said, 'but can get a bit too hot in the summer. We've no aircon.'

'Yeah,' Colin said, 'I think we'll buy a portable unit this year. It's getting insufferable.'

Elaine adjusted her sunglasses and leaned back on the sofa, crossing her long legs and nibbling at her oatcake, washing it down with a sip of beer. I looked at her again, up and down her body, and found myself catching Colin's eyes – we smiled at each other.

'So, Martin,' she said. 'How did you and Colin meet?'

'Back in the late nineties,' I said, frowning at Colin, him nodding; careful careful! I would have to leave some things out, and I could see he wasn't fully relaxed as I spoke. 'I had set up a computer business with a school pal, way back in the late eighties. We were doing well, but everything was moving in a much more serious direction – actually it wasn't nearly so much fun any more.' We gave a rueful grin at each other. 'Everything was online by then, and security was a big issue. We'd always managed to stay ahead of the game, and we learned fast, but we knew we needed a proper, educated guy who understood all the worms and the Trojans and the security risks.'

'And Colin was your man.' She reached to hold his hand briefly.

'Yes.' It seemed best to leave the inference that Colin was there to help protect people from online threats, keep their online transactions and bank accounts safe. But Colin and I knew the true story: he had found the contacts that had led us down the road of cybercrime.

'Interesting times,' Colin said.

'We were making a fortune,' I went on, 'and then Colin decided to turn his back on it all for this life.' I spread my arms to take in the surroundings and Elaine herself. 'Don't know what the attraction was.'

Elaine did that thing again, leaning over and briefly holding his hand, smiling broadly, then sitting back to nibble cheese and sip beer, shaking her long hair away from her face.

'How about you,' Colin said. 'Still enjoying it all?'

I held his eyes, and the amusement fell away from both of us. He knew fine that I had never 'enjoyed' that side of the business. 'I think I'm ready for a change.' He nodded; he understood.

We made more small talk, and Colin came down to the car with me while I got my case.

'How did you meet Elaine?' I asked him.

'I met her in Gib, last summer. I visit the place from time to time – the banks are discreet, you know – and she was on holiday with a friend, a female friend, staying near Torremolinos. We bumped into each other a few times that day, in town and then up at the summit in the café, and we sort of stuck together on the walk down, into the caves. We got on well. She found out I was single, and she said she was separated. She was a teacher, and very pissed off. We made arrangements to meet up a few days later, and I drove her down here to show her the place, and she er... sort of stayed over. She stayed for the rest of the summer, and decided to pack in her job and come out here to stay with me. She had to give a term's notice, so we had a long gap – and I was worried she would come to her senses. But she didn't. We Skyped every day, and she came out to a new life with me.' He laughed. 'She's fantastic. Gorgeous. Great fun.' I realised I had no idea whether Colin had had any relationships with women in Glasgow.

We walked back with my case and rucksack to the flat that connected with his via the balcony, and which he owned as well and let out to people he knew, including Elaine's pals: one bedroom, no TV, the only internet connection via his Wi-Fi, but all perfectly fine. He left me to get freshened up and changed, and then I just sat on my part of the balcony, looking out over the golf course.

So… what could my life be like here, with Helen? I projected ahead, not thinking of the difficulties in our relationship.

Colin came through the iron gate on the balcony to join me, handing me a gin and tonic – 'You still drink these?' 'Damn right' 'Cheers' – and we sat for a time.

'I have a problem, Colin,' I said. 'They're not letting me go. They got me to do a wee job last autumn, in Portugal – just rummaging around on some guy's computer and installing a keylogger – in and out in a couple of hours. But the guy was murdered a few days later. He had connections to organised crime and fraud.'

'I saw the story.'

'What did you hear about it?'

'Not sure of all the details, but from the local press it seems that money vanished from his account, and it was only there being washed. They didn't believe it was nothing to do with him, didn't believe he wasn't leaking names and details. So they shot him.'

'Sandy set it up, through an intermediary. It really scared me, Colin. I'm trying to realise my assets, trying to tuck the money away, not get dragged down by the liabilities that Talbot pinned on me. I need my money somewhere safe, but I need to be able to get my hands on it. I have to live.'

'They'll notice. Ken Talbot has clever accountants working for him.'

'I know. My financial adviser has been doing things softly softly, tracking down businesses and cut-outs, trickling things out, but I've asked him to up the pace. So, yes, they'll notice. But they're not the fucking CIA – they haven't got eyes and ears everywhere.'

We sipped our gins, and watched a couple of golfers drive off from the tee out in front of our apartment, across the small burn, then climb into their golf cart and speed away. Did Colin lie awake at night, expecting a knock from some hit man who wanted to get even for something we'd done? How had he first reacted when I'd called his mobile?

'How did you get out, Colin?' My voice was soft.

He coughed. ‘Two ways. One, I knew too much for them to hassle me: I’ve got documentation, papers, names, dates, a whole map of Talbot’s organisation tucked away with a bank in Gib. I have a solicitor whose company have instructions on what to do with it in the event of an accident to me. Talbot and Sandy know this. I told them roughly what I had, and what I had taken out of the company. I wasn’t greedy, and I’m sure they respected that. So they didn’t chase me when I slipped away. Have you seen Talbot recently?’

There was something else he wasn’t telling me, but I let it go for now. ‘No, not for years. Sandy runs the company to all intents and purposes now, along with a twat called Graham Turner; there are the guys along on Argyle Street still, but we’re using the same system you left us with for the other stuff. I do the business on that, and I supervise, troubleshoot, keep myself up-to-date, give advice. Haven’t seen Ken Talbot since the accident. Sandy hints that he isn’t a well man, heart trouble, but I don’t know.’

‘The accident. That broke him, I think. So – you say Sandy set up the Portugal job?’

‘I think he was behind it, but I was approached by a woman: small, blonde – absolutely stunning wee thing. And a guy, big, heavy features – called himself Jimmy Anderson. He looked like he was running it, and she played dumb at first, but she was the one that came over to the house with us, had the house key and the password to the computer: he was just there to frighten me. Her name is Charlene.’ I looked hard at him. ‘You know them?’

‘No.’ Not a flicker of hesitation, but I wasn’t sure if he was telling the truth. Colin had lied to me for most of our working relationships: I didn't know what he looked like when he was being honest.

We fell silent again for the rest of the gin.

'I can't help you,' he said at last. 'You can stay here as long as you like, but I can't help you get out. And I'm really sorry about the past, truly I am, and I'd like to make it up to you, but I can't help you with Sandy and Ken Talbot.'

'I'm not asking for help in that way. Just advice – financial advice.'

He nodded. 'No chance of an ID change?'

I shook my head. 'No. Did you manage that?'

'Sort of – I have a couple of identities for different bank accounts, different credit cards, a few different addresses – properties I own – but only one passport: never mastered the whole Bourne Identity thing – didn't really need to.' He took a deep breath. 'My advice is probably the same as your adviser would give you: get the money into online banking, different banks, different accounts – different usernames, different passwords – some in Gib, a sort of nest egg – we can go down there for the day if you like. But keep moving most of it around; the UK government is suddenly getting twitchy about tax avoidance, people and companies using offshore accounts. It may be just political opportunism, but you never know – you might get caught it the fallout. And get ready to run, away from your life in Glasgow. When you do, take multiple journeys, double back, try to use cash for ferries, car hire. Get well away, somewhere they won't think you'll go. Somewhere remote, cold.'

I nodded. 'Do you ever see anyone suspicious wandering about, checking on you? Maybe the CIA have found out about the cybercrime.'

He smiled. 'It's the FBI that investigate cybercrime, as you know, and they tend only to worry when US citizens are involved as victims, and as far as I know we didn't ever screw over any American businesses or individuals. If I was paranoid about all the possibilities, I would have to shoot myself – it's no way to live. No, Ken Talbot and Sandy know that I'm not a threat to them, not while I'm happily ensconced here, and they leave me alone. I've earned them more money than I ever took from them. They're gangsters, always have an eye out for the main chance, but they don't fight hopeless battles. I never knew Talbot to take revenge just for the sake of it. If you make reasonable efforts to get away, get your money safe, he won't pursue you – not worth the hassle for him. Probably. It would help if you tucked away some details about him though, as security.'

I nodded at that thought, and wondered whether I could start to document all the infected computers we had set up, all the people and businesses we had compromised – would that work as security, or just make me more of a liability to them? 'How about Talbot's rivals in Glasgow – if one of them gets a hold of information about you?'

He pursed his lips and then shook his head. 'Nah. Not worth worrying about. If it happens it happens.' He stood up, stretching. 'I'm going to have a wee siesta – we'll go into town in a couple of hours, get some food, I'll show you around. Beach tomorrow. Gib on Wednesday. OK?'

I nodded. Sounded like a plan. Options? Including what Colin and I had discussed, I had a total of one option.

*

We took my hire car, just Colin and me, and set off early. The hour's run down the motorway was fabulous, and the familiar huge shape of the rock came into view surprisingly soon. We followed the road past it and back, and joined the traffic jam heading into Gibraltar, stopping on the Spanish side of the border in a big, expensive dust bowl of a car park, and then walking in, my eyes fixed on the rock, the marina, the sea of people around us. I knew what the rock looked like, of course, but wasn't prepared for the whole environment, the mass of humanity pouring across the border.

We got through passport control without a hitch, waited at the edge of the runway that separated the main peninsula from the Spanish side while a small jet came in, and then crossed it and went along past modern housing, including rather run-down blocks of flats, down a tunnel through the old city walls with a busker playing a saxophone, and found ourselves in a long London street dropped into the Mediterranean. London bobbies walked about here and there, and the air was filled by a curious blend of English and Spanish – I saw one bobby talking Spanish to a café waitress who replied in English, and so it went. We passed Marks and Spencer's, and stopped at a cafe, paying in pounds.

Colin had arranged the meetings with three banks. Gibraltar had basically become a centre for online banking, online gambling, money laundering and Internet fraud. Everyone was discreet: if you could prove your own identity, and show them the money was real, you were in. Two banks gave us accounts with online access; another was a deposit account where I would have to turn up in person, but under a different name. I reckoned my money was safe, and mostly accessible. How traceable it was, I wasn't sure: I just needed to do lots of little transfers through different accounts in different names, so that it would be as difficult as possible to track it back or forward. As and when I decided to get away from the company, whatever the circumstances, I would be well off.

From a computer in the bank I transferred some money over from my UK accounts; other money would go by a different route. I'd let the money settle in Gibraltar, but maybe move it on later. All I needed was Andrew, back in Glasgow, to track down my shares and move them around, out and over.

I began to feel better after that, more secure. And not too morally bankrupt, because I'd resolved that some of the money would go to Davey's family.

From the top of Gibraltar rock, after a visit to the café and looking wonderingly at T-shirts that proclaimed 'British since 1704' on the front, we stood looking over the Mediterranean to the east, across the merchant ships at anchor, and then walked round to look across to Africa, and then round to look over the sprawl of the city and the port, and an EasyJet flight coming in away below us. It was an interesting place, but something about it didn't sit well with me. And those famous apes were an irritation, sitting around like bored, surly teenagers, glowering as they were photographed, trying to get into the café to shoplift.

'How are relationships these days?' I asked.

'Gibraltar and Spain? Still tense – usual thing: governments like to have an enemy. Still the usual restrictions: only UK flights can land here, mobile phones registered in Gib won't work in

Spain, stupid stuff. But almost everyone who works here comes over the border in the morning: they depend on Gib, so they have to make it work. It's a crazy place.'

We took the long walk down the rock, in and out of caves, doing the history and the pre-history bit: world war 2 gun emplacements, Neanderthal dwellings. Again, I felt the whole history put my life in perspective.

As we walked back across the runway and the border, Colin was reflective. 'Have you simply asked them if you can retire gracefully?'

'They made it clear a long time ago that I couldn't get out. I thought of asking again, after that business in Portugal. But even if I retired, they'd be able to get back to me for 'one last job'. No, I have to grab the money and run. Otherwise I'll end up doing jobs for him forever.'

'How's Davey doing?'

'Still the same.'

'Sorry to hear that.'

We reached the car, and fought our way back into the traffic jam streaming out of Gibraltar. As we drove back up the motorway, I glanced back at the rock. We drove in silence.

*

Late that evening, when Elaine had gone to bed and Colin and I sat on the balcony, our skin covered with mosquito repellent, sipping a last gin, I asked him about the online fraud. We were both pretty drunk by this point.

'How did it all happen, Colin?'

'It was my idea. After I got the job with B&D, I made contact with a couple of hackers from London – I'd met them at another conference: I was doing the rounds, exploring options. I was flat broke and my record ruled me out of a lot of jobs. They did the coding and set up the system more or less as you see it now: we never had to meet after the set-up, never even make contact except in an emergency.' He took a deep breath. 'They had the contact with Gregorius. I never knew who that was, never saw anything online about him. It didn't worry me. I stuck to my plan. Gregorius paid us a fee for each computer we sold him, and if he wanted to keep it on his network he paid an on-going fee.'

'I assume he got his money's worth.'

'Oh yes. Not just cash down the line: access to these computers gave him power, potential. Once he had enough – not just from us, of course – he could blackmail people, threaten them with denial of service.' Colin shrugged and sipped at his gin. 'I always felt threatened by Gregorius, somehow. I was glad when I got out of the business.'

'Has he contacted you since?'

'He doesn't know I've left B&D.' Colin turned to look at me. 'He will be under the assumption that you are me.'

I took in the implications of that. 'So what would happen if *I* left?'

There was another deep breath and a gulp of gin. 'I don't know, Martin.'

Chapter 12

Glasgow– the early 90s

Frank and I were hunched over a PC as we heard Charlie breeze into the front shop. 'Hi gorgeous!' and a squawk from Sam as he grabbed her – he usually gave her a squeeze and a grope, but she didn't seem to find it appealing any more. He had moved on.

'What's happening, guys?'

Charlie was wearing an Armani suit, a big gold watch, gold cufflinks. As he came through the back he waved a set of car keys. Frank and I couldn't avoid looking at them.

'Fuckin' bimmer, boys.' We looked blank. 'BMW 3-series – the 325is.' His mouth dropped open as we didn't react. 'You poofs no interested in cars?'

Frank shook his head, and I said: 'I don't even drive, Charlie.'

Charlie appealed to Davey, who shook his head also.

'Aw, for fuck sake.' He put his keys away. 'So, anything new?' He poured himself a coffee from the big jug on its heated stand and pulled over a chair to look at the monitor.

Frank nodded and mumbled something. Charlie frowned at me.

'The world wide web,' I said.

Charlie, for all his cash and posturing, wasn't entirely stupid. 'I've heard about it.'

'Computers can communicate over the phone lines – the network is called the Internet, and it's been around for years, mainly used by the US military and universities. But now there's the World Wide Web, which makes it easy to share content.'

'It's early days,' Davey cautioned.

'There's a lot of fun stuff going on – people discussing weird TV programmes and computers – ' Davey nodded seriously: he was an avid user of this, and wouldn't have thought of it as being frivolous. 'But,' I went on, 'businesses are beginning to see the potential. Some banks are allowing you to do your banking online, travel firms are doing bookings, some wee shops are starting to sell stuff online. And more people are using email: you can send messages, instantly. It hasn't been mentioned all that much on mainstream news because none of the reporters can understand technology properly, but it will change the way we all live.'

Charlie sat back with his coffee. 'Where do we come in? How can we make money out of it?'

I got myself a coffee too.

Davey chipped in: 'We need to push modems – the things that connect to the phone lines – as part of the PCs we sell, and help people get onto the web.' He still looked down when he spoke, but it was less of a mumble. Even Frank was known to speak occasionally.

I nodded. 'There are loads of big companies out there who can build and sell PCs cheaper than we can. We're making money just now because Microsoft's programming is basically shite: they design their software on huge, fast mainframes, which causes problem on PCs, even when they've got as much as 256K of memory and maybe even a fast 500 meg hard drive. So we're getting the premium by sorting out all the software problems, and selling additional hardware that customers didn't know they needed, like the hard drives we fit. But we're still really hitting the home computers, the hobbyists, with only the occasional business. We need something better.'

Charlie grimaced as he reached the end of his coffee. 'So, what's the idea?'

'Instead of selling a little hardware, and software, and fixing stuff they've bought elsewhere, we can do an all-in-one service. We talk about what they need for their home or their hobby or their small business. We put together their perfect hardware and software package – maybe buying in basic PCs and selling them on with all the extra bits and peripherals they really need. We install their software and guarantee to keep it running, for some kind of on-going fee. And we train them to use the software – either ourselves or buy in some lecturer from the college, or a school even. We fit anti-virus software too, to keep them safe.' Viruses were becoming more common, and a complete pain in the backside. I'd been researching them, and had even written one myself as an exercise, horrified at how easy it was and what it could do.

Davey cleared his throat. 'We sell a complete working system, train them to use it, and sort out problems that come up.'

Charlie was nodding. ‘So, we charge a premium for the hardware and software, because we’re tailoring a package, and we charge a fee to keep it all sweet. Sounds good.’

‘We can also design websites for people.’ I’d done some work on this too: it wasn’t difficult. ‘But we also need to expand to do all of this.’

Charlie looked round the crowded workshop. ‘Yeah, it’s a bit tight.’

‘And not just that. This place has all the air of a hobby computer shop. If we want to attract proper business people we need a different place, with desks and PCs on them, so we can show them what we can do. OK, we can make and install stuff here, but we need a better image. Another shop, bit more flash.’

‘Close by?’

‘Not necessarily. It might be useful for us to go back and forth, but there’s really no need. Somewhere a bit more upmarket might be better – Byres Road, or in the centre of town even. But the overheads there would be higher, I think.’

‘OK. Right, could you boys write all of that down, and I’ll speak to dad, Sandy and Tom. Then we can all meet and work out the details. Oh look!’ He had spotted a blocky photograph appearing on the screen, slowly building up and resolving, and was grinning like mad.

We worked on our main jobs through the day, and then in the middle of the afternoon Davey and I put together the plan for the new part of the business, including what the new place would have to look like, and thoughts about staffing. Frank listened, and softly suggested the occasional idea. We printed off three copies for ourselves to think about overnight, and I phoned Sandy to organise a meeting the next day, at lunchtime – typically, Charlie hadn't yet got round to mentioning it to him. Davey left – he and Jane were going to the pictures – and eventually Frank left too.

I drank coffee and played with my new software that could display text and photographs from computers faraway, and let myself dream of what this could all look like in the future, what the potential might be.

I had to put the lights on after a time, and then I sat in the one soft chair we had, and stared into space. The future was strange, unknown. I looked at my watch: Fiona had an appointment with her GP. She was still losing weight, and was tired all the time, but insisted it was the after effects of the miscarriages. She'd been for blood tests, and the doctor had asked her to come in as soon as possible to talk about the results.

The phone interrupted my thoughts, and Sam answered – then waved urgently to me. I went over and took the receiver from her.

It was the doctor. She had phoned an ambulance for Fiona, because she'd collapsed while he had been examining her.

'Christ,' I said. 'But nothing serious. Is there?'

She hesitated. 'There are some issues with your wife's blood tests. She's on her way to Gartnavel Hospital, ward 5B. If you get there and report to reception, they'll fill you in.'

My mouth was dry. 'What is it? Tell me something.'

She took a deep breath. 'We think your wife may be very ill. The hospital will tell you more.'

'What's wrong with her? Tell me.'

The voice went soft. 'I shouldn't say anything over the phone, but we think your wife has ovarian cancer.'

'Is it operable?' My heart was slowly thudding, and I could feel my head growing light.

'I hope so. They'll do what they can. You need to get over there as soon as possible. You need to be positive for her.' And then the deadly coda that I can remember to this day: 'But you need to prepare yourself for what might happen.'

Sam took the phone from me, and I sat down before I could fall. 'Could you get me a taxi?' I asked her. I looked around in despair, and then the tears came.

*

I can still recall those short few hours: the taxi driver wittering on about the football; me stumbling through the hospital, trying to find my way; the talk with the nurse in the fluorescent-lit empty day room; the waiting while they operated on Fiona – I hadn't had a chance to see her. Someone told me where the coffee machine was, suggested I go for something to eat.

Davey appeared from somewhere, at some point: he seemed to know what was happening. He brought me a sandwich and a drink, and went back and forth to talk to the nurse, and a doctor. He was suddenly in control, while I sat gazing at the pale green wall, miserable, trying to come to terms with what was happening to me. My wee brother, my dad – and now my wife. What had I done to deserve this?

Two guys appeared, men hardly any older than me, and sat down beside me. They introduced themselves: they were doctors. In quiet voices, they told me the story: the cancer had been very well developed, but they'd made the decision to operate, to try to excise them, to give her a chance because there would have been none otherwise. But it had been too much: she'd had heart failure on the operating table, and because of the cancer and the tissue they'd cut away they'd known it was hopeless: they had tried to resuscitate her for a short time, but given up.

She'd passed away. Peacefully. She was gone. Just like that.

'Would you like to see her?'

'No,' I said at once. It wasn't her. She was gone.

I gazed at the world around me: all different, everything I had wanted gone, the love of my life gone. I gazed at Davey, and the greyness around me. Tears flowed down my face.

*

Planning the Catholic funeral – well, Fiona's mum did it; I just nodded to everything – and then sitting through it, numb, eyes open and cursing a God I didn't believe in, was rough. The funeral was almost the same as the wedding, such a short time before – same people, same priest with his fatuous condolences, Fiona's sister Janine in a short black dress, a black veil over her face.

The weeks and months after that were the worst ever, a descent into a lonely hell. I started drinking a lot. The flat was empty, Fiona's absence like a vacuum, following me around. The world was flat grey. There was no end to the misery, and something cold settled in me.

Chapter 13

This spring - Glasgow

I got back from Spain to a chilly, gloomy Glasgow, with a feeling of certainty in my gut of what I wanted to do and how to do it. The only uncertainty was around Helen and her mood towards me.

Andrew phoned and gave me a name and a number. 'This guy is a private detective in Glasgow. For £200 he'll get you the name of a policeman working on Operation Lockdown who will talk to you about what they've found out about Ken Talbot's business interests.'

'Just like that.'

'Just like that. If you give me the nod, I'll organise the payment and then text you the contact details. After that it's down to you. You just give me anything you get from the police.'

'What if the information is rubbish?'

'That's the chance you take.'

'OK, Andrew.' I flipped through options in my head. 'Go ahead.'

An hour later I had a mobile phone number and a name: Detective Sergeant Amanda Pitt, working out of Stewart Street police station up in Cowcaddens. I sat looking at the text, and then went to get a coffee and brought it back to my desk.

I started searching online for information about her. She was in her mid-thirties, single. I found a photograph: a slim, severe-looking woman with short brown hair. Her Facebook account wasn't well protected – she'd obviously missed all the changes to security settings over the years – and I found other photographs, many with her smiling, some with her in bars with an arm round someone, always another young woman.

I scanned her newsfeed: comments on TV, asking for advice on a planned holiday to New York, and a host of responses to that. Messages to and from a 'Rose Brown', but no pictures or details: her Facebook account was locked down, with not even a profile picture. It sounded like they were an item, but keeping it very low key. As I watched, Amanda sent a private message to Rose Brown to say she was just heading down to the GFT – the Glasgow Film Theatre – for coffee. The reply came immediately: a triple kiss.

I sat still, counting the seconds, wondering if I dared go through with this. She would walk, I was sure. So I gave her a minute or so to get clear of the police station, and then I took a deep breath and phoned her mobile, withholding my own number.

She answered, the voice cautious, traffic noise in the background: 'Hello?'

'Hi there,' I said, trying to keep my voice calm. 'Is that Detective Sergeant Amanda Pitt?'

'Yes. Who is this?' Her voice was level, but wary, her breathing deep as she walked.

'I'd really like to have a chat with you,' I said, 'about Ken Talbot.'

And it was obvious the name meant something to her. Good. 'Where and when can we meet?'

Shit – I hadn't thought that far ahead, had expected to have to persuade her. Somewhere quite busy, but not too busy. 'How about the foyer of the Hilton – the one up from Anderston Cross?' And I cheekily decided to rattle her a little. 'In about an hour – once you've finished at the GFT?'

I heard the moment's hesitation as she caught the implication of what I'd said, then smoothly ignored it. 'See you there.' And she hung up.

I sat back. Did I really want to go through with this? She might simply arrest me, get what I knew out of me in an interview room. I was sweating suddenly. I sat still, letting the time pass, trying to decide, my fingers trembling.

I told Claire I was going out, and headed into the stale city air, and down the hill towards the Hilton, by the M8. I walked round the corner, and up into the wide lobby and over to the bar to get myself an over-priced lager. I sat at one of the low tables across from the wide reception desk, and watched people come and go.

A woman came in and sat on a low chair at the other side of the foyer, taking out her phone, checking it, looking round. I was pretty sure it was Amanda Pitt, but she looked different from her Facebook photos: an angular face, a neat figure in a dark trouser suit with a white blouse under it. Her hair was mid-brown, with blonde highlights. I phoned Amanda Pitt's mobile, and the woman across from me answered: 'Hello?' At the same time, she looked across, and I gave her a wave. She switched off her phone and came over to sit beside me, shaking hands with me as

I half-stood and bobbed my head. She put her handbag on the floor at her feet, and brushed her hair back from her face with her hand. Then she sat composed, hands loosely clasped on her lap.

'OK,' she said. 'Who are you?' Her voice was low and calm.

I thought of all the things I could say, but simply said: 'My name is Martin McGregor.'

She nodded. 'How did you get my mobile number?'

I took a deep breath, wondering what her reaction would be. 'I got your number from a private detective – I don't know his name, but he claims you'll be willing to give me information about Ken Talbot, what you know about his operations. Is that right?'

She pursed her lips. 'And how did you know I was on my way to the GFT?'

'I found you on Facebook: you haven't done your security settings properly. I saw the message from Rose Brown'

She nodded, with a brief closing of her eyes. 'OK. So… Who are you?

'Would you like a drink?' I asked.

She shook her head. 'No. Who are you, Martin McGregor?'

I took a deep breath. 'I'm a senior manager in two computer companies in Glasgow, B&D Software Solutions, and also Bytes and Digits. They're both connected to Ken Talbot – he really sort of set them up and financed them.'

She nodded. I could see she either knew of them or understood exactly the purpose of them. 'So why are you talking to me?'

‘I’d like to know the extent of Ken Talbot’s business interests. I’d like to know what you know – assuming he’s one of the people under investigation in Operation Lockdown.’

‘Why?’

I gave a cough and had to look away briefly from her steady gaze, her complete lack of emotion. ‘I have shares and interests in a lot of these companies. I want - ’ and my voice stumbled. I looked at her and then away again. ‘I want to get out of the situation I’m in, get away from Ken Talbot.’

‘Taking as much as you can,’ she said.

I squirmed. ‘I suppose so. Yes.’ I cleared my throat again and tried to sound more assertive: ‘Much of that money is legitimately mine. I’ve worked hard all my life.’

Now she raised an eyebrow. ‘For criminals, helping to launder money from theft, smuggling and drugs, and prostitution.’

I shook my head. ‘I didn’t do any of that.’

‘But you knew it was going on.’

‘No. No I didn’t. Not till relatively recently.’

She held me in the cold stare, her brown eyes boring into me. ‘So what are you offering me?’

‘I can give you money. Or information about more of Talbot’s interests. There are probably things that you don’t know about.’

‘Such as what?’

‘There is some online criminal activity going on.’

Her expression changed subtly. The eyes narrowed, and the mask of indifference slipped. ‘OK, let’s say we make a deal. How much information? How much money?’

I began to worry that this was an elaborate sting, entrapment. I felt a shiver run through my body, my confidence dribbling away. I wished I hadn't made the call. 'Everything I know for everything you know. And name a price.'

'Five thousand pounds,' she said.

I took a deep breath, pressed my palms hard against my thighs to stop my fingers quivering. 'Fine,' I said.

She raised her eyebrows. 'OK,' she said, picking up her handbag and standing up. 'I'll see what can be done. Give me a couple of days, then I'll be in touch to take this further.'

I stood up and we shook hands. 'Good to meet you, Martin.' Her grip was firmer this time, and her eyes held mine, before she turned away and walked out of the hotel.

I sat down, my hand shaking as I finished my lager. It was going to be a long two days. And maybe at the end of it I was just going to be hauled in by the police and locked up for years.

*

I treated Helen to a meal out in her favourite fish restaurant in the Merchant City, and promised her a luxury weekend in Skye. But I could see she still wasn't happy. She knew something was going on, knew that I was keeping things from her, knew I wasn't relaxed and happy. My trip to Spain, the whole business in the Algarve, had built a barrier between us. Incredibly, I wondered whether our relationship was over: could that be? I thought I still loved her, but had I killed it all because of the crime that surrounded me?

'Catherine saw you earlier,' she said suddenly over her wine glass. 'At the Hilton.' Her eyes were wide on me.

'Oh – never saw her.' Thinking fast, going for the big lie because that's often what works. 'They're clients of ours. They have the big Hilton corporate system of course, but also their own internal one for the conferences they run there.' Absolute bullshit, I thought, not remotely believable – but Helen nodded. 'I was just talking stuff over with one of their sub-managers – nice lady.'

She nodded again – I'd got away with it. Maybe. Her phoned beeped with a text message, and she fished it out of her handbag. She unlocked it, and her eyes grew wide again, and then narrowed.

'What's up?' I asked.

She turned the phone to show me. It was a photograph of a small, blue Portuguese fishing boat, with a small blonde girl in short shorts, wearing a baseball cap, leaning over a man and smiling – the man was me. The photograph had been taken as we sailed across to the house in Portugal, when Charlene had stood up and stumbled.

'You didn't mention romantic boat trips with the wee blonde.' Her voice was calm, cold.

'This is a set-up,' I said. 'That was the day we went over to do the computer job. She stood up and pretended to fall towards me – must have been for the photograph.'

But then I saw on Helen's face that this wasn't the main problem. 'You didn't tell me she was with you that day.'

I blustered. 'I didn't think it mattered. I thought you'd be irritated if you knew. Helen!' At this point she snatched the phone back and pushed her chair back from the table.

I thought she was walking out, but she went to the toilets. Five minutes later she was back, her make-up obviously repaired, topping up her wine glass and taking a big drink. Oh shit. I cradled my head in my hands. Someone had taken that picture, and then sent it to Helen with the express purpose of destabilising our relationship. Why? Did they realise how precarious that relationship was right now?

Shit shit shit.

*

The next day, after a chilly evening at home, I went into the office, and grabbed a coffee while I asked Claire about the plans for her wedding. She told me Sandy was in and wanted a word, so I knocked on his office door – Colin's old room – and went in.

I noticed he was getting bigger these days, more of the muscle turning to fat and multiplying, his face a bit florid. He looked up from his computer and waved me to sit down. We both sipped coffees, and looked at each other.

'How are things, Martin?' he asked.

'Fine,' I said. 'Everything is working away like it should.'

His eyes narrowed, picking up that I really wasn't happy.

I decided to get it off my chest. 'The bottom line is, Sandy, that you got me involved in something in Portugal that I don't understand, and I helped steal information from a guy who got murdered a couple of days later. And someone send a photograph to Helen – a photograph that shows I lied to her, which is bad enough, but which also looks like I was having a wee something with a tasty wee blonde girl. It's causing difficulties with my relationship with Helen.'

Sandy spread his arms. 'Shit happens, Martin.'

'Who was she, Sandy? The wee blonde girl, Charlene.'

'She works for some people who work with us. She knows Ken – from the old days.'

'From the old days? She's only in her mid-twenties!'

'Yeah.' He raised his coffee cup to his lips, his eyes on me, narrowed.

'How is Ken, by the way?'

Sandy grimaced. 'Not good. He spends all the time in his house in Bearsden, hardly goes out. He's tired and old.'

'How about his business interests?'

'I'm handling those,' Sandy said, without a pause. He was still directly looking at me.

I decided not to pursue that. 'Life's complicated,' I said. 'It's not good at the moment.'

'Is that why you're selling off your shareholdings?'

I shrugged, trying not to panic that he'd noticed what I was doing, as Andrew had said he would. 'Just moving some assets around. Keeping my options open.'

He shrugged in turn. 'It's not a good time to sell. Are you still thinking of retiring, Martin?'

I gave an unconvincing yawn. 'Would that be a problem? We spoke about it before, I remember, but things have moved on.'

His eyelids drooped as he looked at me. 'Tell you what, Martin, I'll make a deal with you. One more job for us and then you can retire. We won't stop you.'

'For fuck's sake, Sandy. That thing in Portugal was creepy – I don't want to get into something like that again.' Part of my mind wondered whether he could 'stop me' now, but I was pretty sure he could make my life hell if he chose; at the very least he could have me beaten senseless, and probably killed.

'One more job. It's part of a link with European interests, and doing a favour for some friends. Then we'll let you retire, clear of debts. B&D will be bought by another firm, and they'll take on all assets and liabilities. You'll be clear, free. Go where you like, do what you like. I'm told the south of Spain is nice.'

I debated this inside my head. Maybe… 'Who are these "European interests"?'

'A group of Romanians. They've got various things going on out there, and they're interested in the sort of thing we've got going on here. I've offered to explain what we do, how we work. In turn, they will explain how things work over there – they're connected.'

I mulled that over; East Europe was in many respects the centre of cybercrime, so I wasn't sure what I would be able to tell these people. But maybe they didn't trust their own friends, or were trying to branch out on their own into the west. Sandy's pitch made some kind of sense. And if he was about to let me get clear then I had made a mistake in contacting Amanda Pitt. I wasn't in a position to get away just yet, though, so I nodded. 'OK, Sandy.' He smiled. 'When are they coming over?' And what would happen with Gregorius if I left?

'They want you to go over there.'

'Oh. OK.' I had never been to Eastern Europe before.

'In a couple of weeks. I'll organise the details, let you know.'

‘How long for?’

‘Depends.’

‘OK. As long as this is the end of it.’

Sandy smiled over the rim of his coffee cup. ‘I promise.’

*

Amanda Pitt phoned the office three days later, and Claire put her through to my desk. ‘How did you get my number?’ I asked.

Her tone was sour. ‘I’m a detective, Martin. I find things out. I detect.’

‘So…’ And I let that hang, unsure, frightened almost.

‘We can work together,’ she said, her voice matter-of-fact. ‘Can you meet me in the Counting House at four o’clock this afternoon – near the St Vincent Street entrance, down the road from your office.’

‘I’ll be there.’

‘Good. Bring me a personal cheque for £5000 made out to Rose Brown.’

*

She was there in the huge, very busy pub bordering George Square, in a corner on her own with a glass of coke – at least, I assumed it was just coke. Once I’d spotted her, I got myself a beer and squeezed through the crowd to her table. I was relieved to see that she was on her own, that I wasn’t going to be arrested just yet.

Her manner was brisk. ‘I’d like a note of your bank account and sort code.’

‘Why?’

‘I’m going to pay you for the information you’re going to give me.’

‘But I’m…’

‘Otherwise someone will wonder what I gave you in return. They may even suspect I gave you sexual favours.’ She gave a pantomime shudder. ‘God forbid.’

‘Thanks very much.’

‘You’re not my type, Martin – as you know.’

‘So we’re on.’

‘Yes. In this – ‘ she handed over a pastel blue cardboard folder, stuffed with sheets of paper, printouts and hand-written notes – ‘is most of what we have on Talbot and his business connections across the city, and wider. We’re investigating what we can, tracing companies real and dummy, shareholders, real and dummy. We thought you were a dummy, but you’re real.’

‘Thanks very much,’ I repeated. I drank some beer, and showed her my bank card: she copied the details into her phone, then put it away. Then I handed her the cheque, from my personal account, made out to Rose Brown. She scanned it before putting it away in her purse.

‘A lot of the companies are not designed to make a profit. We don’t know much about B&D.’ Her eyes looked hard at me. ‘I assume this is what you’re going to tell me about.’

I nodded.

Amanda went on: ‘We also note that there has been a steady flow of share dealings in recent months from some of Ken

Talbot's companies on our list – the real and the fake. We thought that he was getting ready to finance something major, maybe arms or drugs, but it's been you, hasn't it? This is all about you getting out, with your money, and blowing a hole in Talbot's empire so he can't come after you.' Her voice had a scathing edge to it.

'It's not quite like that,' I tried to protest. 'As well as the assets in those companies –' which I'd never bought, but I didn't feel it was useful to tell her that – 'I have massive debts, and they aren't mine. These debts were nominal when we signed up, but they've become real. I'd be broke if it all came down.'

She frowned. 'Correct me if I'm wrong, but you are a criminal. How much money do you think you legitimately hold?'

I drank more beer. 'Look, I'm not getting into an ethical argument with you, of all people. My conscience is clear. I was dragged into this by accident – all we wanted was to run a small computer shop, earn some money, do what we loved doing. None of this was part of the plan.'

Her brown eyes were blank as she looked at me. She didn't know the whole story, and I couldn't begin to tell her.

I shook away the past. 'Look, I'll take this. I'll get you the details you need about the online stuff. It'll take me a while to pull it together.'

'I'll give you a week. Don't leave the country.'

'Actually I am going away… holiday, Eastern Europe. In a couple of weeks. But I'll be back, and I'll see you then.'

'How about something in good faith? Apart from the money.'

'I'll email you stuff tonight.'

'You want my…' and then she paused. 'But you know my email address.'

'If it's on your Facebook profile I do.'

She closed her eyes momentarily.

'Don't you guys train people on how to stay safe online?'

She nodded glumly.

*

I phoned Andrew and met him that evening in Blackfriars at a table by the window, and gave him the folder from Amanda Pitt. He flipped through the sheets of paper, and nodded. 'Yes, this looks pretty comprehensive. This will help. I take it things went well with the policeman.'

I nodded. 'Just fine.' I was tense, my heart thudding, the adrenaline racing through me. I tried to hold it all in check, because there was still a long game to be played here.

'So you want me to keep doing what I've been doing?' he asked over his gin.

I nodded. 'I'm going to Romania in a couple of weeks for a few days with work. When I come back, I want to shift all the money you can get out for me over to the bank accounts where I can get them. Don't worry about leaving loose ends or some stuff – just get what you can. I'll pay your fee, and then I'm out.'

I'd go somewhere with Helen, repair our relationship, start the next phase of my life. I'd be relatively well off. We could be happy together, we really could.

'Be careful in Romania,' Andrew said.

I nodded. 'It'll be fine.'

That evening, I emailed Amanda Pitt with a very carefully worded document: I didn't want her bosses rushing off at half cock to raid B&D and spoil everything before I could get away.

I told her the basic outline of what we did at B&D, but not the details of any companies we had compromised. I made up a story that we had a network of hackers who were buying and selling lists of credit card numbers, email addresses, and mobile phone numbers, and were compromising and selling details of machines that could be used in botnets, to mount cyber attacks on institutions and governments. I didn't mention that we actually had a single link through to this Gregorius character.

I said that I would email her much more detail when I got back from Romania.

After I sent the email, I stared at my computer. Had I handled this the right way? Had I given her enough but not too much? Would I be able to get clear, or would the Scottish police just drag me down with the rest of Talbot's empire? Should I have just sat tight and assumed that Sandy would honour his promise to let me go after the Romanian job? How would Gregorius react? What could he do to me?

Finally I gave a shrug. I didn't trust Sandy, and I didn't trust Amanda Pitt either. But I'd started the process. I couldn't go back now. The clocks were ticking.

Chapter 14

Glasgow and London – the nineties

Bill Gates had discovered the World Wide Web, and Steve Jobs was back at Apple. Professionally speaking it was an exciting time, everything was opening up, everything was changing.

In my lucid moments, I thought up daft ideas for websites, and designed them. Everybody wanted to do things on the Internet suddenly. I spent all day dealing with email – much of it meaningless – and evenings writing code. I discovered I could write programs that got through the rudimentary security in Microsoft's browser and pick up email addresses. Once I wrote an email to a batch of these addresses, pretending to be Lloyds Bank, asking for their full details as a 'security check', even though it was unlikely they actually banked with Lloyds. Three people sent me the information by return, and another two 'corrected' my information by giving me the actual names of their banks and their sort codes, and their account numbers. I was amazed.

But my personal life was like my flat on Argyle Street: cold and empty. A cleaner came in once a week, though I had no idea how that had been arranged or who gave her a set of keys. I slept there, coming home late after several beers alone in the pub, having a glass of wine before going to bed, to help me sleep. Then strong coffee in the morning to get me up.

Davey and Jane got married. My mum and Alan got married. I sat drunk through both weddings. Davey didn't trust me to be his best man, got a stumbling Frank to do it instead. I didn't mind: he was right – I could barely handle being there, never mind speaking.

One side of life was going really well, the rest was crap.

Sam interrupted my thoughts. 'Are you finished for the day, Martin?'

I looked at my watch. 'Shit, Sam, sorry – didn't realise it was so late. You get off, I'll lock up.' She had a life out there, I had nothing to go to. Except the pub.

'I've closed the till.'

'Thanks.'

But she didn't leave. She stood looking at me with almost a sad expression on her face, and I looked back at her. 'Are you wanting something to eat? You haven't had anything all day.'

'I suppose I should. How about you?' I would normally get hungry around eleven at night, and have something in the pub. I'd never asked Sam to join me, and she'd never shown any hint that she wanted to.

'We could share a pizza,' she said.

I looked at her again. She'd filled out a bit over the last few years, in a good way. She still had the Goth look, but it was less angular and angry. The black jeans and the black T-shirt were tighter, her lips less black, her face less white, the hair cut back a bit to show more of it. There was only one small nose ring, and only three rings in each ear. As I watched her, I suddenly felt a sexual desire. But no, I didn't want a relationship with her: we had nothing in common except working here. It wouldn't be fair to use her for sex. And Charlie had been there before. And, of course, she had never shown any interest in me.

'Want me to phone out for a pizza?' she asked.

'Yeah – great,' I said.

We shared a Quattro Formagio, and then went across the road to the pub, her with her usual vodka and coke, me with my beer. And another round, and another. It was always like this: I wanted to stay where it was warm and there were people. I didn't want to go home to that void.

We talked, possibly for the first time. We talked about the business, and I mentioned ideas for expansion, sharing some ideas, telling her that she'd be OK if she wanted to stay with us – did she want to stay with us? Oh yes, she was happy here.

Then we got onto personal stuff. She said she was sorry about Fiona, but never had a chance to properly say it. I spoke about the days before she had died, not realising how ill she had become – though it was obvious now, looking back at holiday snaps of our honeymoon in the Algarve, and comparing them with the photos of our last Christmas together.

I began to cry, and Sam held my hand and buried her face in the nape of my neck, her other hand on the back of my head. I could smell her perfume, feel the softness of her body. After she went to buy more drinks – I gave her the money – she picked up my hand again and sat close to me, our hips touching.

Sam spoke about her family: her big sister had had a second baby and then separated from her 'two-timing shagger' of a husband. Sam lived with her mum in Partick; her mum worked in a shop; her dad had left a long time ago. Sam didn't have a boyfriend at the moment.

'Did you and Charlie ever…?'

She grimaced. 'Yeah. He's a good-looking guy, but he's such a flash twat. He moved on.'

'Must have been awful for you.'

She looked blankly at me with her dark brown eyes framed by heavy mascara. 'It was good fun. He took me up to a hotel near Loch Lomond for the weekend once. Treated me really good, like a princess. But I think he shagged one of the waitresses when we were there.' She shrugged.

We spoke about music: I didn't listen to much, but knew one or two of the bands she mentioned. She didn't read books, I didn't have time. She liked going to the cinema with her friends, but I didn't know any of the films she'd seen.

We had almost nothing in common, apart from working in the same place.

Out on the pavement, I looked around for a taxi for her. 'You just going home?' I asked her as we waited in the darkness and the light rain.

She grimaced. 'Suppose.' She didn't look at me.

'Want to come back to my place…?' I had no idea why I suggested that, and waited for the refusal.

She linked her arm in mine. 'OK.'

We crossed the road through the traffic, along and upstairs, while I wondered what sort of condition I'd left it in that morning, couldn't remember when the cleaner had last been in.

Once inside, I went to the toilet and urged her to make herself a drink – there was beer and coke in the fridge, an old half-bottle of vodka in a cupboard in the lounge. I tidied up the bathroom a bit, but luckily it wasn't too bad.

In the lounge, she had shut the curtains, and was sitting on the sofa with her vodka and coke, a beer poured into a glass for me. 'This place needs a bit of a makeover, Martin.'

I sat beside her, looked round the tired decor, and agreed. 'Cheers.'

I took a sip of my beer, and then reached to touch her arm. She didn't respond for a minute or two, and then she just finished her drink in one go and put the glass on the carpet, and leaned towards me. I kissed her on the mouth, and my hands were around her, and hers were around me, holding me. Nothing was said. I just let my desire run away with me, not thinking about the next morning, not thinking that I didn't love her in any sense but that she must have some kind of feelings for me after all.

Amongst the tangle of limbs and hands we somehow got each other undressed, and my lips were everywhere on her white body, and she held me and let me wander over her.

'I don't have any condoms,' I said.

'Don't worry. Just pull out, OK? Please?'

I was worried for a moment that I wouldn't be able to function at all, because of the ghost of Fiona in the room, but my young hormones won the day.

Finally we slept, a blizzard of tissues scattered round the lounge and the bedroom. In the morning I woke with a splitting headache and a profound sense of guilt, thinking that this was a betrayal of Fiona and also a betrayal of Sam. At one point during the night she'd whispered: 'I always fancied you, Martin. I thought we'd never get it together.' And she'd snuggled her body close against me. I did enjoy holding someone during the night, a warm soft body next to me.

Now, in the morning, her fingers were working on me and, as she climbed on top of me with the biggest smile I'd ever seen on her face – and almost comical panda eyes from smudged mascara – I found I couldn't refuse her, and decided to deal with my guilt later.

*

Sam and I continued our relationship, though 'relationship' makes it sound more than it was: we had sex, lots of it. And she kept my flat tidy, and stayed there almost every night. She looked so happy it made me miserable, but every time I thought of breaking it off she would reach down with her cool, soft hands and I would again concede to short-term gratification. She obviously thought that my odd manner was the after-effects of Fiona's death, and that I would come out of it in due course. I hadn't ever realised she had wanted me, that her liaison with Charlie had been to spite me, get my attention. I didn't love her in any sense, and we hadn't anything in common out of bed, and it wasn't fair letting her think there was hope, but I just couldn't break it off. Part of me had wondered whether Fiona had been the only one that would ever want me, and that what I had with Sam was probably as good as I was ever going to get now – so, being young, I stayed with what I had.

The business soldiered on. The new office along St Vincent Street had opened up, under the name B&D Software Solutions. It was bright, glossy, cool and, well, business-like – not like the workshop in Argyle Street. We acquired a young receptionist with good people skills and a working knowledge of computers; she was pretty too, and expert at fending off unwanted attention.

At first there weren't any customers. I discussed this with Sandy, but he said Talbot wasn't bothered – give it time. They would come.

Along on Argyle Street, we were still doing OK, but I was aware things had changed again. There was still a group of gamers and hobbyists, but mainly we were getting people who used their computers for word-processing and spreadsheets, 'looking at things on the Internet', and sending emails. We tried to push some of them towards St Vincent Street, and gradually it seemed to happen, with the enthusiasts staying at Argyle Street.

Gradually I was spending more of my time in St Vincent Street as that side picked up – installing Windows 95 and finding drivers for the peripherals punters wanted, making sure they bought a much bigger hard drive than they needed – at least three gig, and preferably five – and the anti-virus software, an email client. We would phone after a few days, check everything was working fine. Word got around that we did a good job, cared for our customers, were in for the long game, not a fast buck.

Davey and I were still drawing a very nice salary, and cash payments and bonuses kept appearing, along with mysterious forms to sign that had the names of strange companies on them: Sandy said it was just a way of avoiding tax, not to worry about it. I couldn't quite see how we the company was making so much money. Every time I spoke to Sandy, he shrugged and just repeated that Ken Talbot wasn't bothered, so I should just enjoy the ride.

I joined a gym. I'd always been stick-thin, and walked everywhere, but a lifestyle of big meals, taxis, junk food and loads of alcohol had given me a little tummy and a general flabbiness. I went three times a week, building up my stamina on the running machines, enduring the hell of the cross-trainer. I began going out for runs, round Kelvingrove Park, and along the river, faster and further each time. The exercise left me with a high, but there was more booze afterwards, and despair. I felt trapped by my relationship with Sam, and I felt guilty: beyond the sex, there was nothing. I was using her. And, given that, the business success felt hollow, the money meaningless. I felt I was drifting from day to day.

*

In the trade press there was an advert for a 3-day conference in London – 'exploiting the world wide web', and I asked Davey if he fancied it. He didn't want to leave Jane for that length of time, so I went myself, flying to Gatwick, into Victoria on the Gatwick Express, and a taxi out to the big hotel in Kensington. I hadn't visited London before, and it was all so busy and noisy; warmer than Glasgow, but with many more people packed in, and indecipherable accents.

That evening we had an 'ice-breaker' in our groups in the main conference suite, and initial discussions about what we thought the Internet could be used for – everyone used the phrase 'blue-sky thinking'. We had dinner with loads of wine, and then a presentation in the main conference room, using a digital projector showing PowerPoint slides fading into each other, flashing and twirling. I watched the effects, and realised a couple of things: I hadn't been keeping up with developments as well as I'd thought, and I had no idea what the presentation was about.

I paid closer attention and started to note down things B&D had to do. My mind began to work, and I realised there was a whole dimension out there that I had been missing. I'd been moving on day to day, but there was a leap to be made. The stupid ideas I'd had for websites weren't stupid at all – or, rather, they weren't stupid enough. I sat up in my seat, and exchanged smiles with the woman sitting beside me.

The delegates were of all ages, with relatively few women, most of whom kept quite quiet. We were all dressed in suits, though some of the young men didn't wear ties, and I discreetly took mine off at one point. As the evening progressed, I began to notice who the really smart people were, who were the bullshitters, who were the guys with the cheque books, and who were the thinkers, taking it all in.

I wasn't sure what anyone thought of *me*, but, after we'd changed following the final evening presentation and drifted back down to the bar, I found I had attracted a couple of the men and one woman, all of whom I had badged as 'really smart'. I bought an eye-wateringly expensive round of drinks for us, and we tucked ourselves in a corner, away from the others, forming a tight group that defied anyone to break in.

The woman was called Elizabeth Davidson – she'd been beside me at the presentation. She was tall, a few years older than me, into her thirties, and was now wearing a dark denim skirt and a loose, checked shirt. She had light brown hair that brushed her shoulders, and a strong, calm, handsome face that lit up when she smiled, showing perfect teeth. She sat very still, sipping white wine, but the fingers on one hand played with the engagement ring on her left hand; I took that as a sign that she was drawing everyone's attention to it. She worked in a large bookshop in York, and had declared an interest in early signs of Internet shopping. She had a classless accent with hints of Yorkshire in some vowels.

One of the men was called Raymond Jones. He worked for a bank in London. Once you got past the gelled, spiky hair, the casual jacket and trousers that looked smarter than my suit, and the public school accent, he turned out to be quite a sharp guy. He was exploring banking online. 'There's been some available since the early 80's,' he told us, 'but very much a niche market. We are ready to manage credit cards online, deal in shares – not just check your account.'

'Won't people worry about security?' Elizabeth asked.

'There are lots of ways to make it secure – the maths is all in place: there are systems for secure log-ins and for making transactions secure with short-term one-off passwords.'

We nodded. 'But,' I argued, 'the biggest risk is the soft fleshy thing attached to the keyboard.' They laughed, especially Elizabeth. I was thinking of the replies I'd had to those spoof emails where I had pretended to be a bank and just asked for people's details.

'Pornography on the Internet too,' Raymond said.

Elizabeth grimaced: 'Oh god no!'

The other man was Colin Strachan, shorter than me and several years older, with greying hair. He actually contributed little, but he asked questions and listened carefully to all the discussion on online security. He was a 'consultant', which apparently meant he knew a lot but didn't have a job.

I told them about myself and our company, and the need to move up a gear, ride the Internet thing properly.

'Are you married, Martin?' Elizabeth asked as Raymond went to get drinks, quickly lifting her glass, averting her eyes but then flicking them back to hold mine.

'Widowed,' I said. 'A few years ago now.'

'In a relationship?'

I grimaced: 'That's a complicated story. I see you're engaged.'

'That's a complicated story as well.'

We all went our separate ways to bed, knackered, excited, and a bit drunk.

The next day was longer, lots of brain-storming, presentations, alcohol to keep down the critical faculties, and an hour in the hotel gym – Elizabeth was there, her full figure suddenly noticeable in tight Lycra as she ran on the machine beside me, her long legs matching my pace.

The ideas came thick and fast: banking on the internet (from Raymond), selling books, selling groceries, selling CDs, playing music (laughter here, but I told them about those two guys in the US who had created IUMA, the Internet Underground Music Archive, and the compression of audio as MP2 files, and the ever-increasing speed of modems, that all made distributing music on the internet feasible), sharing photographs (shouted down – modems were far too slow), playing movies (hysterical laughter from everyone), sharing information, being able to have group discussions, collaborate on documents.

Again, the four of us formed a closed group in the bar after dinner – others had gone out to find different pubs, but we had tacitly agreed to stay here. We picked up on the ideas we had listened too. Elizabeth knew of an American company which had been formed to sell books online, and the idea terrified her. 'Customers will come in to browse our stock and see what they like, and then go away and buy it cheaper online.'

We offered her suggestions. 'Set it up yourself: send out catalogues of your stock – or let them browse your shop online, and deliver the books yourself. There will always be people who trust the local bookshop more than an online retailer. Anyone over, say, fifty isn't going to shop on the Internet unless he can walk round to physically complain afterwards that he never got the right book.'

'Online banking,' Raymond said. 'Easy to move money around, pay bills.'

'How do you deposit money?' Elizabeth asked, and we laughed as I described people shoving fivers into their floppy disk drives.

'No no no. Everybody gets their salary paid directly into the bank these days.'

'Some don't. Some get paid in cash.'

'Ah, fuck them.'

Cue a sharp intake of breath and laughter, and another round of drinks.

Colin Strachan had been thinking more and talking less. 'Businesses will need people to help keep their money and their information secure,' he said quietly at one point.

I saw what he meant. We installed anti-virus software, but there was more to be done if our business clients were going to be doing serious financial work online. We needed to keep their system running – do their backups for them? And make sure they were secure from people grabbing their email addresses and their bank details – and stop them being stupid, like the people who had cheerfully sent me their account numbers and sort codes. I felt that Colin knew a lot about the field: maybe we could bring him in to advise us.

'Great possibilities for fraud,' Elizabeth said, and Colin pursed his lips and nodded. I caught his eye, and he seemed to know what I was thinking.

After that, we drank more, and Raymond started to hit on Elizabeth; she crossed her legs and sat back as he opened his and leaned forward. Colin and I talked a bit more about how the Glasgow business could be built up, and he gave me his card – 'that's my mobile phone number,' he pointed. 'What's yours?' I shook my head, and resolved to get one, as soon as I could. 'I'll talk to my partner and give you a call next week,' I said.

'I'm off to Spain next weekend. I have a place out there – two places, actually. But I could come up to Glasgow, say, Thursday, and fly out directly to Spain on Friday. If that suits.'

I nodded. Yes, it suited. I could see how it could all work, but first Sandy needed to meet Colin.

I stood up – my evening was done, and, for the first time in years, I really didn't want another drink. 'I'm off to bed – see you all at breakfast.'

Elizabeth stood up too, draining her wine. 'I'll come with you, get you those papers we spoke about.'

I hesitated for the merest fraction of a second. 'OK. Well, goodnight all.' Several thoughts slipped through my mind.

In the lift, Elizabeth smiled at me: 'Thanks, Martin – Raymond was getting a bit serious there.'

'I don't blame him.'

She smiled again, but not a warm smile, and looked away to our reflections in the door of the lift. 'My engagement is falling apart,' she suddenly said, 'but there's no way I'm going to let myself be fucked by a stranger at a conference.' Her voice was flat, emotionless.

I wasn't quite sure how to take that, so I tried a joke: 'Especially not by Raymond.'

And she laughed. 'Did you see him slip off his wedding ring last night? Little shit.'

The lift stopped at her floor and she fumbled in her handbag.

'Well, goodnight,' I said.

She pressed a business card into my hand as she stepped out of the lift and turned – I held the doors open with my foot, wondering what was going to happen, what she was going to say. She didn't look too sure herself.

'I'm going up to Edinburgh for the book festival in a few weeks. If you're available, if you'd like to meet up… Well, that's the number of the shop in York, and my mobile. Call me. If you want. You can tell me about your relationship.'

'There might be nothing to tell by then.'

She leaned forward to give me the lightest of kisses on the cheek, her breath warm. 'Goodnight, Martin. See you at breakfast.'

Chapter 15

May this year - Romania

Helen dropped me at Edinburgh airport at half past seven for the 9:10 KLM flight to Schiphol. I got out of the car, with my case, and she gave me a long, tight hug – one of the few I'd had for weeks; we'd hardly spoken, and the sex had stopped completely. When she released me, there were tears streaming down her cheeks. She tried to smile, and it almost worked; she looked like she was trying to say something, but couldn't get anything out. She turned away and got into the car.

I heard the engine start as I walked across from the drop-off bays to the bright confusion of the terminal building, dragging my suitcase behind me, my rucksack over my shoulder, wondering what was going to be at home when I got back.

I had checked in online, of course, but still had to join the queue at check-in. No one around me could explain this. No one got annoyed at the young American couple who came in at the front, bypassing the queue, and proceeded to take forever to check in overweight bags, parts of which were re-distributed – slowly and carefully. I sighed inwardly.

Finally I was through. Security wasn't too bad, and I scrambled a coffee and pastry in departures before the flight was called. Then it was up through the clouds to a blue sky, and eventually back down to the grey wetness; from my side of the plane I could see only flat land and fields, and roads.

I switched on my mobile as the bus took us on the long drive to the terminal building, and texted Helen to say I'd got there. As I typed, a text came in from Vodafone, welcoming me to Holland and telling me how much they were going to charge me to use my phone here.

I stood looking at the huge departure board at Schiphol, trying to find the Bucharest flight and dodge the policemen on Segways, and I wondered how I could retrieve the situation with Helen. I could understand why she was angry that I'd lied to her – because I had, and had been lying, by omission, for years – but did she really think I'd been unfaithful to her with Charlene? I wouldn't have done that, I really wouldn't.

I got through security at the gate after an age. We were processed one at a time, and many passengers didn't seem to have flown at all since everything tightened up. They had to be told to take their jackets and belts off, and get their laptops out. One old guy was just confused, and was body-searched twice before they gave up on him. And of course they all took an age to get all their stuff back together again on the other side of the screening machine. I forgot to take my mobile out of my trouser pocket, so that held us up a bit too – I got scowls from people behind me.

At last we were through, the flight was called, and we wandered down the walkway. We stood at the door of the aircraft, filtered on board, and waited while somebody put his case in the overhead luggage bin, took his jacket off and his newspaper out, and sat down. Then had to get up because I was sitting in the window seat beside him.

By the time I slumped down, I was exhausted. I had forgotten to take my jacket off, but decided to leave it on because of the disruption it would cause. I looked out of the window at the cloudy, wet day, and tried to tune out of the noisy bustle of the aircraft filling up.

Was I really alone again? Was it really over with Helen? It almost took me back to losing Fiona, but this wasn't nearly the same. Sam? A youthful, lustful episode, a reaction to Fiona, to needing someone, and I still felt bad that I'd never had any feelings for her beyond the sex. I wondered where she was now. Elizabeth? Then Helen, built on a dream, a memory of Fiona.

We pushed back from the gate, and were taxiing. And taxiing, and taxiing. We taxied across a motorway, and I began to the think that the pilot maybe wasn't fully trained and was therefore going to have to drive all the way to Bucharest. But finally we stopped, settled, revved up, and hammered down the runway and into the sky.

I shook away the thoughts of Helen. Let's get this job – whatever the hell it involves – out of the way, and get back and either make amends with her – should be easy if I left the company – or start again, on my own, without her. That thought brought tears into my eyes.

I dozed off and on. At one point I fished out my Romanian phrasebook and the man beside me smiled. 'Is not too difficult,' he said. I smiled back. It was *really* difficult. I don't have a good ear for language, but I can usually pick up key phrases like hello, please, thank you, good-bye, and come back here and give me my change you robbing bastard. But nothing in Romanian was sinking in. Maybe it would be better when I actually heard people speak.

When lunch came – bizarrely, a cheeseburger – I put the phrasebook away. 'Finished?' the man beside me grinned. I nodded. 'Simple.'

The flight passed quickly, and I looked down as we dropped through the clouds and approached Bucharest. It was different from Scotland, or anything in Britain, or anywhere else I'd been. First impressions were of flatness, though everything looks flat from altitude. Strip-farming. Houses clustered along straight roads for mile after mile. Thick clumps of forest – houses that had either, impossibly, been shoe-horned into think clumps of forest, or, equally impossibly, have had the thick forest grow around them.

And we were down, after those seconds of flying just above the runway when you feel the pilot is shouting at the rookie co-pilot 'down a bit more you idiot or we'll run out of runway', then the brakes and the reverse thrust, peering at the terminal building as we taxi up as if that gives you any idea of what a foreign country will be like. We bobbed to a halt, and I yawned. I was really, really tired. I wanted a beer and to go to bed.

As we lurked by baggage reclaim, I switched on my mobile. Vodafone welcomed me to Romania, and again told me how much using my phone would cost me. Nothing from Helen, but I texted her anyway to tell her I was on the ground safely. I put my phone away and sighed with relief as my bag came round the carousel.

The folk on passport control were straight out of a cold war movie; the pretty blonde woman was stricter than anyone, as if trying to demonstrate that pretty blondes really can give you a very bad time. Everyone was scrutinised very closely, but those who looked in any way Middle Eastern were scrutinised more. One guy got ten minutes of close discussion before being let through. The next guy got fifteen minutes of close discussion, and then had to go to talk to someone higher up. As a result, my queue was very, very slow to clear. But I know that if you jump to another queue, it will be slower. Other people behind me didn't know that, and as a result that rule didn't apply. But it would have if I'd done it. I yawned. What was I doing here?

I got was processed relatively quickly and went out into the exit area. I experienced that feeling you get when you arrive in a new country: confusing signage, voices loud in a foreign language, different toilet systems. You're abroad. You don't know anyone. You can't speak the language. (You haven't any currency – I had brought Euros before finding out Romania wasn't in the Euro-zone.)

There were loads of people holding up signs, and finally someone with my name. I went up to him and he smiled. 'Hello. I'm Martin McGregor.'

He smiled again. 'I am Aurel.' He was a bit shorter than me, a little bit overweight, with brown hair and a friendly smile. 'How was your flight?'

'Good thanks.'

'Let me take that.'

He wheeled my suitcase and I carried my rucksack. We went out into the heat of the car park across the road from the terminal building, with a black sky and flashes of lightning in the distance. Taxi drivers tried to persuade me to go with them.

A young Romany girl appeared at my side and flashed a bright smile in a pretty, dark-skinned face. 'Money?'

Aurel muttered something sharply to her but she stuck with us. 'Do not give her money, Martin,' he said.

'Don't worry. I haven't any.' He smiled as if that was a joke.

Aurel had a small, silver Toyota saloon. He manoeuvred my suitcase into its boot, and I dropped my rucksack in too. 'Please.' He ushered me towards the front passenger seat. I looked around. More lightning flashes, and a rumble of thunder in the distance. The Romany girl was helping another couple get into their hire car: she manoeuvred their trolley, and wheeled it away to the trolley park. A Romany boy materialised by me. He showed me some notes crumpled in his hand: 'Money?' I ignored him and slumped into the car. Aurel started it up, and the air conditioning blasted at my face.

I relaxed for a few moments as Aurel got us out of the car park and through the junctions and roundabouts to the main road. Then I ignored the past and started to worry about what was to come. I knew nothing about arrangements or plans: I had been told I'd be met, and that everything would be organised by the people here. I wasn't in control at all. I took a deep breath and let it out slowly. 'So,' I said. 'What now?'

'I have good hotel.'

'Good. Good.' Another deep breath. 'Where is it?'

'Not far. How was your flight?'

'Good. Thanks.' The déjà vu passed as I realised that he really had asked me that before. His kind face smiled at me, then he went back to looking ahead at the road.

I turned to look out of the side window, wondering whether I could sleep. But the scenery was too different. The houses didn't seem to stop, and every one had a fence, with a gate. There was almost a continuous line of fencing, some wooden, some rusty metal, and some very smart indeed. The houses were similar: some – literally – falling down, some very nice and smart, and some quite luxurious. Here and there I saw a wrinkled old peasant woman dressed in black and sitting outside her fence; it looked like she was just passing the time in a scene that could have been from any time in hundreds of years.

I didn't know too much of the history of Romania, just the basic Eastern European thing and the orphans. Now it seemed they were in that twilight zone between communism, with its corruption and its patronage and its universal poverty, and capitalism, with its corruption and its patronage and the schism between rich and poor.

As I sat beside Aurel with his inscrutable smile, I felt unsure, alone. I didn't know how these people thought, how they worked. Back in Glasgow, I could talk to someone for five minutes and get a pretty good grasp of what their background was, and hence their basic nature, what their needs were, and what drove them. I could judge how clever they were, whether streetwise or academic. Which gave me a good idea of how safe I was with them, how I should behave to keep myself safe. But not here. It wasn't even like Portugal or Spain – it was different.

We were reaching another city, even though there had been little discernable countryside. We crossed over a mass of railway lines: I saw a huge station, and an oil refinery in the distance, and then we were onto a broad boulevard with trees, and a long park alongside it. We passed a mixture of modern buildings and big old red ones, and then we were off the boulevard, past some banks – RBS! – and came to a halt, illegally, in a tiny car park in front of a tall, fairly modern hotel. Most of the cars around were Renaults or Logans.

'Where are we?'

'This is Ploesti. Important city in Romania.'

We got out of the car into the heat. 'Oh?'

'Oil fields, all around. In the war, allies bomb us. Then Germans bomb us.' He smiled. 'Very bad time.'

Aurel helped me with my case up the steps and into the open reception area, a restaurant away to my left, and a bar area – I really needed a drink. Aurel went up to long reception desk, and there was much murmuring and checking of computers and paperwork. I stood yawning. Then he called me over, and I showed my passport and signed the registration form, and got my room key.

'OK,' Aurel said. 'You rest, Martin. I pick you up here – ' he pointed to the leather sofas near the window – 'tomorrow morning at eight thirty. Then we start work. OK?'

I nodded, fighting another yawn. 'OK.'

'You put all drinks and meals on your room, I pay.'

'Great.'

We shook hands and he smiled and left, and I made my way over to the lift and upstairs. My room was big and comfortable, and clean. I stood at the window and looked out over what I could see of the city – which was the car park and the tall banks just beyond. It was late in the afternoon, so I decided not to go out for a walk, just have a quiet evening and an early night.

Dinner was good, though odd – a fillet of salmon dressed with cheese sauce – and the wine was OK. The waitress was a tall young girl with long dark hair and a short red skirt. The local Ursus beer was tasty too, though I don't regard 0.4 of a litre as 'large'. The restaurant was almost empty, the main noise coming from a parrot in a cage.

I sat on the comfy leather chairs in the reception area in a cloud of drifting cigarette smoke, watching people come and go, getting my beer regularly topped up by the barman – who now responded to a simple lift of my eyebrows, and brought small bowls of nuts and other vague salty snacks to keep me thirsty. There was free Wi-Fi in reception – and a free wired connection in my room, which was better than most British hotels – so I caught up with my online life. Not that there was much: there were no emails from Helen, no Facebook activity, no texts. The cold shoulder in cyberspace, I thought. I texted Helen that I was in my hotel, and told her it was very comfortable.

Eventually I realised I needed a good night's sleep, and the cigarette smoke was getting to me – amazing how we had got used to the smoke-free environment in the UK – so I shook my head as the barman spotted me finishing my beer and gestured to the tap, and rode the lift upstairs. The two hours time difference was big enough to make me feel strange; I felt jet-lagged.

I set the alarm on my mobile, and got to sleep after an hour of over-tired thrashing around, and an overwhelming misery.

*

I was in the reception area dead on 8:30 as Aurel came through the door with his smile.

'You sleep well, Martin?'

‘Yes – not bad,’ and I yawned. ‘Lots of barking dogs outside.’ And people emerging from a nearby nightclub in the small hours.

‘Is big problem in Romania. Not so bad now. Please, you come.’

I put on my sunglasses and shouldered the rucksack containing my laptop, and the two of us, in our suits, headed out to the heat of the anarchic car park and into Aurel’s Toyota. We didn’t drive far – maybe ten minutes – across vague junctions where only the fastest survived, around rattling trams that looked like they dated from before the war. I looked at the large red sandstone houses fallen into terminal disrepair, and the dirty grey concrete blocks of flats, some with balconies windowed off to become part of the main flat.

I commented on the fine houses now falling down. ‘Communists,’ Aurel explained. ‘They put families without homes in big houses. Owners move out. No one takes care of building.’

We parked up behind an old building that looked like it might have once been a school. The back door was open, a notice with a string of Romanian words pinned to it, including ‘USA’. I asked Aurel about it, thinking maybe it was some political comment. ‘”Usa” means “door”,’ he said. ‘”Please keep door closed.”’

We smiled, and he led me through the open door and up a narrow staircase, past a reception desk with a middle-aged, grey woman who gave us the briefest look, and along echoing linoleumed corridors, past half-open doors, up stairways, and finally into a carpeted room, with half a dozen office desks and chairs, a collection of filing cabinets and cupboards, and four people, all formally dressed. An air-conditioning unit hummed away at the top of the high windows.

’Martin,’ Aurel said, ‘I present to you Bianca, Coralia, Tudor – and Gheorghe.’

I smiled, and shook hands with them. This felt more normal, like my usual work.

Bianca was middle-aged, with shoulder-length mid-brown hair. She had an attractive face, and an intelligent smile; her handshake was firm. Coralia looked about eighteen, but must have been older; she had olive skin that suggested a Romany heritage, and huge brown eyes, full lips and thick black hair pulled back in a knot at the nape of her neck. Tudor was tall, with a handsome face, bright eyes, a full head of hair combed back and showing distinguished grey at the temples. Gheorghe seemed to be the boss: they all stepped back when I shook his hand. He was short, squat, balding, with a round face; his suit hung badly on him, and he smelled of cigarette smoke.

Gheorghe was silent as the others asked about my flight and the hotel, and was the weather warm enough for me – I explained about Glasgow weather, and they laughed.

Then they all chatted together in Romanian, and Coralia eased herself to my side and put her face close to mine. I looked into her eyes as she almost whispered: ‘They would like to start the meeting now. I am the translator.’

‘Good.’

We pulled the office chairs from out behind the desks, and sat in a rough circle. Gheorghe spoke something gruffly to Bianca, who smiled and responded, and they all laughed. Then Bianca said something to Coralia, who said to me: ‘They would like you to tell them about computer fraud, and what the best ways are to deal with it.' She smelled of perfume and cigarettes.

'How to prevent it?' I asked.

Coralia spoke rapidly to the others, and there were smiles and rapid-fire statements. Bianca spoke to Coralia, who said to me: 'In order to prevent fraud they must understand how to carry it out, so they want to know that.'

OK, I thought: we're going to pretend this is legitimate, but we all know what's really going on.

Bianca said something else with a broad grin, and Coralia added to me: 'They would like to spend today talking in general about what might be done, and what they would need. For the rest of the time you will work with them to get things… working. Then you fly back to England.'

'Scotland,' I corrected automatically. 'Who are these people?' I asked her.

Tudor interrupted: 'Is better you do not ask, Martin. Let us just say that we work for a large computer company, like yours.'

I held up my hands and nodded. So, they could understand what I said most of the time, but I couldn't understand them. Nice.

*

We spent that day with me going through the main elements of computer crime, from simple phishing scams, through keyloggers and Trojans, to programs like Zeus which could intercept and redirect online banking transactions; denial of service attacks and botnets; the need for contacts with hackers and carders. They listened carefully, took notes, and had regular chats amongst themselves – usually, but not always, prefaced by a polite ‘Excuse, Martin – we talk.’

There was a break for lunch: a platter of cheeses, cold meats and bread, with coffee and water.

Towards the end of the afternoon, when I was getting really tired – I had been the focus all day, answering questions, talking – they put a simple question to me, originally from Gheorghe but through Bianca to Coralia: ‘What do you think we should put our attention to?’

‘That depends,’ I said. ‘Do you want to make money, or do you want to disrupt someone else’s online life?’

That took a bit of translating, but I think we got there. They wanted to make money.

‘OK,’ I said. I thought for a minute. ‘I’ll come over tomorrow morning – with Aurel?’ He nodded. ‘And I’ll work on some ideas, then discuss it through Coralia with – Bianca?’ A nod. ‘Then in the afternoon we can all go through those ideas, and take it from there. See if they fly.’

This last statement caused puzzled looks when translated, so I waved it away. They agreed to my plan.

That evening I went out for a walk and found the bizarrely named London Pub, which, of course, sold Italian lagers. I had one, and then walked back to the hotel to be served dinner by the tall waitress with an even shorter skirt tonight, the parrot even noisier. Then it was another couple of beers and up to my room.

I checked my emails: nothing from Helen. I emailed Sandy to tell him everything looked fine. Absolutely exhausted, I went to bed, falling asleep to the thoughts that I wanted to go back, back to the day before that Alvor thing, back to my relationship with Helen, back to my comfortable, safe life.

Outside in the streets, the dogs started barking.

Chapter 16

Glasgow and York – the mid nineties

Mid-morning, Davey and I met with Sandy at St Vincent Street, and I gave my impressions from the conference.

'Online security,' I said. 'It's bigger than we thought: there's a whole market in keeping people secure, stopping their details being stolen. We can really establish a name for ourselves, and help people and businesses.'

I told them about Colin Strachan, and Sandy reached for his mobile and disappeared into an office while Davey and I went for a coffee.

'I'll need to get a mobile,' I said.

Davey frowned. 'Why?'

I shrugged. 'I want one.'

'Like one of these?' Charlie came from nowhere, making one of his rare appearances. He'd hung around a lot at the beginning of the B&D office, mainly trying to get off with the secretary. He'd either given up or, possibly, completed his mission and lost interest. He grabbed a coffee and sat with us, showing us his little mobile phone. 'Can't function without this boys – the office can get me wherever I am.'

I could see how that might be useful: he was never in the office. However, I wondered who would ever contact him, and why: he still contributed nothing that I could see, though he was the major partner in B&D.

We sat for a time, then Davey said: 'Sam didn't come in today.'

'You still shagging her?' Charlie asked, lighting up a cigarette.

Davey looked up at me, puzzled, and I just looked embarrassed, and ashamed… and a mixture of a lot of emotions, but certainly not any pride.

'It's all over,' I mumbled. 'It was just a fling. For both of us. Nothing more.'

That morning, I had told Sam it was over. We hadn't seen each other since I'd got back from London – I'd taken the day off, and she'd then been at college. I'd suggested a drink and a meal the night before. My intention had been to tell her that we couldn't continue, but she'd babbled on, not letting me get a word in edgeways. But I'd got a bit drunk, and she was looking damned sexy. So we'd gone back to my flat, and one thing had led to another. And another.

In the morning, as she stood naked by the window, looking out, drying her hair, she asked what we would do that evening. I looked at her, trying to analyse my feelings: physical desire for her certainly, but beyond that? Conversations in the pub were just a prelude to sex.

I said I'd let her know about 'later'. I'd be in St Vincent Street all of today, probably till very late. She took that happily, and got dressed.

Then she climbed over the bed to me, and grinned. 'How about tomorrow?'

'Sam... look – it's great being with you, and the sex and everything is fantastic, but…'

She sat up, her smile fading to a frown. 'Martin? What are you saying?'

'We've nothing on common,' I blurted out.

The beginnings of awareness and horror crossed her face, and I felt like a shit. 'Is there someone else?'

'No.' Which was technically true at that moment.

'Are you saying you don't want to go out with me?' Awareness, horror, puzzlement were all there.

I closed my eyes. Tell her, tell her. 'I think we should have a break. Our relationship is all about sex, we need to explore…'

But she was already on her way to the bathroom door, sobbing, slamming it behind her and loudly locking it. I clenched my fists and swore at myself for being such a complete shit.

I'd managed to get out of the flat without seeing her, and, just as importantly, without needing to go to the bathroom. I'd used the facilities at the office, after grabbing a bacon roll from a shop a few streets away from the office. I was looking dishevelled, and I ached inside. I hadn't done this before, hurting someone who apparently loved me. It felt awful, and god knew what effect it would have on Sam: I was no better that Charlie had been – worse, in fact.

Sandy came out of the office and beckoned the three of us in, rescuing me from Davey's censure.

'Want to run through the main details for Charlie?' Sandy said, so I did.

Charlie really paid attention for a change, and tried to think about what I was saying, but I could see the bafflement behind his eyes.

'OK,' Sandy resumed, 'I've checked out your man Colin Strachan, and had a word.' He sat back in his chair, and took a drink of his coffee. 'He seems to be an expert in his field, all the qualifications, an MBA no less, and he has his own consultancy firm. Which consists of a wee flat in Highgate, and a mobile phone number – no staff. One man show – not that there is a problem with that. He has a conviction for fraud, and is a discharged bankrupt.'

My heart sank, and looked at Davey. 'Ah well. Sorry, Sandy. He sounded like the real deal.'

Sandy was smiling. 'Let's interview him tomorrow, as planned. You and Davey talk to him first, and see what he's like, whether you could work with him. Then Charlie and I will have a word.'

'You're not put off by his dodgy past?'

'On the contrary, Martin.' He smiled. 'On the contrary.'

*

That afternoon I found a Vodafone shop in the city centre and got myself a wee Nokia mobile phone on a contract, then went to the big pub on George Square to wonder what to do with it.

My first phone call was to Elizabeth.

'Hi. It's Martin, from the conference.'

'Oh. Hi.'

'You free to talk?'

'Yes.' I heard footsteps and a door closing, and the background noise went away. 'That's better. How are you, Martin?'

'I'm good. I – eh – sorted out my complicated relationship.'

'That's good. I sorted out my complicated engagement.'

There was a silence.

'So what do we do now?' I asked.

'I'll be at that book festival in Edinburgh in a few weeks.'

'Of course. It would be nice to meet up before then.'

'Yes it would. We're busy in the shop, though. Getting ready for the festival. I'm not sure I could take time off.'

'I'm busy too, but I could come down to York. If that would help.'

'Yes, that would help.'

'I could find a hotel.'

'Don't worry about that – I've got plenty of room at my place: I live just outside York, a village called Upper Poppleton.'

I laughed at the name.

'We have a railway station and a pub and a shop – all I need.'

'Sounds lovely.'

'So when can I expect you?'

'I could probably get there Friday evening – I'd need to check the times of the trains.'

‘That would be perfect. I’m working Saturday, but you could browse around, and we could meet for lunch, and there’s a concert at night at the University Concert Hall. You like classical music?’

‘Of course,’ I said. Maybe I did.

‘OK – let me know when your train gets in, and I’ll meet you at the station. Looking forward to seeing you again.’

‘And me.’

I worked out how to finish a call, and sat with my beer. Yes, this was the right decision. Elizabeth was cultured – classical music! – and intelligent. She was attractive and funny. Sam was a lovely wee thing, and a sexual athlete, but she wasn’t what I wanted.

I thought about the options, and agreed with myself that I’d made the right choice. I needed to properly move on from Fiona.

*

Two weeks later, Colin was in place as a full partner of the St Vincent Street business. Charlie was CEO of B&D Software Solutions, and Bytes and Digits, with a remit to stay out of the fucking way. There was another company mentioned on the paperwork – ‘Software Support Services’ – and Charlie and I were partners in it, but Sandy told us not to worry about that: it was just a tax thing.

And I’d had my first weekend with Elizabeth, in York. I’d got there on the train just before six – not a bad journey: change at Waverley, less than four hours in total – and she’d met me at the station, and taken me to a little pub for a drink, and a tentative embrace and a kiss on the lips. Then we got the train to the small town and the bungalow where she lived. I dumped my bag in her spare room, got changed, and we went to the local pub for food and wine.

We talked. We talked about books and films and music and the theatre, and uncovered all the gaps in my knowledge. I'd been buried all these years in computer magazines, and now geeky websites and discussion forums, and so much had passed me by. Elizabeth said she'd broaden my education.

She spoke about the business, and the threats to it.

Then, a good bit drunk, we linked arms and went back to her home, where we sat in the dark lounge, listening to a classical CD, sipping wine, talking more, sharing our past: Fiona, my dad and wee brother – the tears came again and she held me tight – and Sam, and the business. She told me about two failed engagements: one she admitted was her fault – too busy building the bookshop, and an ill-judged one-night stand with a colleague – but the other was his fault: serial infidelity, though maybe her continuing obsession with work had been a factor.

And then we starting kissing and stroking, and undoing catches and buttons.

'Did you bring any condoms?' she gasped.

'No – didn't want to make assumptions.'

She reached for my hand to stand up. 'I've got some in the bedroom – let's go to bed, Martin.'

*

And it just went on from there, effortlessly. Weekends in York, which meant taking Friday afternoons and Monday mornings off, but that was no problem. She was very busy with work, and some Fridays when I arrived in York I had to sit in a pub in a narrow, winding street with a couple of pints of Theakston's and a book, but that was no hardship. Most Saturdays she had to go into the bookshop for at least part of the day, sometimes staying late, but again I loved wandering the city. Sometimes I just stayed in her bungalow, doing some of my work online.

We agreed we needed a break, a holiday to get us off the treadmill of work, and, with some misgivings I suggested the Algarve. We went to a place called Carvoiero, but took a trip along the coast to Alvor. There, on the beach there where I'd been before, as I held onto Elizabeth, I believed I'd finally put Fiona to rest. She was gone, Sam had been a blip, Elizabeth was my future.

Taking time together, with no work to get in the way, Elizabeth and I properly fell in love, and spoke about commitment. She taught me about wine and food. Our lovemaking became less frenetic, except on a Friday when we hadn't been together for a week: we took the time to get to know each other, and what we both liked. I learned that she liked what she liked, and no more, but that was fine with me. I had no complaints. My life was back on track. My future, like the sky above us, was clear and wonderful. I had it all. Nothing would go wrong this time.

*

Colin Strachan sat with two men at a table in the lounge of the hotel on North Bridge, above Waverley Station in Edinburgh, a lounge so large that you could easily have discreet conversations without being overheard, and probably wouldn't even be noticed.

They sipped their coffees, and Colin kept them topped up from the cafetiere.

The two men were young, younger than Colin. They were thin and quite short, wearing jeans and jackets, shirts with no ties. Their faces were clean-shaven, their hair short. Colin looked a bit young to be their father, but could possibly be an uncle.

One man looked at the other, and then asked Colin: 'So what's your idea?' He was English, educated.

Colin cleared his throat. 'I have access to the computer systems of various businesses in and around Glasgow – and our client base is growing all the time.' He was exaggerating a little: the business was in its infancy. 'I am in a position to influence the installation of these systems, and I will have the master password for the networks and individual computers.' That too was a slight leap of imagination, but he felt it was highly feasible.

The men nodded. 'And?'

Colin sat back. 'You tell me. What would you be able to do with such access?'

One of them shrugged. 'You heard the speakers at the workshops. Anyone with that access could install any kind of malware and make sure the anti-virus program ignored it. The malware could do anything: capture credit card details, bank accounts, passwords, email addresses. Those could be used or sold on. Network ports could be left open at particular times of day, which would allow anything to happen in future. Just need to tweak the firewall.'

'Could you two organise all of that?'

The men looked at each other. 'We can do the software and use it to get everything off of the machines.'

'But,' the other one added, 'we don't ourselves have direct access to the dark markets where such things are traded.'

'Oh.'

'But we have a contact: a network called Gregorius.'

'So you would have to contact them and negotiate.'

'It won't be difficult. They would pay a set fee for every machine we infect.'

'But they might get nothing off some and a fortune from others.'

The young men smiled. 'In this situation, where we could guarantee a regular supply of new machines, we could work a new system.'

'Such as?'

'Charge per machine, but make it renewable. After one month, say, Gregorius either gives up access to the machine – and you change the master password – or they pay again for another month, at a higher rate.' Both men shrugged. 'Because we can turn off the tap at any time, we can ensure a steady return. Obviously we take a part of the monthly fee, as well as a big chunk up front.' He indicated himself and his colleague.

Colin nodded. 'That sounds OK. 'When could we start?'

'You identify your next client, and we will be with you just after you install their system. You need all the details of the computer and any passwords to access it – your IT people will have all the info. We can take it from there. We will also need to come to your office and look at your system. After that, we can work remotely.'

'How about communication?'

'We'll each buy a new pay-as-you-go mobile, and use it only for this project.'

Colin nodded and took a deep breath. It was going to work. The chance meeting with Martin McGregor and his open-minded criminal boss Sandy Lomond, and now these guys. A few years of this and he could retire to his Spanish flat permanently.

Chapter 17

May – Romania

At the end of the third day, when everyone was looking as tired as I was, we decided to take a day off. We'd reached a stage where they had choices to make, and Bianca and Gheorghe seemed to want to go off and meet with other people to talk about things. They were nearly ready to implement the plan, beginning with a fake corporation with lots of fake subsidiaries with websites – all basically short-term, unsustainable scams to generate quick money, leading on to the strategy to begin harvesting email accounts, mobile phone numbers, bank details – all very like what we had in Glasgow. They seemed to know some criminal gangs based in the old communist bloc who could simply trade email lists, customer details, and rafts of credit card numbers: some of these would have been detected by their owners, and stopped, but enough of them would work. It was probably the same people who picked up the stuff from B&D's activities: Gregorius or similar.

They were really excited by the possibilities for exploiting what Facebook had opened up, where people happily published their phone numbers, home towns, and current locations.

'Ceaușescu,' Bianca smiled, 'he would have love Facebook. Securitate not required.'

I was looking forward to a day off to wander the city, away from them, but Tudor and Aurel said they would take me for a drive, to see something of the countryside. I couldn't refuse.

The next morning after breakfast they picked me up and we drove north. As soon as we were out of the city, the traffic thinned, and horses and carts appeared on the road. At a level crossing, a set of feral dogs materialised from the fields and sat at the car drivers' doors, begging for a couple of minutes then moving down the line when nothing happened. We passed two Romany camps, and Tudor expressed his distaste for them. 'Lazy. Young girls only want good husband. No ambition. Thieves.'

Eventually, after driving up a long valley and past a dam, we turned up a dirt track and climbed to a large, modern wooden building, and parked.

I got out and looked back, away down the enormous green valley to the mountains in the distance. It was stunning, and felt remote, like nowhere else.

Aurel took me inside, and the three of us sat at a big polished table by the picture windows, looking down the valley. A platter of cheeses and meats and bread arrived, along with a small carafe of white wine, and a smaller carafe of a pale liquid. 'Romanian whisky,' they smiled. It tasted fine, if you drank it fast enough, but it certainly wasn't whisky.

We ate and drank.

'We are poor country. We want to do well,' Tudor explained. Despite this being a day off, he wore his dark suit. Aurel had on a jacket and trousers, I wore casual clothes. 'We need to educate our cleverest people. We need to learn from other countries. We need ambition. That is why we need you.'

'But what you are doing is criminal,' I said.

They shrugged. 'We need money to invest in new businesses.'

'But you're stealing it.'

'Like you. But you do not need to steal. We do.'

I couldn't explain how I had ended up in this position: I hadn't set out to steal, to be a criminal. I had just been a kid, having fun with computers, not savvy enough to recognise the evil in other men's eyes.

We drove back to the city, and they dropped me at the hotel, back into the heat of the city. 'Eighty thirty tomorrow morning,' Aurel said in his gentle voice. Tudor pointed to a building down from the hotel, a black frontage and two silhouettes of naked women: The Pussycat Club. 'If you want go there, give me call. I know manager.' He passed me his card, which had only his name and a mobile phone number.

As I wandered into the hotel, yawning and sleepy with wine from that small carafe that had never run dry, I wondered if I should visit that club. As I passed the reception desk, the men smiled at me. I went upstairs.

*

I slept for an hour, then showered. It was now mid afternoon, and I decided to get out for a walk. The place was busy, the day hot. The city dogs which barked all night were spread on their sides on the pavements, flanks rising and falling as they slept.

Old men sat at tables in the gardens off the main boulevard, playing chess and backgammon.

I dodged the traffic – they had a system like the US where cars could turn right through red lights, but here they were much more aggressive, almost nudging bonnets against pedestrians, trying to run over any dog that was up at this hour.

There was a small shopping centre, but nothing of great interest. With a heavy heart I realised that there was nothing I would have bought as a present for Helen. I'd checked my mobile: nothing from her.

I found a little café on the corner of a big, old hotel on the main boulevard, and went in.

'Bună ziua,' I attempted, which earned me a big smile. I ordered a cappuccino.

'Mulţumesc.' 'You are welcome.'

I sat in a corner, connecting to their Wi-Fi and surfing emails and the news back home. And I now wanted to get back home, I really did. I felt alone here.

I was vaguely aware of someone sitting close beside me – despite the fact that the café was almost empty – and then a hint of perfume and the crossing of legs. I looked sideways, catching an impression of a low-cut red T-shirt and a gold necklace reaching to the edge of a lacy red bra. I looked up to a young pretty face with blue eye shadow around impassive blue eyes, a touch of red lipstick, all framed by short blonde hair.

The context threw me, but then I realised it was Charlene, the girl from Portugal.

'Could you get me a coffee? An Americano. No milk.'

I took a deep breath, and went and ordered it. The waitress indicated that she would bring it over to me, and gave me a conspiratorial smile, indicating Charlene.

Charlene, who had caused the death of a Portuguese gangster and what looked increasingly like the break-up of my relationship with Helen.

I sat back down beside her, and we waited till the coffee came – Charlene checked her phone, not looking at me. Finally it was there, and she took a tentative sip.

'Fancy meeting you here,' I offered. My mind was trying to work it all out: this wasn't any coincidence.

'How is it going?'

'None of your business,' I suggested.

'Yes it is.'

We had another few moments of silence and thinking and sipping coffee.

'It's going fine,' I said.

'Good.'

'They're very nice, polite.'

'They would be. They need your help. When will you be finished?'

'We haven't said. My return ticket is for Tuesday.' This was Saturday. 'We had a day off today, but we'll be back at it tomorrow. I think we finish when they are ready to go ahead on the basis of what they know.'

I turned to look at her full on. 'I seem to be dangerously close to the end of my relationship with my partner,' I said.

She gave no reaction.

'Why did you text her an innocent photograph of you and me on a boat in Portimao and make it look like something was going on between us?'

'I didn't send it.' She put down her cup, and crossed her legs the other way, to match mine. 'We took the photograph as insurance, just in case you had a crisis of conscience and spoke about that trip to anyone. It should have been deleted. Somebody pressed 'send' by accident. Sorry.' There was no apology in her tone. 'Weren't you able to explain?'

'I tried, but she wasn't happy that I hadn't told her what the trip was about – she knew I was lying to her, and just assumed that you were part of the lie.'

'She really thought you and I were fucking?'

I was shocked by her tone and language, and not sure what to make of it, so I just let it pass. 'Anyway… what was Portimao really all about?'

'That guy was managing and laundering money for various people. We wanted to find out who they were, which we did, and siphon off some of the money that he was sitting on, which we did also. But there was money that was due to pay off somebody's debt, and its disappearance, with no credible explanation, caused some problems. Somebody got grief, and got really pissed off, so they shot him out of spite. Stupid, but there you go.'

'How did you get that guy's password for his computer?' I was genuinely interested.

'We broke in one day and tried all sorts of background data – things like mother's maiden name, first wife's name, the usual –

it let us keep trying, but we got nowhere. So one evening a girl got herself picked up by him in a hotel bar in Lisbon – he has a house there too. One thing led to another...'

'He told her his password?' I was incredulous.

'She watched him type it in while she was draped naked round his neck, and then checked she'd got it right. And she got a copy of his house key. Easy.'

'As long as you're prepared to shag a stranger.'

'People shag strangers for less.' And she turned her cold blue eyes on me.

I suppressed the shiver that ran through me – lust? Fear? Had she been 'the girl' in Lisbon? Or was she just trying to stir my emotions and confuse me? 'So, why are you here in Romania?'

'Just keeping an eye on things. These people have gang connections that run deep into Russia, and Gheorghe goes way back to communist times – corruption, fraud: dangerous pastimes in those days. After the collapse of the Eastern Bloc, he got involved with mafia-type groups here and in the former Soviet Union.'

'I didn't think they were boy scouts,' I muttered. She had said 'we'; who else was working with her? The lumpen guy from Alvor? Sandy? Why was he so cagey about her?

'Don't forget: they've grown up in a world where, if you don't take what you want, you don't get it. They've grown up with a ruthless streak, that makes any Glasgow gangster look like they have the moral high ground.'

I absorbed that. 'Surely they wouldn't have a problem with me?'

'You know rather a lot about their plans and organisation. Another coffee?'

I let all of that sink in while I watched Charlene stand at the counter, and found myself staring at her backside, my mind trying to work out what she was trying to say to me, and what I could do about it.

I became aware that she was talking in French with the woman behind the counter. When she sat down again with the coffees, I said: 'How did you know she spoke French?'

Her eyes stared at me. 'Older Romanians learned French as a second language at school, in communist times. They study English now as well.'

She held my look. You think I'm stupid, her eyes said: but I'm not, am I?

I swallowed. 'OK. What can I do?'

'I have a plane ticket for us both for Monday, to Schiphol, two pm. I'll be on that plane. See how it goes over the weekend, but it might be sensible if you got out with me before your planned departure on Tuesday. Keep your passport with you at all times, just in case.'

'Wouldn't it just annoy them if I pissed off?'

She shrugged. 'Probably, but you could just say there had been a change of plan. Retrospectively.'

We finished our coffee and walked outside into the heat. 'Where are you staying?'

She indicated the long hotel building we were beside. 'It's crap, but it'll do for a few days. You'd better take my mobile number, text me yours.'

I keyed in the number as she spoke it to me. ‘Can we meet later, for a meal or a drink, or something?’

She didn’t respond to that offer. ‘There’s a sex club right beside your hotel – if you’re bored.’ And she turned on her heel and walked away. I watched her go.

On the way back to the hotel, I tried to work out where my biggest danger lay here – the Romanians, who seemed friendly and helpful, or Charlene, who might have broken up my relationship with Helen, and whom I still knew nothing about: I wondered if that ‘accidentally sending the photo’ was genuine, or had she just done it out of badness. And in what way was she involved with this business? I wanted to go back and ask her more questions.

But getting back to Glasgow as soon as possible sounded like a good idea. And then I had to just get out from under all of them, and go away with all my money, like Colin Strachan had managed to do. Finish the plan with Andrew, get out with what I could, repair things with Helen, hope nobody came after me.

Back at the hotel, I had a drink in the bar. Later I had my dinner, and another few drinks. I looked around, but the place was now full of families here for the weekend, and what looked like a few small groups of men in the city for a weekend’s hard drinking; the place was full of cigarette smoke.

Regretfully, and lonely, and a bit scared, I went up to bed and had a fitful night of drunken footsteps in the corridor, doors slamming, dogs barking outside and the crowds spilling out from the sex club.

I really wanted to get home, where the loneliness might not be quite so stark.

*

Charlene sat with Gheorghe and Bianca around the table in the bar in her hotel. Around them, the décor was faded and shabby, communist austerity overlaid with someone's idea of sixties trendy, all badly done.

The women sipped their gins and tonic. Gheorghe sat slumped with a large whisky, his eyes half-closed, a cigarette between his fingers – a waitress had come over to tell him he was in the non-smoking area of the bar, but he'd looked at her coldly and she'd apologised for disturbing them and backed away.

Bianca smiled at Charlene. 'All is going well,' she said.

Charlene nodded. She was tense, and conscious that Gheorghe was staring at her chest. 'So, Martin has been helpful.'

'Very helpful. We will be able to start next week, after some tidying up. Some people we do not need any more.'

'You still need me,' Charlene said, as gently as she dared.

'Oh yes. We still need contacts with England. We still need access to your English companies.'

'And you still need Martin.' Anyone listening would not have been sure whether that was a question or a statement.

'Perhaps. But not some of the others. We need insurance also.' Bianca's smile was still wide.

Charlene nodded, understanding what she meant.

Chapter 18

York and Glasgow – the early 2000s

Elizabeth had been texting every ten minutes to say that she was delayed. When she finally arrived in the little pub, I was on my third pint. 'Sorry, darling.' There was the exhausted slump into her chair and the cheek held for me to kiss. 'Get me a wine, would you?'

When I got back with it, she drank most of it down. 'God, what a day. Some guy is trying to buy us over – bastard.'

This had happened regularly, and she'd always ridden out the storm. But Amazon was hurting sales, and the big boys – Waterstones, Borders and Ottakar – were trying to beat Amazon by going large. Elizabeth's big shop suddenly looked either too big or not big enough. And her city centre location was attracting interest.

'I don't want to be a niche market selling odd little titles like 'Trainspotting in Romania for left-handed vampires'. I want to have a business that people know about, I want my grandfather's name to stay on the big sign in the Shambles.'

'What about dinner?' I asked.

'Shit, I forgot to get anything. How does the pub sound?'

'Good.' The pub in her village sold good beer and good food, and we always went there on a Friday, because she always forgot to get something in.

We finished our drinks, and caught the train out to the village, and walked up the lane to her bungalow. Inside the door, we embraced and kissed, but as I responded a bit too much she intercepted my hand: 'Sorry darling, I am bushed. I'll get changed and we can go to the pub.'

We chatted about her week, and her business hassles over wine and food, and talked with the regular Friday night professionals-on-the-weekend crowd, most of whom I was getting to know.

It was late when we got back to the house and fell into bed. She was suddenly demanding, and I did my stuff, and then she held me tight. 'I love you, Martin,' she said. 'You're the best.' And her breathing became a regular, soft snore.

I listened to the peaceful village. I could never sleep here the first night – too quiet; I was used to traffic going past in the street below, and the occasional car horn, police siren, and shouts of drunken neds. English country life took some getting used to.

The travelling was getting me down, and we had discussed it. But there were too many big uncertainties in her life to make plans. Could I live here? No. Could she live in Argyle Street? She gave a grimace.

But was there something almost half way?

In the morning, after breakfast, she drove us over to Harrogate and we went for a walk around the town to clear our heads of too much wine and beer the night before. We talked of things, in amongst relaxed silences.

We had lunch in Betty's, and then drove out to another village where we stopped for a drink. 'You really must learn to drive, darling. I can't believe you never learned.'

I explained again that my dad had died before I got to that age, and that mum and I had simply got rid of his car – we didn't need it. Now I had plenty of cash, but still no need for a car: the thought of driving round Glasgow terrified me. Davey was learning, now they had the baby, and was dragged out to admire every new car Charlie appeared in. It seemed Charlie owned a car dealership somewhere in Paisley, and had told us that Davey and I were partners.

I yawned over my lunchtime pint, and Elizabeth reached for my hand. 'Is this travelling getting to you?'

'It is a bit,' I confessed. 'But it's worth it.' We grinned at each other, and she reached under the table to stroke by thigh.

'Sorry about last night – I was really tired. And a bit pissed.'

I registered the ego-flattening fact that she hadn't noticed we'd actually made love last night. Ah well.

'I don't know,' she suddenly said. 'Maybe I should just sell up, start something somewhere else. To hell with my grandfather's name.'

'What would you do?'

'Remember at that conference? You suggested bespoke online retail. I couldn't stand being in a pokey little bookshop selling obscure titles, but online, selling lots of obscure titles from different lines, acting like it was a whole set of pokey little bookshops…' She sipped her wine. 'Old titles, early editions, new authors… '

'It might work,' I suggested.

'And it wouldn't have to be in York.' Her eyes met mine, and my body began to tingle.

'You could do it anywhere. My work has to be in Glasgow, but we could be based anywhere reasonably handy for there.'

'Living together? I sell the house here? Buy something decent in Glasgow?'

I ignored the suggestion that my flat wasn't 'decent'. 'There are some luxurious places off the top of Byres Road,' I said. 'I'll show you round when you're next up.'

'This sounds like commitment, Martin. Long-term commitment.' She sat back, finishing her wine.

I got another beer, and a coke for her.

'Yes, commitment,' I said.

'I've been there before. It didn't work out. Twice.'

'This would be different.'

'Are you offering to commit to me? Do you know enough about me? Are you enough in love with me?'

Those were curious, serious questions. 'Ah, well... Taking those questions in order: yes, yes, and yes.'

She smiled, and reached to hold my hands. 'Think about it for a couple of weeks, then we'll talk again.'

'OK.'

*

I got back to Glasgow on a high, and thought through the new future that had opened up for me. Living with Elizabeth. And the unspoken thought that was there: marriage? She had had two broken engagements, I was a widower. Would marriage bring us closure?

Then reality struck. Hard.

I was spending most of my time in St Vincent Street, with Davey at Argyle Street. We had hired another young guy, whose name was Ben but whom we called Frank II. They got on with things with minimal supervision in their OCD way, and Davey was just so happy with Jane and the baby, and mucking about with hardware all day. He didn't go to the pub any more of an evening, not even on Fridays. Drinking with the Franks was hard work, so I stopped going too on those weekends when I stayed in Glasgow, when Elizabeth was out and about with publishers, or down in London.

Then we had the incident in Argyle Street. Davey phoned me, his voice trembling. 'Two guys came in – young guys – smashed one of the computers, said they'd be back tomorrow.'

Sandy and I went straight up there in a taxi, and into the shop. I was shocked. There wasn't too much of a mess – one computer smashed, and some stuff pulled off shelves – but it represented an invasion of our orderly lives. Davey was still shaking, the two Franks stood close together as far into the workshop as they could go, their faces frozen in surprise and fear. Our receptionist Gertrude was sitting down, tears on her face.

Sandy didn't look shocked, or particularly surprised. 'What did they say they wanted?' he asked. When no one answered, he repeated: 'What did they say?' His voice was calm.

Davey's voice trembled. 'They said they'd be back tomorrow morning. They want money, otherwise they'll beat the shit out of us. One grand. Every month.'

Sandy smiled and gave a snort. 'Not a problem,' he said.

'Are we going to pay up?'

Sandy looked at Davey. 'No, Davey, we are not going to pay up. These guys are amateurs, so we'll just teach them a lesson, and they'll go away.' He thought for a couple of minutes.

'I want you all in here tomorrow.' He turned to Gertrude to indicate that he included her, and she nodded, then tried to dry her tears again. 'Working as normal. I'll be here too, with another body, and Charlie. We'll see what they have to say. Were they armed?'

'Baseball bats,' Gertrude said.

'Huge baseball bats,' the Franks said, as one.

'Not a problem,' Sandy repeated.

*

The morning dragged. It was wet outside, so every customer came through the door as fast as they could, and that made us jump. Sandy sat on a chair just inside the workshop, reading the paper and then a paperback thriller. The other man was introduced as Ted: he was mid-twenties, small thin and muscly, with very short hair and a stubbled face, and cold, dead blue eyes. He sat motionless, his hands in the pocket of his ancient brown leather bomber jacket, chewing gum. Charlie hadn't shown up.

Finally – and I was almost grateful for the release of tension – the two young guys came through the door. They were in their late teens, scrawny kids who moved jerkily, nervily, eyes darting.

They came in, flipped the sign, and snibbed the door. Then they pulled out their baseball bats from under long black coats. One went to the counter: 'You got our money, gorgeous?' The other guy stood in the middle of the office, looking through to me, Davey and the Franks, a slight frown on his face.

Gertrude turned towards the workshop, and Sandy got slowly to his feet and into their view. 'I've got what you need boys.' Ted stood up too, just out of their sight.

The first guy came towards Sandy: 'OK, you old fucker, hand it over.'

'What's the deal here, boys?' Sandy replied. 'If we pay you, do you go away?'

'Aye – ' he attempted a laugh. He held the baseball bat like he was ready to swing it, obviously sensing something wasn't quite going the way he'd planned: Sandy's confidence had rattled him. 'Till next time.'

Sandy shook his head. 'I'm afraid that's got a good enough deal, boys. So why don't you pair of cunts just fuck off and never come back here?'

The second kid, who looked the more wired of the two, suddenly leapt forward and swung his bat: 'Fuck you, you old - '

Sandy stepped inside the wild swing and his arm jerked, and the kid dropped to the floor, letting go of the bat and clutching his throat. Ted was suddenly at the other kid, grabbing the bat and kicking the kid's legs from under him. Then he stood over the kid and started hitting him with the bat, again and again. The kid tried to protect himself, but there was a crunch of bone and screams.

'That's enough,' Sandy said.

The second kid was on the ground, absolutely amazed by what had happened, trying to take it in, still gasping for breath. The first kid was almost unconscious, rolling from side to side, trying to clutch what was obviously a badly broken arm.

Sandy crouched by the second kid: 'You boys working for anybody?'

There was a shake of the head.

'So you dreamed this up on your own?'

Nods.

'OK.' Sandy reached inside his coat pocket and produced an odd-looking handgun, which he pointed at the kid's head. I was sitting terrified and frozen, along with Davey and the Franks. 'Now,' Sandy went on, 'that's a lovely couple of baseball bats you've got there, but I've got this.'

The kid was trying to back away as he lay on his back, but Sandy held his leg. Then he laughed and stood up. 'Up you get.'

The second kid got to his feet, his eyes darting from the gun to Sandy's eyes, up and down, hands still at his throat, trying to swallow, trying to breathe properly.

'You'll need to help your pal here down to the Western. They'll take good care of him. So, off you go. And, we'll never see you again, will we?'

They hobbled out, the second kid almost dragging his mate who was moaning and giving the odd scream.

Sandy turned with a smile to us all. 'Thanks, Ted. OK, that wraps it up – we won't see them again.'

'How can we be sure? I asked.

'They're just wee guys that thought they'd chance their arm. They're not going to risk getting killed for a grand a month. No, I've dealt with this situation often enough, I know the type.'

I didn't doubt it, but I hoped that he hadn't got it wrong this time.

The shop door opened, and we all leapt back, except for Ted and Sandy, who looked like they were bracing themselves for a renewed assault.

Charlie looked round, and then put a concerned expression on his face. 'Aw fuck, have I missed all the fun? Jeez, sorry guys. Did you manage to handle it all, Sandy?'

Sandy didn't say anything as he eased past Charlie and outside with Ted. We watched them cross through the traffic towards the pub, looking in the direction of the Western.

We all sighed with relief of the tension. Charlie was grinning. 'So what happened, guys? Did Sandy sort them out?'

I went over to Gertrude: she was still shaking. 'I can't work here any more,' she said to me, in a husky, soft voice: 'I really can't.'

'See how you get on today,' I said. 'Nothing else will happen today.'

Charlie was pacing around like he'd won the battle of the OK Corral single-handedly. He picked up a discarded baseball bat and weighed it appreciatively.

'Where were you?' I asked, as my fear turned to the need to show some aggression towards something, somebody.

'Picking up my new car,' he said, swinging the bat and making Star Wars whooshing noises. 'Fuckin' Tigra 1.6, man. What a beast.'

I shook my head.

'Anything else happening?' Charlie asked.

'There's a company in Inverness,' Davey said, his voice still trembling. 'They're wondering if we could go up there and set up their system. Should only take a day. They've got the hardware, just need it wired up and installed.'

I frowned. I really didn't fancy going all that way. 'Could you do the software side?' I asked Davey.

'Yeah, no problem. If there is, I'll phone you. I'll get the train up, maybe stay overnight.' He didn't look particularly happy about that, though.

'Tell you what,' Charlie offered, 'let's take the Tigra, see what it can do. I'll even give you a shot of driving, Davey. Up and down in the one day.'

'I haven't passed my test yet.'

'Bring your L-plates.'

'OK.' Davey was smiling, excited.

'Right,' I said, 'I'm off home. I'll be down at St Vincent Street tomorrow.' I turned to the Franks: 'You guys OK to run the show here?'

They nodded, eyes still wide.

'Gertrude?'

She looked at me, arms hugging her chest.

‘Can you do tomorrow for us? We can probably start a temp in a day or two, but you’ll need to show her the ropes.’ There was no way the Franks could explain how the shop worked. ‘Please?’

She gave a tight nod, blinking away tears.

*

I was alone in St Vincent Street the next morning when the receptionist put through a call from what turned out to be an irate customer: he ran a small business just off Byres Road, selling a range of niche products like fancy – and very expensive – oils, vinegars and spices, mostly online. We had set up his website with everything he needed for secure online selling, and I’d been monitoring it from time to time; everything seemed to be working fine. I couldn’t understand what he was on about on the phone, so I went over there.

He had closed the small shop to customers, and sent his two staff away for the day. Raging, he told me about the problem, without offering me a coffee. Bill was in his fifties, receding, greying hair, short and round.

‘Three of my customers have had their credit card details stolen and used. And others have been double-charged for some of my products.’

‘That happens to a lot of people these days.’

‘They think it has something to do with using my website – they all ordered online, though some came in to collect. They *all* came in to complain.’

I pursed my lips and shook my head. ‘Very unlikely – your system has the latest security and encryption. What is more likely is that they’ve used some dodgy website somewhere else, had their credit cards stolen from there.' But it was a coincidence right enough.

'It happened just after they started shopping with me.'

'That doesn't mean anything. Credit card numbers get stolen and then stashed, or sold on – they may lie for months without being used. The timing isn't significant. And they'll get their money back.'

He was calming down. 'Could you check my system, Martin? Just in case. Reassure me.'

'No problem.' I took off my jacket and sat down, using my B&D master password to get administrator rights and delve through his system. I downloaded a small checking program from our own website and ran it, looking at the results as they scrolled up in a text window. And my frown deepened.

I was handed a coffee. 'Anything odd?'

I took a drink. 'Have your staff been installing anything on this machine?'

He shook his head. 'Sometimes they'll surf the Internet in their lunchtime, but that's all.'

'I think they've managed to infect your machine by doing that – you have a virus, or something.' But the virus checker wasn't showing anything untoward. 'It might be…' My voice tailed off. 'Look, could you leave me to this for a couple of hours? I need to have a close look.' It looked like there was an unknown process running, but our anti-virus software hadn't picked it up, which was odd.

Two hours later I was sure about what was happening. While credit card details were being entered by customers through his secure, encrypted website, something else was going on. Another program was running which captured raw credit card details, and sent them to a server somewhere. It also looked like random checkouts were double-charged. The proper, secure shopping website, which I had designed, was overlaid by something else. That should not have been allowed by the software.

This all indicated that there was something seriously wrong with our system, and if Bill had a problem then undoubtedly others did too.

'Look, I think we do a re-install. I can save your customer list, but I think it's best if we delete any credit card information that they've stored. I'll add something to the home screen to tell customers that you've got additional security.'

'Thanks, Martin.'

'Someone will come round this afternoon, then I'll come and check it. I suggest you stop your staff surfing the Internet from this machine, and educate them about dodgy websites.'

Bill shook my hand gratefully.

I phoned Argyle Street and told Frank what I wanted him and Frank II to do. Then I went down to St Vincent Street.

I went into Colin's office, to talk to him about what had been going on, and to investigate whether the breaches in security were coming from us in some way. But he stopped me before I could begin.

'They've been in a crash.'

'Who?'

'Charlie and Davey.'

I sat down. 'How are they?'

'We don't know yet.'

We stared at each other.

*

I sat down opposite Ken Talbot and took another drink of my beer. I realised I hadn't actually seen him for years, but he had always been there, in the background. His appearance was a shock: his face was gaunt and grey, his hair thin, his body stooped. His eyes were far away, no shine to them. He wore a suit and black tie, but he looked old and crumpled, the shell of the man I'd met half a lifetime before, the power and threat that he had always carried now dimmed.

'Hellish business, son,' he said, lifting his glass of whisky to his lips, his fingers trembling slightly.

'I'm so sorry,' I said.

'It was his own fault, the stupid wee cunt.'

'Davey was driving.'

'Aye, but it was Charlie's car. He knew Davey was just a learner – no way he should have let him drive the Tigra.'

'The cops say the guy coming the other way was at fault. The road had changed to single carriageway, but the other guy didn't seem to notice.'

'Must be a stupid cunt as well then.' The shaking fingers raised the glass again.

I looked round the dark pub that had been hired for Charlie's wake. All the people from both our offices were there, out of respect rather than any mark of friendship or particular liking for Charlie, but I didn't recognise any of the others: men speaking in rough Glasgow accents, women – with fake tans and excessive make up – smoking and sipping from small glasses.

They'd crashed that day on the way to Inverness. Davey had been driving. He was still in intensive care, but Charlie had died instantly – he hadn't been wearing his seat belt. I could imagine him urging Davey on, and maybe Davey responding just a wee bit to keep him happy, probably not realising how fast they were going. The police had reckoned the Tigra was doing over seventy on the single carriageway, and the Mondeo coming the other way over eighty, just coming off the dual carriageway down the Drumochter Pass but still overtaking despite being unable to see. The Mondeo driver had been killed outright. Someone said that Davey had swerved to the right, which was instinctive in a kind of a way, ending up saving himself but killing Charlie; the car being overtaken had collided with the Tigra, but its driver was OK.

We didn't know whether Davey would survive, what the long-term damage would be. He was on life support – 'critical but stable'. One arm broken along with four ribs, one leg shattered, the other one with several fractures; multiple internal injuries, serious head injuries. I'd gone up to the hospital to see him, but once I got into the intensive care ward and saw him lying there at the centre of a network of wires and tubes, a stack of machines by the bed flashing numbers and traces, I could only visualise Fiona there and remember my visit the day she had died, and I backed away in tears, Jane holding out her arms for comfort from me, comfort that I couldn't give. I phoned her later to explain, forcing out the words over her sobs.

That night I went round to see her in their home in Partick, and she hugged me, inconsolable. The baby was at her mother's, over in Clydebank.

Finally she pulled it together and we had a drink.

'So, you're in a relationship, Martin. How is it going? Thinking of getting married again?' Her words came in a rush, and she flapped her hands as she spoke.

Ah, I thought – good question. 'It took me years to get over Fiona,' I said. 'I had one disastrous relationship – just for sex: it wasn't fair on her.'

'Was that Sam, your receptionist?' She nodded at her own words, frowning.

'Yes – Davey told you? Anyway, it was never going to work out. Then I met Elizabeth. We got on really well – she's a bookseller, setting up an online business. We're having a bit of a distance relationship, me here going down to York most weekends, her down there coming up occasionally – it's harder for her. She's away at a conference just now, couldn't make the funeral.'

'So, is it going well? Thinking of wedding bells?'

I could see she was desperate to talk about anything except Davey and his prospects, so I repeated: 'She's very busy with her business, I'm very busy with mine – ours, you know. There's a lot of things we don't have in common, but we get on really well.'

'I'm glad. You deserve to be happy, after Fiona.'

I offered to get us another drink, and went off to explore her cupboards. I had no idea what to say to her, how to console her.

I'd been there myself, but this was worse: Fiona's death had come quickly, but god knew how long Davey would… I found a couple of beers in a cupboard and opened them.

Jane had given up talking about me, and had returned to the big black shadow over her life. 'What do you think will happen to Davey?' she whispered, choking slightly as she gulped her beer.

'You mustn't ask that.' I reached to hold her hands. 'You mustn't think anything. Just take one day at a time.'

'It must have been awful for you when Fiona was taken into hospital – Davey told me.'

'Listen, listen. This is different. Davey's stable, there's hope. There was no hope with Fiona, it was quick. Davey will be fine.'

'Maybe it's worse that there's hope. Maybe it would be better if I just knew.'

'Listen. Listen. Don't. You must keep hoping.' I held her tight.

'I don't know what I'd do without Davey.'

'I thought the same about Fiona. But life moves on. Anyway, you're not in that position. You must keep hoping.'

She forced a wan smile onto her face. 'Thanks, Martin. You were always a great pal for Davey – his only pal, really.'

'Same for me. It was always me and Davey at school, the geeks who did all right, to everyone's amazement.' I remembered some stories about school, and she laughed and cried as I told her them.

I prised myself away eventually, and went back along Argyle Street to my flat, wishing Elizabeth wasn't at that conference in

London, that she'd managed to get out of it. The flat was empty without her. In fact, the flat was empty without *Fiona* – that thought came from nowhere, and shook me.

I poured myself a whisky and sat in the lounge, only one light on, and remembered Fiona. And I thought about death, and the nothingness that was there. Fiona had been Catholic, so maybe she was up there, but I didn't believe. If there was a God, then he was one vicious bastard.

I dozed on and off through the night, becoming almost fully awake around four in the morning, standing up stiffly and undressing. Then throwing up in the toilet, and falling face down onto the bed, back into the dreams and the nightmares: dreams of Fiona, the life we'd had – strange how I hadn't remembered her so clearly for so long – and nightmares of Charlie with her in heaven, his cock out – 'C'mon hen, just a wee suck.' And Davey on life support, me beside him willing him to live.

I woke up around ten in the morning, absolutely exhausted, my mouth dry and foul. I made myself some cereal and a cup of tea, and was sick again, then got dressed and sat it the lounge. I texted Elizabeth, asking how she was and hoping for some words of comfort, but she didn't reply. A phone call went to voicemail – I hung up without leaving a message. I didn't really know what to say to her, what to ask from her, what help she could give me.

I slept in the chair, in front of daytime TV, till the early afternoon, then began to feel more like my normal self. I headed out, and went to a café for a large latte and a panini. When that stayed down, I reckoned I was probably OK, so I walked on aimlessly, my thoughts on the past.

I found myself at the Kelvingrove Museum – I hadn't been there for years. I went upstairs to the art exhibitions, and walked aimlessly from room to room, sometimes sitting gazing into the middle distance, memories swimming towards me. Gazing at the big Dali, Christ of St John on the Cross.

Then I came through a doorway and saw Fiona.

Fiona. Standing at there with her short dark hair and her dark clothes, a smile on her lips, no different. Fiona.

'Woa – careful.' 'Steady.' 'Catch him!' 'Give him some air.' 'Hold on – get him upright.' 'No, put him on his side.' 'On the chair, head forward.'

I was sitting on a chair, and Fiona was crouching in front of me while two women held me straight. 'You OK?' she asked. My breathing was shallow, I felt clammy and shaky.

'Fiona?'

She frowned. 'I'm Helen,' she said. 'Who's Fiona?'

And of course, she wasn't Fiona. I could see that now. But she looked so like her, and sounded like her.

They got me a taxi which took me back to my flat, and I lay on my bed, bathed in complete embarrassment and self-pity.

I tried phoning Elizabeth, but got her voicemail again. I asked her to ring me. Then I managed to sleep, off and on, waking up very hungry and desperate for a drink. It was well into the evening, streetlights on outside.

I phoned Elizabeth again.

'Hi darling.' There was a babble of voices around her, glasses chinking, laughter. 'Just having a brilliant time here – heaps of contacts, lots of meetings set up. I'll be another couple of days. How are you?'

'I was at the funeral,' I said.

Her voice became sad. 'Oh, of course. How was it?' Then, her voice fainter, 'Yes please – white – that's fine; thank you.'

'Pretty grim,' I said.

'Poor you.' Then again she was saying something to someone near her, and he laughed.

'So,' I said dully. 'See you in a couple of days.'

'Yes, absolutely. I'll phone tomorrow. You get some rest.' Waves of laugher in the background and then silence.

I put the mobile away in my pocket.

Chapter 19

May - Ploesti

The Sunday went as planned. Gheorghe spent most of it on his mobile, often outside at the back of the building in the car park, smoking. Tudor and Bianca were working on different projects, and I split my time between them, Coralia glued to my shoulder, whispering translations, her lips millimetres from my ear, her perfume mixed with stale cigarette smoke. Today she was wearing combat-style trousers and a thin jacket which zipped up the front.

We had the usual pause for lunch, and general chat about the UK. They hadn't travelled much. Tudor had once been to Dublin, for some kind of conference, and he spoke about the Guinness and the pubs, but sadly I had never visited. Bianca spent all her time in Romania, holidaying at the strip of Black Sea coast that belonged to her country, or in the mountains – Transylvania.

'Of course,' I said, 'Dracula.'

'Vlad the Impaler, from the Dracula family – not like the vampire fiction,' they laughed. 'He lived when Transylvania was Hungarian, so is not our responsibility.' But he confessed they did milk it for tourism.

Again, when I got back to the hotel, I was exhausted. I Skyped Sandy, and we spoke about the weather – glorious here, wet and cold in Glasgow, no surprises; apparently this was the best time of year to be here in Romania: winter was too cold, summer too hot. We also chatted about what was going on.

'Seems OK,' I said. 'Have you got anything you're worried about?'

He shook his head. 'Nothing this end. You finish up and get home on Tuesday as planned.'

'I bumped into that wee blonde Charlene,' I commented.

He ignored that. 'See you back here on Tuesday, Martin.' And he disconnected.

I shut down my laptop and stared at my face reflected in the empty screen. I'd have been happier if Sandy had said he was worried, if he'd mentioned a contingency plan. But he hadn't. So what the hell was Charlene up to?

I had my dinner –the waitress' skirt was, impossibly, getting even shorter – and then sat in the bar area with my laptop, surfing and just generally passing the time, drinking beer and nibbling snacks. There were no smokers around tonight, so I could breathe. Only one more night after this, I thought.

Two young women came into the bar area: one sat on the leather couch beside me, and the other sat on the leather chair at the end of the low table. I looked up.

Beside me was a very thin girl, dressed in a diaphanous green blouse and a short leather skirt. She had a pretty face with high cheekbones, framed by light brown hair. The other woman was Coralia, smiling at me as she crossed her legs – she was wearing the same clothes as she had been earlier that day, the zip of her top pulled down slightly to show some cleavage.

'Martin, this is Rodica.'

The thin girl smiled at me. On first impressions she looked about sixteen, but I could now see under the make-up that she was a little bit older – maybe mid-twenties. She gave me a limp, slightly nervous handshake, but said nothing.

The barman appeared and spoke Romanian to them, and they replied. Then he looked at me: 'Large beer?' I nodded and he turned away.

'How are you enjoying your visit?' Coralia asked.

'Very interesting,' I said, 'but I've had very little time to explore the city.' I closed my laptop and put it down by my chair.

'Have you visited the Pussycat Club? Rodica works there.'

I gave her another look and she smiled back, and I shook away the too-obvious thoughts.

Our drinks came, and we managed some small talk. Rodica seemed to relax. She said nothing to me, but offered a comment in Romanian to Coralia from time to time, and both women giggled. As we had another couple of drinks – I moved onto gin and tonic – Rodica seemed to lean closer to me, her body touching mine, our thighs together. We traded anecdotes about tourists, speculations about what other countries were like, what famous people were like, all the time Rodica never speaking English.

Time wore on, more drinks came, punctuated by visits to the toilet by me, and I suddenly realised I was incredibly drunk – really bad. I was swaying in my seat and laughing like an idiot as Rodica lightly stroked my thigh and I spilled my drink and bent to lick it from her knee. I tried to calculate how much I'd drunk – not too much, surely. But god, I felt great. I reached over to pull open the front of Rodica's blouse and peek down, and we all laughed like drains.

Then I fell sideways on my seat and struggled to get up, still laughing like a crazy man the whole time. 'I really have had too much to drink,' I slurred.

They laughed too. 'We help you to room.'

Which they did. I opened my eyes and I was at the lift door, then when I opened them again I was outside my room and they were searching for my keycard in my pocket, and then I was lying on my back on the bed, with Rodica standing at the foot of the bed, taking off her blouse and the short skirt. I looked at her tiny breasts, the pale skin, the narrow strip of pubic hair. Someone else was pulling off my trousers – my, what an erection I seemed to have developed.

Rodica knelt on the bed and leaned over me, holding my penis. 'We have good time, Martin.'

I smelt the perfume and cigarette smoke from her, and heard myself groan and slur the words: 'Yes, please, Sam.'

Chapter 20

The 2000s - Glasgow

Elizabeth relocated to Glasgow and started her online business. She kept the shop in York: the retail side of it specialised in travel and local history books, but was also a showcase for some of the online stuff, getting tourists hooked in; most of the building was now a warehouse for the online selling. She needed finance for the online business, and I supplied that, and did most of the work on it. I didn't want B&D to have anything to do with it, and didn't even have myself named in her business documentation.

Things started slowly, but kept building up. She was busy, and enthusiastic, and it rubbed off on me.

The flat in Finnieston really wasn't her style, so we looked around and settled on a place off the top of Byres Road: a much more upmarket area, and much more expensive. Elizabeth's house in Yorkshire would sell for a lot, but there was a reluctance in her to sell it. Sandy spoke to Ken Talbot, and the Finnieston flat could be sold and B&D could buy half of Byres Road. All the economics of that left me baffled, but I went for it.

It turned out that Elizabeth's reluctance hinged on commitment. So we got married before we closed the deal and moved into the Byres Road flat. The wedding wasn't a big affair, just work colleagues, Davey's wife Jane, my mum and Alan, and Elizabeth's mum and dad – they were a very elderly couple, very polite, very correct, very dull. We honeymooned in Florida, on the Gulf coast. I learned to drive.

We developed a circle of friends, largely through her work: literary agents and publishers, but also neighbours. We went on the occasional trip together, where she would go and meet people, and I would be a tourist. We made love regularly.

Life was just fine.

Davey was out of hospital, but they said he was badly brain damaged, would never walk again, could barely move his arms and hands, and could hardly communicate. I went to see him when I had time, but I hated it, watching him stare at me, his brain locked away, his hands useless, having to be fed and toileted. Jane kept smiling, but as I left she would hold me tight and cry. My visits got less frequent – I would find any excuse – and I hated myself for it.

Another customer – a jewellery shop – phoned B&D with a story of customers being ripped off. I went down, investigated, found it was the same story as before; I sorted it again, and went in to talk to Colin Strachan.

He looked nonchalant as we drank coffee and I explained that we needed to up our security.

'There's no need, Martin,' he finally said.

I frowned. 'We can't allow these breaches in security – it's not fair on our customers. We're leaving them and their customers exposed.'

He looked tired, his skin pale, eyes bloodshot. It looked like stress to me. I could see him try to think of something to say, like he was arguing with himself. 'Ah, fuck it,' he said.

'What?'

He ran his hands roughly over his face. 'Martin, we're not leaving them open to breaches of security: we *are* the breach in their security.'

I tried to work that out for a minute. 'I don't understand.'

'Yes you do – you know all about Internet fraud.'

He looked at me and I looked back, still not understanding.

He lifted his mobile and dialled. 'Hi, Sandy. Could you come over? ASAP. Martin is here, and we're having a serious chat. He's found out what's going on.' He switched off the call and put the phone down. 'We build in the security breaches, Martin. Those rich clients of the retailers we target, those are the ones whose credit card details get stolen. It's how we make the real money.'

I looked at him like he was insane. 'This business runs on honesty and trust, and good faith, and… and… and providing good backup services.'

'Absolutely. They trust us, which is how we get away with it. And if we're found out, we provide backup – we fix the retailer's software.'

'How about the clients' money?'

‘They get that back from their credit card companies and their banks. Nobody loses. We gain.’

His breath-taking lack of any sign of remorse or shame left me stunned. ‘Are you doing this?’ I couldn’t believe he had the knowledge.

‘I have contacts and they have contacts. The systems are set up leaving holes, and down the line credit card numbers and bank accounts get syphoned off.’ He rubbed his eyes. ‘It’s really not difficult.’

I wanted to get angry and kick something, or shout or swear. ‘So who knows about this?’

The door had opened as I spoke, and now it clicked shut again, and Sandy sat down beside me, and lit a cigarette. ‘Who knows? Just Colin, and me. And Ken, of course. And the people down the line.’

‘OK,’ I said. ‘Look, I’m out. I don’t want to be any part of this. Just give me my share of the business and I’ll leave you to it.’ I stood up, catching their eyes. They didn’t look rattled like I’d thought they would. ‘I mean it, I’m out. I can’t be part of this.’

Sandy leaned further back in his seat. Colin sat forward, elbows on the desk, head in his hands.

‘Sit down, Martin,’ Sandy said. His voice was mild, and I did what he said. ‘You’re not going anywhere,’ he added, looking at me carefully.

‘I won’t do it.’ The words poured out of me, without any thought behind them: ‘I want to sell my side of the business. I’ll leave you to it. I won’t tell anyone what’s going on, but I can’t do this kind of work.’

Sandy pursed his lips, shifting his big frame in the chair. 'Do you ever read the small print on those contracts, Martin?'

'Of course I do.' No, I didn't read the small print, never had. I just knew I had plenty of money coming in, plenty in the bank, few outgoings, and part-ownership of various businesses, but I probably couldn't have named any of them.

Sandy nodded. 'You have a lot of assets, Martin. On paper. You are a director and shareholder in businesses ranging from cafes to restaurants to car dealerships to garages to scrap metal dealers and taxi firms, all over Central Scotland – and some of these businesses actually exist, they trade. But you also have liabilities. And, if you want to get yourself an accountant – and he'll need to be fuckin' good to track through all of this – he'll find that your liabilities vastly outweigh your assets. It could easily happen that some of those businesses folded or vanished, and your assets would disappear – leaving your liabilities. Could easily happen, Martin. And where would that leave you? Flat broke. Mid-thirties, no qualifications, no money – and probably a very poor credit rating, and maybe even a criminal record.' He paused. 'It could easily happen.'

I recognised his words for the direct threat they were, and I was stunned. All of my successful life was an illusion: I hadn't been successful at all – Sandy and Ken Talbot had fixed everything behind my back. I had no money, not really. 'So all of this…' I flapped my arms and watched him give a grim smile.

'Then there's poor Davey,' he went on.

'What about Davey?'

'This company pays for his care: for all the technology in his wheelchair that's helping him to talk to the full-time carers that make life tolerable for his wife and their wee boy. If you go, he goes. He's in the same financial boat as you are.'

I couldn't think of anything to say. The silence lay amongst us. Colin looked at me, Sandy lit another cigarette.

Finally Sandy stood up. 'Go home, Martin. Have a think. Take a day off. When you come back we'll carry on exactly as before, and pretend this conversation never happened.'

*

I visited Davey. Jane was glad to see me, didn't complain that I hadn't visited for so long. He was in a hi-tech wheelchair which he could move and steer. He was learning to operate the voice synthesiser, and spoke to me for the first time since the day before the accident.

'We need touch screen,' he said, in the American robot voice. And he lifted a finger to show how he would operate it.

The nurse who was there smiled. 'He's getting really good at using this – I have to unplug him to get peace.' We laughed, tears in my eyes. 'He seems to understand the technology.'

'You don't say,' said Davey's computer.

I stayed for a couple of hours, and then Davey had to be toileted and given his medication, so I left them to it.

As I walked the long walk back towards town – it was a warm afternoon, patchy cloud, a slight breeze – I realised that I couldn't just get out just like that, but I couldn't stay. They wouldn't let me just walk away, so I had to do something cleverer. I needed *someone* cleverer, someone who understood the financial web that Sandy had trapped me in. Then I could maybe plan how to get out of this.

Or maybe I couldn't really ever get out, not taking the things that mattered to me.

*

The following day I phoned Sandy and met him in an up-market, middle-class bar down the road from B&D for a late afternoon drink. We sat amongst stainless steel and glass and drank expensive lager.

'So all of my whole life has been a sham,' I said.

He pursed his lips. 'You want to do this?' When I nodded, he went on: 'OK. Yeah, your original wee shop was a money-laundering operation. Ken was fuckin' amazed when you made money. So he let it run, still laundering money but also making money. Win-win. And your name was handy for some documentation on other businesses round the place. Most of them are real, but a lot don't actually exist. Money gets moved round, guys get paid. Drugs get smoked, prostitutes get shagged, loans get repaid, kneecaps get broken.' He shrugged. 'But you kept away from that, Martin. You got your money – a fuckin' *heap* of money – but you didn't get your hands dirty.'

'And B&D?'

'Started the same way: ran at a terrifying loss for years, which was good. Then it picked up a bit with your drunken Internet ideas, and then Colin appeared and got us on the yellow brick road.'

'Who does he work with?'

Sandy gave a sigh. 'I've no fuckin' idea, Martin. When we first interviewed him he told us about the possibilities. Then he found the contacts and set it all up. He runs it, and the money comes rolling in. Meanwhile, we're still officially operating B&D as a tax write-off.'

I shook my head in disbelief.

'We don't hurt anyone through B&D, Martin. Insurance companies and banks take the hit, we take the money. You just need to help manage the legitimate side of the business, keep it all running, let Colin do his stuff with his network.'

There was nothing I could think of that would get me out of this, but I knew I had to, somehow, some day. I had the resolve, and I just needed to find the means.

*

I had agreed to meet Elizabeth in a café off Byres Road. She was meeting an agent for coffee and a snack, but had said I could join them if I wasn't doing anything else in particular. I went along because it was one of the rare chances I had to talk to my wife.

I looked in the window as I came to the door of the café, and did a double-take: Elizabeth was sitting talking to Fiona. I went into the café, and it wasn't Fiona, but – almost as bizarre – it was the young woman from Kelvingrove Museum that I had previously mistaken for Fiona. I said hi to them both, checked that they were OK, and got myself a latte. Then I joined them at the small table, juggling their cups to make space.

'Helen, this is my husband Martin. Martin, this is Helen.'

'Hi,' I said and reached for her hand.

She was laughing a musical laugh, with her pretty face lit up. 'We've met,' she said.

I interrupted her as she looked like she was about to tell the story: 'That's right – Kelvingrove Museum, last year. So, you're an agent – Elizabeth trying to sign you up for her website?'

Helen barely paused before skipping the events at the museum. 'That's right. We've a very small client base, just a little esoteric group of authors. We're looking at ways to get new writers published.'

I looked at her over the rim of my coffee cup, and she looked back, and we exchanged smiles.

'I understand you had the original idea for Elizabeth's venture,' she said.

I demurred. 'Easy to have ideas, especially after a night on the booze when your critical faculties are switched off, but it took a single-minded lady to pull it off.'

'Must have been a lot of work.'

'Dedication,' Elizabeth said. 'Like Martin says, I had to be single-minded.'

I looked at Elizabeth, and thought about what she'd said. Yes, 'single-minded' covered it. The business was what mattered to her. I looked at her with her strong face, the brown hair, the dark suit. And at Helen: short black hair, a black jumper, black trousers. Her eyes sparkled, her face was smiling and alive with joy. Just exactly like Fiona had been, that first night at the party, and at the museum. Even Sam had had something of the look, but not the nature. My heart took a lurch, and I realised Helen was looking at me as Elizabeth spoke to her; I looked back. And she quickly looked away, back to Elizabeth.

Elizabeth's mobile rang and she checked the display: 'Have to get this – sorry.' She had it to her ear as she stood up – 'Hi

Camilla. No, not busy at all. How are things with you?' Her half of the conversation faded as she went outside.

Helen and I looked at each other, and then we both laughed.

'You didn't tell your wife about fainting at the museum.'

'No.'

'Why not? I take it you're OK now.' She reached out and touched the back of my hand, and I turned my fingers to touch fingertip to fingertip, and we both withdrew, and drank our coffee. 'Does that happen a lot?'

I could see Elizabeth pacing up and down outside the big window, on her mobile.

'Just the once.' I thought for a moment, and she waited, knowing I was making an important decision. 'I had been at a funeral.'

'Oh dear. Someone close?'

'Someone I knew well, but really didn't like. He was killed in a car crash. But a very close friend of mine was very badly injured in the crash – he's permanently disabled, in a wheelchair; brain damaged.' I coughed away what was almost a sob, blinked away tears; Davey and Jane were being so positive now, so optimistic, I had no business being maudlin. Helen's fingertips reached, but pulled back. 'So, that day I had been really very drunk, on a bit of a bender I suppose: no sleep, no food.'

'Understandable.'

'I was still drunk and really hungover, really tired, when I went into the museum.'

'No wonder you fainted.'

‘Well, there was more to it than that.’

Outside, Elizabeth had finished her call – but she was dialling another number. She looked through the window at me as she raised the phone to her ear, and I could see her beginning to talk excitedly.

‘You looked like someone I used to know.’

‘Ah.’

‘My first wife – Fiona.’ Something made me want to just tell her everything, made me want to trust her. ‘I met Fiona at a party when I was seventeen, and – eh, well, she was the first girl I slept with. But we lost contact after that night – I tried to find her. And one day, a few years later, I walked into Kelvingrove Museum, and there she was.’

‘That’s lovely.’ She was using both hands to hold her coffee mug – no fingertips now.

‘She got pregnant and we got married. And we were so happy, and she lost the baby, and another two, and she got quite ill but we didn’t know why, and then she went for tests and they found she had very advanced cancer, and they operated on her, but she died. They couldn’t do anything.’ My voice faded away as I spoke the last words.

I couldn’t see Helen any more, couldn’t even see her as Fiona. There was a mist around me, and an echoing voice. But, for the first time, I didn’t break down talking about it.

‘You OK, Martin?’

And I was back in the room, Elizabeth sitting down. ‘Great news – Camilla is on board, and it looks like Mairi is interested now too. So, Helen, how about you – interested in joining us in the world of e-publishing for your authors?'

Helen was looking at me, and I was looking back at her. Her eyes shone, and I felt a strange sensation in me. Then she turned to Elizabeth. 'Sounds like there is huge potential there. I'm interested.'

*

I was surfing the Internet one evening, when I came across a relatively new website called Friends Reunited, which seemingly existed for old school-friends to link up and establish that they had nothing in common any more. I browsed my school, looking at some of the people who had left at the end of fourth year, remembering them – including a couple of girls whom I had lusted after from a distance: now divorced with children, one looking attractive still and working as a secretary, the other bloated and run-down and currently unemployed. I read the details, and the comments, with mixed feelings and some perverse satisfaction at times.

I clicked on to the year after me, the people from my year who had stayed on for sixth year – the relatively successful and the highly successful. There was Andrew Russell. The photograph showed how he had improved with age: his hair properly styled, no longer the unruly mass of curls; a bright, confident smile rather than the downcast hesitant, fearful expression. He'd got his first class honours from Glasgow University, and his accountancy qualification, and now had his own business, working as an independent financial adviser.

I sat back and stared at the photograph. Sandy had told me I'd need a clever accountant. Would an old school-friend, a fellow geek and loner like me and Davey, be interested in helping me? How much could I tell him?

I sat looking at the screen, playing out all the possible scenarios in my head.

Chapter 21

May - Ploesti

I woke up at six in the morning, face down on the bed, a hammering in my head like the worst hangover I'd had in my life. In fact it was like *all* the hangovers I'd ever had in my life, all together at once.

I tried to sit up, but flopped back down – then had to make a run for the toilet to be sick. When I was sure there was no more to come, I went back to sit on the bed, then slowly keeled over onto my side, closing my eyes gratefully, the last thought in my head wondering just how much I'd had to drink last night.

The alarm on my phone woke me half an hour later and I sat bolt upright. I didn't feel too bad suddenly; I tentatively stood up, and then went through to shower, and got dressed.

Gradually things seeped back into my mind as I surveyed the hotel room: a mess of tissues, and two used condoms. That was when the headache came back, and more of the memories. I closed my eyes and let the pictures flash around: Rodica naked, over me and on me and under me, Coralia whispering in my ear, stroking me, Rodica's wet mouth on me, her moans and cries, flashes of bright light. Unzipping Coralia's jacket, counting the line of beauty spots along the inner curve of her left breast with my finger till she pushed me away and zipped herself up again, turning me back towards Rodica. My laptop! But it was there – thank god.

Jesus. What had I done?

I remembered Charlene's talk of an early exit from Romania on this afternoon's plane – I could get away from this nightmare, today. I packed my suitcase and stuck my passport in my jacket pocket. I took the case down to reception, and spent ages explaining that I wasn't checking out, but that a friend might come to collect it later. I had a slow breakfast, with lots of their strong acrid coffee, the parrot in its cage staring pityingly at me. Still the memories came, and the headache deepened.

Oh shit, what had I done, what had I done? Helen… I groaned aloud, and people at the other tables looked round.

Aurel was there at eight thirty as planned, and his whole demeanour was the same as ever; it looked like he had nothing to do with last night. We walked out to another sunny day with me carrying my rucksack, and drove the short distance to the building where we had been working.

'You enjoy your visit, Martin.'

'It's been very interesting.'

'You go to Pussycat Club?' He grinned.

'No – no, I didn't.'

'Many nice girls in Romania. You young handsome man – many girls would want to be with you.'

'Aye, right.'

We reached the car park at the back of the building, and saw that the fire door was propped open, with its USA notice, which saved us going round to the front.

I followed Aurel up the narrow staircase, along the linoleumed corridor smelling of cheap disinfectant that reminded me of the hospitals I hated, and up to the office we had been using. No one was about, the building was silent except for distant echoing footsteps – someone running, slowly and heavily, the footsteps growing fainter.

I paused at the door as Aurel tried it: it was locked. He knocked, and pressed his ear to it. He frowned. 'I get a key. Wait here, Martin.'

It took him fully ten minutes, and then he was unlocking the door and I followed him in. The room was almost dark, the blinds down, and there was a smell I couldn't place. Once my eyes got used to the darkness, I saw it, and Aurel did at the same time – I heard his gasp. We both leaned forward to check that we were seeing correctly, and then we recoiled in horror and stood up. I could feel the image burning into my mind as I stared.

There was a naked body stretched across a desk – Coralia. Her wrists and ankles were tied round the legs of the desk, wide tape across her mouth. Her face was frozen in terror. There were knife wounds in her stomach and chest: she was covered in blood, and it had run from her over the desk and formed small puddles on the carpet; a large, bloody kitchen knife lay there. I saw blood and fluids around her pubic hair, the line of beauty spots on her left breast – and had a flashback to last night, unzipping her jacket. And there was the jacket, and her trousers and underwear, on the floor – she hadn't gone home to change after she'd left my hotel with Rodica.

My eyes followed the pool of blood and saw the other body, sprawled on its back on the floor by another desk: I recognised the distinguished greying hair and the slim face – Tudor. He was naked from the waist down, and his jacket and shirt were open. And then I saw the gun in his hand, and the small hole in one temple, and the blood and bone and brains leaking from a massive hole in the other.

What had happened here? I stood looking, trying to imagine a scenario – Tudor tying her up and raping her, murdering her then, overcome with grief, killing himself.

I shook my head. Bollocks. Tudor had been a quiet man, a gentleman. I'd never noticed him show any interest in Coralia over the past few days. Gheorghe, on the other hand…

Aurel was half leaning on a desk, the knuckles of his right hand jammed in his mouth, tears running down his cheeks, staring at Coralia's body. I was standing breathing very deeply, and then suddenly the smell of blood gripped my throat and stomach and made me feel dizzy and sick, the noise of my own blood roared in my ears, the hangover slammed back into me, the overpowering fear and revulsion grabbed me and shook me. Aurel slumped a little lower, closing his eyes and putting his hands to his face.

Dazed, and still not sure if I was going to be sick, I was aware of my mobile ringing, and I answered it, turning away from the scene as I imagined Coralia's dead eyes were appealing to me for mercy.

Charlene's voice: 'Where are you?'

'I'm in their office – it's… it's… there's been – '

'Get out of there now. I'm out on the road, in a blue car.' Her voice grew even firmer, calm but urgent. 'Get out of there now, Martin.'

'Something's happened,' I said. 'It's awful…'

'Get out. Now.'

I fumbled to put my phone away. 'Aurel…' I began, and then I simply turned and went out, down the stairs, along the corridor, not running in case that attracted anyone's attention, but walking very quickly. There was no one on reception. I went outside and slipped on my sunglasses, shouldering my rucksack. Across the road, at the kerb, was a blue Logan, engine running, the small driver with a baseball cap and huge shades, but unmistakably Charlene. I dodged a couple of cars as I sprinted across to her. She slipped the clutch as I climbed in, pulling the door closed as we moved off. I saw another man emerge from the building, running towards us, shouting something; he wore a brown leather jacket, but I made out nothing else – then we were round the corner and away,

'How are you?' she asked.

I looked at her profile. 'Two of them are dead, the others aren't around.' My breathing was still rapid, my heart racing. 'Coralia – the translator – and Tudor. Murdered.' The scene came back to me, and the smell, and I fought down the rising bile.

At the next junction she turned the car round a line of shops and following a sign for Bucharest, driving fast, cutting up two other cars and a tram.

'My case is at the hotel,' I said. 'I left it at reception.'

'We haven't time to go back for your luggage – we have to get to the airport, get checked in, through security. Got your passport with you?'

'Yes. What do you think has happened?'

She took a deep breath. 'The translator obviously knew everything that was going on, and maybe they decided they couldn't trust her to keep silent.'

I swallowed. 'Oh God. What about Tudor?'

She gave a shrug. 'Maybe he tried to protect her, or maybe he was having second thoughts about the project. Doesn't matter.'

'Aurel is still back there.'

'Good luck to him.'

I watched her drive over the railways, out of the city, and then we were on the main road, following that ribbon of houses behind fences that stretched all the way to Bucharest.

'So Gheorghe and Bianca are really running the show.'

'I told you he is a serious player.' She overtook traffic smoothly – not being stupid now, but getting us far away from the scene as quickly as possible.

We were silent for a time, and then I said: 'So you really were here to rescue me.'

'So it would seem.'

'Thank you.' It was hard to say those words.

'We still have to get out of this country.'

We reached one of the rare open stretches, with a field on our right and bizarre masts that might have been just radio relay masts or might have been some relic from the cold war. She pulled the car into the side, switching on the hazard lights, and reached down to pick up a small package in a plastic carrier bag from the footwell. I watched her get out of the car and tuck the bag into the wilderness on the other side of the fence. Then she got back in the car, and we pulled into the traffic.

We made it to the car-park at the airport where Aurel had first picked me up, and she simply left the car keys above the visor. A couple of the Romany kids who were begging saw us arrive, and I'm sure one of them clocked what Charlene had done with the car keys. She pulled a holdall from the boot and we walked quickly over to the terminal.

We were very early for the flight to Schiphol of course, but they let us check in. Then we went through passport control and security, and managed to find a corner in the departure lounge. We looked at our watches: three hours to kill. I found I was shaking, staring out through the big windows to the aircraft, clasping my hands together, my mouth dry, my brain pulling away from the inside of my skull with dehydration. Charlene sat back and pulled out her phone, her little fingers flying over the screen, then pausing, then flying some more.

'Someone will meet us at Edinburgh,' she said, 'take us to Glasgow.'

'What was that you threw away when we stopped?' I asked.

She ignored the question.

'You were prepared – you thought something like this might happen.'

She put her phone away and settled down in the seat, pulling her baseball cap over her eyes. Then she kicked the holdall over to me. 'There's a man's sweatshirt in there and a baseball cap. Take them to the toilet, ditch your jacket, and come back wearing them. It's not much of a disguise, but it might help.'

I did as I was told. The sweater was grey, the cap black, no logo on either. I was as anonymous as I could be. She looked me up and down, and said: 'It'll have to do. Now, get me an Americano, no milk.'

I got one for myself, though I really felt that this was a good time to have an alcoholic drink, a strong one. We sat drinking coffee, carefully watching everyone who moved around, everyone who came anywhere near us. I don't know what we thought we would do if something happened. Time dragged on.

Finally they announced the gate and the flight was ready to board. We both went to the toilet, and then boarded, and waited till everyone came on to the very busy plane, watching the faces from our seat over the wings.

The first officer introduced himself and the pilot over the intercom, the cabin crew gave us the safety briefing in English and Dutch as we taxied, and we were away.

I was by the window, looking down at the narrow fields, the clusters of houses, the dense forests. I breathed freely for the first time since entering that room, my heart rate slowing.

'Last night,' I whispered, 'the translator came to see me, brought a young woman – a girl.' I wanted to tell someone this, and Charlene was going to be the only person I ever confessed it to. 'Very young, skinny – pretty. They got me drunk, took me up to my room. I think I shagged the girl – or she shagged me.'

Charlene looked at me, a look that said: 'So?'

'Why do you think they did that?'

'Did you leave any DNA?'

'Loads. Well, you know... Why?'

She appeared to think about my situation. 'Maybe they were planning on setting you up. No chance you were photographed?'

I remembered the flashes of light – yes, a camera with a flash, Coralia with a camera. Oh fuck. 'I think they did. But why would they do that? Blackmail? You had already wrecked my relationship.'

She had the decency to look just a bit apologetic about that.

'What should I do?'

'Just keep watching your favourite porn sites. You might be a star.' At that she settled down to sleep.

I tried to sleep too, but every time I got close to it my mind leapt into action with half-remembered events from the night before… on top of Rodica, my hands reaching for Coralia… and then Coralia lying tied up and covered in blood. Who had tortured and raped her? Why? Poor bitch.

Our airline lunch arrived: another cheeseburger, and weak coffee. I ate glumly and looked out as we came to the clouds of central Europe. Later we circled Amsterdam and I watched the lines of wind turbines standing in the water as we waited to land, traffic running across the dams. Nearly home, I thought. Nearly home. But what was there for me?

A young man picked us up at Edinburgh airport, and took us through to Glasgow on the busy M8. He didn't speak, didn't acknowledge us. He dropped Charlene at the front of Central Station, and took me out to the west end, to the street outside my flat – all of that without any instructions or directions.

The flat was silent and empty. Helen wasn't there.

I grabbed a lager from the fridge and switched on the TV in the lounge. Nothing on the news channels about murders in Romania, not yet.

I texted Helen. No reply. I called her several times; after a few rings it went to voicemail, every time. So it wasn't switched off: she was declining my calls.

Then I looked around the flat. Her toiletries were missing from the bathroom, along with some of her stuff from beside the bed and the drawers there. Her half of the wardrobe looked a little sparse. And one of the suitcases was gone from the hall cupboard.

I sat on the bed with my beer. Surely to god she didn't know about last night. Please, no.

*

Bianca sipped her gin and tonic, and frowned as Gheorghe blew cigarette smoke across the table towards her. 'You don't think that you were excessive?' she asked.

He shrugged. 'She was a very beautiful young woman. I needed to see what was there, needed to enjoy her.' He gave another shrug. 'It was messy but worth it.'

'And Martin McGregor?'

'We'll see. I have the photographs and the mobile number.

She sipped her drink. 'Poor Tudor.'

He ground out his cigarette. 'The man was an idiot. Trying to protect her like that.'

'I'm not sure this was sensible. It is a big story – the newspapers will enjoy it, the police will be forced to investigate. You could have taken her somewhere, disposed of the body.'

He waved her objections aside. 'The police will be busy, but they will find nothing – except Martin McGregor.' He lit another cigarette and checked his watch.

Bianca had been shaking her head. Now she raised an eyebrow. 'The prostitute Rodica?'

He nodded and blew more smoke across to her. 'All being taken care of.'

She nodded and gave a sigh. 'Let's hope we can now get on with the main business.'

'Charlene beautiful too,' he murmured. 'Very sexy.'

Her eyes narrowed, warning him, and he shrugged again.

Chapter 22

May - Glasgow

After a day recovering from Romania, I texted Helen and begged her to meet me. I couldn't just let her go like that: apart from Fiona, Helen was the best thing about my life and I needed her more than ever right now. She texted back, and said she'd meet me the next day, but not in the flat. It didn't sound promising: if she'd wanted to meet straight away, that would have been better, but this sounded like she was in no rush. Still, I dared to hope.

I went down to St Vincent Street and met with Sandy, and we sat in one of the offices and I told him everything that happened in Romania. Everything. He didn't flicker at any of it, not the murders, not my night with Rodica – 'Sounds like you were drugged and raped,' he said drily, one eyebrow raised.

'It was all bloody terrifying,' I said. 'I still don't know whether they'll come over here to get me, for whatever reason. Someone ran after me as I got away – no idea who he was.'

'You finished the job?'

'Yes – as far as I know. Gheorghe and Bianca have all they need for their online work – they can do it. I assume they have other connections with organised crime over there. So, on the face of it, they've no beef with me – us.'

He shrugged, and sipped his coffee. I noticed a tremor in his fingers.

'Why do you think they murdered Coralia and Tudor?'

He paused before replying. 'The translator was probably always going to be got rid of – depending on whether they had any other way of making sure she kept quiet. Tudor was maybe just in the wrong place at the wrong time – maybe he disturbed them torturing her. Maybe…' He sipped more coffee. 'Lots of maybes, Martin. Hard to tell with so many bad bastards around – no code of ethics.'

I let the irony of that remark slip by.

'Nah, no point speculating, Martin. Now, do you want to spend your life worrying about who's behind you? No. So fuckin' forget it. Just get on with things as normal. We'll talk next week about what we agreed.'

'Who is the blonde girl, Sandy? Charlene. Who the fuck is she?'

He shrugged and sipped, looking away across the room. 'Don't worry about her, Martin. She's not for you to worry about.'

As I walked down into the city centre, I wondered what the hell that last statement meant.

*

I met Helen in Starbuck's on Buchanan Street. She was late, and I thought she'd reconsidered meeting me. I'd bought her a latte, and I sat watching it cool down as I sipped at mine.

But she appeared, her face expressionless.

She squeezed in beside me at the bench in the window, and we said hi, and looked out at the street busy with shoppers, the guy busking on electric guitar, young folk in red tops, with clipboards and cheery smiles, trying to get people's attention to talk about something important.

We didn't kiss or touch in any way, but I wanted to hold her – and it hit me how much I'd missed her, how much I wanted her. We acted like we were strangers, meeting for the first time, but with no interest in each other.

'How are you?' I asked.

'Fine.'

'At your mum's?'

'Yes.'

'You've taken a lot of your stuff out of the flat.'

'I'll get the rest this weekend when I've time.'

My heart dropped. 'Helen, please. That photograph wasn't what it seemed – she just fell across me on the boat. She set it up.'

'Where were you going?'

'It was a business thing – there was this guy we needed to talk to, about computers.'

'Was that the guy who got shot?'

I gulped. 'Yes – but that was nothing to do with us. Me.'

She drank her coffee. 'You're a crap liar, Martin. That's one of the things I always loved about you.'

'Look, I had nothing to do with that guy getting shot – you must believe me.' I kept my voice low, but some people looked round, fascinated. 'And the blonde girl and me are nothing. I love you, Helen.' And my voice choked and I had to stop.

She looked at me over the rim of the big cup, her eyes cold, giving nothing away.

'Please, Helen. Whatever you think I did, please let it go. You're the only one I want.'

'So you've never been unfaithful to me.'

I felt cold inside. No no no… 'No,' I said, with all the sincerity I could muster, watching her pull out her smartphone and unlock it. Then she flipped through some screens, and held up the phone for me to look at.

It was a picture of me lying on the bed in the hotel in Romania, with a skinny naked body over me, her head level with my groin.

No no no…

Then a swipe of Helen's thumb and there was a picture of Rodica astride me, her head back in posed ecstasy.

'That's not what it looks like,' I croaked. But of course it was.

'Game set and match,' Helen said. 'I'll get the rest of my things this weekend.' She put the phone away. She stood up without another word and walked out, bumping into people as she went. I saw her walk away up Buchanan Street, head high, no backward glance. She disappeared amongst the crowds.

I finished my coffee and covered my face with my hands. I was alone now, really alone. And scared.

*

I took the next few days off work. I met Andrew, and he told me we were well down the road of shifting things. In fact, I could probably go any time I liked, and I thought of doing just that. 'No,' I said to him: 'Give it a few more days.' Meanwhile, I transferred money around accounts, and out to Gibraltar, and wondered whether Sandy would honour his near-promise to let me go.

I phoned Amanda Pitt. 'Give me a few more days,' I said. 'New stuff has come up. I'll meet you on Saturday – I'll phone.' I needed her off my back.

'OK,' she simply said.

There was nothing in the papers about any murders in Romania, and nothing online.

The flat was empty – Helen gone, Fiona gone, Sam gone – even Elizabeth's presence would have been welcome. At night I would see shadows as I imagined someone was following me home, and I would look out of the lounge curtain, conjuring wild nightmares about a man standing smoking under a streetlight, talking into a mobile phone, looking up at my window.

Then one evening I got to my front door and there *was* someone behind me. 'Mr McGregor?' he asked, in a heavily accented voice.

I was too slow to deny it, and he took that as a yes – like he didn't already know who I was.

'Please. I need to speak with you.' And he showed me his ID. 'I am Inspector de Politie in General Directorate.' Then, unnecessarily, he added: 'In Romania.' I stood transfixed, my key in the door, the door ajar. 'Please, I need to speak with you.'

I let him follow me up to the flat, switched on the lights, and made him a cup of tea. I had a can of lager. I sat opposite him in the lounge. He was a tall, big man, wearing a brown leather jacket and jeans. His hair was very short, the same length as the stubble on his chin. He had a black leather document wallet with him, which he unzipped and laid flat on my coffee table.

'My name is Adrian Stancu.'

I slumped back on the sofa. I was very depressed, and very tired. There was no doubt what he was here for, but I had to put up some kind of pretence. 'Pleased to meet you. How can I help?'

'You were in Romania some days ago.' I nodded. 'You came back to UK on Monday 23rd.' I nodded again. 'You were also booked on flight on Tuesday 24th.'

'Yes I was.' He was waiting patiently for me to explain. 'I wasn't sure when I'd have the job finished, so I made two reservations.'

'Very expensive.'

'The client was paying.' And I now saw that I'd opened up the next line of questioning.

'Who was your client? What was the nature of your job in Romania?' His tone was calm, polite.

Oh hell, I didn't have a story ready. I hadn't expected to be quizzed on this, especially not by a Romanian policeman. I had to give an answer, something believable, something quite near to the truth. 'I work for a computer company here in Glasgow. We were helping a Romanian client set up security for their system. I'm afraid I can't say too much – client confidentiality.'

'Of course. What was the name of the company?'

I swallowed some lager, my head aching now, my heart thumping, my hand trembling. 'Eh – I can't remember for certain.' I had to make one up. 'I think it was 'Bucharest Software Solutions'.' Brilliant, I thought. He'll know this is a lie, and he knows this whole thing is dodgy anyway. My last pretence of denial evaporated.

He reached over to the document wallet on the table and lifted out an A4 photograph: Gheorghe's face, round and bald, humourless. 'Is this the man you dealt with?'

I knew my expression had already registered that I knew Gheorghe, so I nodded. 'Yes – Gheorghe. He was in charge.'

Another photograph: Tudor's face, tanned and handsome, greying hair and a confident smile. There was a numbness creeping up from my toes. 'This man?'

'Tudor – I worked with him operationally, developing the systems. Excuse me.' I went to the toilet for a pee, but at one point thought I was in danger of throwing up. I controlled it, and came back to the lounge with another lager. I'm stuffed, I thought: no way out of this. He's going to take me away.

And a photograph of Coralia's face, the olive skin and lips perfectly rendered. 'This woman?'

'Coralia – she was the translator. They understood English very well but preferred to speak in Romanian, and she translated for me.' OK, that was it, I thought, but another photograph floated onto the table to join the others: Rodica, looking calm and innocent. My heart dropped, and I felt myself beginning to panic. But I controlled it, and frowned. 'No, she wasn't someone I dealt with.'

'But you meet her.'

I frowned again and shook my head. 'No. Don't think so.'

'Coralia and she come to your hotel, and stay. They go up to your room, leave early in morning.' Every time he referred to someone his finger prodded the appropriate photograph. 'The hotel ordered a taxi for them in the morning. She work as escort girl, in sex club, and sometimes in pornographic movies. You have sex with her.'

I closed my eyes, not sure whether his last statement was a question or an assertion.

The Romanian policeman sat back in his seat, his tea untouched on the table beside the collection of photographs. 'What happened on Monday morning, the day you left Romania, after these women leave your hotel?'

'I – eh – ' Think, man, think! 'I was picked up as usual and taken to the building where we had been working. The job had finished the day before – I met the girls in the hotel bar that evening. I got a bit drunk, and I'm not sure exactly what happened that night. I didn't pay for sex – I had no idea she was a…'

'A prostitute. You are married?'

'No. My relationship was – eh - so… Anyway, the plan was for us just to have a social chat and then I would get off to the airport. But when we got to the building, no one was around. The door of our office was locked. So I got them to call me a taxi and went to the airport.'

'You did not go into that office?'

'Not that day, no. Of course, I had been in it every day before, so my fingerprints will be all over it.' Belatedly, I realised I hadn't asked the obvious question: 'Why? What happened?'

'These people – ' prodding the photographs of Tudor and Coralia – 'were found dead in that office, murdered; the girl was assaulted sexually. This girl – ' pointing to the picture of Rodica – 'was found dead in a hotel room the next day: she had been with a client, but he had checked out early, leaving her in room. We found her in the bath: her body had many drugs – cocaine – and much alcohol. She drowned in bath. She was murdered too we think.'

My breathing was seriously laboured now, my heart thumping madly, every muscle in my body twitching.

'I had nothing to do with any of that,' I said, as forcefully and as calmly as I could. Oh fuck, I thought: my luggage, they must know I left my luggage at the hotel – no way my departure could be painted as being planned. I was fucked.

He shrugged. 'You know these people. We need to take statements from you. You must come to Romania with me. Now.'

'Hey, whoa. I've given you my statement. I can write it down if you want, but that's all there is. What I've said is the truth.'

He gave a slight smile. 'Perhaps. Some of it. But there is much we want to know. You work in computers. My directorate investigates cybercrime. These deaths are important, of course, but this man was a criminal, this girl was a prostitute, and – ' he shrugged over Coralia's picture – 'this girl was involved with criminals. Their deaths are not so important. But I believe Gheorghe is involved in major cyber crimes.' And his eyes looked straight into mine. 'I think you help him. Scottish gangsters are involved in companies you work for. Not as bad as Romanian gangsters, perhaps, but evil men.'

I scratched my chin, trying to clear away clouds of tiredness and alcohol. How did he know all that? It couldn't end like this, not in some Romanian prison – mind you, would they be any worse than Barlinnie? I didn't want to go to either kind of prison.

'Why do you do this,' he asked. 'You are smart, good-looking man. Why you work for gangsters?'

By accident, I thought, all by accident. I didn't ever mean it to happen. 'You've got it wrong,' I said. 'I'm innocent. My company is entirely above board – we've never been investigated by the police.'

'OK.' He stood up. 'I go now. I come back with Scottish police, and they arrest you. I take you to Romania, and we investigate your links to these people.'

I followed him to the door. 'You've got it all wrong,' I said.

He didn't look back as he went downstairs, with his comment floating back: 'I do not think so, Mr Martin McGregor.'

*

I phoned Amanda Pitt.

'What is it? I'm busy. It's late.'

'What's happening with the investigation? Have you started on B&D?'

She sighed. 'I've mentioned to my boss that B&D is part of Talbot's empire, and that I have an informant who is getting inside information for me. That's you, Martin. I've said I'll have the information before Saturday.' The last remark was pointed.

'So what are they doing now?'

'Just what they have been doing for years: trying to identify key people, build up a case. Slowly slowly. Why?'

I didn't know how much to tell her. I felt we had some kind of trust, but she was a police officer and I was a criminal.

After a moment of my silence, she repeated: 'Has something happened?'

That Romanian policeman *must* have been in touch with the Scottish police…

'Martin? You still there?'

'Yes – sorry. Look, have the Romanian police been in touch with you? About B&D?'

'I've no idea – I haven't heard anything. Why? You were in Romania – did something happen?'

'I was working with some people there… there was a…'

'What?'

'There was a murder,' I said suddenly. 'Three murders.'

'Oh for fuck's sake, Martin.' She took a deep intake of breath. 'Look, you need to tell me what you know – right now. Jesus fuck, what a mess you're in.'

'First thing tomorrow,' I said. 'I'll write it all down tonight and give it to you in the morning. Where do you want to meet?'

'The Thistle Hotel – it's not far from my station. Nine o'clock.'

'OK.'

*

By midnight I had five pages of names and companies whose systems we had compromised. I outlined how it worked, and stuck it all a big envelope.

Then I fired up my browser to book some journeys, and packed a small suitcase.

Chapter 23

Glasgow and Amsterdam – a few years before

I'd had little to do with Colin Strachan since he'd told me about what was really going on with the company. We worked together, and I let him do what he did; I would do most of the software installation, and then pass it over to him and whoever he used out there.

But we had no personal relationship. I felt that he had used me, betrayed me. I saw him as sided with Sandy and Ken Talbot, criminals – while I, of course, was an innocent man who was an *accidental* criminal, through circumstances. When we didn't have to speak, we didn't. I knew nothing of his life outside of work, and didn't want to. I hated him.

My marriage to Elizabeth had kept going, and we kept doing the things that married people do: holidays, travel – often in connection with finding publishers and second-hand bookshops – theatre, concerts, meals with friends. We didn't ever discuss having children: Elizabeth never mentioned it, and I was still haunted by the memories of Fiona's miscarriages, and whether that had contributed to her cancer or been a result of it – either way, I couldn't face the danger again.

I was becoming happily middle class, and could talk of films and plays and music, though my new iPod was full of old and new singer-songwriters, and some modern guitar bands. I was also developing a love of art, part of me thinking of what Fiona would have been doing and achieving. More and more often I thought of Fiona, and saw her every time I looked at Helen.

There were three couples we regularly went out with, and one of them was Helen and her long-term boyfriend Neil, who was an author; I hadn't heard of him, but he'd had two novels published and won some short story competitions. We often went round to his place while he cooked us dinner and we sat in his lounge overlooking the Clyde. We never ate at our place; I could cook functionally but not for guests, and Elizabeth just couldn't be bothered - when it was our turn to entertain, we took people out.

On those evenings, Helen, Elizabeth and Neil discussed the intricacies of writing and selling books, self-publishing, though Helen would often break off to talk to me about music and art.

Helen and I swapped mobile phone numbers, and began to visit art exhibitions together. We would meet Elizabeth or Neil, or both, afterwards for a coffee or a drink. And we thought that it would be nice to visit art galleries in other countries.

'You love Van Gogh, Martin – so you must go to Amsterdam.'

Elizabeth agreed. 'Absolutely. Let's have a weekend away there.'

So the four of us arranged a weekend in Amsterdam, staying together in the same hotel. With Helen, it was going to be partially work: 'There are some interesting Scandinavian crime writers appearing – they're getting snapped up by the big guns, but I have found a couple of Dutch writers: I think they could ride the wave.' But there would be time for the museums.

Elizabeth was also looking to link up with a small online bookseller in Amsterdam, with an idea of a network of traders, able to fight the Amazon behemoth. We would meet up in the evenings for drinks and food – we were advised that we had to eat Indonesian over there.

But the day before we were due to leave, Elizabeth said she couldn't go: the Amsterdam bookseller was away suddenly, and anyway, she had loads of other work that had come up. Neil couldn't go either: another short story had won a competition and he had to go to Bristol to get the prize, do a reading, and take part in workshops.

Helen and I were disappointed, but Elizabeth said: 'Why don't you two just go? Enjoy it.'

We flew out from a cold damp Glasgow, got the fast, quiet double-decker train from Schiphol into Centraal Station, and walked through the warm autumn afternoon down to the small hotel on Prinsengracht, chatting and laughing, planning the days.

The hotel had misunderstood our communications: Helen and Neil's double room had been entirely cancelled, leaving the twin room Elizabeth and I had booked. The rest of the hotel was full. There were dozens of other hotels around, of course, but we couldn't face trekking round them, and being in separate hotels was, by unspoken mutual agreement, out of the question.

So we agreed to take the twin room, and went upstairs to unpack and change, and text Elizabeth and Neil to say we'd arrived, agreeing not to mention the room mix-up. In the room, we dodged round each other, exaggerated gestures of covering our eyes while we changed into cooler trousers and tops, and headed out to explore: 'Van Gogh museum first,' she said, 'then play it by ear.'

The city was busy. We marvelled at the mass of bicycles and the traffic on the narrow streets as we walked over to the museum, and went round it, standing close together, pointing and speaking in hushed reverential tones, agreeing that seeing it all for real was so much better than in a magazine or a print, that we didn't like his early dark stuff.

Then we meandered back through the town, having drinks in street cafés, picking an Indonesian restaurant on Rembrandtplein at random, guessing at what to eat and going with their suggestion of the rijsttafel, and marvelling at all the flavours and the tastes.

And we went back to the hotel after a last nightcap, exhausted, and into our twin room. She went to the bathroom first, and then me. As I brushed my teeth, I wondered what to do. I had realised that evening that I really enjoyed being with her and wanted to develop our relationship; there was a physical aspect to it too. But I didn't want a one-off furtive encounter. I didn't even want a succession of furtive encounters, hiding from Neil and Elizabeth. And what would I do if Neil asked her to marry him?

But I was getting ahead of myself. I grinned at my reflection and shook my head. Let's just get a good night's sleep, I thought. She's a good friend. Don't spoil it. Unless I walk out there and she's sprawled naked on the bed…

When I emerged from the bathroom, she was standing by the window, still dressed, looking out, streetlights reflecting up on her face. 'The canal is so beautiful,' she said.

I stood beside her, very close, and looked out. There were couples and singles walking along the cobbled street between our hotel and the canal, bicycles zipping past, and the distant sound of a tram rattling along the main road.

'It's magical,' she said. 'I'm so glad we came.'

And she turned to look at me, and I looked back at her. Our bodies moved fractionally closer, and I could feel her breath on my cheek. She put one hand on my shoulder, as if to steady herself, and her eyes closed as her lips parted. I touched my lips against hers, and the hand on my shoulder gripped tighter.

'We shouldn't do this,' she whispered.

'I know.' And I kissed her properly.

'Martin…'

'It's OK,' I said. 'Why don't we just get into bed and hold each other, all night. Not do anything.'

She nodded.

And that was what we did, holding each other tight in one of the single beds. In the morning, I woke to see her face looking down on mine, smiling. 'Come on, sleepy head, we've got a lot of exploring to do.' I watched her walk to the bathroom in her T-shirt and knickers, and I slowly breathed out, my mind tumbling confusing thoughts and possibilities while at the same time feeling a sense of gentle happiness through my body.

After breakfast, we walked round the shopping district, and then had a tour on a canal boat. In amongst that we had snacks and lunch, and spent time at pavement cafés by busy junctions, watching the world go by. We talked and laughed. We held each other's hands, and linked arms, as we explored the city.

She caught up with her prospective Danish authors for a couple of hours, while I just wandered, alone but strangely happy. I met them in a bar near Dam Square, as they were finishing their discussions. I watched the two men shoulder their leather bags and walk off, and I held Helen's hand tightly. She yawned.

'We need a time out,' I said, and she smiled and nodded sleepily.

We went back to our room in the hotel. I went to the loo first, and then stretched out on one bed. When Helen came back she lay beside me, smiling and nestling into my shoulder, arms round me. I bent to kiss her, and she responded. Unthinking, my hand went to her breast. I hesitated for a fraction of a second but she didn't pull away, and she ignored my mumbled 'Sorry' through the kiss. In turn, her hands began to run across my chest, and down.

It wasn't frenzied drunken passion. It was two people who wanted to make love to each other, and that's what we did. Afterwards there was no regret, just holding tight and smiling, content. We spoke about what we might do that evening, and then her hands were moving and we made love again, and she nearly crushed me as we orgasmed together this time.

We found another Indonesian restaurant, every bit as good as the first one, and wandered through bars and the red light district, and sniffed cannabis in coffee houses. We laughed and cuddled and kissed all the time, and back at the hotel we made love again and slept.

I awoke at four in the morning, and I looked at Helen's sleeping face and smiled. I felt… happy, truly happy for the first time in years. It was almost like Fiona had been reincarnated in this woman. I knew at that moment that I couldn't give Helen up, that I didn't really love Elizabeth – it had been almost like Sam: something I needed at a time and place, but never sustainable and never totally fulfilling. I had hurt Sam when I finished with her – I had never heard any more about her, and sometimes I felt guilty about that – but I felt Elizabeth was more resilient. Either that or she would kill me.

Helen and I spoke about what we might do as we walked around the Sunday city until it was time to head back to Schiphol and our plane to Glasgow.

'I'll need to split up with Neil,' she said. 'I couldn't lie to him. I couldn't sleep with him again, not now.'

I nodded.

'What about Elizabeth?'

I wondered whether I was brave enough to tell Elizabeth face to face and absorb her wrath – should I move out? I suddenly saw all the divorce proceedings rolling out in front of me, and Helen could see my turmoil.

'That's assuming you want to leave Elizabeth,' she said. 'I don't do sharing – remember that, Martin. I don't do secrets, or lies, or sharing.'

I reached to hold her. 'I want you,' I said. 'I did from the moment I saw you.'

'Yes, but that was because I looked like Fiona.' Her voice was muffled against my chest.

'That was the initial moment. But you are your own person, you're not Fiona. I've grown to love you. And now I know you want to be with me, well… that settles it. I never want to lose you.'

'You never will.' She pulled her head back and looked up at me. 'As long as you're honest with me.'

'I promise.'

At arrivals in Glasgow, Helen phoned Neil to say she was sharing a taxi with me, and would call him tomorrow. Her tone was flat, but if I'd been him I would have spotted that there was something not right. I phoned my place, but it rang out. Elizabeth's mobile went straight to voicemail. I said I was at the airport and sharing a taxi with Helen into town.

Helen's flat was south of the river, a modern, bright two bedroom place. The taxi dropped her there and I said I'd phone tonight.

My place was cold and empty, like no one had been there for days. The dishwasher still held a cup that I remembered putting there before I left.

I unpacked and put a load in the washing machine – again, the wash basket had clothes from before I'd left and nothing recent. Bemused, I got myself a lager and sat in the lounge with the TV on. I tried Elizabeth's mobile again, twice, but just voicemail. I tried to rehearse what I would say to her: how had I done it with Sam? Oh yes – very badly. What words to use… what tone to adopt.

And then the door of the flat opened and someone came in, and it slammed shut. There was a rush of someone in the corridor, and then Elizabeth was in the lounge, looking flustered, unsure, still with her coat on, clutching her handbag, as if she wasn't stopping. Had Helen told Neil already, and he'd contacted Elizabeth?

She stood looking at me, and I looked back. 'Martin. You're back.' Her voice was agitated.

'I phoned you from the airport.'

'Oh, right. My mobile was off. The battery ran out.' She took a deep breath. 'You had a good time?'

'Yes.' A pause, and then I decided I had to say something: 'Elizabeth, there's something I have to say. There's something we have to talk about.'

She nodded. 'I know. I'm sorry, Martin. I knew you must have realised. I'm sorry. It's being going on for a while now – I just… I just couldn't stop it.'

I took a long drink of lager while all my brain cells went off to have a meeting to work out just what the fuck was going on here. 'So…'

Now she sat on the arm of a chair, not looking directly at me, holding her hands together tightly. 'His name's Joe – he's the chap that has the chain of small bookshops specialising in military history. It's a niche market, but there's lots of potential. I've spoken about him before.'

I vaguely remembered a 'Joe' being mentioned, and excitement about the possibilities of such niche products having significant online sales, while physical stores struggled to make pin money. And her having to go to publishers and meetings to support him. But I also registered that I had long ago stopped paying close attention to what Elizabeth talked about.

She swallowed. 'He's outside. I've just come for some more of my clothes. I meant to have done it before you got back.' She took a deep breath. 'Anyway, how was your trip?'

'Good, thanks.'

'Good, I'm glad. Right. I… I don't know what to say, Martin. I'm so sorry. I hope we can be civilised about… about dividing up everything. The divorce.'

Another gulp of lager, and I nodded. 'I'm sure we'll be able to do that. You get your stuff. We'll talk after a few days, sort things out.' I kept my voice cold and calm.

She stood up, almost coming towards me for a hug and then thinking twice about it. 'I'll get that stuff. Thank you for being so good about this.'

'No problem.'

Endgame

Chapter 24

Spain and onwards

This time when I arrived at Malaga airport, I knew exactly where to go to get my hire car, beating the queues. Satnav in place, I was out into the sunshine and driving down the coast in no time at all. I had my suitcase and my technology with me. I just had to visit my bank in Gibraltar, find somewhere to stay for a couple of nights, and then finish my already tortuous journey – I had decided on Orkney, because it was far away from the too-obvious Spain.

I'd given my information to Amanda Pitt, sitting in the hotel lobby with my suitcase and rucksack, making no secret of the fact that I was getting out. She looked at the stuff, and took notes. Finally she nodded. 'This is useful, Martin. Thank you.'

'What happens to me?'

She looked at my suitcase. 'I'll pass this stuff onto colleagues and they'll investigate the cybercrime and all those associated with it. I assume you are planning to go somewhere warm, out of the way, and that you have managed to accumulate enough money to live on. We may very well never find you.'

I nodded and swallowed, daring to hope, daring to think that she was going to try to protect me.

'But no guarantees. I don't know what happened in Romania, and I don't know what our investigations will turn up concerning you. We might very well not pursue you for theft and fraud, but murder would be something else. I'll try to play down your role, but ultimately the decision will not be mine.'

I nodded. 'I appreciate that. I won't tell anyone you took money from me for information.'

She looked straight at me. 'There is no trace of any money coming into my bank account.'

I nodded: it had been a cheap shot, trying to get extra insurance like that. 'The people in Argyle Street,' I said, 'are innocent. Don't waste your time there, don't give them a hard time.'

She nodded.

'And there is someone you might be interested in – a young blonde girl, early twenties – first name Charlene, possibly Charlene Anderson. She knows Sandy Lomond, has connections with Talbot, but I'm not sure how she's connected.' Amanda was looking straight at me and nodding. 'She's very pretty,' I added, and she gave me a look.

'I'd better go,' I said.

We stood up and she politely shook my hand, but she must have noticed the relief on my face, because she repeated: 'No guarantees, Martin – ever.' And added, with an acidic tone: 'You realise you'll never sleep soundly again: you'll always be afraid that someone will come for you.'

I swallowed.

I phoned B&D, but Claire said no one had come in – Sandy hadn't been in touch for a couple of days. I said I'd see her later.

I phoned Andrew and told him I wouldn't be able to have any more meetings, and told him it might be better if he just stopped doing anything more with my shares and interests. 'The police are involved,' I told him, 'try not to get sucked in.'

'Fine, Martin – appreciate the warning. Have fun. Going somewhere warm?'

'Oh yes.'

'Sun sea sand and sex,' he suggested.

'I'll settle for three out of four,' I said. 'Cheers, Andrew. Thanks for everything.'

I emailed Jane and then phoned her, moving away from the reception area and down a long corridor. We exchanged pleasantries – 'Still the same, but the new wheelchair is really good'. I told her to check her email.

'What is this, Martin?'

'The business is going tits up, Jane.'

'Oh dear – is it the recession?'

'Not exactly. Some of Ken Talbot's dealings were dodgy, and the police are onto him. There's a danger that they may freeze all the company's assets.'

'Oh no,' she wailed. 'That would –'

I interrupted her: 'The info on the email I've sent you is for an online Santander account. It will give you all the money you'll ever need to look after Davey and yourself. It gets topped up monthly from another account by standing order – the reference you'll see will be Fiona Jobs. Nobody knows about the accounts except me. Take a note of the log-in details and password somewhere safe and then make sure you delete all trace of the email.' I thought for a second and decided to tell her about Andrew, in case she arsed things up and needed help. 'If you ever run into problems, contact Andrew Russell. He was at school with us – he's an accountant. Davey will remember him.' Davey would remember him as the nerd who got bullied worse than Davey himself.

'Why – what are you – where – ' She stuttered to a halt.

'I need to get away, Jane. It's very complicated for me – the police would nail my arse. But they won't touch you and Davey.' God, I hoped that was true.

'So – '

'Yes. Promise me you'll give yourself some time out from looking after Davey. Treat yourself.'

There was silence on the phone, and I had nothing more to say. 'Look, Jane, I've got to go. Bye for now.' Yeah, bye for ever. I switched off the call.

Hotel reception got me a taxi, and it arrived a minute later. 'Glasgow Airport,' I said.

As Gibraltar came into view, with a clear blue sky and all my physical possessions in the boot of a black Seat, and millions in the bank, I felt free but with a heavy sense of hopelessness.

*

Amanda Pitt walked up from the hotel where she'd met Martin McGregor, towards the police station where she worked, her mind churning. She crossed the main road, down to the old buildings, the original Cowcaddens area, and stopped to fish her mobile out of her handbag. She stood with it pressed thoughtfully against her lips, listening to the traffic on the road.

What to do… So, she said quietly, you've been playing Martin McGregor. Did you sleep with him too to get what you wanted?

She blinked away an unexpected tear. You were never in love with me, she thought. You just used me to get to Talbot, like Martin did. He gave me money, you gave me sex.

She dialled a number, which went straight to voicemail. 'It's me. We either need to talk honestly about what's been happening, or I need you out of my life completely.' She swallowed, and her tone grew softer. 'We're nearly ready to move against Talbot. You need to be careful.'

Back at the police station, the CID room was buzzing. They were nearly there, nearly ready to start raiding Talbot's main businesses and pull in the main players.

Her boss called her in, and asked about Martin McGregor, what she'd got.

'Not much, sorry. I've got some details on some minor cybercrime activities, but nothing else – and I don't think what I have will give us anything much. Martin McGregor is not important in Talbot's business – he just works on the computer side. He's not important,' she repeated.

Her boss sat back, looking coolly at Amanda. 'I'd like you to stay with McGregor and that cybercrime angle.'

Amanda frowned. 'I know very little about cybercrime.'

'I'd like you to look after it for now. We'll attach an expert to you, and if anything pans out we'll get a team organised.'

Amanda nodded and understood. She was being kept away from the main Talbot team. Did they suspect her?

Chapter 25

New York

Mark Grosvenor took the packed A train from his home in Brooklyn, got off at Fulton Street and walked up through the welcome shade of the narrow Nassau Street into the sunshine of City Hall Park. He bought a black coffee and a bagel with cream cheese and smoked salmon from a stall there, and headed on towards Federal Plaza. He was warm in his jacket, holding his briefcase, his arthritis not so bad now in the warm weather. Away to his left, the One World Trade Centre had now relegated the Empire State to second place once more, and still had three hundred feet to go. Grosvenor didn't think about that day any more. He was still preoccupied with his son and family staying in his home, the child getting ever larger and louder.

He made his way up to the 23rd floor, and along to the small conference room. Kurt Jackson was already there, with Maxwell Stuart, both of them in crisp light blue shirts, checking their phones. Grosvenor hung his jacket on the back of his chair, and sat down, loosening his tie and starting on his breakfast bagel.

The three of them had a meeting every other Friday to look at where they were, share ideas, document progress. The rest of the time Grosvenor and Stuart worked mainly alone, with email conversations and occasional discussions.

'OK,' Jackson said. 'What have we got today?'

Grosvenor, his mouth full, indicated Stuart.

'OK,' Stuart said, 'we may be getting somewhere.'

'At last,' Jackson sighed.

'Can't be rushed,' Grosvenor commented, spitting crumbs.

'Of course. Apologies. Didn't mean to imply you guys were dragging your feet. Carry on Max.'

Stuart stroked his laptop, and a map of the world appeared on the screen. 'As you know, I've been looking at cybercrime implications of the Portugal hit. I've been through the code and the cards, trying to track the numbers back to whoever harvested them and sold them on. It's taken time. We've found links with many of the usual suspects across Europe and into Russia, but we've also stumbled on some new kids on the block. And we've found some interesting connections.'

As he spoke, marker flags appeared on the map, with lines connecting them till the map was almost obliterated. Jackson showed his irritation: the graphic told him nothing.

Then the map was overlaid with a man's face: round, balding, Eastern European. 'This is one of the significant names we got: Gheorghe Angelescu,' Stuart said. 'He's Romanian, but has worked mostly with criminal gangs in the former Soviet Republic. Intelligence on the ground said he had dropped out of sight – they thought he was dead, in fact. No one said he had any links with cybercrime prior to this.' A stroke and a press, and a new face appeared, soft blonde hair, high cheekbones.

'This is another of the names the Portugal people had. He is Charlie Talbot, and it seems he runs a computer company in England.'

Grosvenor sipped his coffee. 'That's Glasgow, England,' he said to Jackson.

Jackson waved away his sarcastic comment. 'Slip of the tongue – I'm sure Max knows where Glasgow is. Carry on, Max.' He looked past the handsome face on the screen to the cold eyes and the cocky, sardonic smile.

Stuart sat back. 'That's pretty much it from me just now.' He turned the laptop and pushed it across to Grosvenor, who plugged in his encrypted thumb drive and started typing to unlock it.

'So,' Jackson said, to fill the gap, 'we've got connections between Portugal, Romania and Scotland. A known face, not previously involved in cybercrime, and new people, whom we haven't seen before.'

'Right. That in itself makes it all worthwhile.'

Jackson didn't look convinced. 'Mark?'

'OK.' Grosvenor put up a text document and scrolled through it. 'That's all the names I checked,' he said. 'All hotel guests around the time of the Portugal killing.' He scrolled and scrolled.

'OK, Mark. I get the point. Cut to the chase.'

Grosvenor closed the document and opened a new one. 'I was searching for names that matched anything that Max was finding, and then exploring the connections. I always find it remarkable how many coincidences there are with so many people in such a small planet. Anyway, this guy dropped out.' The name on the screen was Martin McGregor, one of a short list of names on a new page, but highlighted bold and italic. 'He was in Alvor, near the scene of the murder, for a few days either side of the event. He works for the same computer company as Charlie Talbot. All of that could be coincidence, but last weekend this guy goes to Romania – Ploesti, around thirty five miles north of Bucharest.'

Jackson nodded and frowned. 'And…?'

Grosvenor pushed the laptop back across the table to Stuart, who stroked and clicked it. A line of three photographs appeared.

Grosvenor said: 'We contacted the police in Ploesti, and asked if they knew anything about McGregor, why he had been there, what he had been doing. They checked, and after a couple of hours a guy called Adrian Stancu, an Inspector de politie in the General Directorate, got back to us.'

Jackson was now sitting forward, his eyes narrowing, feeling the excitement that they really might be getting somewhere. Grosvenor watched him.

'It seems McGregor left Romania rather quickly.' Grosvenor went on. 'He had booked two air tickets: Monday and Tuesday. He left on the Monday, leaving his luggage behind.'

Jackson was looking at the three photographs on the screen: the handsome, greying, middle aged man, the beautiful dark girl, and the thin, pretty girl with soft brown hair.

'And what he left behind were three dead bodies – these two, who were associates of Gheorghe Angelescu, and a prostitute. The man himself was on the scene at the time. Stancu went over to Glasgow to speak to McGregor; he denied everything, but rather unconvincingly. Stancu went home – didn't even speak to the Scottish police. Off the record, he said that he thinks people in Romania are protecting Gheorghe.'

Jackson went to get more coffee, and to think. When he had sat back down, he said: 'So McGregor is our hit man.'

'Not necessarily, sir,' said Stuart. 'McGregor's profile doesn't fit that at all. He has no qualifications, but seems to have computer skills – not gun skills.'

'And remember what I said about coincidence.' Grosvenor said. 'We have someone else who happened to be in Portugal and Romania at the same time as McGregor, and we checked her out. Her name is Charlene Anderson, aged twenty three, but she is a hairdresser in Wales. No connections whatsoever to McGregor, or computers.'

They all gave a smile.

'Anyway,' Grosvenor went on. 'I agree with Max. McGregor doesn't look like a killer – he looks like a hacker. I've now been in touch with the police in Glasgow, and they're preparing to close the net on an organised crime gang, run by Ken Talbot – Charlie Talbot's father. There's a criminal empire of drugs, prostitutes, stolen cars – hell, stolen anything – illegal cigarettes, hooch, and a whole heap of money that needs laundering. Max here thinks that the young Talbot is the cybercrime mastermind, and McGregor is his key man.' Grosvenor sat forward. 'I spoke to the police in Glasgow – they put me on to a Detective Sergeant Amanda Pitt, who is dealing with what they know about the computer company where Martin McGregor works. She doesn't think McGregor is a big deal. The police are mainly after Ken Talbot and his sidekick Sandy Lomond. Pitt doesn't rate McGregor.'

'And yet he is linked to four murders.'

Stuart sat back from the laptop, looking at Jackson. Grosvenor got himself another coffee, and then sat looking at Jackson too.

'We've been in touch with the NSA again to see what they have from McGregor's email or Facebook activities. Nothing had been flagged up. They had another look at my request, but came up with nothing: no links to any known carders out there.'

Jackson pursed his lips. 'Which means he's either clean – which we know he damn well isn't – or he's covering his tracks so well that he really is into something deep.'

They were silent for a time.

'So,' Jackson added at last. 'Do we just leave it to the local cops there to reel in the whole gang, including Charlie Talbot and McGregor, and the Romanians and the Portuguese can come in on the murders. Do we need to do any more here?' He frowned. 'Did she *mention* Charlie Talbot?'

Grosvenor raised his eyebrows. 'I don't think we should just leave it to them. We know more about the whole story that they do – the Brits aren't on top of the cybercrime issue – I don't think they've got hold of the implications; they seem to think it's just a little side-line over there. They're interested in local gangs, not international fraud.' He shrugged. 'Furthermore, there is one strange twist to it all that *we* don't fully grasp.'

'What's that?'

Grosvenor nodded to Stuart, who put up the photograph of Charlie Talbot on the screen again. 'You hinted at it yourself just now, boss,' Grosvenor said, his voice slower and deeper. 'This guy is the key man in his father's criminal empire, and is the main man in the computer business, and by implication in any cybercrime. His name is all over the documentation. But he's been dead for ten years – Amanda Pitt told me that when I asked, wondered what I was interested in him for. Automobile crash in the Scottish Highlands.'

Jackson swallowed. 'So there's a hole in our overall picture.'

'Oh yeah. A big one.'

The silence hung in the room while they all thought of the possibilities.

'What do you think we should do?' Jackson eventually asked, when it was clear to the others that he had made his own decision.'

'I would like to talk to McGregor,' Grosvenor said over the rim of his coffee cup. 'The Scottish police are picking him up as we speak, along with the others. I'd like to go over there in a few days and talk to him, and Sandy Lomond. And I'll try to find out what's going on with Charlie Talbot's ghost.'

Jackson nodded. 'I'll set up the formal arrangements. Early next week?'

Grosvenor yawned. 'Yeah. I have a family weekend, and anyhow, there's no rush. McGregor won't be going anywhere.'

Stuart coughed softly to remind them he was there.

'You carry on with your stuff, Max. No need for you to travel. Mark will let you know what he finds out and you can follow it up from here. You can liaise back and forth.'

They all understood that, while the cybercrime was really Stuart's expertise, Grosvenor had much more experience of working out in the field, interviewing suspects, getting them to talk and tell what they knew – even though they didn't want to talk at all.

'OK,' Jackson said, 'we'll get folks here to arrange the travel.' He took a deep breath. 'We'll see how close this gets us to the answers, and maybe the bigger international guys. Good job, guys. So far.'

Grosvenor tossed his empty coffee cup over to the trashcan. It missed.

Chapter 26

Kirkwall and onwards

I was into my third week in the hotel, slowly becoming institutionalised and feeling ever more alone. Nicola had never returned,

I spent some days exploring: Sanday with its incredible beaches, the anomalous mountainous Hoy, and around what I had learned to call Mainland – walking and thinking, gazing in wonder at the remains of coastal defences from the wars.

Late one evening I got back to the hotel, and collected my key.

'Did you ever catch up with Mr McAllister?' the lady on reception asked me. I stared back at her blankly. She smiled. 'He was in the bar, looking for you. No?'

I shook my head. 'I didn't see him.'

I stood frozen for a moment, wanting to ask her what he looked like: not Romanian, or she'd had surely commented. Not police – again, she'd have said. So who was he? And why had he hung around and then simply gone?

I found out when I got up to my room. I had no idea how he'd done it, but he'd got into my room and searched it. He'd been careful, but I could tell that the stuff in my drawers had been moved. He'd attempted to get into my laptop, but the password had defeated him.

I sat on the edge of the bed. They'd found me. If they were the police then why hadn't they moved to arrest me? If they were gangsters then why hadn't they hung around to beat me senseless in the car park?

So who were they then? What did they want?

I spent an hour sitting there, my mind freewheeling, racing. It was over. I was, to all intents and purposes, caught. At some point they'd come again and take me back to Glasgow to face whatever it was I had to face. Maybe escape as a minor accessory to Ken Talbot's criminal world, maybe get the rap as a key figure in it. How much would they nail the cybercrime on me? Would I face murder charges in two countries?

And then I stood up, shaking away the torpor, the despair. No, it wasn't bloody over. I wasn't going to let it end like this, not without a last push. I was hungry after my walk, so I went down for dinner, washed down with a few pints of Scapa Special, and then back to my room and onto the Internet. Then I started packing.

I checked out after a very early breakfast, paying for a few extra days in lieu of notice, and then drove round to the hire car garage. I settled my bill there, and they phoned me a taxi and wished me a safe journey and hoped they'd see me again. I said I hoped so as well. The taxi came and took me the short journey to the airport. As we curved down towards it, I could see the runway and then the sea, clear blue, glinting in the morning sunshine.

'Going to be a bonny day,' the driver said in the accent I had become so familiar with – at first it had been incomprehensible, like Norwegian.

I agreed.

I checked in, and then grabbed a coffee and sat on the comfy chairs looking out through the big window at the apron and runway and the water beyond, with half an eye on the TV, and both ears listening for heavy footsteps behind me. On my laptop, I booked a hotel in Aberdeen for two nights, paying in advance.

One of the tiny 8-seater planes with the Highland Park logo departed to Westray, to be followed by that little hop over to Papa Westray, the shortest scheduled flight in the world. After it buzzed away into the sky and disappeared, the larger Flybe came in, parked and emptied, and our departure was announced.

Security was strict, and then I was in the little departure lounge, and boarding – the flight was full – and away, through the clouds into a clear blue sky.

I relaxed, but knew this was an illusion. The police would easily be able to check the flights and ferries, and find I had gone to Aberdeen. I planned to try to confuse them there. But for the next hour or so I was safe. I accepted my free coffee, drank it, then closed my eyes and slept for the rest of the trip.

At Aberdeen airport, I took a taxi into the city, to the Union Square shopping complex which contained the big Victorian railway station. All the time, I expected to hear a cough behind me and a hand on my shoulder. But I hoped they might be waiting at the hotel I had booked, but had no intention of staying in.

I walked into the railway station, and bought my ticket for Edinburgh, first class, cash. As the train hurtled down the rugged east coast of Scotland, the day turned back to rain, I enjoyed the free snacks and the endless coffee, and I slept some more. But all the time I knew it was pointless: they'd found me before, and they could do it again. I was done and I knew it. I actually just wanted to go home, to that empty flat in Glasgow.

In Edinburgh, I went down to a hotel in Grassmarket – they had a room. I booked it for three nights, and gave them my credit card.

I drank and ate, and drank again in the hotel, and went to bed quite early. I couldn't sleep for the unfamiliar city noises, and for the fear that at any moment someone would walk through my hotel room door and either arrest me or kill me.

But I'd done what I could today to get clear, and in due course I'd move on again, and just keep running, for as long as I could.

*

It was my third night in Edinburgh. The city was cold, and made me feel lonely as I walked around. I gazed in disbelief at the on-going tramworks cutting through Haymarket and along Princes Street. There were still traces of the Festival – fly posters everywhere, baffled tourists stumbling around, the hotels still very busy and expensive.

I liked being alone in the pubs on and around the Royal Mile and down on Rose Street, but I usually left when they get really busy with drunks, because by then other lonely people would want to talk to me. I didn't want to talk to anyone; I couldn't make friends, couldn't talk about my life. I craved female company, but all the girls out in the pubs were far too young – like Sam, back in the day: short skirts, high shoes, and squawking, drunken laughter and shouts, hen parties everywhere. Once I heard a loud foreign voice at my shoulder at the bar, and I jumped; false alarm.

I ended up back on Grassmarket, in one of the pubs across from the hotel. I had a last beer there, feeling safe somehow in that crowd. Then I went back over to the hotel, and had a gin and tonic in the bar – the barman knew me now, and it was just a nod to get my drink poured and brought over to my table, just like in the hotel in Ploesti.

Tonight another resident came into the bar from upstairs, and I heard a gravelly American accent as he ordered a 'double Scotch with water' – I recognised the accent from the movies and TV: New York. He talked to the barman briefly, asking about the best places to drink in town, and the barman gave him some tips.

I looked up. The man was somewhere around sixty, with a mass of white hair and a big white beard. He was wearing jeans and a thick, loud lumberjack shirt.

'Much obliged, son,' he said to the barman, and I watched him come over – walking with a stiff right leg like he had an old injury – and sit at the table next to mine, unfolding a newspaper with a flourish, giving me a slight nod. 'Hi there.'

'Hi,' I replied.

I settled back in my seat, looking around the rest of the open plan bar area. Every time someone came in from outside, taking off their coats and jackets immediately as they hit the warmth, I looked hard, trying to guess whether it was someone after me. I was tuned in to East European accents, and was scanning for a young pretty blonde, with a mixture of desire and fear.

A good night's sleep, check out in the morning, go somewhere else. I contemplated the last of my gin, saw the barman raise his eyebrows. I thought for a second, then shook my head. Where would I go tomorrow? Back to Spain? God, I needed somewhere warm.

I finished my drink and stood up, gathering my coat, heading for the lift. I heard the voice – 'Night – thanks for the suggestions' – and the white-haired American was in the lift with me, asking for the same floor.

'Cold,' I said, because you have to say something in a lift.

'I'm from New York,' he said, 'so I'm kinda used to it. Not this early though.'

He let me get out of the lift first, and I heard him behind me as I went down the corridor: I looked round as I walked, and saw him pulling his keycard from his pocket, juggling his newspaper. The corridor was empty – too late for many, too early for some. I reached the door of my room and opened it.

I heard two swift footsteps coming towards me, too quickly for me to react, and then I was suddenly and firmly pushed inside my room, and the door closed behind me. I staggered and turned, wondering what had just happened, and saw the American lock the door and stand motionless at it, listening.

'Anyone following you around?' he asked. 'Anyone looking for you?'

I shook my head, confused by the question, baffled, wondering what to do. I stood holding my keycard, then leaned past him to put it in its slot. The lights in the room came on, and the TV. I grabbed the remote and turned it off.

‘Take a seat, son,’ he growled pointing his newspaper at the comfortable chair squeezed in beside the bed. I went over and sat on it; he sat on the upright chair at the room’s desk.

I looked at him, and he stared calmly back at me.

‘Sorry,’ he said, ‘remiss of me.’ He groped in his back pocket, pulled out a slim wallet, and flipped it open to show me his ID. ‘I’m Mark Grosvenor. FBI,’ he added unnecessarily, because I can see that clearly on his ID. He put the wallet away. ‘I’d like a talk with you, Martin, and I have a proposal. I’ll give you time to think about the proposal, but I’ll tell you right now: it’s your only choice, son – your only way out. So don’t go running off in the morning. We need to talk details when you’re sober. OK so far?’

He stopped, and the silence fell.

Finally, I shook my head. ‘I haven’t a clue what you’re talking about.’ The FBI? How the fuck did the FBI fit into any of this?

He leaned back, crossing his legs. He was shorter than me, and clearly a bit overweight and with a limp – probably a gunshot wound, I now thought – but I didn’t feel like trying to get past him and out of the door. He knew who I was, but I didn’t know what he knew about me. It was probably a mistake – I maybe had the same name as a New York crime lord.

I didn’t know what he was talking about with this ‘way out’, and ‘I’ve no other options’.

‘Sorry, son, I’ll start at the beginning.’ He cleared his throat. ‘Mind if I use the bathroom?’

I didn’t move as he went into the toilet and unleashed a waterfall, then flushed, washed and emerged.

‘That’s better.’ He eased himself back down onto the chair. ‘I can see you’re a mite unsure, so I’ll just run through some of the main details of the past fifteen years or so, and you make minor corrections where necessary – maybe fill in a couple of gaps. But that’ll get us past the ‘I don’t know what you’re talking about’ crap, OK? We both know what’s going on here.’

Silence again. I felt some response was appropriate, so I nodded, but I didn’t say anything.

‘Anyhow, you work for a computer company in Glasgow, B&D Software Solutions. There is another company called Bytes & Digits – love to find the asshole that made that one up – which is pretty much legit, and performs a useful service. But B&D is bad. We know how it’s set up to syphon off customers’ credit cards, bank accounts, passwords. So far so good: that brings in cash, and mostly the banks and insurance companies take the hit, and most folks think they deserve it – causing the recession and all. But the people out there are major criminals and terrorists, everywhere including Portugal to Romania, and you’re funding them. You’ve opened up dozens of computers that can be hijacked, used for everything from spam emails to denial of service attacks against legitimate companies or governments. How am I doing so far, son? Pretty much there?’

I gave a shiver and closed my eyes briefly. The fucking FBI knew *all* about me. Well done Martin: the Portuguese police, the Romanian police, the Scottish police, Romanian gangsters, Glasgow gangsters… bad enough. But the fucking FBI! I felt myself shaking slightly, and I folded my arms, tight. I had no doubt whatsoever that he knew absolutely everything. I knew the stories of young hackers being extradited to the States, given huge prison sentences. Oh fuck.

'OK, I'll take that as a yes. At the back of it is a gangster called Ken Talbot. He originally used it all as a way of laundering money – one of many businesses he had: typical Glasgow stuff – scrapyards, taxi firms, ice cream vans, laundrettes, money lending, drugs, rented property, prostitution, blah blah blah; cash goes in and out, and ends up in legitimate investments: you've got quite a portfolio yourself. But somewhere along the line B&D became less of a front for that and became a cash cow in its own right.'

He reached for a bottle of still water in my mini-bar – I shook my head when he offered me one, I was cold enough. He twisted it open and drank half of it in one go.

'So, what else? Ah yes, Portugal - and the dead guy.'

I swallowed.

'In case you're wondering, that's how we got involved. The Portuguese police managed to get some information off the guy's laptop, and it led to a couple of US citizens who had had their credit card details stolen. So the Portuguese asked for our help, it fitted with our workstream, so we went to work: and we got more stuff off the laptop. This led to some pretty big international criminals, so we got *really* interested.'

He finished the bottle of water, and set it down on the desk unit. I still felt cold but beginning to sweat now; I stuck my hands deep in my pockets, where they continued trembling. My heart was thudding, slowly and strongly, in my chest. My breathing was difficult.

'We cooperated with the Portuguese police, and started digging. We went through everything we could make sense of from that poor dead guy's laptop, and we went through all the people that were nearby in Portugal at the time, looking for any connections we could find. It was a lot of work.'

He gave a yawn, and scratched at his thick beard. 'And then what happened… oh yes, Romania, and the three dead people there.'

The thudding of my heart was now more pronounced – I wondered whether he could hear it – and I felt slightly dizzy.

'The Romanian police were helpful too – really encouraging, all this international cooperation, don't you think? Anyway, the dead people had links to a guy known as Gheorghe Angelescu, who is very well known to us – I assume you met him.'

I tried to frown like I had no idea what he was saying, but none of the muscles on my face would work.

'Which was interesting. And you just happened to have been in the two places at the two times. Big coincidence, don't you think?' He reached into the minibar for another small bottle of water, and started drinking it.

'I…' I tried to say, but he raised his eyebrows, and then my tongue stopped functioning.

'So we did some exploring, found out about Ken Talbot and Sandy Lomond, and spoke to the Scottish cops – Detective Sergeant Amanda Pitt. She told us they were getting ready to pull down Talbot's whole operation.'

A mobile phone started ringing somewhere in the room, slightly muffled. We looked at each other, until I realised it was mine, the one I'd bought in Orkney and never used. I pulled it shakily from my trouser pocket, fully expecting someone from the CIA to be on the line.

‘Hello?’

‘Martin?’

I didn’t recognise the female voice, so I gave a cautious: ‘Yes?’

‘It’s Nicola.’

Nicola? ‘Yes?’ My brain cells stirred. Why was that name familiar?

‘From Orkney – Kirkwall – the hotel.’

Oh shit. Nicola. ‘Oh hi.’ I tried to moisten my mouth. ‘How are you?’ She’d kept my number, the one that the receptionist had given her.

Grosvenor sat drinking his water, watching me, face impassive.

‘I’m fine, Martin. Sorry I haven’t been in touch, it’s just… well, it’s been complicated. I’m in Kirkwall again, in the hotel. I – er – wondered if you fancied a drink in the bar.’

She’d kept my number, but bloody awful timing using it now. ‘I’m afraid I can’t – I’m actually in Edinburgh right now.’

‘Oh.’

‘Yeah – it’s to do with that stuff with business I told you about, remember? It’s got even more complicated. Well, it turns out the FBI have been after me.’

She gave a laugh. ‘It’s good to hear your voice again, Martin.’

‘And yours. Listen, I’m being interrogated by this FBI guy right now, so could I phone you tomorrow?’

She laughed again. ‘Of course. I’m back home on Friday – if you’re still in Edinburgh… It would be good to talk to you.’ She took a deep breath. ‘Things have moved on in my life.’

And in mine, I thought. 'It's a date,' I said. 'I need to go. Bye just now.'

'Bye, Martin. See you soon.'

I switched off the phone and put it away in my pocket. Grosvenor continued looking at me, no expression on his face. I had no idea whether he knew about Nicola or not. Suddenly I wasn't just scared, though, I wanted a way out: I wanted to see Nicola again, to see where it took us. I took a deep breath, and felt some of the clouds of uncertainty lift away from me.

'So,' Grosvenor eventually said. 'Summing up, I have enough on you to link you to international cyber criminals, who are operating against US citizens – et cetera et cetera. And I could throw in terrorism charges too: these guys regularly try to bring down major US websites, so that counts as terrorism too.'

I found my voice. 'The US seems to do that as well, to other countries.'

He gave a wry smile. 'Yeah, well… that's another agency. I see myself as one of the good guys here. So,' he let out a sigh, 'the point is that I could get you to Prestwick airport by tomorrow morning and onto a Gulfstream out of there, no questions: your government would not raise a finger. In fact, I think the Scottish police would not be unhappy to see you leave.'

I nodded, believing him. 'You said there was a way out.' I was beginning to think, seizing on his offer.

'There is, Martin. There is. First of all, I'd like a bit more information on one or two things. Who were the main players here?'

I swallowed; he must know everything, so there was no point holding back. 'Ken Talbot was the boss, but Sandy Lomond did all the day-to-day management, including the computer stuff. And Colin Strachan was the main guy who started up the cybercrime – he had the contacts originally, someone calling themselves Gregorius. Colin retired a few years ago, left the country.'

Grosvenor showed no reaction to any of that. 'You know where Colin Strachan is now?' His voice was even.

I tried to shake my head, but ended up giving a strange bob and then a nod.

'OK,' he said. 'We'll talk more about that tomorrow. How about Charlie Talbot?'

I frowned. 'Charlie died in a car crash ten years ago.'

'Apparently. But he was pretty big, yes?'

I couldn't understand what the hell he was talking about. Was he trying to trick me, to see how honest I was being? 'Charlie's brains were in his cock. He spent all his time chasing – ' I was about to say 'fanny' but changed it – 'pussy. He was officially in charge of Bytes and Digits, and a director of B&D, but he did fuck all – which suited us fine.'

Grosvenor was staring impassively at me. Then he took another sip of water. 'OK. Who else?'

'Well, you'll know about Charlene.'

Again there was an impassive stare, and a sip of water. 'Tell me about her.'

'Well – you know she set up the thing in Portugal when we got into that guy's computer, and she was in Romania, watching what was going on. She got me out. I don't think she was directly involved with the murders, but…'

My voice tailed off because he was unlocking his mobile and checking his watch as he dialled.

'Hey, Max, how you doin'?'

I couldn't make out any words from the other end.

'Max, remember that other name we picked up on? … That's the one. I think we may have missed something there. Could you go back and really dig deep on that one. Thorough. … Yes, I do. … And another couple of names: Colin Strachan, who worked at B&D and made the original contacts with the hackers but left town a few years ago, and someone calling himself Gregorius, who may or may not be a big player out there. … OK, Max – call me when you have something.' He hung up, and stared at me again.

Then he seemed to rouse himself from his thoughts. 'You asked about the way out. We'll start talking about that at breakfast – 0800. Don't try to run away: we'll find you, and I'll be really pissed. But what I want you to do for now is go back to B&D and help us trace the bad guys at the other end of your operation, including 'Gregorius'. If it doesn't work then we'll just lock you up somewhere. If it does work, then – ' and he shrugged. 'We'll see.'

He yawned. 'You have no bargaining power, Martin. On the one hand you have the Romanian police, the Portuguese police, the Scottish police, and the FBI. On the other hand you have various global criminal organisations and gangsters. Between a rock and a hard place, son. I think there's a Scottish word that covers your situation, I believe: 'fucked'.'

He stood up and stepped to the door. 'But don't do a runner, Martin. I'll see you at breakfast. 0800.'

I stood up too. I was still shaking, alternately cold and hot, questions tumbling through my head.

He let himself out, and I locked the door behind him and put on the chain, then stumbled back to my chair, and sat there, staring at where Grosvenor had sat.

Options?

I had to do what Grosvenor wanted – no choice. Could I cover myself?

I looked at my watch: after ten.

I hadn't had my old mobile on since I left Glasgow; I plugged it in to charge, and thought. Then I switched it on, and watched the text messages and the emails pour in, and the missed call count rack up.

Amongst the spam and the crap and the routine daily updates on things, there were several texts and voicemails from Sandy Lomond, all basically saying the same thing: 'Where the fuck are you?' and 'What's going on, and what do you know about it? Fuckin' phone me, Martin.'

Sandy would have thought that I had somehow brought the police down on the company, and gone into hiding with their blessing, and to an extent he wouldn't be far wrong. But what had *he* done? What had happened when the police had gone in to rake through our files? Nothing at all had appeared on the news. What about Ken Talbot? What about the other staff – Claire and Graham?

No sure what I was really doing, or why, I dialled Sandy's mobile. But I just got weird electronic beeps. I guessed that would have abandoned his mobile somewhere so that he couldn't be traced.

I checked the dates on his texts and voicemails: all of them from the few days after the police would have moved into St Vincent Street, and nothing after. So, was he hiding in the sun somewhere, while Talbot was near death? Was anything functioning in B&D or up on Argyle Street? What about the dark network out there - Gregorius?

I had to do what Grosvenor said, and hope somehow that I would prove useful enough to them that they didn't want to just sling me in jail. But their track record on this wasn't good: the FBI had extradited and imprisoned a lot of hackers, many of them vulnerable young men. Why should they take pity on me?

I couldn't think of any plan B, though.

And Charlene was out there somewhere – even the FBI hadn't known about her. What was she up to? How was she really involved?

I went to bed, exhausted but unable to sleep. Partly this was the alcohol I'd drunk – I was up and down to the toilet all night – but mainly it was the thoughts swarming and tumbling inside my head. Finally, around four o'clock in the morning, I focused on something I wanted and managed to get to sleep, all my thoughts aiming for it. Fiona was dead and gone; Helen had left me, and would never trust me again. But Nicola liked me, and seemed to want to give some kind of relationship a try. That was what I wanted too.

Alone in my bed – alone in the world – I seized the possibility that this could all work out somehow, and I could be with Nicola. I resolved that I'd pretty much do anything for that to happen.

Chapter 27

Edinburgh and Glasgow

I wandered into the breakfast room at exactly 0800. I'd slept for approximately three hours, was woken by my phone alarm, and had tried to shower away sleep and my hangover, and residual memories from Romania. I really needed to think clearly, and here I was knackered and fuzzy-headed.

I gave my room number and pointed across to the table – 'Joining colleagues', I said – and went over to sit beside Grosvenor, still in his jeans and thick, checked shirt, and Amanda Pitt, wearing a dark jacket and pencil skirt, looking thin and tired; she'd had her hair cut very short. Grosvenor was working his way through the full Scottish, Amanda sipped a coffee.

She looked at me over the rim of her cup. 'Hello again, Martin. You look dreadful.'

Grosvenor checked his watch as he shovelled bacon and egg into his mouth with the fork in his right hand. 'Good to see you,' he mumbled through a mouthful of food. He poured me out a cup of coffee from the pot on the table.

I fetched some cereal, and sat trying to eat it.

We were all silent, looking at each other and then out to the castle, its grey walls almost obscured by the thick, grey rain. Around us came the excited chatter of many languages. Two young Japanese women were up at the window, documenting every angle of the view.

Finally Grosvenor wiped his lips, Amanda re-filled her coffee – and got the Polish waiter to bring us more – and I pushed away the last of my cereal.

'Well then,' Grosvenor said. 'You've met DS Pitt. She kindly came over on the train for an early breakfast so we could talk. Let's find some privacy.'

We managed to find comfy chairs in a corner of the empty lounge bar, and sat with the new, fresh jug of coffee and our cups, our backs to the grille protecting the bar.

'Well then,' Grosvenor repeated. 'This is another fine example of international cooperation, within certain vaguely defined boundaries of course. We're not sharing absolutely *everything*. Except for you, Martin: you don't have any chips left, so you just give.'

I grimaced.

'Have you thought about what we said last night?'

I looked at Amanda, and she looked back at me.

I nodded. 'I'll do what you want.'

Grosvenor nodded, and now Amanda looked at him and gave an almost imperceptible nod, which he returned.

'What's been happening?' I asked Amanda.

She took a deep breath. 'Ken Talbot is out on bail. He had a major heart attack last week, and they are planning a quadruple bypass, but the prognosis is not good. Sandy Lomond was questioned for twenty four hours and finally we attempted to charge him with some minor offences, but there was a cock-up with how the arrest was dealt with: he wasn't charged with what we arrested him for, so we had to release him. And then he vanished: he's somewhere in mainland Europe, we think; looks like he's ditched his mobile phone, so no joy there.'

She continued: 'Talbot's empire is fragmenting: we've rounded up a number of people – involved in drugs, prostitution, taxi firms, scrapyards – and closed down some of what he was doing, but, as usual, others are moving in. We've got some of our people undercover, and we're well-placed to keep an eye on developments and pick off serious players as they emerge.' She took a long drink of her coffee. 'We're processing a lot of information, but, following some discussion at top level, we've left B&D's cybercrime activities alone.' And she half-turned to Grosvenor.

He yawned and scratched at his beard. 'The Scottish police – and the Romanian and Portuguese police – have agreed to leave that all to the FBI for now; we're better equipped to deal with it at present. We'll keep them informed, of course.' He nodded to Amanda, and she returned the gesture, her lips tight. 'First we need you back in your office, then we'll see what happens.'

I nodded. I knew I had only the one tenuous link through to all of that side, and it might very well have been shut down since my unexplained departure, but I didn't want to tell Grosvenor that, not now. 'Then what?'

'Then we'll see. We'll see what you can do. You might be able to play them. If not,' and he shrugged.

I drank my coffee. I was sure it wouldn't work, but what choice did I have? I couldn't run away again. I visualised life in a prison in America, and shuddered.

'You're sure you don't know where this guy Colin Strachan is?' he asked.

I shook my head. 'What about Charlene?'

Amanda looked intently at Grosvenor as he explained: 'When we started investigating the Portuguese murder, we picked up on a few names. Two of them reappeared in Romania: Martin here, and Charlene Anderson. We checked on her, and she is a hairdresser in Mid-Wales. So we – I – discounted her. After speaking to Martin last night I realised we had made an operational error there, so we checked again.' He gazed into his coffee cup.

'So what do you know about her?' Amanda asked again. Her voice was calm, her body still.

'It turns out the hairdresser she works for is owned and managed by Charlie Talbot. We had been checking – like you were – on Ken Talbot's businesses, and Charlie Talbot's name was all over a lot of them, and also many that didn't seem to have any other direct connection to Ken Talbot, apart from the name.'

'Yes,' Amanda said, 'but Charlie Talbot's been dead for ten years. His name was obviously just being used as a placeholder: it wasn't really him.'

Grosvenor shifted again. 'We thought Charlie Talbot might still be alive.'

‘Impossible,’ I said.

‘And is a sense he is. Charlene Anderson – Martin’s Charlene, who pops up here and there at crucial times – is Charlie Talbot.’

‘What?’

‘Charlene Anderson is Charlene Talbot, calling herself Charlie in business documentation. She’s Charlie Talbot’s daughter.’

‘Oh shit,’ I said, shutting my eyes. ‘Of course she is. She looks just like him.’ The fine blonde hair, the high cheekbones. Shit fuck. ‘How old is she?’

‘She’s twenty three.’ Grosvenor looked baffled by the question.

‘Do you know anything about her mother?’

Grosvenor frowned. ‘She works in the hospitality trade, has done all her life, all over Scotland. We haven’t had time to speak to her, and I don’t think there’s any need. She’s currently managing a restaurant in Aberdeen; married, with a teenage son. Charlene was adopted by a couple who moved to mid-Wales when she was still a baby.’

Yeah. Charlie must have had the relationship, or one-night-stand or whatever, with Charlene’s mother around the time he was bedding Sam. Maybe she had been working at the hotel on Loch Lomond where Charlie had taken Sam. And Ken Talbot would have been able to pay for the child. Was that what Sandy had meant when he’d spoken about Charlene and Ken going ‘way back’? Was Charlene actually working for Sandy or Ken Talbot?

I noticed Amanda’s fingers were shaking as she put her coffee cup down and reached in her handbag for her mobile, holding it against her lips.

'We're trying to find her, and I think it would be good if we kept our eyes open for her. I don't know how much she knows, or what she might want out of this. It's untidy, I know, but it can't deflect us from the main plan.'

Amanda had composed and sent a text, and now she had dialled and was speaking to someone. 'Hi, it's Amanda here. In connection with the whole Talbot enquiry, there is a person we want to trace: her name is Charlene Talbot, though she's going under the name Charlene Anderson, and for business purposes she uses the name Charlie Talbot. Does that make sense? … Yes, she's Ken Talbot's granddaughter. … Yes, she's involved in a lot of stuff: we'd like to find her. … No, just keep a watch and if you find anything let me know straightaway – *I'll* decide what to do. Thanks.' She hung up.

'You think she's dangerous?' I asked.

Amanda raised her eyebrows. 'Do *you* think she is?'

I didn't know. 'No,' I said. 'Charlene didn't kill those people.' But I was sure she had a ruthless streak to her: I had seen her close up. But I didn't really think she'd killed people. 'Can I ask a question?' I said. They nodded. 'In Romania, I was… well, I think I was drugged and – er – seduced, in my hotel. Coralia, the Romanian translator, set it up; Rodica was the girl – the prostitute. Coralia photographed us in the act.'

Amanda was glowering at me, Grosvenor looked like he was concealing a smile in that big white beard.

'A few of the photographs were texted to my partner Helen. And she dumped me because of that. Do either of you know how that happened?'

They shook their heads. I absorbed that: if they hadn't done it then it was down to the Romanians, or Charlene – maybe she had got hold of Coralia's camera, or the memory card, or copies of the photographs, and sent them to Helen. She'd done something similar with the Portugal photograph.

'OK,' I went on. 'In Orkney, someone broke into my hotel room and had a rummage around, and tried to get into my laptop.'

Grosvenor raised his hand. 'That would be me – well, a private detective I hired. He wasn't much use.'

Amanda was looking daggers at him.

I nodded. OK. 'You knew I was in Orkney.'

Amanda and Grosvenor nodded as one. He spoke: 'Of course. You left a card trail all the way. We were just waiting to decide what to do. Then we saw your route to Aberdeen, where you went off the radar a bit, and on to this hotel.' Grosvenor set down his empty cup. 'By then I had a plan, and didn't want you to mess it up by skipping off again. Hence last night.'

I gazed blankly at them. All those weeks I'd thought I was free, and they were sitting on my tail, the whole time. I felt like an idiot.

'OK, what now?'

They stood up. 'We check out, get the train back to Glasgow – you can go back to your flat and dump your luggage, then we'll go down to B&D and start work. We have a computer expert coming over – he'll be in Glasgow by this afternoon.'

'I'll see you at reception,' Amanda said, and stepped away from us, dialling on her mobile.

*

We got a taxi down to Waverley station, and Grosvenor bought tickets for him and me. The three of us found a table in first class on the Glasgow shuttle service, and we hurtled across the central belt. The compartment was empty apart from us and an old English couple. He sat with his hearing aid and walking stick, staring out of the window. She had a newspaper, and loudly read out letters and articles; he didn't acknowledge anything she said.

I gazed out at the fields after we left the city, the cooling towers and flares of Grangemouth, and then on towards Glasgow, the high rises slipping away from view as we entered the tunnel and slowed and ground our way into Queen Street station. We joined the massed bodies on the concourse, dodging out of their way as their platform was announced with only minutes to spare and they piled through the barriers.

Amanda said: 'I'm going down to B&D now. You two follow later – let me know when you're coming.' This was to Grosvenor. To me she added: 'Anything you need down there?'

'How about Claire – our receptionist?'

'We interviewed her. She seems clean.'

'Yes she is – where is she?'

'At home, I assume. Maybe she's found another job. You want her back?'

'If you can. And Graham Turner?'

'We talked to him too, briefly, and we've told him to stay away for now but keep in contact. Not sure what to do with him just yet. What do you think?'

'Keep him away from the place for now. Any word on Charlene?'

Amanda looked at Grosvenor, then back to me. 'No. We haven't had any credit card activity, and her car is still in Wales. She's still in this country from what we can see.'

I thought back to Romania, and our check-in at the airport: I couldn't remember whether she's given her own name at the desk, and I hadn't been able to see her passport. Had she got herself another ID?

The noise of people around us was giving me a headache. I was tired and thirsty. And starting to get hungry. This was a nightmare, and it felt like it was going to go on for ever.

'Anything else?' Amanda asked.

I shook my head.

Amanda went out of the front of the station, pulling a tiny red umbrella from her big handbag and opening it as she went down the steps. Grosvenor and I went out of the side entrance to the taxi rank.

*

The flat was cold and empty. I lifted the mass of mail and dropped it on the table in the lounge, and turned the heating back on. Grosvenor left his bag by the door, and had a good look around – I noticed him staring up into the corners of the high ceilings, and behind pictures and under tables and chairs. I watched him for a few minutes, then rinsed out the kettle and put it on.

I unpacked and stuffed as much dirty clothing as I could into the washing machine and started it up. I made us both an instant coffee, which he grimaced at, and I sat on the couch and flipped through my mail, looking for anything significant. Nothing. I tore up the junk mail, and left the rest for later.

'Which is my room?' Grosvenor asked.

I looked up at him.

He grinned. 'Just kidding. I've got a hotel. Our guy Steve will be moving in here for a few days though – you two might need to work real close. Shouldn't be for too long.'

We sat opposite each other in the lounge, sipping our coffees, leaning forward, tense.

'Tell me about your family, Martin. What are they like? What's your relationship with them?'

I took a deep breath, surprised at his question. 'My dad died a long time ago, when I was in my early teens,' I said. 'I had a wee brother – Peter; he died a couple of years before that. He was very clever.'

'Must have hit your mom real hard.'

'Yes.'

'So you were her last hope.'

I nodded glumly, looking into my coffee cup. 'And I let her down.'

'Where is she now?'

'She remarried – a schoolteacher. They live on the south-side - ' I clarified: 'The other side of the river. I don't really keep in touch. She wouldn't have noticed anything unusual in me being out of contact for a few weeks. I don't really rate my step dad much. But he knew there was something dodgy about Ken Talbot, right from the start. He guessed what I was into.'

'You can atone for all of it now,' Grosvenor offered.

'You think?'

We sat in silence for a time.

'We've never mentioned David Collins,' he suddenly said.

'You know about him.'

'Sure we do. Disabled in the automobile accident that killed Charlie Talbot. Living with his wife and child in Glasgow. Seems to have plenty of money to support him. She looks after him full time, and they have a full time nurse too.'

'Leave him alone,' I said. 'Just leave him alone and I'll do what you want. But if you spoil what quality of life he has, I'll fuck up all of your plans, no matter what.' I was aware my voice had got louder. I was angry.

He raised his hands. 'Hey, easy tiger. We've no reason to touch Collins. We're not doing anything out of spite here – we're just trying to nail some bad guys, as high up the tree as we can go.'

I nodded, satisfied.

Grosvenor checked his watch and stood up. 'OK, Martin. We need to get to work. Let's rock and roll.'

I sighed and got to my feet.

Chapter 28

St Vincent Street

Grosvenor and I climbed out of the taxi into the cold drizzle and walked across the pavement and up the steps to where a police constable stood with rain dripping from the brim of his hat, a small crowd of people at the nearby bus stop idly watching us. The PC looked at us dispassionately as Grosvenor flashed his ID, and he then led us through the door and up the stairs to the door of B&D Software Solutions. I noted the damage around the shiny new deadlock: it looked like they'd broken into our offices and then replaced the lock.

We went inside. Amanda was standing in the middle of the reception area, her umbrella propped against the desk and developing a small puddle on the floor. She was on her mobile. She killed the call quickly as we came in, and it rang again immediately. 'Yes, tell her to come over soon as she can.'

I looked around. Like my flat, it was silent and cold, with a film of dust everywhere. The two filing cabinets each had a random drawer open – and I could see they were empty – and Claire's desk drawers were all open and empty. The doors to the individual offices were closed and had police tape across them.

The policeman stayed by the main door. Grosvenor walked slowly around, and leaned over the tape to open the doors of the three offices. He ducked into each in turn, and looked around. 'You didn't touch these computers?' he asked.

Amanda grimaced. 'We tried to get into them, but they are all password protected. When we got enough potential evidence from the paper files here and at Talbot's and Lomond's homes, and their home computers, and we'd spoken to you, we decided to leave them here rather than take them back to the forensic IT guys. My boss OKed it.'

Grosvenor nodded. 'Good.' He stroked the keyboard of my Mac, and the PC beside it, and stood still, thinking, then looked at his watch.

'What now?' I asked.

There was silence for a couple of minutes. Then he said: 'I think we need lunch. Can we get take-out?'

Amanda pulled out her purse and gave the policeman a couple of twenties. 'Could you get us a selection of sandwiches and some soft drinks – bring them back here? Enough for five people. Anybody veggie? No? OK.'

He pocketed the money and left, looking proud of his new responsibility. I went into my office, ducking under the tape, and sat at my desk. The drawers had been forced open and emptied. Grosvenor was still deep in thought. Amanda started pulled the tape away from the doorways, stuffing it into the bin.

'Martin!'

I stood up at the sound of Claire's voice, and she came through to hug me. 'You're safe. Thank god.' She held me at arm's length to look at me, then held me tight again.

'I'm OK,' I mumbled into the mass of her long red hair. 'How are you?'

She let me go and looked at Grosvenor and Amanda, who was looking hard at her with a raised eyebrow. Claire was dressed in jeans and a green fleece, her hair wild. 'What's been happening?'

'Come and have a seat,' Amanda said, leading Claire back to the outer office and sitting her down at her desk, perching herself on the edge of it, legs crossed. I stood in my doorway and watched.

Claire looked up at Amanda, then past her to me. 'Martin? What's going on?'

'It's OK,' I said. 'What have you been up to?'

'Just stayed at home – after the police interviewed me when you and Sandy disappeared. I haven't been doing anything. What's all this about? What's been happening? Nobody's told me anything. Was something going on with Sandy?'

Amanda was still just staring at Claire, so I answered. 'Sandy worked for a gangster named Ken Talbot. This whole business was a scam to get credit card numbers, bank account details, the works.'

'Oh god!'

Amanda reached to hold Claire's hand. 'I'm Amanda. I'm with the police. We've got all of that business cleared up now.' Her voice was deep and smooth. 'We know you had nothing to do with it.'

'So what happens to the business now? What about my job?'

Grosvenor smiled at her. 'Your job is safe for now,' he said. 'Martin here is going to see if he can run the business as a legitimate concern. If it works, everything will be pretty much back to normal – except it'll be legit.' His smile widened, but hers was tense.

'Who *are* you?' she asked.

'My name's Mark Grosvenor,' he said, reaching to shake her hand. 'I work for an IT company in New York. We dealt with B&D, and they screwed us over. I came over to try to sort things out, and ended up being interviewed by DS Amanda Pitt here – scared the hell out of me, I can tell you. Anyway, the Scottish police have asked me to stay on and help find out what was going on with the business, and maybe even find some of the guys out there that were working with Sandy Lomond and Ken Talbot. I'll just be here for a few days – but I need to get back to New York soon as I can.'

Claire nodded. 'So what do we do now?'

Amanda stood up, smoothing her skirt down, still focused on Claire, her eyes all over her; she seemed to hold her breath as Claire struggled out of her fleece, revealing a tight green halter-neck top. 'We've got some lunch coming in, and then we'll try to get everything up and running. We'll get your switchboard live, switch on the computers, and then, over the next few days, see what happens.'

'What do you want me to do?'

'Same as before: take calls, arrange meetings, field enquiries, troubleshoot. Except that Martin will be in sole charge.'

'And we're bringing in a colleague of mine, an IT expert from the States – guy called Steve Roberts.' Grosvenor's smile was still wide, his voice soft. 'Is that all good with you?'

Claire nodded, and gave a smile that was only a little strained. 'Yes. As long as I have a job.'

Amanda leaned over and almost touched her hair. 'You still have a job, Claire. Here, take my card. If you're ever worried about anything, you just call me.' She handed Claire the small white rectangle from out of her jacket pocket, pressed it into Claire's hand, and clasped it tight.

The young policeman arrived back with a bag of sandwiches and some juices and cokes, setting all out on a side desk, and explaining what it all was. We helped ourselves and then spread out in the room to eat and drink, in almost total silence. There was no small talk to be had in this gathering, nothing to joke about. Grosvenor took a couple of calls, moving as far away from us as he could to mumble and listen. Amanda spoke on her mobile to someone who was obviously her boss, but I couldn't make out anything.

I texted Nicola from my Orkney mobile, and gave her my main mobile number. I told her I really wanted to see her again, and that things were complicated with work but that I hoped to get through to see her at the weekend, or maybe she could come to Glasgow.

Then, after lunch, Claire started up the switchboard and started to listen to some messages, making notes. Amanda smiled, whispered something in Claire's ear, then said goodbye to us all, leaving Grosvenor the keys. The policeman hovered by the door. Grosvenor worked out how to start the coffee machine, and grimaced at the pack of stale coffee but used it anyway.

I went into my office, sat at my desk and switched on the Mac, and held my breath and logged on. Grosvenor set a cup of coffee beside me, and pulled a chair over so he could sit watching what I did. 'I need to keep the business going first,' I said to him.

The emails started coming in, private messages started appearing, and Claire's phone started ringing.

Grosvenor watched and sipped his coffee. I replied to what looked like the most urgent messages and enquiries, apologising for the interruption to service because of a major server breakdown. Claire brought through messages from people who had been having problems, and I got her to phone them back, give the cover story, and, arrange for work to be done, prioritising it all as best she could. I checked our bank accounts: nothing had been paid into the Argyle Street account for over a week, but that wasn't sinister – Argyle Street was legitimate.

After about two hours, with Grosvenor there all the time except when he used our toilet, I had covered all the outstanding legitimate enquiries, scheduling and re-scheduling weeks of work. On that level, things looked good. The business was still afloat, and our clients were still out there, speaking to us.

I phoned Argyle Street. 'Bytes and Digits. Ben speaking.' The voice was hesitant.

'Hi, Frank,' I said. 'It's Martin. Martin McGregor.'

His tone didn't change. 'Hi, Martin.'

I smiled. Ben – the one we used to call Frank II but had started calling Frank+1somewhere along the line – didn't react to someone who had vanished from his life and been out of touch for almost three weeks. 'Who else is there, Frank?'

'Just Frank and me,' Ben said.

'Who's manning reception?'

'No one. June left eight days ago.'

I closed my eyes. 'So who's been sending out invoices, banking cash, doing the books?'

There was a silence. 'June left eight days ago.'

'OK. Have you and Frank been doing work, Frank?'

'Yes.'

A pause. 'Right. Claire is going to send down a schedule of urgent jobs – forget everything else and get right on those. Understand?'

'Yes.'

I waited for a follow-up enquiry, but nothing came. 'Fine. I'll get over later, or tomorrow.' I hung up.

I called Claire through and told her to send the work schedule up to Argyle Street. Then I turned to Grosvenor.

'OK,' I said. 'That's all the legitimate enquiries dealt with for the moment.'

'Talkative guy, your Frank.'

'Hmm. Right, do you want me to try to contact the others side of the business?''

Grosvenor pulled his chair closer, his breath on the back of my neck. 'Let's go,' he murmured.

I switched on the PC and booted into our version of Linux, and logged on with my password. I typed 'strangle10' at the command line, and that program started up, giving no clues that anything was happening at all until it put up two numbers, a nine-digit and a six-digit. On my phone, I sent a text to the contact called Straiton containing those numbers. This should allow whoever it was to access the identified bank account, and transfer whatever money was there to the other accounts, including mine. This was all normal procedure, and it seemed to work.

Now I typed Woz84. Again there was just a long pause while the program went out to somewhere on the Internet. Nothing happened: I just got the command line prompt back again. I stared at it and swallowed.

'OK?' asked Grosvenor.

'No,' I said. 'I should have got some IP addresses. These would be ones Gregorius wanted to keep contact with. The fees for them would go into that bank account, and dispersed from there – I don't know how that works. '

'What would you do with the IP addresses?'

'I'd leave the admin passwords for them alone and change the others that we'd previously given access to him for.'

'Locking Gregorius out of them.'

'Yes.'

'But he'd already have installed malware in them.'

'Yes, he just no longer needs to harvest other details. If people change their passwords then they'll be safe. More or less. And if it's a business computer, then it won't grab details of new customers.'

'Pretty neat.'

'I suppose so.'

'But it's not working today.'

‘No. They’ll probably be suspicious about the three-week gap in contact.’

I typed Gregory on the PC, and got a ten-digit number back from somebody somewhere, and a question-mark prompt. The number was *not* divisible by nine. I gulped.

‘What does that do?’

‘If it’s divisible by nine then the whole setup is safe. This number isn’t.’

‘Yeah, I can do the math.’ He sat back. ‘What now?’

‘Emergency contact,’ I said. ‘I’ve only had to do that before going on holiday.’ Like Portugal and Romania. But always in advance and never after a failed attempt to make normal contact. This was all going to look very suspicious to those people at the other end of the line.

‘So what does that entail?’

I started the graphical interface on the PC, and clicked on Skype. The phonebook there had two entries: Strangle10 and Woz84. I clicked on Strangle10, choosing a voice call. Even so, Grosvenor shifted his chair to the side, well away from the webcam’s line of sight. The call went unanswered. I tried Woz84.

‘Hello, Colin.’

‘Hi,’ I said. I swallowed. ‘I’m sorry I’ve been out of contact for a few weeks: unexpected holiday – couldn’t let you know.’

There was a short silence. ‘Where were you?’

‘Ah – Orkney.’

‘Interesting.’

I swallowed and shared a glance with Grosvenor. 'What do you mean?'

'We understand you've been in Spain. For four years.' I could make out more of the voice now: a foreign accent, East European I thought.

Oh fuck. 'Ah. I should maybe have mentioned that to you. Colin retired and I took over. My name's Martin McGregor.'

'Martin McGregor. Who are you, Martin McGregor?'

'I worked with Colin. I took over when he left.'

'You explained nothing of this.'

'I thought there was no need. Nothing changed, did it?'

There was a pause. 'But something change now, Martin McGregor. What has been happening?'

'Nothing. Nothing at all. Honestly.'

'No police activity?'

'No.' Shit, I should have said yes and explained.

We could hear a whispered conversation at the other end, and then the sound of a phone dialling. 'Hi…' and the person turned off the microphone.

Grosvenor and I looked at each other. I raised my eyebrows, but he shook his head. We waited.

Then the voice was back. 'Goodbye, Mr Martin McGregor. For now.'

'Hang on a minute. There's no problem. Yes, the police were here but…'

The reply was garbled, unintelligible – bandwith problems?

Claire appeared at the door. 'Internet's down,' she said. 'I can't get anything done.'

'Oh fuck,' I said.

Grosvenor stood up, pulling out his mobile and dialling. 'Hi, Steve. Where are you? … It's urgent now, we have a problem. The plan hasn't worked, and I think we're currently undergoing a DDoS attack. What should we do? … OK, I'll tell him – get here soon as you can.'

I went back to my Mac, opened the terminal and typed DDoS-catcher, and sat back. The screen exploded with text and symbols and angled brackets, scrolling up fast. I switched off the PC and pulled out the USB stick.

Claire was still there, waiting for a response from me. 'Someone's started a distributed denial of service attack, a DDoS. It's flooding our servers with requests, so fast that nothing works – it can't deal with it. I'm going to let it happen for a while, ride it out. Then we'll re-boot everything.' I turned to Grosvenor. 'I'm letting the attack happen, trying to capture any details from the computers doing it. I know they'll all be hijacked as part of a botnet, but maybe we can get something.'

'Steve will be here in an hour – you're doing what he suggested.'

I stood up, unsettled, edgy, and started pacing the room, glancing back at the screen and the scrolling text, with some IP addresses appearing amongst it all.

Grosvenor had said 'the plan hasn't worked' on his mobile. That would be the plan to put me back in touch with the dark network out there. And if that wasn't going to work, then he didn't need me. And if he didn't need me, then he might choose to just take me to jail as an example, along with the other hackers that the US had ruthlessly prosecuted over the years.

'Let's leave it till Steve gets here,' he said to me.

'We're fucked,' I said again, rubbing my face with my hands, raising my eyebrows at Claire's look of concern: she was still standing, watching us. What I meant was: 'I'm fucked.'

'Not yet,' Grosvenor said. 'Steve is good – no offence, Martin, but you're a self-taught amateur. Steve is a pro. He's worked with the NSA – he knows how computer attacks work. He's fended them off many times on behalf of the homeland.' He checked his watch. 'I suggest we let Claire here get home – come back in tomorrow morning. OK? We'll wait for Steve.'

I nodded to Claire. 'Yes – good idea. We'll be up and running tomorrow.' My voice didn't sound convincing, and she didn't look convinced, but she tried a smile, and switched off her computer – not bothering to try to shut it down properly – and let herself out after a quiet: 'I'll be in around eight thirty'.

I looked again at the text scrolling up my screen, and turned away in anger. Strangely, Grosvenor's words had cut me: yes, I was an amateur – I had no qualifications, no proper education; I was the lucky amateur who had stumbled into this through a series of circumstances. I'd maybe always been out of my depth, but Jesus, I really was now.

I went through to sit on Claire's chair, and slumped back as much as I could, with my feet up on her desk. Within moments, I was asleep.

*

I dreamed of Orkney and the evening with Nicola – except that she was really Fiona, and she was in my bed. I made love to her over and over; she left the room, closing the door loudly behind her and speaking through it in an American accent, and then came back into the room: 'Martin… Martin…' I could feel her breath on my cheeks and I reached for her, falling towards her. 'Martin. Hey, Martin – careful,' she said in a deep American voice.

I opened my eyes and saw the office sliding sideways and the floor coming up to me, strong arms catching me. I blinked away sleep and stood up, helped by Grosvenor.

'Hey, you were gone there, son.' He pulled me to my feet.

I swayed and then managed to get my balance back and stand up unaided. I rubbed my eyes, and yawned. It took me a minute to remember where I was, what had been happening. I closed my eyes briefly, wanting to go back to my dream.

'What's happening?'

'Steve is at your computer, working. Come on through.'

I walked stiffly, my body sore and my left leg almost dead below the knee from where it had rested on the edge of the desk.

'Steve, this is Martin. Martin – Steve.'

I reached to shake his hand, but he gave me only the briefest of glances as he to scrolled and clicked on a laptop open by the Mac; an Ethernet cable ran from it down under my desk, a USB stick was plugged in, its LED flashing. This guy was like the American cousin of the Franks and Davey, separated at birth. He was skinny, wearing a faded corduroy jacket and old jeans, with a dark polo shirt underneath. His hair was black and wild, like he cut it himself. His face was gaunt, a short badly-trimmed beard hiding most of his pale skin, lit by the LED screen.

'Good program, Martin,' he said, with a soft accent that I reckoned was from the deep south.

'Can you do something with it?' Grosvenor asked.

Steve didn't reply for a minute, so Grosvenor repeated the question.

'Think so. Yes, indeed.' He suddenly sat upright and started typing.

I looked at his screen. He had two terminal windows open. One looked like it was doing what my program on the Mac was – capturing everything from the DDOS attack. On the other he was typing commands.

'You know what he's doin'?' Grosvenor asked me.

I shrugged. 'A DDoS overwhelms the server with requests from dozens or hundreds of computers that have been hijacked as part of a botnet – probably ones we effectively sold to Gregorius. The standard response is either to go offline and then try to restart, or to heavily filter traffic – even block it all together.'

Steve bobbed his head. 'Blackholing,' he murmured.

'But Steve isn't doing that. He seems to be letting the attacks carry on but try to capture the IP addresses of the computers – which is what my program did too. That way he may be able to do a reverse attack. I guess governments do this kind of thing when they are under attack.'

Steve glanced up at me with a smile, then concentrated again on the screen. Finally he sat back, still looking at the scrolling white text on my Mac and his laptop.

After a few minutes I said: How long will it take?'

He looked up at me and shrugged. 'Couple of days.'

'Oh shit,' I said.

Grosvenor gestured with his head, and we went through to the outer office. He made another jug of coffee, but I declined: I really needed a beer, and some proper sleep.

'What do we do now?' I asked. 'And what do we do afterwards?'

'What do you mean?'

'My contact with the dark network has been cut off. Even when Steve sorts the DDoS out, I'll still have nothing.'

Grosvenor nodded. 'How about Charlene?' he asked. 'Can we find her? She might be involved in this.' He drank coffee in silence, standing by the window, looking out. 'Any ideas?' he asked.

I closed my eyes, trying to think, but nothing came. 'No.'

Steve came through and helped himself to coffee; he had very long legs which made him surprisingly tall, though he walked with a stoop. He didn't look at either of us, or say anything, and then went back to my computer. Through the door I saw him staring at the screen, gulping his coffee.

Grosvenor took out his mobile, stared at it, then put it away again and drank his coffee, gazing out at the wet afternoon.

I slumped on Claire's chair and closed my eyes again.

'Hey,' Grosvenor said. 'Might as well get you home for a proper night's sleep, and I'll find my hotel.'

'Have you found somewhere?' I couldn't recall him organising anything.

'Booked it three days ago,' he said, and smiled at me through that big white beard.

I nodded glumly. 'How about Steve?'

'I think it would be good if he stayed with you for a couple of nights – it's an intrusion, I know, but it'll get you two talking about what B&D did, let him tune in, give him ideas.'

I looked through to Steve, and thought back to my time sharing a flat with Davey. 'OK,' I sighed.

*

We had a meal in an Italian restaurant just off Byres Road. Grosvenor and I ate hungrily, but Steve picked at his seafood spaghetti dish, reading his iPad beside his plate, occasionally wiping a dollop of sauce from the screen. Grosvenor and I split a bottle of Rioja; Steve drank a Peroni. We were all tired, and the restaurant was busy, so we couldn't really talk about the reasons we had come together, and weren't inclined to small talk either.

'You got a GPS tracker app on your phone?' Grosvenor suddenly asked.

I shook my head. He asked me to download one, and then we set up permissions to track each other's phone.

'Why am I doing this?' I asked him.

'Just in case.'

We checked it was working.

'You're in a restaurant just off Byres Road, Glasgow,' he said.

I nodded. 'Hey. Well done. So are you. Isn't technology wonderful.'

We both looked at Steve, gulping Peroni and swiping his iPad, and we shook our heads.

Afterwards, Grosvenor grabbed a taxi to his hotel in town, agreeing to meet at St Vincent Street at around nine the next morning, and Steve and I traipsed across to my flat.

Inside, I showed him the spare room – the sheets would be clean, but probably could have done with being aired – and grabbed a couple of beers from the fridge and offered one to Steve; he declined, so I put it back and went through to the lounge, slumping on the couch with the TV on, trying to let my body and mind to relax. My PVR had been religiously recording the crime programmes I liked, so I started playing an episode of CSI, feeling my eyelids droop.

Steve came in with a thin laptop open on his arm – he'd left his other one at my office, connected to the network – and he sniffed the air and frowned. I sniffed too, but couldn't detect anything other that pretty stale air.

'Wi-Fi?' he asked.

'Code's by the router,' I said, nodding to the corner.

He frowned more, and went over to key in the wireless key code from the sticker by the router, and sat down on the chair opposite me, typing on his machine. My eyes dropped again.

I jerked awake when he jumped up and went to the window again. 'Neighbours?' he asked.

I nodded, baffled. 'Yes, I have neighbours.'

'All flats occupied?'

'Yes – as far as I know.'

He scanned the street for a minute, and then sat down again, put a USB stick into his laptop, and started typing.

I sniffed the air again, but still could detect nothing.

'What's the matter?'

'Have you used your computer since you got back?'

'No.'

'Someone's monitoring your Wi-Fi. A woman.'

I stared at him. 'How the hell do you know that?'

'Perfume – not yours.' He sniffed again. 'Broke in, read the code.'

'Shit. How do you know about the monitoring?'

'Not passive - there's someone probing.' He frowned at his screen. 'Shoot,' he said, and leapt to his feet and went over to pull out the leads from the box on the wall that connected me to the Internet, and stood up. 'Need to change the router password. Change the channel too.' He stood at the window again, looking out.

I joined him at the window, not perfectly sure what we were looking for, but guessing that the eavesdropper was in a car out in the street, though I supposed they might have broken into a neighbour's flat. The street, as ever in this part of Glasgow, was lined on both sides with parked cars, nose to tail; I had no idea how these people got parked or how they got back out again. At this time of evening most cars were there for the duration.

'Dark VW Rabbit,' he said.

I looked down and saw the Golf he meant. 'What about it?'

'It was parked six cars down earlier on.'

'So? They may have gone out and then come back.' But I doubted that myself – not at this time of evening: when you went out, you went out till late.

He pressed his face to the glass, cupping his hands around his eyes. 'Someone in the car.'

This was flimsy – a product of Steve's over-deductive brain – and I wasn't paranoid enough to phone Amanda Pitt. 'I'll go down,' I said. 'You fix the router. Admin password is Fiona#01 – capital F.'

He immediately plugged an Ethernet cable into the router, and I went out of the flat and down to the street, pausing at the bottom of the main steps.

I casually looked up and down the street like I was expecting someone, and stepped into the road, still scanning but taking a few steps towards the Golf, trying not to stare at it.

A car engine started up, and now I could look: it was the Golf. I got an impression of a big man behind the wheel as the car went back and forth, edging itself out from the cars hedging it in. Back and forth.

I continued my pretence of scanning the street, and pulled out my mobile and pretended to talk to someone.

The Golf was now free, and I stepped out of its way as it accelerated hard up the street. I got the number, and noted what I could of the driver behind the raindrop-covered windows: a tall man hunched over the wheel, short dark hair –really nothing else beyond that impression. But I had the registration, safe in my phone, and I was sure Steve had been right.

I ran back upstairs. 'Has the monitoring stopped?' I asked.

He typed at his laptop. ‘Can’t tell yet.’

I phoned Amanda Pitt. She answered after many rings, with a sleepy, exasperated voice. ‘Yes, Martin.’

‘Sorry to disturb you, but there was someone eavesdropping on my Wi-Fi. They’ve been in my flat. They were outside in a car – I’ve got the number.’

I heard her yawn and cover the mic and murmur something to someone who was with her, and there was a distant – sexy – female chuckle from someone else. ‘OK, I’ll get it traced. What is it?’

I read it out.

‘I’ll get back to you when I know something.’ And she hung up.

Steve was reconnecting the router and restarting it, and he typed and watched his laptop. Finally he nodded.

‘Are we OK now?’

He nodded. ‘Pretty sure.’ He began typing furiously again.

I phoned Grosvenor and told him about the eavesdropping.

‘Interesting,’ he said. ‘I’m sure this is Charlene. Gregorius would be confident that the DDoS would knock you out.’

‘So what can we do?’

‘My guess is she’s on her way to Glasgow – maybe to try to salvage some of her grandfather’s business, maybe talk to him. She took two hundred British pounds out of an ATM in Dumfries an hour ago. She might easily have had someone local ready to do the surveillance when you resurfaced.’

‘Should I be worried?’ I thought of the dead bodies that followed Charlene around. OK, I still didn’t believe she actually killed anyone, but there was too much of a correlation between her and dead people.

He laughed. 'Relax, Martin. You're safe.'

I hung up, not believing him for a minute, for all sorts of reasons. He wanted the big international men driving the major cybercrime, and he didn't care about me. Amanda and the Scottish police wanted to finish off Talbot's empire and get him in jail before he died, so they didn't really care about me either. Charlene was someone who looked after herself.

I was alone on this.

I finished my beer and went to bed, leaving Steve pale and wide-eyed in the darkening evening, staring into his laptop, typing, scrolling and clicking.

Chapter 29

Glasgow

Amanda Pitt heard the buzzing of her mobile and slipped naked out of bed, padding softly through to her lounge and retrieving the phone from under Claire's green top. She sat on the sofa.

'Yes?' Her voice was soft. She still couldn't believe how the evening had worked out. Normally it took days or weeks of patient seduction, and Claire was massively heterosexual and engaged. But the phone call had come early in the evening – 'Can I ask about what's been going on? Martin and that American haven't told me the whole story, have they?' – and they'd met for dinner and talked, got on famously, discussed the events around B&D and Talbot and Sandy Lomond, and then about Claire's controlling fiancée and her deep underlying unhappiness with the relationship.

And now Claire was in her bed, sound asleep with a mass of red hair on the pillow, and Amanda just felt so… satisfied.

So the voice on the phone wasn't welcome: 'What's been happening?'

Amanda shivered and pulled Claire's discarded top across her lap. 'The FBI are here, and they're trying to get Martin to get everything up and running again. They're in control, and they know everything that's been going on – Martin told them everything. I don't know what they're doing exactly – I just know it's proving difficult for them. I don't know what they plan to do with Martin afterwards. I suppose you know he found out you were eavesdropping on your Wi-Fi. I'm supposed to be tracing a VW Golf.'

'Oh dear, that's awkward.'

'Yeah, look – I suggest you just go away and hide somewhere. It's not working out for you here, and I can't protect you. The FBI guy is smart; he might suspect me.'

The voice was more seductive. 'Don't you miss me?'

Amanda reflected on that for a moment. 'I've moved on – I had no choice.'

'We had some good times.'

'Tell me about Romania and what you did with Martin McGregor. Tell me about the dead people, Rose. Or Charlene, or Charlie.'

There was a laugh. 'Oh, I see. That was all just business. I didn't hurt anyone.'

'Did you sleep with Martin to get him to do what you wanted?'

The laugh came again. 'I didn't have to. And I seem to recall you very much enjoyed what we did together. What's happening with Ken Talbot now?'

'We're sweeping it all up best we can. But they know exactly who you are now.' Amanda shook herself and sat upright. 'Look, I have someone here. I have to go. All I can do is advise you to stay away – it's too dangerous. For both of us.' And she killed the call and flicked on the do not disturb setting, and went back to the bedroom.

Claire flinched as the cool body enveloped itself round her. She murmured something sleepily, and Amanda shushed her and held her tight. It took her an hour to get back to sleep.

*

Needless to say, I slept very badly. Steve woke me around two am: 'No toilet paper.' I told him where the spare rolls were, and tried to get back to sleep. When I did sleep, I was repeatedly haunted by a very attractive, naked blonde woman who seductively came up to me and then did an alien-style attack on my throat; I woke up sweating every time that happened. Sometimes, for variety, she knelt before me and then tore off my penis with her huge teeth. Sometimes it blended with that night in Romania, and it was Rodica undressing and attacking me.

I woke at seven, feeling more shattered and hungover than I had the day before. Steve was lying on his bed, still dressed, his laptop beside him, his mouth wide open, snoring, as I passed the spare room on my way to the bathroom.

The shower and then breakfast revived me. Steve yawned his way past me and opened all the cupboards till he found the cereal and a bowl. He poured himself some, added milk, found the cutlery drawer, and went through to the lounge, shovelling spoonfuls into his mouth.

I made instant coffee – Steve declined when I showed him the jar – and he went off to shower, though it looked like he put the same shirt back on afterwards.

We headed out into the cool, dry morning – a classic autumn feel in the air. I took him over to a café to get a couple of proper coffees to take with us, and we caught a passing taxi into town.

I texted Nicola: 'You OK to talk?'

She texted back immediately: 'Just leaving the hotel for my last appointment. Getting the afternoon flight back to Edinburgh. I'll call you when I get home. Can we meet at the weekend?'

'Hope so. Speak later.'

I smiled inside: something positive to look forward, something to counter the mess I was in.

Claire was at her desk with a cup of coffee, wearing the same clothes as yesterday; she looked happier this morning, almost radiant. Her computer was still off, though she'd started up the switchboard. Grosvenor was in my office, holding a cup of coffee and staring at the scrolling white text in the two windows on the monitor. Steve gently eased him aside and sat down on the chair.

'Any idea how long now?' Grosvenor asked, his voice sounding deeper and rougher this morning.

Steve gave a slight shake of his head. He set up his other, thin laptop with a 4G-modem stick, and started typing, still half-watching the Mac and his other laptop as the brackets and the alphanumerics shot up the screen.

Grosvenor and I went back to Claire's office. She had plugged a landline into the phone socket now, bypassing the mini exchange, and was answering calls now, fielding enquiries.

'Not much we can do,' I said. He nodded.

I helped Claire with the enquiries, and sent an updated list of jobs to do along to Argyle Street. But mainly nothing happened. Nothing at all.

By eleven o'clock we were seriously bored. I checked the Internet on my phone, and we talked about maybe getting something for lunch later – 'Yesterday's sandwiches were good.'

Amanda Pitt still hadn't shown, and then we discovered why. The BBC Scotland twitter feed had the breaking story of a man being shot dead in a supermarket car park, and vague references to his being a local businessman but also a 'prominent figure in the Glasgow underworld'. I phoned Amanda.

'I'm busy, Martin,' she said, the wind crackling across the microphone of her phone, loud voices all around her.

'I saw the news.'

'And?'

'Who is it?'

I heard her moving, and then her voice was quieter. 'Ken Talbot. His driver took him out to Tesco. A car pulled up behind them, a guy got out with a handgun and fired everything into Talbot's car – killed him and the driver.'

'Jesus. Obviously couldn't wait till he died naturally'

'Soft target – someone making a point, starting the takeover. We're expecting mayhem over the next few days. I'll be tied up completely with this for a while: we need everyone on this.'

'Right. Did you trace the number of that Golf that was outside my flat?'

'Eh – no. Haven't had time. Look, I have to go.'

'What about the ownership of B&D, with Talbot dead?'

'I suppose lawyers will make a lot of money deciding that over the next few years. Got to go,' and she hung up.

I looked at the mobile, and wondered about the legacy of Talbot's empire – his legitimate empire. How much did I really own? And if Charlene was his granddaughter, how much could she grab? And I thought about Talbot's dying…

*

The black BMW turned into the parking bay at Tesco's, and the driver switched off the engine. He half-turned to speak to Ken Talbot – a final check on the shopping list – when they both heard a car braking and stopping at the back of them, its engine still running fast.

A scrawny man wearing a long-sleeved T-shirt and jeans, his face ravaged and angry, his hair cut back to the scalp, was at the window by Talbot. Talbot pushed the button to lower the window, and he looked up at the man. Heroin, he thought; wired to the moon, after some money. He reached into his jacket.

The man had one badly withered arm, the result of a severe beating some years before in a computer shop that had caused multiple fractures which had never healed properly. In his good arm, he held a handgun, which he raised. It shook as he pointed it at Talbot.

'Look, son,' Talbot said, calm, unafraid, resigned. 'You're wasting your time. I'll be dead in a couple of months.'

'Nah,' came the reply, strangled by adrenalin and a set of rotten teeth. 'You're fuckin' deid now ya cunt.'

And the gun began to fire till Talbot was slumped and dead, and then turned to fire into the head of the driver as he tried to duck away and cover himself. A minute later and the other car was racing out of the supermarket car park, while people nearby looked up, mystified at the noise, unable to make sense of the sounds. Until someone went over to look at the car, and called the police – and then took some photographs on his phone.

*

Grosvenor was helping himself to more coffee – I noticed he'd brought in new stuff, and was keeping it in the small fridge we had. I joined him, got one for Claire, and explained what had happened.

'Did you know him well?' Claire asked, when I told her about Talbot.

I shook my head. 'He got us started in B&D, me and Davey, but he was just interested in using the company for laundering money. I never had dealings with him; just Sandy.'

'Actually,' Claire said, 'I don't know much of the story. It was only ever Colin and Sandy I worked for, and he said nothing about Ken Talbot,'

So I explained about my gradual awareness of what was really going on with the companies, the leaking of customer details to some 'people' out there – I was vague about it all. And I explained about my moral dilemma: I had earned a lot of money, but much of which was not rightly mine. I didn't mention what I had managed to park in Gibraltar.

I suddenly noticed Claire wasn't wearing her engagement ring. I was about to ask, when she realised I'd spotted it. She gave a quick shake of her head, and then the phone rang and she answered it.

I looked at my watch. ‘Will Charlene be in Glasgow now?’

‘Undoubtedly. We have to wait till she does something,’ Grosvenor said.

I looked at my phone, scrolling through it, and suddenly realising. ‘I’ve got her mobile number,’ I blurted out.

‘How the hell did you get that?’

‘In Romania – she gave it to me.’

Grosvenor thought for a minute. ‘Call her cell now. Speakerphone. Through here.’

We went into Sandy’s old office – stripped of files, drawers empty, his computer sitting dead on his desk.

I dialled. It rang out and went to voicemail. Unsure, I said: ‘Call me when you can. We need to talk.’ And hung up.

Grosvenor frowned at me. ‘You watch a lot of cop movies?’

My mobile rang a moment later: it was Charlene. ‘Hello, Martin. How are you?’ I recognised that slight Welsh accent. Her voice was confident, calm.

‘I’m fine. Can we meet up and chat about how things are going?’

‘Good idea, Martin. How long will it take you to get down to Wales?’

‘Ages. But it won’t take long to get to your hotel in Glasgow.’

She gave a short laugh. ‘Who have you got there with you, Martin?’

'Just a couple of guys. You heard about your grandfather? He was shot dead today, in a supermarket car park.'

There was silence for a time, and her voice was less cocky this time round. 'I think you're right, Martin. We need to talk. Why don't we have dinner this evening, at my hotel?'

'What time?' I was conscious Grosvenor was frowning hard.

'Six this evening? Meet in the bar.'

'Where are you staying?'

'I'm in the Crowne Plaza. See you at six.'

'Looking forward to it.'

I hung up and turned to Grosvenor. 'Right – what do I say to her?' But he was already on his mobile.

'Hi, it's me. I need to check the guest list at the Crowne Plaza hotel, Glasgow, Scotland. I'm looking for a Charlene Anderson aka Charlene Talbot aka Charlie Talbot. Asap.'

He hung up and turned to me. 'You just talk to her, find out what you can about what she's up to. Try to see if you can persuade her that the situation she's in is hopeless, but we're willing to talk to her if she'll cooperate.'

Just like they did with me, I thought. 'Can't we get her arrested?'

'We have no evidence that she's done anything wrong, and I don't think that's necessarily the best approach. But it's a possible threat. Just meet her.'

'Will I tell her the FBI is involved? That might impress her.'

'I don't think she'll either believe you or act on that: she's not yet feeling as cornered as you were; she probably still thinks she can have a slice of Talbot's empire – she is his natural heir, after all. Save the FBI bit till later. How tough do you think she is?'

I thought back to that first sighting on the beach at Alvor: the pretty blonde with the pert breasts, who didn't speak at all, and so we assumed she was stupid, someone's trophy wife. Given her background, did she feel the world had cheated of her rightful inheritance – had she felt abandoned by her family, making her angry, deeply resentful – 'tough'? 'I don't know,' I said.

I was pacing the room, checking my watch. 'I need to do something,' I said. 'I'm going along to Argyle Street, see how the Franks are getting on. Do you want to come?'

He looked between me and my office, where Steve was still staring at his laptop and flicking back to my Mac and his other machine. He shook his head. 'I better stay here with Steve. You go – but get back here in good time to get over to Charlene. I'll try to find out what I can.' His mobile rang. 'Yeah? … OK … Can you check the rest of the hotels in and around Glasgow? … Yeah, I appreciate that, but I need to find her. It is important. … Good, thanks.' He put it away. 'She isn't registered at that hotel.'

'Fake ID?'

He shook his head. 'Don't know. We'll go ahead with the meeting. You head off, but get back here good and early.'

*

It was strange being back in the shop up at Finnieston, where it had all started – that promise of a hard-working but rewarding life, the lucky start that had turned out to be fatally flawed. All the disasters that had befallen us since.

As I walked in the door, I remembered seeing Charlie with his cock out in the drunken hope that it would prove irresistible to our secretary; the neds who'd tried to run a protection racket on a company owned by one of the biggest gangsters in the city, and who'd ended up in A&E as a result; the fun we'd had, working till all hours, Davey at his desk, totally focused; Sam with her black hair and clothes – which led me to remembering having sex with her. Where was she now? And poor Fiona – seeing her at the museum. Helen – who looked so like her. 'Never lie to me, Martin…' The doomed marriage to Elizabeth that Helen had rescued me from – then losing Helen. The night with Nicola in Kirkwall: the promise of a relationship. Charlie's death, Davey's horrific injuries.

All of it washed back and forth through my mind as I closed the door behind me and sensed the history of the place, everything me and Davey had done and achieved, all of it made frictionless by a gangster's money and intervention. Had I achieved anything in my life that was truly down to me? Could I ever right the wrongs? Were the disasters that had befallen me down to some balancing of the universe?

I looked around and felt myself go weak with the weight of all the memories and the baggage, tears welling in my eyes.

There was a cough. Ben was standing near me, looking at the floor. 'Hi, Martin,' he mumbled. He looked less thin these days, though his skin was still pale even by Glasgow standards.

'Hi, Frank,' I said. 'How are things?'

'Frank's out on a job. I'm working remotely on a system we repaired in June for a small independent record shop on Otago street; the owner is fifty six and has …'

I managed to stop him with several waves of my hand. 'But no one on the front desk, no one handling invoices. What happened to June?'

'She left nine days ago.'

'Yes, but did she say why?'

'Said this place was too weird.' He flapped his arms.

'OK. You go back to work.'

He went through to the back of the open-plan workshop, where I could remember Davey clearly, hunched over open computers, wrestling with their innards, plugging tiny connectors into circuit boards.

I spent an hour there. The till was stuffed with cash and mysterious IOU notes; I counted and took the bank notes but left enough money for a float and also the IOUs, not feeling up to asking Ben for an explanation of their existence: he'd explain each and every one at length, and I'd be none the wiser.

I looked around the stock – graphics cards, processors, motherboards, cases, a few printers and monitors, hard drives, a small stock of ink cartridges, a few USB sticks and SD cards, assorted leads, keyboards and mice. We couldn't compete with the nearby PC World or Amazon for the mainstream stuff, though a few people would just do an impulse purchase when passing the door, so we carried specialised equipment that the enthusiasts would be interested it, because we could talk to them about it, genuinely help them decide what they really needed, and help them sort out their inevitable disasters. Ben said we didn't need anything right now.

'OK. Give me a call if anything happens.'

Outside, with the breeze picking up and chilling the air, I walked the short distance to Kraweski's pub, our old haunt. It was quiet – just a few students and some locals – so I bought a pint of IPA and a packet of crisps. I sat in one of the booths near the back of the pub and looked around, letting all the ghosts come back. All those nights sitting here with Davey, starting with the day we'd first seen the shop; here with Sam that night when she'd ended up in my bed; working all those hours, coming in knackered and getting quickly drunk on two pints because we were so tired; moving into our flat just up the road; living with Fiona in the flat, that all-too brief time, maybe the happiest of my life. More thoughts of Sam… and Elizabeth. Then Helen.

I finished my beer and wandered out into the street. I walked all the way along Argyle Street to where it crossed the M8 and morphed into St Vincent Street, my thoughts tumbling and surfacing in my head.

By the time I climbed the steps to the office, I felt something like resolve forming inside me. I'd get out of this, doing whatever it took, and I'd make a go of things with Nicola – no way back to Helen now. I'd keep in touch with Davey and Jane, and I'd keep in touch with mum and my step-dad. I'd get it all sorted, get some kind of life together.

*

'Keep your phone on, son – just in case,' had been Grosvenor's last words to me. 'Scottish police are tied up with the Talbot case; there's no backup for you.'

I walked down to the river, and then all the way along the path to the hotel, joggers and cyclists streaming past me, the cool evening breeze tugging at me, light rain falling now. I passed the angled road bridge known to Glaswegians as the 'squinty bridge', the huge Finnieston Crane which was a memorial to the vanished shipbuilding industry, the Hydro Arena overshadowing the Clyde Auditorium, BBC Scotland headquarters and the science centre across the river, a car – bizarrely – in the middle of the Bell Bridge, which I had thought was for pedestrians only. All of it completing the transformation that had its beginnings with our own, back in the day.

I pushed through the main door into the warmth of the hotel, and turned right, walking round the island bar. Just a few people there, reading Kindles or iPads, or talking on phones – sometimes all three. The barman looked at me expectantly, and I looked at my watch; I was five minutes early.

I ordered a pint of very expensive Czech lager and sat at a table near the window, where I could look out but also see anyone coming in from the front door or from reception. I drank my lager and waited, all the memories that the day had stirred up still washing back in forth in my mind.

I had spoken to Nicola earlier, just when I had begun to wonder whether she would call. She talked of her visit to Orkney, some creep trying to chat her up at dinner in the hotel – I winced at that – and the poor weather. I told here I was really tied up with business, but should manage through at the weekend. 'I hope so, Martin. I really want to see you again, for all sorts of reasons.' 'Me too.'

And now I was wondering how much I could tell her about my life, and how that would affect her. If we could sort out the computer problems, then I need hardly lie to her at all – might even tell her the truth. But if things didn't change…

My mobile rang, jerking me from my thoughts. It was Charlene. I swallowed and answered. 'Hi there.'

'Come up to my room,' she said, breathing heavily. 'I'm in 214.' And she hung up.

I stared at the phone, and then texted Grosvenor telling him where I would be. I gulped down the rest of my lager and burped across to the lifts, pressing the button till one came. As it rose quickly, I could see down the river, the way I'd walked earlier; I watched the cyclists and runners, the city dark under fading light and thickening clouds. I came out of the lift and then through the doors into the corridor – her door was opposite, beside the ice machine. I knocked, wondering just what might happen, what Charlene was really like, what motivated her.

The door opened, and she was there, still the young blonde with the pretty face and enigmatic gaze, and the neat figure in tight black lycra. Her face and hair were damp with sweat, and she was still breathing hard.

She showed me into the huge room and pointed me to the soft chair by one of the double beds. She stood by the desk and poured two gins-and-tonic, complete with ice, handing one to me. 'Sorry there's no lemon. Cheers.' She took a big swig, and I did the same. Then she took a bigger drink from a collapsible blue water bottle with MOMA written on the side. 'I need a shower. You watch TV.' She tossed the remote onto the bed beside me.

The bathroom door closed behind her and I heard the shower start up. I turned on the news and listened to various items about the English education system, and then a brief mention of a shooting in Glasgow of a man, and an interview with the BBC's Scotland correspondent, who said that a shooting was unusual even for Glasgow and that there were no clear details available but the man had been under investigation by the police. Then we were onto the state of the NHS in England.

The shower went off, and a few minutes later the door opened and Charlene came out, a big white towel wrapped round her – I saw the reflection in the wardrobe mirror first, and then the reality. She bent from the waist to delve into a drawer, retrieved what she wanted and went back into the bathroom, the reflection showing her unwrapping the towel as she back-heeled the door closed.

When she emerged again, she was wearing a short black dress with a broad white belt. She sat at the desk, took a sip of her gin-and-tonic and a big gulp of water, and began drying her hair.

I sat with my drink, watching her. Was she really trying to seduce me, I wondered, or simply wanting me to desire her? Or was she really just innocent of her attraction?

The Scottish news came on, leading with the story of Ken Talbot's murder, pictures of his car in the Tesco car park, its windows shattered. The reporter looked serious; there was an interview with a chief inspector, pictures of a forensic team working round the car, policemen walking slowly in a line looking at the ground. Charlene's hairdryer drowned out any words; she didn't so much as glance at the screen.

She finished with her hair, put on some moisturiser, eye makeup and lipstick, a white plastic watch and pearl earrings, little white shoes, and stood up. She drank the rest of her gin-and-tonic, and I finished mine and stood up too. She leaned to switch off the TV.

We walked to the lift in silence, and down to reception and along to the restaurant area; she gave her room number – 'Good evening, Miss Brown,' the woman said – and we were taken to a table in the far corner by the angled window, below the mural depicting the heyday of a shipping industry now gone. We sat down with the menus.

'Any drinks to start with?' the waitress asked.

'Two gin-and-tonics,' Charlene said, without looking at her. 'Tanqueray. Doubles. Diet tonic.'

'Certainly.'

We read the menus, and I realised that I was not in the slightest bit hungry. I was nervous of Charlene – unsure of what was going on.

Our gins came, and we ordered food – just a main course: chicken for her, salmon for me – and she ordered a bottle of red wine: a Chilean merlot. We sat and looked at each other, sipping our gins, and I looked at her impassive face, just the way it had looked when I'd first seen her in Alvor.

The waiter brought the wine and showed Charlene the label, but poured some for me to taste. Charlene reached for my glass, sniffed the wine and rolled it round the glass, then sipped it and nodded. 'That's fine.' She gave me the glass back. The waiter, embarrassed, filled our glasses and set the bottle down.

'Can we have a jug of tap-water too?' Charlene asked.

'Certainly, madam.'

'Cheers,' I said. We paused on our gins and chinked wine glasses.

The restaurant was quite busy, but there was no one close by. Once our food arrived, and then the follow-up visit to confirm it was fine, I felt able to talk – but I didn't know what to say.

'What will you do now Talbot's dead?' I finally blurted out.

She flicked her eyes over me. 'Who have you got working with you, Martin?'

'Just a couple of guys.'

She nodded, sipping her wine as she held the glass cupped in her right hand. 'We could work together,' she finally offered.

'Yes we could, but I'd need to know a lot more about just what the fuck has been going on for the last year or so.' I hadn't meant to let any anger show, but I couldn't help it.

'What brought you back to Glasgow?' she asked.

'They found me. I tried to run, but they knew where I was all the way. So I let them bring me back here. No choice.'

'Where were you hiding?'

'Orkney.'

She raised her eyebrows at that.

'I did a bit of a detour round Spain and the rest of the UK, but I thought Orkney would be the last place they'd think of.'

'So you're back in B&D, trying to make contact with your network. Who have you got working with you?'

I wondered how much to say to her, how honest to be. 'I'm helping the authorities. To track down the online criminals out there.' I gave a shrug. 'I have no choice,' I said again.

Her face was impassive. We ate our meal for a few more minutes.

'So,' I said, 'what really happened in Portugal?'

She shrugged. 'Just what you saw and what I told you. The guy was killed by his former partners when some of their funds disappeared. Nothing to do with me – I was as shocked as you were.'

'But you arranged for that photograph to be taken and then you sent it to Helen.'

She nodded, no apology on her face.

'How did you get involved with that situation?'

A sip of wine and a calm gaze. 'I needed funding. I wanted that guy alive so I could keep getting funding.'

'And what about Romania? What happened there? What did you do? Was that funding as well?'

She finished her meal and eased the plate aside, then topped up our wine glasses with a steady hand. I couldn't eat any more. The waitress materialised, and we assured her that everything had been fine and we didn't want any dessert or coffee. Charlene indicated the near-empty wine bottle – 'Certainly, madam.'

Charlene pursed her lips. 'Romania got complicated. It started off with me wanting to get into the East European carders' society – the UK scene was too crowded, no one needed another partner. So Sandy helped me out with contacts – Gheorghe, who was a major player in the Russian criminal scene and was setting up an online operation using some Romanians he had recruited, in a genuine small computer company – just like B&D. It all started just the way you saw it: you were there to help train the group, and it all went swimmingly at first.'

'Till I was date-raped and three people were murdered.'

The waitress arrived with the fresh bottle, catching the end of my sentence; she checked the label with Charlene and opened the bottle, and Charlene took it from her and waved her away.

'None of that was anything to do with me.'

'You were around, you must have known something like that might happen. You knew what Gheorghe was like.'

'I was looking out for you, Martin – honestly.' She took a deep breath, and I could almost see the internal struggle. When she spoke, I wondered whether she was about to be honest or to lie. 'My guess is that it was set up to look like Tudor raped and murdered Coralia and then killed himself.' Her voice was a low whisper. 'But either Gheorghe himself did it, or he had help from one of his thugs. He lusted after Coralia in a big way – I'm pretty sure he would have wanted to be there when she was stripped and assaulted. I'm sure they would find his DNA all over her. But he hasn't told me directly, and I don't expect him to.' She swallowed, and looked me in the eye. 'I thought they were probably planning to frame you for something too, to do with Rodica – her murder. That's why I had to get you out. And I was right. She was expendable to these people – she was just a sex worker, not important to them. Photographing you having sex with her would be part of the frame-up. When you left the country *before* she was killed, well… I think they sent the photographs to your girlfriend out of spite – revenge.' She gave a shrug.

I looked hard at Charlene. Maybe she was being honest now. Maybe. OK, so she had got me out – but she'd also got me in.

She topped up our wine from the new bottle. I realised that she had told me she was still in contact with Gheorghe: that was interesting – but what would their relationship be, since she had virtually double-crossed him? I was starting to feel quite drunk, my brain trying to cope with everything I was being told, trying to work out what I *wasn't* being told; however, she didn't seem to be suffering any effects at all from the gins and the wine.

'So,' she went on. 'That's what happened. You never properly thanked me for rescuing you.'

I raised my eyebrows.

'Now, Martin. Your turn. Who is working with you?'

I ignored her question. 'With Talbot dead, do you have a legitimate claim on his estate – assuming the police don't manage to confiscate the whole shebang?'

'We'll see.'

'I take it some of shareholdings and companies are really in your name, and not Charlie's.'

'Some.'

'I knew your dad,' I said. 'I don't suppose you ever did.'

She shook her head. 'He was only my biological father.'

'Are you in touch with your real mother?'

'No.'

'When did you find out about Charlie?'

She was gripping her glass firmly, and her jaw was taut as she spoke: 'Five years ago, when I was told I had been adopted – when I noticed I was nothing physically like my parents or my brother. Then I did my research.'

'And got in touch with Ken Talbot.'

'I visited him at his home – thought he'd be delighted to see his granddaughter, especially since his son was dead. Turned out to be totally wrong. But he passed me on to Sandy, to get some kind of financial settlement worked out. I told him I didn't want to be bought off, so we made a deal: he used me – 'Charlie Talbot' – as a named shareholder in various companies that they were using for money laundering – you know the kind of thing they did. I went away for a while, happy with the arrangement: but then I realised I could get more, and I came back. He told me about the situation that you all had at B&D, and suggested that I could maybe set up the same kind of thing – but elsewhere. I went off to get some computing courses under my belt so I could understand more of what was going on, and set up a hairdressing business back home in Wales – cover. Met a few people in the field.'

I nodded. That all seemed logical and believable. 'Who was the guy with you in Alvor? Is he really your husband?'

She shook her head with a wry smile. 'Jimmy's just a guy: a bit of muscle.'

'While you play the dumb blonde.'

She looked at me with wide eyes. 'I find it helps to be underestimated and patronised. So,' she said yet again, 'who is working with you?'

'A couple of guys from the FBI.'

She nodded. 'Who are they?

I noted that she hadn't registered any surprise. 'Guy called Mark Grosvenor is in charge, and Steve Roberts is the computer expert. The Scottish police are around, but they're letting

Grosvenor and the FBI take charge of all the cybercrime aspects.'

'How did the FBI get onto all of this?'

'Grosvenor told me a bit about it. He says the dead guy in Portugal had credit card numbers on his computer – as you know. The Portuguese police were trying to investigate it all. But a couple of the numbers belonged to Americans, so the Portuguese got in touch with the FBI, who deal with such things. They investigated. Later on, when the Romanian thing happened, two names popped out as being in both places at the right time.' I pointed to myself and then her. 'So they contacted the Scottish police – DS Amanda Pitt – and sent Grosvenor over to find me and talk to me. And he brought Steve.'

And suddenly I could see she looked a little rattled, the calm enigmatic façade cracking for the very first time. There was a milder version of my reaction when Grosvenor had told me who he was.

'So,' I went on, 'you see my problem. Working with you would be difficult.'

She seemed to have nothing to say to that, holding the big wine glass in front of her face, focusing on it.

'But I guess that you could come in with us, with the FBI, help them get into the network. You must have useful information – your contacts with Eastern Europe.'

'Have you discussed this with them?'

'Not as such.'

We sat in silence for a few minutes, sipping our wine. I had a big drink of water too.

'How much money do you have, Martin – cash?'

'Loads actually, I suppose – plenty to be going on with. I could have managed, if I'd got away.'

She pursed her lips and nodded, a faraway look in her eye. 'I don't have much, beyond what I got from Portugal at the start, and what Sandy gave me. It's all tied up in the companies. I hoped to get more out of Ken Talbot, but… well, his accounts are all frozen now. I have to carry on, Martin. I don't have a choice.'

'Yes you do. You can work with the FBI.'

I looked at her, her new vulnerability making her almost attractive to me. Inside my trouser pocket my mobile phone vibrated; I ignored it.

She finished her wine and shook her head when I reached to refill it, so I filled my own glass. God, over a bottle of wine and a couple of large gins; last night's hangover was gone, but tomorrow's was building up. I had no idea what I was trying to do here: I needed to get home, talk to Grosvenor, and go and see Nicola and have a break from all of this. I'd thought I had Charlene worked out, but now I saw a young woman who was as trapped as I was.

'I need to go,' I said.

She nodded.

We stood up and walked by the desk at the entrance to the restaurant area, where Charlene stopped to sign the bill. I looked at her in the slim-fitting black dress, and thought of her emerging from the bathroom in the towel… and I took a deep breath said: 'I'll speak to Grosvenor. I'll phone you tomorrow.'

She didn't look up, and I walked away, out of the hotel into the cool wet evening.

I headed up past the SECC and across the covered footbridge over the expressway and the railway, making my way towards the west end via Finnieston, and phoned Grosvenor as I walked.

'How did it go?'

'She's registered under the surname Brown, room 214. She's still got working connections to the Romanians, but I think she would work with us if you and the police could give her some kind of immunity from prosecution, and income of course.'

'She said that?'

'Not as such. But she's cornered, she doesn't have much cash, everything she has is tied up in Talbot's companies. With him dead, she can't get at it. She's cornered,' I repeated.

'Mmm – I don't buy that, son. Where are you now?'

'Going home. I'm pissed and I need to sleep. How's Steve getting on?'

'No idea. He sits there with his laptop and grunts when I ask him. I'm bushed, so I'm going to chase him out and lock up. He'll come over to your place, I'll go to my hotel.'

'Anything from Amanda?'

'She's snowed under with the fallout from the Talbot killing. I'll maybe try her tomorrow.'

'OK. I'll come down in the morning.'

I hung up.

I passed the Kelvingrove museum, and found some more memories rising into my tired, drunken mind – the red wine was catching up with me. Then along Dumbarton Road and turning into Byres Road.

I saw a couple walking the other way through the dark night and the increasing rain, not holding hands or linking arms, but their bodies close together, eyes down as they spoke and laughed. As I passed them, I caught a glimpse of the woman's face and recognised the laugh and the voice: it was Helen.

I kept my head down and walked quickly by, hearing their continued conversation and laughter recede behind me. More memories, the past haunting me.

I turned into my road and along by the lines of parked cars, fumbling for my keys as I reached the steps up to the entrance of my close – desperate for a pee, and feeling full of the wine.

I heard the running steps, and half-tensed by instinct. I'd never been mugged before, but the possibility was always there in the back of my mind. Still, when the heavy weight of a body crashed into me, knocking me against the railings, I was surprised. I had an impression of a man in a hooded top, and then a fist hit my stomach hard, and I gave up the bottle of wine in a parabolic stream, some of it over him. He hit me again in the side of my head, and pulled me off my feet onto my knees on the wet, cold paving stones, and dragged me across to the kerb, one hand in my hair, the other on my arm. There was a rattling diesel engine nearby and a door opening. I tried to struggle, but any balance I'd had was lost as I came off the kerb and hit the bumper of a car and another pair of hands grabbed me. My shins hit the sill of the car door as I was dragged and pushed into the back of it, and the door hit my feet as it was slammed shut.

As we moved off, I tried to sit up was pushed flat again, my head and upper body behind the driver's seat and pressing against the legs of the man who held me.

I stopped trying to struggle. God, my body ached. I listened. The car was moving fast, turning corners, accelerating and braking. After a few minutes I had no idea where we were.

'What's going on?' I asked, my voice thinner and more scared than I'd meant it to be.

A hand cuffed me across the side of my head, and there were a few words in a language I didn't understand. A sense of terror settled in me.

Chapter 30

Glasgow

Mark Grosvenor climbed out of the taxi outside the Crowne Plaza hotel, paid the driver, and made his way through the smokers and into the bar area. He ordered himself a scotch and water, and took a seat while he steeled himself for what was to come, and thought through his plan, his pitch.

Upstairs in her room, Charlene sat in the chair between the bed and the window, looking out at the lights of the car park, the river, the science centre and its tower on the other side, the old paddle steamer tied up. She regretted the second bottle of wine: it made it hard to think. She crossed and uncrossed her legs, folded and unfolded her arms, stood up and paced the room then sat down again.

Her mobile rang. 'He's left,' she said, and listened. 'On his way home. Just do it'.

She dialled. 'What's the latest?'

She heard the sound of Amanda Pitt moving away from noise and discussion, whispering into the phone. 'I told you not to call me again.' Then an intake of breath. 'I've told you. It's out of my hands. I've no strategic command with the Talbot case any more, I can't do anything. All Talbot's business interests, including Charlie's, are frozen. If I'm not careful I could come under suspicion.'

'Have you any idea where Sandy Lomond is?'

'We think he might be in Spain somewhere, but he's lying low – no mobile activity. Look, I need to go. Sorry – I can't help any more. Please don't call me again.' And she disconnected the call.

Charlene sat motionless once more, continuing her scan of the skyline out of the hotel window, her thoughts unclear. Could she really handle Gheorghe on her own as a business partner, without Sandy behind her?

When the room phone rang, she jolted out of her thoughts and reached across the bed to answer it. 'Yes?'

The deep New York accent growled. 'I think you know who this is, Charlene. We need to talk. I'm coming up.'

She put the receiver down and stood up, waiting patiently for the knock at the door, again regretting the wine, and breathing deeply to try to push away the effects: god, she needed to be thinking clearly. She kept the chain on as she opened the door and looked at the face of the man with the white hair and the bushy white beard – not what she had expected. He held up his ID for her to see, and she nodded and opened the door.

'Drink?'

'Only if you're having one yourself. Scotch and water, thanks.'

'I've only got gin,' she said, splashing it into the glasses – a very large one for him, a very small one for herself – and adding tonic and the last of the rapidly melting ice from the machine outside her door. She went back to her seat with her glass and crossed her legs, looking at the American as she sipped her drink. He was old, limping, but there was an authority and intelligence about him, a presence, and something in her found all that attractive, which surprised her.

Grosvenor sat on the chair by the desk. ‘Cheers.’

‘Cheers.’

‘So, Charlene. How you doin’?’

‘I’m fine, thank you.’ She kept her voice controlled.

‘No you’re not. Your plan – though I confess I’m not perfectly sure what that plan was – is a bust. You need to re-group, Charlene. Re-think your strategy. I can help you.’

She forced a small laugh. ‘I don’t need your help.’

He looked at her and gave a moment’s pause. ‘I think you do, and you’d be wise to recognise that.’ They sipped their drinks, and then he turned to put his glass down on the desk, and pulled his chair closer to her, holding her gaze. ‘Tell me about those years, Charlene. When you found out about your real father and mother, when you discovered you were Ken Talbot’s legacy through his useless womanising son. How did it make you feel?’

She looked straight at him, her lips tight, her body tense, her hand gripping her glass.

‘Will I tell you what I think?’ He wheeled his chair back a bit, found his glass again, crossed his legs. ‘First of all you wanted a share of the money – you deserved it, didn’t you? Your adoptive parents didn’t have all that much, though they got by real fine. But you thought of what big money could give you. And Ken Talbot was happy to cough up, to get rid of you – he had no love for his son's bastard – probably didn't feel any obligation at all; you're likely one of many. But it wasn't enough, was it? Did you go to Sandy Lomond? Did you work your charms on him and get him to tell you more of how Talbot's operation worked, what B&D was really all about? Or was it somebody else in the company? Or someone else – ' he was examining her expression, searching for a clue – 'someone in the police maybe?' There it was: the tightening of the jaw, holding his gaze just a little too much. It didn't matter whom, so long as he knew – and suddenly his imagination made a leap as he remembered the long running police operation against organised crime in Glasgow and the key role held by Amanda Pitt: shoot, had she…

'So,' he went on, reigning in his imagination, 'you went back to the buffet. You managed to persuade Lomond that you could be the new Charlie Talbot, and that tickled him – did he even tell Ken Talbot? But straightforward protection and smuggling and prostitution and money laundering wasn't for you: you needed something more, something cleverer, something with an edge. And when you found out about the cybercrime at B&D, that appealed to you. You didn't have much knowledge and hardly any skills, but you could beguile almost any man.' He tried the long shot: 'Or woman,' and saw the jaw tightening again. 'So you put your good looks, your prefect figure, and that enigmatic expression to work. Lomond gave you some contacts and ideas, a bit of muscle for protection, and you started up on your own. But it didn't quite work out, did it? The guy in Portugal got murdered, thus depriving you of a flow of cash and intelligence.' He sipped some gin and waved the glass at her. 'You just join right on in any time you feel like it.'

She sipped her own drink, her body visibly tense, telling him he was right.

‘So you tried again – you found a guy, Gheorghe Angelescu, who had split from his Russian pals, was trying to set up a cybercrime network from Romania. Where did you get that from, Charlene? Did Sandy Lomond make contact for you?’

Charlene swallowed.

‘Both times, Portugal and Romania, you needed just a little bit of expert help, so Lomond sent you Martin McGregor. Poor Martin, always ending up in the wrong place at the wrong time.’ He saw Charlene glance at her watch. ‘I hope you don’t mean him any harm, Charlene.’

‘I’ve never meant to hurt Martin.’

‘What then?’

She shook her head and closed her eyes. ‘Look, I could see that Gheorghe was thinking about tidying everything up once he had what he wanted. He raped and murdered the translator, and then tried to make it look like Tudor had done it and then shot himself. He had always planned to kill the prostitute, putting suspicion on Martin – Gheorghe could buy off the police and do what he wanted with Martin after that. I got Martin out of Romania – don’t forget that.’

‘Was Martin immune to your charms, Charlene? Was that what made you pissed?’

‘Of course not. I manipulated him, like the rest.’ She pursed her lips, annoyed that he had made her say that.

Grosvenor gave a laugh. Once again he put down his glass and moved the chair towards her, leaning forward, elbows on his knees, hands held out. ‘So what can you do now, Charlene? Your grandfather’s empire is collapsing, his money is tied up - most will be confiscated by the state anyway; if you ever see a penny of it, that’ll be years down the line. You going back to Romania, take your chances there? Alone? With killers like Gheorghe? No backup? It’s cold and lonely out there, Charlene. You’re one self-contained lady, some might say you’re a cold and heartless bitch – that’s understandable: nobody gave you anything, you had to take it all.’

She had finished her drink, and now she looked into the empty glass.

‘It doesn’t have to be that way.’

She looked up and gave a sarcastic laugh. ‘Martin suggested I could work with you.’

He spread his arms. ‘Is that so crazy? What do you want, Charlene? Money? Power? Excitement?’

She crossed her legs the other way, sitting back on her chair, putting her glass on the windowsill, half-looking away.

‘Let me make you a proposition,’ Grosvenor said. ‘We’ll let you go, back to Gheorghe but working for us. Or…’

She turned to look at him as he sat back with a half smile. ‘Or what?’

His mobile rang. He checked the display and then answered it. She made out the urgency at the other end, but not the words themselves. Grosvenor’s voice was calm. ‘That makes it interesting,’ he said, and raised his eyes at Charlene. She saw anger in them, for the first time, and she felt physically afraid.

Chapter 31

Near Glasgow

We stopped driving after a time, and the engine was switched off. I could hear the silence outside; when I managed to turn my head slightly, I could see that there were no streetlights.

The car door at my feet was opened and I was dragged out, the man who'd been sitting in the back pushing me with his feet. I lay on stony, muddy ground, my arms and legs stiff, and turned onto my back, while the two men stood and looked around.

There were farm buildings not far away. In the other direction I could see the lights of the city reflected in the clouds. I reckoned I was somewhere to the north of the city, but had no idea exactly where. It was cold but not raining.

One of the men gave a kick at my ankle – nothing particularly vicious – and connected with the bone; I swore and clutched at it. He then kicked me in the side, harder this time, trying to hurt me. I swore again.

A mobile phone rang and the kicker lifted it to his ear and walked away a little. 'We have him,' he said, the voice heavily accented – East European I guessed, just like the Romanians.

And my feeling was that that was exactly who it was: the Romanian gangsters, tidying up the loose ends, taking revenge.

'What you want? We hurt him? We kick fuck out of him? We bury him here?'

I shivered. Oh fuck, I thought. Oh fuck, oh fuck, oh fuck.

'OK.' He put his phone away and came across towards me, and without any warning or ceremony kicked me in the side of the head,

I rolled away, my head throbbing, my eyes tight shut but still seeing blazing lights and swirling patterns. I got to my knees, clutching at my head, and then felt a double kick in the ribs and I rolled onto my side, huddled, trying to escape. Then another kick to the head, and one in my kidneys.

Oh fuck, I thought.

'Don't,' I managed to gasp. 'I have money. Don't.'

The sequence of kicks was repeated, head and kidneys, and they paused again while I rolled on the ground, sobbing in agony, trying to cover my head, curl up tight, tears rolling down my cheeks. Then there was a long pause while I maybe lost consciousness, when the kicking seemed to stop.

I heard the phone rang again, and I heard the footsteps walk away as I came to my senses. I moaned, tried to gather my strength. I'd never felt so much physical pain. At this point I *wanted* to die.

While one man spoke on the phone, the other one repeated the sequence of kicks and started once more before there was a sharp shout from the other in a foreign language and he stopped.

I was face down now, pressed against the cold damp earth and the stones. I could feel the strength ebbing from my body, along with the will to live. I'm sorry, I found myself thinking; I'm sorry, Helen, for the wrong I did you and the lies I told you; I'm sorry, Nicola, for the life we're not going to have. For a moment I wished I believed in heaven: how nice it would have been to think I was going to join Fiona, at last.

The two men shouted something at each other. Nearby there was the sound of a car engine, revving hard, getting louder. I turned onto my back and tried to get up onto one elbow. Headlights suddenly appeared round a corner and were coming up the hill towards us. The men started shouting at each other again. I heard their footsteps scrabbling on the loose ground, the car door opening, and then something stamped on my right wrist and I the diesel engine starting and two car doors slamming shut as I gave a scream of pain. I just had enough sense and strength to roll to one side onto long wet grass, hearing and feeling the car tyres an inch from my face, before I felt my body shut down and everything went silent. I dreamed of a car crash, hands lifting me from it, soothing me, soft reassuring voices, the pain burning.

I'm sorry, I said. I'm so sorry.

*

Charlene was shaking as she spoke on the mobile: 'Call it off. Leave him – the police are on their way. Don't kill him – I need him.' She stood staring out of the window, still shaking as she gulped at another gin.

*

Colin Strachan laughed as he reached into the fridge for a beer. 'You?'

Elaine shook her head and yawned. 'I'm going to bed – read my book.' She reached to hug and kiss him. 'Don't be too late.'

'I won't.'

She went through to the bedroom, and he heard her undressing – it still gave him a thrill, watching her or even just listening. He sat on the sofa with his laptop, and woke it up, sipping the cold lager and listening to the sounds of the night.

As he scanned his emails, he suddenly shivered. There was one from a property company in Glasgow, which he remembered was one of B&D's clients. Oh no, he thought. No no no. After all this time.

The email simply gave a mobile phone number, with the 49 country code. Colin drank more beer before dialling.

The slightly accented voice answered. 'Hello, Mr Colin Strachan.'

Colin swallowed. 'I got your email. You wanted me to call.'

'Ah yes. I wanted your advice.'

The beer bottle was freezing cold in Colin's fingers, but he gripped it tightly. 'Advice on what?'

'Your colleague Martin McGregor.'

Colin shook his head. The fine meal, the wine and the gins, the company down at the marina, the musicians playing… all of that faded, leaving him with the cold fear. 'What about him?'

'Is it correct that he is now running your end of our operation?'

'Ah – yes. I retired a few years ago.'

'Yes, of course. You are living in Spain now.'

Colin swallowed.

'You did not think to tell us about your change of circumstances, your change of management.'

'I didn't think it mattered. It didn't affect anything.' He tried to keep his tone light, like there was nothing to fear.

'Perhaps not. But we know little of this Martin McGregor.'

Colin tried to think how they had discovered about Martin: what had happened in Glasgow? He had thought Martin might try to escape, but it looked like he hadn't done that at all. So what was going on? He cleared his throat. 'Martin's been running that end of the operation for a few years now. Have you any reason to believe there is a problem?'

'He went out of contact for a few weeks, without telling us.'

Colin tried to think about that. 'Perhaps it was an unexpected holiday.'

'Perhaps.'

'Anyway, what can I tell you? You haven't had a problem with Martin for years, so why the worry now? Is there any other reason you should be worried?'

'So we should trust him.'

'I can't see any reason why not.' What had Martin been up to? Had he made his escape but been caught by the police…? He pushed that thought away.

There was a silence. 'Very well.' And the call ended.

Colin put the phone on the sofa beside him. Elaine shouted through from the bed: 'Who was on the phone, darling?'

'Just an old colleague. Nothing important.' He closed his eyes, feeling suddenly vulnerable.

*

The man at the other end of the call dialled a mobile. 'Stop the attack. We will trust Martin McGregor for now. But be careful.'

He opened the phone and pulled out the SIM card, and broke it in two, and then took out the battery, which he tossed into a drawer, and finally threw the rest of the cheap phone into the wood-burning stove, and watched it thoughtfully.

Chapter 32

Glasgow

I opened my eyes and tried to sit up, but felt extraordinarily weak and detached from reality. 'Fiona?' I shouted, and then realised that was wrong. 'Helen?' I looked around – it was my bedroom at home, I was in bed with my chest encased in bandages, and a cast on my right wrist – and then I closed my eyes and fell back on the pillows. Elizabeth?

'Hello?' I shouted. Somebody had put me to bed, so someone had to be there – surely. 'Hello?' I began to panic that I had been left alone to fend for myself. 'Hello?' My throat was sore and dry.

My head was hurting, and as the memories dribbled back it began to hurt more; I reached to feel the bandages. The attack outside the flat, that I had thought was a mugging; the car journey, the beating, the car driving off, the other car arriving. The voices, soothing, the ambulance, the scratch on the back of my hand and then sleep, a deep deep sleep that I had never known before. Waking up in the hospital, the nurse gradually bringing me round and stopping me from wrenching the mask off my face in a panic, then a porter wheeling me to another room, a woman's face that I recognised but couldn't remember now, a young man blabbering on about bruised ribs and a broken wrist – mine? – a policeman asking questions, and then sleep, sleep.

I'd come round again in the hospital, and the nurse had smiled and reassured me. A man brought me a coffee, and another young man talked to me and asked if I was ready to go home with my wife. I gazed at him, baffled. That woman's face was there again: smiling through tears and concern, holding my good hand. Who was she?

And somehow I was back here in my own bed. Who had been with me? Who was that woman?

I got up on my elbows again. 'Hello? Hello?' And the ache from my head spread downwards, through all of my body, and the waves of tiredness washed through me again

Steve appeared in the doorway, pulling buds out of his ears. 'You OK?'

Oh god, not Steve. Where was Grosvenor? 'No,' I said. 'I'm not OK. Are there any paracetamol?' My voice was weak, and my chest was painful when I breathed in. My whole face felt numb.

He ducked away and came back with a plastic prescription bottle, shook out two big white pills and gave them to me. Then he checked the label and frowned, and gave a shrug.

'Water?'

He nodded, and vanished for a minute, coming back with a mug of water. I managed to get the pills down, and he helped me sit up, rearranging the pillows. Then he sat on the edge of the bed, looking at me.

'What happened?'

He swallowed. 'You were attacked just outside as you got back to your apartment building. Two men. They took you north of the city to a farm and beat you up. We're not sure if they were actually trying to kill you or just hurt you – it was pretty close. I was arriving here just as they drove you off, tried to follow you in the taxi but we lost you. I called Mark and we picked him up from the hotel. We got you from the tracking app on your phone. When we arrived at the farm, they drove off – their car hit our taxi, and almost ran you over, but they got away.'

'Who were they?'

He grimaced. 'Not sure.'

'What's your best guess? They sounded foreign – Romanian?'

He shrugged.

'Could you get my mobile?'

He nodded again and stood up, scratching his head, looking round. Then he held up a hand and nodded, disappeared for a minute, and came back with it.

I unlocked it. 'Could you get my charger?'

There were a few missed calls, including one from Amanda Pitt and another from Nicola, and some emails and texts. I heard the flat's toilet flush and the door being unlocked. I called Nicola. As it started ringing, I heard a phone ringing from elsewhere in the flat. As she answered, I heard a voice from close by, saying the same words.

And she appeared in the doorway, looking worried but trying to smile, and we both hung up. I laughed and she did too, coming over to sit by me, reaching to hold my good hand. She was wearing a blue top and jeans; I looked at her face and her hair, and I felt better suddenly.

‘Hello sleepy. How are you? Are you hungry?’

I thought about that. ‘Yes, but I think I might be sick. How did you get here?’

‘Your friend – Mark? – he phoned me, told me you’d been mugged. I came through straight away. Hope you don’t mind.’

I gave another shallow, painful laugh. ‘Of course not. Thank you.’ It had been her at the hospital; she’d come through to Glasgow in the middle of the night to me.

The pain killers were starting to work, but they were giving me a strange floating feeling. ‘How did they get your number?’ I must have had a general anaesthetic: I could feel it coming back over me.

‘Steve got it from your phone.’

Which would have been locked… I shook that little problem away. ‘I should eat something,’ I said. ‘Before the paracetamol burn a hole in my stomach.’

An hour later I was in the lounge, after awkwardly washing my face and getting dressed, Nicola helping. I toyed with a couple of slices of toast and a cup of tea, vaguely hungry but not feeling like eating. I felt more human but still spaced out. Steve had gone.

‘What’s been happening?’ I asked her.

She shrugged. ‘I don’t know. I stayed with you in the hospital till you were fully awake and they were sure you weren’t concussed. They reckon you just need bed rest and being looked after, but someone has to be with you all the time just in case.’

She gave a smile and reached to hold my hands again. ‘I’ll stay here as long as you need me.’

‘How about Grosvenor – Mark?’

‘Didn’t see anyone else at all. It was only Steve at the hospital when I arrived.’

She helped me back to the bedroom and I lay down and drifted off to sleep.

Some time later I was more awake, though still needing more paracetamol – Nicola frowned: ‘These are strong, Martin.’ ‘It’s OK, it’ll just be for a day or so.’

I lay thinking, and then phoned Amanda Pitt.

‘How are you feeling, Martin?’ But there was no warmth in her voice.

‘On the mend. What’s been happening?’

‘Everything. We’re all deep into the Talbot murder and dealing with the after effects of a weekend of violence and mayhem across the city’s housing schemes. Everybody’s on duty, all over the city and around. It’s going to be bad for some time.’

‘How about the attack on me?’

Her tone was almost sarcastic: ‘How about it? When the PC interviewed you, you couldn’t give any description, or the type of car, or where you were taken. Not much we can do.’

‘It was dark. It was sudden.’

‘Yeah, well, we’ve nothing to go on there, so just count yourself lucky. You’ve still got your money, and the FBI is on your side.’ She gave a snort. ‘You’ve come out of this OK, Martin.’

'You don't think Charlene had anything to do with the attack on me?'

'I have to go, Martin. Bye.' She hung up.

I tried to phone Grosvenor, but it went straight to voicemail. I asked him to call me.

I left my phone to charge, and went through to sit by Nicola on the couch, holding her hand as we sipped cups of tea and I felt my eyes slipping shut again.

She moved closer and put her hand on my knee. 'Martin, can I talk to you?'

I nodded sleepily. 'Thanks for coming through,' I said. 'I appreciate it.' The thought of being alone with Steve as my main nurse did not appeal to me. I turned to half-face her, my hand on hers, enjoying the physical contact, the warmth of her skin.

'I told you about my partner. He contacted me when I was in Kirkwall, begged me to give him another chance, said he would stay off the drink. I said OK.' She shrugged. 'I liked you, but we didn't know each other. And I owed him another chance: I loved him.' She forced a smile. 'So I left Orkney and went back to him.' A deep breath and a rush of words: 'And it was great, really good. Like when we first met. We did things together…'

I shook away the thoughts that sprang into my mind, and gripped her hand as tightly as I could.

'It was really really good for about two weeks, and then he turned up late when we were going round to friends. He was absolutely hammered, staggering and slurring. Swearing and a stupid grin on his face. That was it as far as I was concerned. No more chances. I could never trust him again. I felt betrayed.'

She turned to face me, the beginnings of tears in her eyes. 'I thought about calling you there and then, but I waited till I was back in Orkney. I wanted to tell you about this. I wondered if we could find out more about each other. See if it went anywhere.'

'And I was in Edinburgh being interrogated by an FBI agent.'

She laughed, and then it faded. I wanted to keep that smile on her face, and wondered if I would ever be able to. As I was about to speak, she pressed one finger to my lips. 'I have a feeling you've done some odd things in the past, and it's obvious you're in trouble with the police, and you haven't told me the whole story, and your friend Steve is odd. You've joked about it, but there's something serious been going on with you, Martin. Look at you. I don't want to know all about your past, Martin, but I do want an honest future. From now on. If you can't give me that, then we certainly don't *have* a future. I'll help you get back on your feet, but then I'll go home and pick up my life on my own, and you can get on with yours.' She took another of her deep breaths. 'And I need an instant decision.'

Wow, I thought. Just like Helen: 'Never lie to me, Martin.' Instant decision? Well, I had nothing to lose here. She had cared for me, and that counted for a hell of lot. She had been honest with me, and now it was my turn.

So I started talking. I told her everything, from the beginning, all about Fiona and Elizabeth, and the truth about what had happened with Helen. I even told her about Sam. I watched her face show sympathy and amazement, pity and censure – the screwed up eyes: 'Oh, Martin.' And I told her where I was now, exactly what the situation was with the FBI and the police, and the gangsters still out there.

At the end of it she nodded. 'Thank you for being honest. Wow, what a situation you've got yourself into.' She leaned over to kiss me on the cheek, and we sat like that for some time, just being together. It felt so good, and I felt honest, at last, in a way that I never had been with Helen. Inside, I was strangely calm. I took another two of the painkillers, and drifted off to sleep on the couch again, conscious of Nicola's hand in mine.

*

That evening Nicola fetched a carry-out curry. Steve reappeared, grabbed a plate and helped himself to some of each of ours. We all sat at the table in my kitchen.

'What's happening?' I asked him.

He glanced at Nicola, but I indicated that she was part of this.

'Attack's stopped,' he said, shovelling rice into his face.

'Just like that? What happened?'

He grimaced and took another forkful of curry.

'OK,' I said. 'So what now?'

'You can get back to what you did before, exactly as before. We'll watch, sniff, follow. We'll seed some data and track it around the carders' networks. See what happens. You just do your job. The Scottish police are going to back right off for the time being, though they reserve the right to do some financial forensics on the company at any time in the future.'

'Where's Grosvenor now?'

'Home,' he mumbled. 'Storms in New York – he wanted to get back. Not needed here.'

'Oh.'

'I'm going home in the morning, early flight. I'll send you details of how we communicate, how I'll monitor your system remotely.'

'Oh.' I wondered what it would be like to be alone in the office, with Claire, doing what I did. And what would happen if this didn't work, didn't give them any intelligence? Would they then just discard me?

I shook the thought away. Nicola reached to hold my hand under the table, as if sensing my doubts, and I squeezed her hand and gave her a smile. The future wasn't certain, but there was hope.

'Nicola says you got her number from my phone – how did you unlock it?'

He shrugged. 'Four digit code – I watched you unlock it loads of times: easy to work out what the code was likely to be. Took me two attempts'

After our meal, I was feeling knackered. We watched some TV – Steve in the corner on his laptop, headphones plugged in – and made small talk, filling in the story of her life and the gaps in mine.

I phoned Grosvenor and this time he answered. 'What's it like over there?'

'My house is mostly OK, but the city's a mess. Sorry I didn't get a chance to say goodbye. You feeling OK now?'

'Not too bad – the painkillers are helping.'

'Yeah, well – be careful of them, son. Take the pain – it's part of the healing.'

'Listen, thanks for chasing off those guys – I think they might have carried on beating me up.'

'My pleasure. We need you, Martin.'

That was reassuring, even if I suspected it wasn't entirely honest. 'What are you going to do about Charlene?'

'Charlene?' he asked, as if he'd forgotten all about her. 'Nothing, I guess. Steve will have filled you in on where we are. You just get on with what you were doing, and he'll monitor. The way I see it, Charlene will be tied up trying to get whatever she can out of her grandfather's estate.'

'You don't want her to work with us any more?'

He paused for a second. 'I see no need to involve her in what you're going to be doing.'

I tried to unravel that statement, but wasn't sure I fully understood it. 'How about Sandy Lomond?'

'Still no trace. But he's not mission critical. The Scottish police are still interested of course, so good luck to them.'

Hesitantly, I asked: 'Have you found Colin Strachan?'

'Nope,' he said.

When he didn't elaborate, I went on: 'Who do you think attacked me? Was it the Romanians? Did Charlene - ?'

He interrupted: 'You're safe, Martin. You're working for the good guys: we'll look after you.'

I felt the hollow feeling in my stomach as the painkillers fought with the curry, and my bowels started to protest.

'Anyhow, Steve will give you contact details when he finishes up: he's your case officer – I'm done with it. Good working with you, son.' And with that he hung up.

I put my mobile down, feeling flat.

'You OK, Martin?' Nicola asked.

I held my hand up to her and then made a dash for the bathroom to be violently sick, the heaving causing agony in my chest. Afterwards I washed myself and brushed my teeth and came back through to the lounge. I told her about the conversation with Grosvenor, Steve in the corner apparently unaware. God, this was so like those days with Fiona and Davey in the flat in Finnieston.

'Wow,' she said. 'Are you still in any danger?'

'Grosvenor says no.'

All that night, through sleep broken by a headache and pain, I dreamed of the future I wanted, the future I thought I deserved, the future I should have had with Fiona.

Chapter 33

Spain

Sandy Lomond lit a cigarette and listened to the waters lap on the sand twenty feet in front of him, the noise of the bar behind him. He smiled to himself: smoking was allowed in this bar, but he and the other ex-pats still had that habit of going outside.

It was late - dark, but warm. He closed his eyes briefly and savoured the mood, as he did every evening, and then sat at a small metal table looking out at the calm night.

Another man came out of the crowded bar and lit a cigarette as he sat at the next table. Both men looked towards the sea, the full moon hanging in the black sky. 'Fuckin' brilliant here, isn't it?' The accent was Scottish, Lanarkshire.

Sandy turned his head, then turned back. The man had been somewhere at the back of the bar, chatting to two young girls on holiday; Sandy had noticed them all right, with their bleached hair, their false fingernails and their filmy dresses, but not too much of the man who was chancing his luck. 'Yeah,' he said.

'Where you from yourself, big man?'

'Around.'

'Here on holiday?'

'Retired.'

'Must be fuckin' brilliant, here all the time. Nae work. I'm just here for the week. I'm a taxi driver. What did you do?'

Sandy turned again for a brief look. He was sure the man was just being friendly, a fellow Scot in a strange land, that there was nothing sinister. 'Computers,' he said. 'I was in computers.'

'Fuckin' brilliant, man. Computers! Who did you work for?'

Sandy dropped his cigarette and trod on it as he stood up and turned to walk back towards the bar. 'Enjoy the rest of your holiday, son,' he said.

The stranger got the message.

*

Colin Strachan opened his eyes as the black shadow fell across him, blotting out the early afternoon sun. He could only see the fuzzy outline of hair and beard, but was aware that the man was looking down at him. He held a hand up to shield his eyes, but still couldn't make out the features, and nothing triggered any recognition. 'Can I help you?'

'You sure can, Mr Strachan,' the deep New York voice growled. 'Mind if I join you?'

Colin shrugged. 'Be my guest. Can I get you a drink?' A warning voice sounded in his head, but there was nothing he could do.

'Only if you're having one yourself. Scotch and water, thank you.'

The waiter had caught that, and nodded when Colin indicated his own almost-empty glass. The American sat by Colin. 'Sure is a mighty fine spot here, Colin.'

'You have the advantage...'

'Sorry, remiss of me.' He pulled out his wallet and showed his ID. 'Mark Grosvenor, FBI.' He put it away and continued to gaze across the tiled promenade to the young men playing volleyball on the beach, and the sea washing the edge of the sand.

Colin said nothing till the drinks came, but inside he was suddenly taut; there was only one reason that the FBI would be here speaking to him, but how... When he spoke, he tried to keep his voice steady. 'What brings you here?'

'Oh, just circumstances,' Grosvenor said. 'I don't know if you've heard about all the stuff that's been going down back in Glasgow.' Grosvenor paused, but there was no reply. 'You must have read about the murder of a guy called Ken Talbot.'

'Ken Talbot?'

'He ran what they call a criminal empire across much of Scotland: drugs and cigarettes and booze and extortion. And he had a whole scrunched up bundle of companies, real and fake, to launder his money. Including a couple of computer firms in Glasgow.'

Colin was shaking his head, pursing his lips. 'Nope,' he said.

They both took a good mouthful from their respective drinks, eyes screwed up against the glare of the sun and its reflection from the sea.

Grosvenor smiled. 'Lord save me from criminals who don't know anything. Ken Talbot. You can't remember working for B&D Software Solutions in Glasgow? You were practically in charge.' And he turned to look straight at Colin, who tried to hold his gaze. 'You set up the cybercrime, Colin. You found the hackers. Then, four years ago, you skipped town and came out here, leaving Sandy Lomond and Martin McGregor to work that side of the business, following the instructions you'd left them. You can't have forgotten all of that, Colin, surely.'

Colin finished his drink in two long gulps. He'd had the occasional nightmare about something like this happening. It would have to be the FBI: they were the ones hunting cybercriminals across the world – not for any altruistic reasons, but because criminal forces could be aligned to attack US institutions, backed by foreign governments; China was the current bogey. He'd thought it would be an eager, clean-cut young agent in a suit, not a hairy old man in a lumberjack shirt and jeans, overheating in the sun. He's had the nightmares, and some nights in the early hours, he'd rehearsed what he would say, how he would try to bargain his way out – because there would be no denial. 'What do you want?'

'Are you bored here, Colin? It's sunny and all, and the restaurants look real nice, but don't you miss the thrills, the excitement?'

'What do you want?'

'Or are you still operating? Do you still have the contacts – Gregorius? How about Charlene? You two still in touch? And how's your money holding out?'

Colin frowned, an icy chill inside him.

'How did you get clean away from Talbot and Lomond? Why were they so happy to let you go?'

All Colin could do was frown and swallow. He saw the waiter looking across, and nodded.

'The way I read the timing, Charlene appeared about a year before you disappeared. You knew about her, and you knew what Sandy Lomond set up: her name all over the documentation, 'Charlie Talbot', replacing her poor dead father. You planned to get out all along, didn't you, Colin – once you'd gathered enough money?'

Fresh drinks clunked onto the table. Colin's empty glass was taken away and he grabbed the new one, gulping at it.

'But Charlene was just the little extra insurance you wanted to keep Sandy Lomond and Ken Talbot from trying to track you down – along with what you knew about their operations. So they let you go clear, but not Martin McGregor. They needed him to carry on your cybercrime work. So he had to stay. Is that all correct, Colin? Am I pretty much there?' Grosvenor sat back, looking at the beach. 'Hell, it don't matter, Colin. A working theory is good enough for me. I don't need to prove anything in a court of law.'

Colin swallowed. 'What are you going to do?'

'I tell you what I ain't gonna do. I ain't dragging you across the border into Gibraltar and then over to England, and then to the States. I could do that, make no mistake: I have enough circumstantial evidence to convince my boss that you could give us invaluable intelligence on international cybercrime, and that you have possible links to international cyber terrorism which forms a clear threat to the US, which enables me to lock you up till I get a chance to interrogate you properly – and that could take years, Colin.' He took a breath. 'No, I'm not going to do that.'

There was a pause. They listened to the shouts of the volleyball players on the beach, and a radio somewhere close by, the gentle surf lapping the sand.

'What *are* you going to do?' Colin didn't attempt any bravado.

'I'd like you to work for us, Colin. I'd like you to keep your contact with Gregorius – we'd like to find out more about him.'

'I don't know who he is,' Colin said, the words tumbling out in a rush. 'I can't contact him directly. We haven't been in touch since I left Glasgow. You've got to believe me. I started up with some guys, and they knew about Gregorius – they said that was how we could sell on the stuff we were getting from the computers. But I don't know who he or they are. I can't contact them.'

'But he can contact you.' Grosvenor raised his eyebrows to show this was a question, and Colin looked down, affirming. 'Does Gregorius even know that Martin McGregor has taken over?'

Colin nodded and closed his eyes. 'He does now. He phoned the other day.'

Grosvenor finished his first whisky and reached for the second. He was now sure why the DDoS attack had been called off: Gregorius had spoken to Colin, and Colin had told him that Martin was genuine.

'What's happening in Glasgow?' Colin asked. 'How is Martin?'

'Martin's just fine. He's carrying on with business as before.' Colin gave him a look and Grosvenor smiled: 'And probably best if you don't ask any more questions about B&D. That's all you need to know: Martin is back at his desk doing what you left him doing four years ago.'

Colin nodded. 'So what about me?' He checked his watch – but Elaine wasn't due back from her shopping trip for ages yet, and she would be going back to the flat before coming here for lunch.

'There is a company called Online Business-Lösungen, which is currently seeking investors. I'd like you to buy in and start working with them. It's a very similar operation to B&D. You'll know how it works. We'll get you a couple of hackers to do the business, and then Gregorius will come calling, because he'll know what you're doing. He's bound to be keeping tabs on you.'

Colin frowned. There was almost too much to take in. 'That sounds German.'

'Yeah, well, being in Berlin it would.'

'Berlin? I can't go to Berlin. Why Berlin?'

'Berlin's ideally placed: it's economically vibrant but has enough links to Eastern Europe to make it interesting. And you wouldn't want to be crapping on your own doorstep here in Spain.'

'Berlin?'

'There are three flights a day from Berlin to Malaga. Only takes an hour and a half. You can still have your good life here with your girlfriend, Colin, but you'll be working your Berlin clients through Gregorius. Like you did before in Glasgow.'

'How does that help you, though?'

'We'll monitor the activity. We'll track data through – card numbers, bank accounts. We'll pick some up down the line and track them back. We'll build up a picture of the networks.'

'And what will you do when you've built up 'a picture'?'

Grosvenor sipped his whisky, and then held it up to admire the sunshine glinting through the liquid. 'We have options. And you have options too, Colin. The high life in Berlin and long weekends here, or a lonely cell in a Federal Correctional Institution, probably in New York but it really doesn't matter where it is for all you'll see of the world outside the gates.'

'Did Martin McGregor tell you where I was?'

Grosvenor gave a short laugh. 'Not directly. We found a number on Martin's cell against the name Fred Bloggs. Spanish country code, registered to Telefonica – wasn't hard to work out it was probably you and track you down. So, Colin, do we have a deal?'

Colin Strachan swallowed again, feeling the weight of his mobile phone in his pocket, the impact of the gesture he'd made, leaving a contact route open in case he could make things right with Martin in return for conning the guy and dragging him into his world. He thought about what Grosvenor had said. He sipped his drink, and after a time he asked: 'Do I have a choice about this?'

Grosvenor grimaced. 'Everyone's got a choice, Colin. You had choices all through your life, and the choices you made have brought you to this moment. This is the big one.'

Chapter 34

New York, a month later

Mark Grosvenor had taken the packed A train from his home in Brooklyn, got off at Fulton Street and walked up through the cool, damp day along the narrow Nassau Street into the wider, tree-lined streets of the financial district, towards Federal Plaza. He carried his briefcase and wore his black greatcoat, open and flapping in the breeze. Here and there were traces of the fierce storms that had whipped through the city in preceding weeks. He could feel his limp was bad, not a good sign for the coming winter. His unemployed son, his grandson, and now pregnant daughter-in-law were still living with him, and this was not good either.

He made his way up to the 23rd floor, and along to the small conference room. Kurt Jackson was already there at the top of the table, with Maxwell Stuart beside him, fiddling with his laptop.

Grosvenor shuffled off his coat and got himself some coffee, and sat on Jackson's other side. Stuart closed the lid on his laptop.

'So,' Jackson said. 'Over to you Mark. Sum it all up for us. Where are we?'

Grosvenor blew across his cup and cautiously sipped the coffee. 'We have Martin McGregor at work in Glasgow, continuing what he did before. Steve Roberts has a link through to him and his computer; he's monitoring the data going in and out from B&D. Early days, but we've already identified a couple of credit cards coming up for sale at the Odessa conference that originated from a customer in a wine store in Glasgow where B&D installed the computer system. It's promising. Slow, painstaking stuff, but promising.'

'It's a real breakthrough,' Stuart murmured.

'Max will be case officer for the B&D operation. I assume it's totally sandboxed?' asked Jackson.

'Oh yes.'

'And McGregor's not going to be a problem?'

Grosvenor raised an eyebrow. 'I think he's still a mite scared because of what happened with the Romanian gangsters. He sees us as his protector – the Glasgow gangsters aren't a threat, and the Scottish police are onside, but the Romanians are his worry. McGregor's also afraid that we could drag him over here to face terrorism charges any time we wanted.' He sniffed. 'Which is true. He'll keep straight with us – he's doing well out of this, his private life is going well. He'll be fine for the foreseeable future.'

Jackson waved a hand. 'Right. That in itself justifies your approach – well done.' He gave no sign of that that he remembered the long argument with Grosvenor, when Jackson had wanted to follow the official line and arrest everyone in sight, sceptical that Grosvenor's plan could possibly work. 'What about the rest? The woman Charlene. What's the story there?'

'Charlene's continued working with the Romanian Gheorghe, but she's on our side.' Though he shrugged, as if unsure of what he'd said. 'She's using me as case officer for the moment, keeping me informed, but we need to hand that over to someone full time. She's persuaded them to leave McGregor alone – she got them to call off the beating. But they may change their minds later, of course.'

'Max? Could you run Charlene?'

Stuart cleared his throat and sat more upright. 'Surely. Might be useful to keep it all together, but equally it could be dangerous – too much with one person. Maybe better to split them.'

Jackson nodded. 'We'll think about it.'

'She's currently recruiting for him round Europe,' Grosvenor went on. 'There are lots of graduates with good computer skills and nothing to do in the recession, particularly in Spain and Portugal.'

'Pretty dangerous work,' Stuart murmured.

'Yeah, but she kinda likes it. She's a loner: no relationships, no friends, no family.'

'Profile of a killer,' Jackson commented.

Grosvenor bobbed his head. 'If cornered, certainly. She's cold; she attracts men and women equally, but she's always emotionally detached in any relationship. She's ideal for our purposes, and she wouldn't blame us if we sacrificed her somewhere downstream.' He sipped his coffee.

'Did she explain about the dead people?' Jackson asked.

'The Portuguese killing really fucked up her plans; she got some capital out of it, sure – but she was relying on a regular source of income. I don't think the murders in Romania bothered her, though – I'm sure Gheorghe did all of that, but Charlene understood that the dead people were expendable. Like I say, emotionally detached.'

They were silent for a minute.

'How about this guy Colin Strachan?' Stuart asked.

'Yeah,' Jackson added. 'He came in from left field.'

'He was out of the picture with B&D four years ago, that's why we missed him. He has now begun working for the company Online Business-Lösungen in Berlin, which he invested in heavily, so he's already senior partner. His cover is that he lost a lot of his money in the property crash in Spain, and that's partly true, so he needed employment and investment. He's building up what he had with B&D, and we'll sit tight and wait for Gregorius – or someone like him – to come sniffing round.' He shrugged. 'Early days of course, and no guarantees but I think it'll fly.'

There was more silence while Stuart and Jackson took that in.

'Any questions, Max?' Jackson asked finally.

Stuart shook his head as he sat forward. 'A few gaps, but it doesn't really matter. This is a major breakthrough for us – a much better strategy than simply locking these guys up. We could get really good material from the three sources.'

Grosvenor nodded. 'All the flags in place so none of our teams fuck this up during separate investigations?'

Jackson nodded.

The three men fell silent again.

'I would like to ask about the Scottish detective, Amanda Pitt,' Stuart ventured.

'What about her?' Jackson asked. 'She's really nothing to do with us.'

'Agreed,' Stuart said. 'But she seemed to very…' he fought for the word: 'compliant.'

Grosvenor drained his coffee and stood up. 'I have to get back – guys coming to fix my windows later.'

'OK, Mark. I'll call.' He stood up too and came round the table to face Grosvenor. 'Great job, Mark. Well done. Send me in your job sheet and expenses claim, along with the written report.'

Grosvenor let Jackson shake his hand and then put on his coat. 'You're right, Max. Amanda Pitt was very helpful at all the right times for us, but also before we rode into the scene.'

'So what do you think was going on?'

'I think she was playing both sides of the street, and being played in turn by Charlene. I never had a chance to talk to her, get to her, but my guess is she was feeding Talbot's team information about the police investigation into his empire for years. And I'm also pretty sure that Charlene had a sexual relationship with her and also got information about both Talbot's activities and the police investigation. It was all about knowing what was going on: Sandy Lomond was the main contact for Charlene, but she needed a wider view.'

'Wow,' Maxwell said.

'Anyway,' Jackson said, 'it doesn't affect us. Good job, Mark.'

Grosvenor shrugged, pulled the door open, and stepped out into the corridor.

*

'Do you trust her?' Bianca asked.

Gheorghe shrugged and breathed cigarette smoke across to her. 'For the moment. In due course I want to enjoy her, but for now she is useful.'

'How about Martin McGregor?'

Another shrug. 'We have other things to worry about for now, but if he crosses our path again we may have to do something.' He settled in the big armchair and closed his eyes, thinking of a beautiful, petite blonde.

Chapter 35

Madrid, the following Easter

I took off my straw hat and placed it on the metal table, and ran my fingers through my damp hair. I raised the bottle of Estrella to my lips and took a good swig as I enjoyed the feel of the condensation running down my fingers, and I sat back in my chair, surveying the Plaza Mayor. I had been amazed at how compact the centre of Madrid was – the open-top bus tour had to keep doubling back to give its customers value for money. I loved all the plazas, but this was my favourite, with its bizarre museum of ham in one corner.

Nicola had gone to visit the little Soroya museum. I'd checked online and decided I didn't want to look at pictures of naked boys on beaches with horses. If the guy had been operating nowadays he'd have had his computer seized. So I was shooting the breeze, wandering from café to bar in the sunshine, letting myself enjoy the freedom.

I felt relaxed, happy.

The biggest problem had been to sort out the finances: both Bytes and Digits and B&D had had their accounts frozen by the banks. We kept going on a wing and a prayer, and then the authorities told them that we were OK and they reluctantly let us off the hook. Talbot's accountants had managed to straighten everything out so that it looked legitimate, and mostly it now was.

The Argyle Street shop had really been running at a loss. We trawled for investment, and a young computer graduate called Susanna had come along, bought a half share using her mother's money, and re-booted the whole enterprise. She'd had to let the original Frank go, but he didn't seem to mind. It was now doing fine. I went up there from time to time, but each visit made me sad: I remembered the old days, with Davey slumped and uncommunicative, Fiona waiting at home. I was planning to sell my share to Susanna in due course.

B&D was healthy, but we could now clearly identify the money that was coming in as a result of our cybercrimes. Payments came in from various banks across the country – nothing huge in any single payment, but a sizeable amount in total. I passed on the details to the FBI – my contact was now someone called Maxwell Stuart; I pictured him as young and earnest. I'd re-hired Graham Turner, when the police had let him go; he seemed to have no idea what had been going on or what was happening now, and I didn't tell him. Claire was happy, in a new relationship that she never spoke about; she just smiled enigmatically and said that one day we'd maybe meet 'her partner'.

My personal finances were simplified. The flat we lived in was officially mine, apparently, which was a pleasant surprise. My income was now solely a salary from B&D: no extra cheques coming in, no ghost dividends from companies I didn't know anything about. I felt legitimate. And I still had those bank accounts in Gibraltar. Andrew was still my personal financial adviser, and he'd managed to strike a deal with HMRC about all that tax I'd avoided over the years.

Nicola had sold her house in Bathgate and moved in with me. She was happy, and so was I; the relationship felt solid, and I thought it might last. It was based on the truth, and that seemed to be helping. I had taken her to see my mum and stepdad, and we were forming some kind of family unit there. I was realising, belatedly, that families are important. Friends are important too: I went round twice a week to see Davey and Jane and their son in their new hi-tech home in Milngavie.

I didn't think of the others and the events of the past. Not often. Sometimes Nicola would ask me about Fiona, and I would talk about the happy times, but always with the shadow of her death there. Sometimes we did things that I'd done with Helen, and I always had a twinge of sadness from that; what was she doing now?

I checked the news on my phone, and read about an FBI operation which had broken up an organised cyber-attack on a US corporation. I wondered whether that was anything to do with the information they were getting through the network that B&D was in contact with. The one name that was never in the news was Gregorius; other cyber criminals became notorious, known by some kind of handle, but not him.

I finished my beer and wondered whether to just sit there for a time, or to have another beer and sit there for even longer, or… But I decided to just head back to our hotel on Gran Via and have a siesta, hoping Nicola would come back before I'd gone to sleep.

'La cuenta por favor.' 'Certainly, sir.'

I wandered through the streets, across Calle Mayor up towards Gran Via, letting thoughts – mostly pleasant – turn in my head, and looking forward to the rest of the day, and the rest of the holiday, and the rest of time with Nicola.

A small, pretty blonde woman, wearing tight blue jeans and a tiny white vest top, appeared from a shop doorway. It took me a moment because of the context – and her hair was longer, curling down to the nape of her neck – but then I changed my direction to cross towards her, still not perfectly sure it was Charlene. It was. The memories from her came back: that first sight of her on the beach at Alvor, the hotel room, the beating…

Her eyes widened as she saw me, and then she gave a frown and the tiniest shake of her head. I changed direction again to reach the pavement away from her, and saw her turn to speak to someone, in Spanish. I paused to look in a random shop window, flicking my eyes to look at them. He was tall and slim, with tanned skin, black hair, and thick black stubble that looked like it had been painted on. He wore a white linen suit, sleeves pushed back on brown, hairy arms.

He put his arm round her, resting his hand on her backside as they walked away, looking in the shop windows. She leaned close to him, but kept her arms by her sides.

I walked the other way.

I woke in the middle of the night, random connections firing in my head, set off by seeing Charlene. When we'd gone to dinner at the Crowne Plaza she'd given the name Brown. When I'd first contacted Amanda Pitt, she'd been going to meet 'Rose Brown', the woman she was clearly having a relationship with.

It might have been just a coincidence, and it didn't affect anything, but it made some things from that time clearer.

I smiled and reached to hold Nicola close. Just keep it like this, I thought: I've no other ambitions, this will do me just fine. Don't change anything, not ever.

The End of Digital Circumstances

The author